The

DAUGHTER

of

ROME

The
DAUGHTER
of
ROME

ANGELA HUNT

BETHANYHOUSE
a division of Baker Publishing Group
Minneapolis, Minnesota

Published by Bethany House Publishers
Minneapolis, Minnesota
BethanyHouse.com

Bethany House Publishers is a division of
Baker Publishing Group, Grand Rapids, Michigan

Printed in the United States of America

Library of Congress Cataloging-in-Publication Data
Names: Hunt, Angela Elwell, author.
Title: The daughter of Rome / Angela Hunt.
Description: Minneapolis, Minnesota : Bethany House, a division of Baker
    Publishing Group, 2025. | Series: The Emissaries ; book 3
Identifiers: LCCN 2024036359 | ISBN 9780764241581 (paperback) | ISBN
    9780764244537 (casebound) | ISBN 9781493448913 (ebook)
Subjects: LCSH: Rome—History—Nero, 54–68—Fiction. | LCGFT: Christian
    fiction. | Historical fiction. | Novels.
Classification: LCC PS3558.U46747 D387 2025 | DDC 813/.54—dc23/eng/20240812
LC record available at https://lccn.loc.gov/2024036359

Scripture quotations are taken from the Tree of Life Version. © 2015 by the Messianic Jewish Family Bible Society. Used by permission of the Messianic Jewish Family Bible Society.

This is a work of historical reconstruction; the appearances of certain historical figures are therefore inevitable. All other characters, however, are products of the author's imagination, and any resemblance to actual persons, living or dead, is coincidental.

Cover design by Peter Gloege, LOOK Design Studio

Author is represented by Browne & Miller Literary Associates.

Baker Publishing Group publications use paper produced from sustainable forestry practices and postconsumer waste whenever possible.

25   26   27   28   29   30   31   7   6   5   4   3   2   1

Introduction

In Paul's letters to the churches he founded, we can see his love and concern in the way he praises, encourages, and admonishes the Gentile converts. But although the Scriptures paint an overall picture of the age in which these people lived, the modern reader may find it difficult to fully appreciate the pressures facing the fledgling believers.

THE EMISSARIES series features the stories of men and women who came to faith through Paul's missionary efforts in cities of the Roman Empire. Our own society—which grows ever more saturated with anti-biblical worldviews—is not so different from that of ancient Rome. May we be challenged by the first-century believers' vision, courage, and commitment to Messiah Yeshua.

Since reading involves "hearing" words in our heads, you might find it helpful to know the pronunciation of several names of people and places in this story. The early church was the *ecclesia* (pronounced ek-la-SEE-ah); *aedile* (ee-dile); *salve*, a common greeting (sal-vey); *vigile* (vih-GEEL-ay); and *sestertii* (ses-TER-tea).

Do not fear what you are about to suffer. Behold, the devil is about to throw some of you into prison, so that you may be tested. . . . Be faithful until death, and I will give you the crown of life. He who has an ear, let him hear what the *Ruach* [Spirit] is saying to Messiah's communities. The one who overcomes shall never be harmed by the second death.

Revelation 2:10–11

One

ROME, AD 64
THE 10TH YEAR OF THE REIGN OF NERO
CLAUDIUS CAESAR AUGUSTUS GERMANICUS
THE 17TH DAY OF IULIUS

Ninety years before I was born, for seven consecutive nights a glittering comet swept the northern heavens, gathering nascent souls for eventual delivery to earth. I was one of those souls.

The cosmic transaction was not one-sided, a priest of Jupiter later told me. In return for so many unsullied spirits, the comet ushered an exemplary being into the gathering of the gods: the shining presence of Gaius Julius Caesar, murdered dictator, senator, and aedile, triumphant general, and adoptive father of Augustus, first citizen of the Roman Empire.

The comet returned in the fifth year of Claudius's reign, ushering my stubborn soul to earth and demanding my mother's life in return.

My father never let me forget that I was part of a divine exchange. When I could not sleep, he would kneel by my bed and gently grip my hands. "You were born under the light of Caesar's star," he would whisper, his eyes luminous and tender. "The divine Caesar watches over you even now."

Eighteen years after my birth, I could find no particular evidence of Caesar's guardianship. My father and I lived on the Aventine, a working-class neighborhood of Rome, populated by a fair number of thieves, brawlers, and gamblers. But I had survived the perils of childhood, which many children did not, and I had not been quickly married off to the highest bidder—though I credited my father, not Caesar, for that mercy.

Living with my father, helping him create art for wealthy Romans, was apparently what the divine Caesar had destined me to do. Our lives were simple, but I was content.

"Calandra!" Father called from the other side of the work-room. "How fares the painting?"

"I am still working, Father. Would you have me rush?"

"Cronus awaits his masterpiece."

"The senator can wait. I daresay he is used to it."

I swirled ground charcoal into a drop of walnut oil, then flattened my brush on a stone. With the tip pressed into a fine point, I painted a thin line around the glass eyeball of Lucius Cronus Tuscus, the wealthy senator and elected official who had hired my father to sculpt his likeness in marble.

"We are five days overdue," Father called. "Still, Cronus should be pleased he has not had to wait as long as others."

"One cannot hurry art," I said, repeating my father's favorite phrase. "And I cannot rush these details."

With the tip of my brush I painted sparse lashes on the upper and lower eyelids, then stepped back to survey my work. Father stood beside me, and together we studied the likeness of one of Rome's best-known patricians. Every detail was accurate—the jutting jaw, the haughty brow, the slight smirk on the lips. And of course he was wearing the purple-banded toga of a senator, his fingers tucked into the elaborate folds at his left shoulder.

"He will hate it," Father finally said, his hand alighting on my arm. "Because Cronus is never satisfied. But you and I have done our best, so we have no reason to be ashamed."

"If you knew he would hate it, why did you accept the commission?"

"Because I also knew we had debts." A wry grin lifted the corner of his mouth. "And even though Cronus may say the statue does not adequately represent him, his pride will not allow him to refuse payment for a work that portrays him as more handsome than he is. So we will eat until we run out of sestertii, then we will find another patrician who wishes to see himself immortalized."

"That should not be a problem," I said, wiping my brush on an oiled rag. "The Forum is filled with them."

I dipped my finger into a pot of blue paint, then rubbed the precious mixture on my skin to test the consistency. Few statues bore any trace of the gorgeous color, for few native Romans had blue eyes or wore blue clothing. In any crowd of patricians or senators, white was the predominant color, accented by the reddish purple so well loved by the upper class.

But blue was the color of the sea, and so rare I yearned to use it. "What if I gave him a blue ring?" I asked. "Though you did not sculpt a ring on his finger, I could paint a gold band with a blue stone."

Father exhaled a slow breath. "Better, I think, to paint blue stones on his sandals. One thing is certain—no other senator will have a statue like this one."

"Then Cronus will love it," I said, dipping my brush into the color. "Because I have never seen a senator who is content to remain equal to his peers."

Father snorted. "You are far too perceptive for a girl your age. Are you *certain* you will not entertain a suitor? Several men have approached me."

"Would you lose your apprentice?" I shifted to avoid his gaze.

"I do not want to marry yet. Here I have work and protection. I need nothing else."

"A father is not a husband," he said, his voice softening. "And I am no longer young. You should be thinking of a family instead of sculptures and paints."

"I am your daughter." I smiled as I spread the gorgeous color over the raised stones sculpted on Cronus's sandals. "How could I think of anything *but* sculptures and paints?"

"But I am no longer young. If you do not marry, what will you do when I am gone?"

I cleaned the smudged edge with a fingertip. "I am a daughter of Rome," I said, "so I will trust the gods of Rome for my future."

"I would argue, but I am hungry. Is it not time for you to prepare dinner?"

"I will soon." I spoke the words reflexively, though I did not intend to quit just yet. The statue had received only one coat of paint, and it would need at least two. Marble was absorbent and made even thirstier in the summer heat.

I frowned as a strong gust blew through the open window and rattled a stack of papyri on Father's desk. If I did not hurry, my paints would dry too quickly and crack.

"I will finish soon," I called, quickening my brushstrokes. "Then we shall eat."

Two

Hadrian Cronus Tuscus, son of Senator Lucius Cronus Tuscus, waited for his panting servant to catch up. "Lysandros, we do not have all morning to complete our task."

The slave bowed his white head. "I am sorry, Dominus. I was slowed by the crowd."

Hadrian softened his tone. "We have only five more visits, then we can get out of the heat. Perhaps we will find a breeze once we cross the river."

"I doubt it. The *insulae* block any movement of the wind." Lysandros consulted the wax tablet in his hand. "After we enter *Transtiberim*, the first on the list is Titius Justus. The Corinthian."

Of course—another man convicted of *Lex Maiestatis* because he had refused to sacrifice to the Roman gods. Hadrian sighed. He did not understand how Titius and his pleasant wife could have been convicted of something as heinous as treason. But his job was not to judge; it was to ensure that the prisoners had not fomented rebellion while under house arrest.

The Praetorian Guard was responsible for all the prisoners in Rome, while the job of caring for the mild-mannered Christians had been relegated to the aediles. In turn, Cronus had charged his son with the duty, though Hadrian did not mind.

The task was one of the easiest he had ever been given.

They crossed the Tiber at a narrow footbridge, then stepped into Transtiberim. Home to most of Rome's Jews, a decidedly different atmosphere pervaded this district. On Saturn's day and Jewish holy days, an uncharacteristic stillness blanketed the area while the Jews observed a *Shabbat*. Experience had taught Hadrian not to visit on the seventh day, for no matter how hard he pounded, his prisoners refused to open their doors.

Yet not all the prisoners were Jews. Marcus Memmius Lupus had been a high-ranking Roman official before his arrest.

"It smells better on this side of the bridge," Lysandros said.

Hadrian frowned. "Better?"

"The Aventine stinks of broiled meats. The air is cleaner here."

"Because of the Jews." Hadrian crossed his arms. "Most of the people here refuse to eat meat that has been sacrificed to idols."

"Then it is a wonder they eat at all."

Hadrian pointed to the tall building, where Marcus lived with his wife and scores of other families. "We will start with the Corinthians."

As in all the poorer districts, tall insulae occupied both sides of the narrow, winding streets. Built to house as many people as possible, the structures stood only a few feet apart, blocking all but a sliver of sunlight and prohibiting the free circulation of air. Though the law forbade the construction of insulae more than seven stories high, many enterprising landlords built small rooms in the attics, taking advantage of the insatiable demand for affordable housing.

Hadrian made a mental note—he should remind his father of the unsafe conditions in this area. The rooms on the upper floors were barely adequate, with poor ventilation and no running water. Yet unscrupulous owners rented them out, often placing two families in a space no larger than the room in which Lysandros slept.

When Hadrian and Lysandros reached the apartment occupied by Marcus, Mariana, and their young son, they found that the Corinthian prisoners had guests. Citizens under house arrest were allowed visitors, but Hadrian had been charged with making note of any outsiders in case the prisoners attempted to conspire against the emperor.

Marcus gave Hadrian a guarded smile, then led him into the spacious apartment. Their dwelling, on the desirable second floor, had been decorated with carpets, elegant furniture, and a brazier large enough to cook for a dozen guests. Mariana wore a lovely silk stola, and her handmaid, a woman called Salama, waited at the back of the room, ready to serve.

The two strangers, a bearded man and his wife, appeared startled by Hadrian's appearance, but Marcus gave them an assuring smile. "Before we speak, let me bid farewell to our guests," he said. "They were kind enough to bring us supplies, and we do not wish to detain them."

The couple was about to slip away, so Hadrian caught the man's arm, halting him. "Salve, friend. Do you visit Marcus often?"

The man did not hesitate to meet Hadrian's gaze. "We come as often as we are needed."

"And your name?"

The man's chin rose almost imperceptibly. "Aquila, from the province of Pontus. This is my wife, Priscilla."

Hadrian heard the creak of a metal hinge as Lysandros opened his wax tablet to make notes. "Thank you." Hadrian released the man. "You may go."

Aquila glanced at Marcus and nodded as some unspoken communication passed between them. Priscilla squeezed Mariana's arm before walking to the door.

Hadrian let the couple pass. Unless he found evidence of trouble, he would not interfere with these people. But he cast Lysandros a pointed look and knew the slave had noted the connection between the two couples. Aquila and Priscilla, whoever they were, had just become persons of interest to the Praetorian Guard.

❖

Mariana waited until Marcus closed the door. "They have gone," he said, shifting his gaze to the two-year-old boy in her arms. "Again we have been left in peace."

"I do not know why his visits make me nervous," she confessed. "Every week he comes, we give him the same answers. How long can this continue?"

"For as long as the Lord wills." Marcus knelt on the floor and held out his arms. "Come, Ivan. Come to your *tata.*"

Mariana set the toddler on the floor and watched her son run to his father. "Now, wife," Marcus said, settling the boy on his lap, "what news have you from home?"

"In all the excitement, I nearly forgot." Mariana patted the sealed letter Priscilla had received from Corinth. "Let us learn what is happening."

She broke the seal and spread the folded pages on the small table in their apartment. "The letter comes from my mother," she said, scanning the heading.

"Of course." Marcus shrugged. "My father would not write a traitorous son."

Mariana's brow rose in silent reproof. "He loves you still. Does he not send supplies we sorely need? Did he not allow your mother to provide us with furnishings?"

"My mother and brother live only a short distance from us, but they have not visited once," Marcus replied. "Apparently my behavior has strained the bonds between us."

"But that cord is not yet broken." Mariana smiled. "Now, let us see what my mother says . . ."

Her lips moved as she read aloud. "From Hester, wife of Narkis, magistrate of Corinth, province of Acacia:

"Dearest Marcus and Mariana,

"I was overjoyed to hear how your little son thrives! I know Ivan will bring you great joy, and I pray that he brings light to your hearts even in the darkness of Rome. I pray for you each time Adonai brings you to mind. I ask the Lord to guide you, bless you, and use you for the glory of His eternal kingdom.

"As for us, we are well. Your stepfather continues as chief magistrate, and Governor Memmius has come to depend upon him. I thought this dependence would make Narkis happy, but he has not been himself of late. I find myself wondering if he has begun to reevaluate his choice concerning the gods of Rome—he has given them his full allegiance, but what have they given him? Only earthly pleasures. As Narkis ages, his thoughts turn to the afterlife. I speak to him of my certain home in heaven, but he cannot be assured of any eternal abode. Please keep him in your prayers.

"Your sister Prima is well. The doctors have devised a traveling seat for her, so she is able to leave the house any time we have four slaves to carry her chair. She no longer visits the Temple of Aphrodite, nor does she offer incense at the family altar. She has not yet softened to the point of asking about Adonai, but she is no longer the woman you knew when you left Corinth. Something in her—I believe it was her pride—died when she threw herself off that ledge. If I am right, she is close to salvation. For how can anyone realize their utter dependence upon God if they are convinced they can find their own answers?

"Pray for her, dear ones. Forgive her for the many wrongs she committed against you and demonstrate your love through prayer. If the Spirit of Adonai leads you to do so, send her a letter. Did letters from Paulos not move our ecclesia to repentance? So a letter from your loving and selfless hearts may do the same for your sister.

"As always, you are in my thoughts and prayers. Kiss your little son for me and lead him to knowledge of the God who loves and cares for him. I will never cease to pray for you."

Mariana lowered the papyri and blinked back tears. Though her mother's news brought joy, she could not think of Prima without remembering her stepsister's terrible scheme to destroy Mariana's marriage. Prima's plan had almost succeeded. Though she had not driven Mariana and Marcus apart, she had orchestrated the event that resulted in their exile and imprisonment.

"What say you?" Marcus looked up. "Will you write Prima a letter?"

Mariana caught a breath, then slowly released it. "I will," she said, folding the papyri. "But not today."

Lysandros pointed to the next *insula*, and a moment passed before Hadrian remembered which prisoner was housed there. Petros of Judea had only recently been added to the list, and he could not recall what the Judean had done to deserve house arrest.

The doorman, a retired soldier, recognized Hadrian and opened the door as they approached. They climbed to the second floor, where a wealthy merchant lived with his wife and family. A slave stood outside the door, serving as guard and doorman. Hadrian sighed, ignored the slave, and kept climbing.

With each floor, the walls became dirtier and the brick stairs more uneven. With no windows in the stairwell, the air thickened as they climbed, heavy with the stink of urine and decay. The residents of the upper floors were poorer than their neighbors, with no slaves to haul water, empty chamber pots, or remove trash. Broken pottery, uneaten scraps, and an annoying number of flies, living and dead, lay scattered across the floor.

After climbing the increasingly narrow stairs to the sixth level, Hadrian paused at a rickety door. He could not help noticing that a small fish had been carved into the wood.

"Yet another traitor," he murmured as Lysandros knocked.

"Petros of Judea," Lysandros called, his voice muffled by the stifling atmosphere. "Hadrian, son of the senator, demands your attention."

The door opened a moment later, revealing a tall, bearded man with sparse white hair.

Hadrian consulted the list. "Petros of Judea," he read. "You were arrested for disturbing the peace at a temple."

"A synagogue." Humor lit the man's dark eyes. "Would you like some refreshment? My wife has brought water from the fountain below."

Lysandros frowned, but Hadrian glanced into the apartment and saw an older woman pouring water into cups. A drink, even warm, would be welcome on a day as hot as this one.

"Thank you," he said, entering the domicile. "This should not take much time."

A wave of fetid heat struck Hadrian as he and Lysandros entered. The one-room apartment smelled of unwashed bodies, burning wood, and whatever the woman had cooked for last night's dinner. But though the environment was far from pleasant, the prisoner did not complain.

Petros's wife, a short woman who wore a scarf over her gray hair, gave Hadrian a timid smile as she offered the water. He took the cup and drank, noting with appreciation that she had added a generous serving of honey. He did not know how she had obtained something so expensive, so he had to ask.

"Have you left this house," he began, "to participate in any forbidden meetings?"

Petros's brow twitched. "My wife has gone to the market. Is that forbidden?"

"It is forbidden if she speaks to anyone there."

"How can she bargain if she does not speak?"

"I speak very little," the woman said, lowering her gaze. "I point to what we need and accept the price. Then I leave."

Hadrian glanced at Lysandros, grateful they had finally found a submissive Christian. "Perhaps it would be best if you have friends deliver what you need," he told the woman. "You do not want to be punished for breaking the terms of your arrest."

Her head lowered in a quick motion, then she retreated to a corner of the room.

Hadrian turned his attention to the husband, who had folded his arms. Petros of Judea might have been anywhere from seventy to ninety, so lined was his face, but many Judeans spent most of their lives in the sun.

"You confirm that you are Petros the Judean?"

The old man nodded. "I am, but the Greeks call me Cephas. The Hebrews know me as Simon."

"A man of many names."

"Not for evil purposes, I assure you. My rabbi changed my name many years ago. In our language, my name means *rock*."

Hadrian arched his brow. "Because you are as stubborn as stone?"

The Judean laughed, an unexpected sound. "Probably."

"How long have you lived in Rome?"

The Judean's forehead creased. "A year? Perhaps two. We came here to help friends."

"But you ran afoul of the law, and now you are under house arrest. I assume you know what that means."

"It means," Petros said, his eyes crinkling at the corners, "that you will be visiting once a week. It means my wife and I should remain in this room, but we are free to welcome guests. It means Nero has not had time to hear my case."

"You should be grateful," Lysandros added, but pressed his lips together when Hadrian shot him a warning look.

Yet Petros smiled. "I am grateful to Adonai every day. And I am content to remain in whatever state Nero confines me, for Adonai rules over kings and emperors."

Hadrian sighed, mystified as always by the Christians' unflappable nature. "You people remind me of the stoics. Do you follow that philosophy?"

The Judean's forehead creased. "I cannot say I know much about it."

"A simple concept," Hadrian continued. "The chief task of a stoic is to sort all situations into matters that can be changed and matters that cannot. I do not waste time or energy upon circumstances that cannot be controlled but look within myself to change those that can."

"Do you worship the gods of Rome?"

Hadrian stiffened. "I do what is required."

Petros tugged at the end of his white beard. "But you look within yourself for answers rather than running to the gods. How has that inward look served you? Have you found an answer for all your problems?"

Hadrian turned away, embarrassed to have been stymied by a rustic Judean, a Christian nonetheless.

"I once relied on rituals for salvation," Petros said, his gaze drifting to a distant memory. "But Yeshua, my rabbi, taught us that rituals were only a symbol of the salvation to come. That salvation did not come from myself, for nothing good dwells within me. But in Adonai, I found—"

Hadrian lifted his hand, cutting the man off. "Have you spread the heresy of Christ-worship in Rome?"

"Since being arrested?"

"Yes."

"We have spoken only to our guests. They would assure you that we have not spread heresy."

"Have you disturbed the peace in any synagogue since your arrest?"

"I have not. We worship here, in our home."

"Are you willing to amend your ways and offer incense to the gods of Rome?"

Like Marcus and others before him, Petros smiled at the question. "I am not, and neither is my wife. Is that all, my young friend?"

"It is. Until I visit again next week."

"*Shalom*," Petros called as Hadrian stepped toward the door. When he turned in curiosity, the Judean waved. "The word means *peace*. Surely Romans seek peace as well as power."

Sighing, Hadrian stepped into the stairwell and inhaled air that had been breathed far too many times. The wooden floor above shivered with the thump and bump of footsteps, an inescapable reality in a multistory building.

How soon could they be away from this place?

Lysandros turned. "Why do they smile?"

"What?"

"When you ask if they wish to recant, they smile as if your question is humorous. Why?"

"Perhaps they have been infected by madness. A sane man would leap at the opportunity to restore his freedom."

"Perhaps. Otherwise they seem quite reasonable."

Hadrian led the way down the stairs. "How many more must we visit?"

"One more in Transtiberim," Lysandros answered, "and one in the Aventine."

Three

I cleaned my brushes and tidied my worktable, then lightly touched the paint on Cronus's statue. The second coat was sticky, so I would let it dry a few more hours before allowing the men to move it.

Leaving Father asleep on his couch, I tossed my palla over my hair and left the shop, walking as briskly as possible.

As usual for midday, crowds jammed the narrow streets around our insula, and I had to stop when a slave called, "Make way!" A bejeweled hand parted the embroidered curtain on an approaching litter, then withdrew as if afraid of contamination. I resumed my brisk walk, then crinkled my nose when I bumped into a slave carrying a pot of urine for the fuller's laundry. I moved around the slave, avoided a pair of beggars, and turned into an alley, where the voices of children rippled the air. Huddled in the shade beneath an awning, a handful of youngsters were reciting the twenty-three letters of the alphabet. Their schoolmaster, a tall man wearing a freedman's cap, walked behind them and rhythmically tapped a stick against his open palm.

I strode past the teacher and followed a well-worn path to a *caupona* with rooms to rent. The slave who managed the facility directed travelers to the upper floors; guests who only wanted food remained on the ground floor, where other slaves served food and wine. I stepped to the counter, ordered a cup of honey water and a focaccia bun, and waited. The bun arrived a moment later, served on a plate with a slice of cheese, two figs, and a boiled egg. I slid a bronze coin across the counter and carried my plate to a table where I could sit, eat, and quietly observe my surroundings.

I did not watch the men. I saw them every day because Roman men did nearly all the shopping for their households. They came to our window and argued with me over the price of bowls, decanters, vases, and amphoras. I knew their tactics— their protracted silences, their discreet glances into their purses, and their certainty that I was ignorant of business. Yet *they* were ignorant of my hard-won wisdom.

In truth, I often wondered if those men knew more about women than I did. After all, they had been reared by mothers and most of them had wives. Many of them had fathered daughters and exulted at the arrival of granddaughters. Whereas I had only my father . . .

A freedwoman sauntered over to my table, pitcher in hand. She was well-proportioned, clean, and would make a good model. I would have to mention her to my father.

She twirled a loose curl around her finger. "More water?"

I nodded.

She sloshed water into my cup, then dropped into the empty chair across from me. "You come here often."

"Yes." I took a bite of the cheese.

"Why?" The woman broke into a friendly smile. "The food is not great. You cannot hear yourself think on account of the noise. So why do you come?"

"Not for the food." I lifted my voice to be heard above the raucous laughter from the next table. "Nor for the atmosphere."

Her mouth curved into a knowing expression. "I know. You come to get away from your husband."

"I have no husband."

Her mouth dropped open. "At your age? Bona Dea! How did you escape that fate?"

"I was born under Caesar's Comet. Perhaps he watches over me."

"Someone has blessed you. But watch yourself—soon you will pay a price for your freedom. Rome does not favor those who choose to remain unmarried."

"I know."

The owner called the woman away, leaving me to finish my meal in peace.

That freedwoman would never understand that I ate at the caupona to study people like her. I watched other women sip from their goblets; I studied the way they draped pallas around their heads and shoulders. I marveled at the various stylings of hair and the delicate hues of painted faces. I openly eavesdropped, noting the tenor of voices, the rise and fall of sighs, and the sudden hardening of facial muscles that could signify disapproval or fear.

For eighteen years I lived alone with my father. How else was I to learn about the person I had become? And how would I ever know who I was meant to be?

I considered the question. Roman law required that all female citizens marry by age twenty, but that deadline was still two years away. Until then I would follow in my father's footsteps and continue to study art. Rome was filled with statues created by masters who lived long before me. When I was old and gray—even if I had a husband and children—I would take joy in knowing my hands had created art that would last forever. Works of beauty. Works that would shine through the ages.

When I finished my lunch, I nodded my thanks to the hostess and went home to wake Father from his nap.

Four

PHILIPPI
THE 18TH DAY OF IULIUS

Euodia stepped through the doorway and entered the wind-swept courtyard, then turned to gaze at the house. How she would miss it! The weathered stone dwelling had welcomed her when she arrived as a stranger, and it had protected her when storms raged and the river overflowed its banks. This villa had sheltered Sabina and Ariston, Phebe, Dione, and all the other slaves Euodia had purchased and set free.

"Are you assailed by doubts?" The deep voice came from behind her as a gust of warm breath tickled her ear.

"Not doubts." She leaned back as her husband's strong arms encircled her waist. "But memories. This house has borne witness to so much of my life."

"Now it will watch over Sabina, Homer, and their little ones." Ariston shifted to stand beside her. "It will be a far noisier place."

Euodia couldn't help but smile. Sabina was no longer the frightened slave Euodia had rescued and adopted a dozen years before. Since placing her faith in Yeshua, the girl had recovered from her traumatic past and discovered joy in working with

Euodia and Syntyche, dyers of purple cloth. Sabina would remain in Philippi, working with her husband and Syntyche, her mother-in-law.

"I will miss living by the water," Euodia said, sighing. "They say Rome is so crowded you can barely turn around without stepping on someone's feet."

"At least it has a river," Ariston pointed out. "We will find a place near the shore, if you like."

"I hope there *is* a shore." Euodia lifted her head as Syntyche came out of the house and hurried toward them.

"I am glad you are still here," she said, panting. "I forgot to ask about the order from the magistrate of Thessalonica—did he want wool or cloth?"

"Cloth," Euodia said. "He has never asked for wool."

"Cloth it is." Syntyche stared at Euodia, her chin quivering. "My dear friend. We will miss you."

Euodia stepped forward and drew Syntyche into her arms. The years had bound them together through squabbles and laughter, tragedy and bliss. But as much as it would pain her to leave so many behind, the Spirit had spoken.

"You will write," Syntyche said, pulling away. "You must write and tell us about your adventures—when you place your orders, of course."

"I will write often," Euodia promised. "Because I am certain we will soon outsell every other purple merchant in the city. And you must not worry—you are perfectly capable of overseeing the dyers. You have been doing it for years."

"But not alone." Syntyche's broad cheeks curved in a tentative smile, then she glanced toward the house. "Look at that little one. She resembles her mother, does she not?"

Euodia followed the woman's gaze and spotted Sophia, Sabina's youngest daughter, playing in the sand. Her heart twisted at the thought of leaving the little girl.

"Indeed she does," she said, trying not to weep. "See? You will not be alone. You will have Sabina and Homer, the children, and all the women of Philippi to keep you company. You have made it possible for them to improve their lives, so they will not desert you."

Syntyche stepped away from the *carpentum*, the covered wagon that would shield the couple's possessions on the long journey to the port. "May the Lord bless you, my friend."

"And you, dear sister." Euodia dashed a tear from her eye, then joined Ariston, who waited patiently beside the mule.

"Have you said farewell to Sabina?" he asked.

"Twice," she answered, her voice finally breaking. "And the three little ones."

"Did you forget Dione?"

"I did not forget her. But if we linger much longer, I do not think I will find the courage to leave."

"Then it is time."

Ariston climbed onto the wagon bed and assisted Euodia as she climbed to the space beside him. Together they waved at Syntyche, then Ariston picked up the reins. A moment later they were following the path that led to the Via Egnatia, which would take them to the port city of Dyrrachium. There they would sell the wagon and mule and sail to Brindisi, where they would rent another conveyance for transport to Rome.

Euodia moved closer to Ariston's strong and comforting arm. He had been the first to feel a nudge from the Spirit of God, but by the time he mentioned the matter to her, she had felt it, too. For some reason, Adonai wanted them to leave their home and loved ones in Philippi. He wanted them to move to Rome.

Once they made the announcement, the citizens of Philippi congratulated the couple on their success. Everyone knew that several leading merchants had become enamored with Euodia's purple cloth, and her reputation had spread throughout the Empire. Common sense dictated that they open a shop in Rome, where more people could afford the luxurious cloth.

But while everyone assumed the couple traveled westward to grow their business, Euodia and Ariston were moving for only one reason: God was leading them away.

Five

Under Father's watchful eye, I placed the last of the straw into a wooden crate, then stepped back as Father and two hired freedmen used ropes to lower the life-size statue into its crate. Cassius held the rope attached to the base and Father's hands trembled as he guided the swaying statue. Felix, Cassius's teenage son, finally lowered the head into the bed of straw.

I held my breath until the elaborately painted figure rested safely inside its straw nest, then released a sigh of exasperated relief. "Finally," I said, glad that none of the fresh paint had been scratched. "Now we deliver it to Cronus." I turned to my father, who seemed to have aged in the last ten minutes. "Will you ride with the statue?"

He shook his head. "You should do that. Cronus will be far more charmed by your loveliness than my aging visage. And if he hates the piece, he will not vent his spleen on you."

"He will not hate it," I insisted, but Father had already moved toward the couch where he routinely took his afternoon nap. I turned to Cassius and Felix. "We may as well deliver it straightaway. Cassius, will you and Felix carry the box to the wagon?"

"Calandra," Father called, settling onto his couch, "do not forget to make yourself presentable."

I pushed a spray of sweat-dampened hair from my forehead.

How was I supposed to appear presentable *and* help in the workshop? I drew a breath, about to protest, then realized I had no one to blame for my disheveled appearance but myself. And if I was going to meet a senator, I probably should clean up . . .

"Yes, Father."

I hurried to my bedchamber and rummaged through my trunk, then pulled out a clean tunic. The white linen was wrinkled, but perhaps no one would notice. Another frantic search revealed a looking brass, so I set it on a table and pulled my hair into a bun at the nape of my neck. Loose tendrils of natural curls framed my face, an effect similar to what I had observed on wealthy ladies. I secured the bun with a pair of slender paintbrushes, then stepped out of my oil-stained tunic and donned the clean garment. As a final touch, I pulled a blue palla from the trunk and draped it around my head and shoulders. The scarf was all that remained of my mother.

I hurried to the stable at the back of the shop, where Cassius and Felix waited with the wagon. "You know wagons are forbidden until the tenth hour," Cassius reminded me.

I glanced outside and searched for a sign of orange-tinted sunlight. "If we wait until then," I said, "we will compete for space with every conveyance in Rome. Can we not leave a *little* early?"

"I do not want to be fined," Cassius said, crossing his arms. "But if your father is willing to pay the price—"

"I will pay the fine," I said, "if it comes to that."

When sunlight on the opposite wall carried a slightly orange tint, I climbed onto the narrow seat beside Cassius. "It is time." Then I bowed my head and prayed: "Vesta, gentle goddess, allow us to deliver this without incident. And if it is not too much trouble, spark a flame of pleasure and appreciation in the receiver, so we may incur his favor and speedy payment. If you do this . . ." I hesitated. What would be the appropriate reward? "If you do this, I will sacrifice a dove at your temple."

Cassius grunted in approval and drove the wagon onto the street.

A crew of civil slaves was lighting the street torches by the time Hadrian and Lysandros left the Aventine District. Lysandros always grimaced when visiting the area populated by a variety of merchants, foreigners, and beggars, but Hadrian found it fascinating. The settlement, which had lain outside the city walls in the days of Rome's kings, had been annexed during the Republic, but had retained its unique foreign flavor.

"We should hurry," Lysandros remarked, stepping over a puddle. "I would rather be safe inside your father's house than here when night arrives."

Hadrian ignored his slave and turned onto the Via Appia, the wide road that led to the Circus Maximus. He was tempted to stop at the public baths and wash the day's sweat from his skin, but one glance at Lysandros's anxious face convinced him to keep moving.

"You used to tell me that a truly brave man had nothing to fear," he said, striding around a donkey cart. "I would remind you of your advice."

"As your tutor, I was expected to instruct you in honorable Roman virtues," Lysandros answered. "But as a Greek, I know trepidation can be useful."

"The Aventine is not dangerous," Hadrian said, grinning. "Unless you plan on robbing one of these merchants. If you attempted such a thing, within a moment or two you would undoubtedly find yourself missing a hand."

Hadrian lengthened his stride, reluctantly leading his slave out of the district. They entered a flow of traffic from the Circus

Maximus, home to dozens of merchants who plied their trades in the stalls behind the elongated racetrack. Thousands visited the small shops, called *popinae*, during the daily races and contests. A man could purchase almost anything in the popinae, including pleasure, but Nero had banned the sale of cooked food in the shops, hoping to eliminate fires like the one that had decimated the Circus twenty-eight years before.

Hadrian shouldered his way through the crowd, most of whom were headed toward homes in the Aventine, but one conveyance caught his attention. A narrow wagon occupied the center of the paved street and struggled to move against the tide. A freedman and a woman shared the narrow seat while a younger man walked behind. The wagon bore a coffin-like box, freshly constructed and exuding the scent of fresh pine.

Hadrian gritted his teeth. Why was the wagon on the road at this hour? Nero had specifically forbidden wagons from the city before the tenth hour.

He took a sudden step to the left, intending to walk around the creaking conveyance, but at that moment the wagon hit a loose stone, the bed tilted, and the box slid toward the open back.

"Look out!" he called.

The young man had been walking with his head down, but at Hadrian's warning he stepped forward, arms outstretched, as if to catch the coffin. The box was too heavy, however, and though Hadrian managed to catch a corner, the weight of the load struck the young man and knocked him to the ground.

Lysandros, who had seen everything, hurried forward. "You, driving the wagon. Halt!"

The mule stopped. The freedman and the woman leapt to help the struggling youth. With Lysandros's help, Hadrian heaved the box onto the wagon while the woman knelt at the youth's side. "Felix! Are you hurt?"

"I-I . . ." the young man rasped, struggling to catch his breath. "I am alive, and surely that is the important thing." Groaning, the young man allowed the woman and the driver to help him stand.

The older man regarded the woman, guilt flooding his face. "I am sorry. I did not see the rock in the road. If anything has happened to the—"

"You are not to blame." The young woman offered him a fleeting smile. "I am not worried about the cargo."

"Wait." Hadrian stepped forward, alarmed by what he was hearing. "I do not know who you are transporting, but you show him no honor by allowing his body to be manhandled by a woman and a couple of freedmen. Where are the mourners?"

The woman turned to him, her brows rising like a pair of cranes in flight. He peered at her, unable to place either her face or her station. She did not wear a slave's garment, nor was she dressed like a patrician's wife. She was not young enough to be the driver's unmarried daughter, so who was she?

The woman inclined her head in a polite bow. "I must thank you, sir. If you had not been so quick to alert us, Felix might have been seriously injured."

Hadrian shrugged to hide his confusion. "I am grateful I was able to stop your cargo from causing further harm." He tilted his head toward the coffin. "I do not know who you are carrying to the cemetery, but he must have been a heavy man."

The driver blinked in confusion, and the woman released a peal of laughter. "Oh, Cassius! He thinks we are carrying a body!"

Cassius smiled and rubbed his chin. "With respect, sir, we are not transporting a corpse. The crate contains a work of art."

"What?"

"A statue for Cronus the aedile. We are delivering it to him."

"Do you know the home of the aedile?"

The woman shook her head. "We were hoping to find guidance once we reached the Palatine District. The man must be known there."

"Indeed he is." Hadrian smiled. "And I would be happy to direct you to the senator's house."

Her face brightened. "That would be most kind."

"It would be an honor . . . and my pleasure. But for now, let my slave and I walk behind your wagon in case the box slips again. We would not want a mishap to ruin a fine piece of art."

"We would not." The woman's tone was sober, but her eyes danced beneath the edge of her palla.

Hadrian gestured northward. "Continue in the direction you are traveling. When you pass the circus, turn right before you reach the Basilica Julia. There I will give you further direction."

The woman lowered her head. "Thank you, sir. My father will be grateful for your help."

"And your father is?"

"Pericles Aemilius Claudus, the sculptor."

Of course. The artist chose his daughter to accompany the precious cargo. An odd choice, unless the man had no sons . . .

As the woman and the slave returned to the front of the wagon, Hadrian glanced at the injured youth, who was hopping on his left leg. "Take a seat, lad. You do not need to walk."

Without protest, the boy clambered up and sat next to the crate.

The driver picked up the reins and the mule moved ahead.

"You could have given her complete directions," Lysandros said, slowing his pace as the wagon rattled over the paving stones. "You do not have to provide a personal escort."

Hadrian chuckled. "My father will be delighted to learn that I have personally supervised the safe arrival of his likeness. He has been anticipating this for months."

"Anticipation is a fickle mistress," Lysandros warned. "If he does not like the image inside yonder box, he may think you a fool for escorting it."

"He will approve it," Hadrian countered. "How could he look at that young woman and find anything unattractive? Her beauty gilds everything in the vicinity. Even you, Lysandros, are more handsome in the light of her countenance."

"You have been reading too much poetry," the slave grumbled. "But at least you have not forgotten how to read."

❖

Following the instructions from the striking young Roman who agreed to escort us, I told Cassius to halt the mule outside an impressive domus with a bright red door.

"The aedile lives here," the young man said, striding toward the house. "Wait there and I will see that you are admitted."

I watched, frowning, as he entered the domicile without knocking. The slave who had accompanied him remained outside. He looked up and caught my questioning gaze.

"Young woman," he said, "do you know the man who has gone into the house?"

Mystified, I shook my head.

The slave's mouth curved in a faint smile. "He is Hadrian, son of Senator Lucius Cronus Tuscus, the aedile. This is his home."

I swallowed my surprise. "And you are?"

"I am Lysandros, once his tutor, now his companion."

I lifted my chin. "Yet still a slave."

"Yes. But in many ways, he is like a son to me."

I motioned for Cassius to remain where he was while I slipped from the seat, careful not to entangle my palla on the wagon. Perhaps this slave would be willing to help.

"Lysandros," I said, approaching him, "perhaps you can

help us. With Felix injured, Cassius and I will not be able to lift the crate."

"You have only to wait for Hadrian. He is a most capable young man."

"He would actually help us *carry*—?"

The words had scarcely left my mouth when the red door opened and five slaves strode out, followed by Hadrian. He stood on the curb, his impressive arms crossed, as the slaves pulled the crate from the wagon, slipped leather straps beneath it, and took it into the house.

No, *he* would not help us carry the crate. He would order slaves to do it.

Lysandros and I watched silently, then the doorkeeper stepped outside and indicated that I should follow him.

I instructed Felix and Cassius to wait with the wagon, then I entered the house, steering clear of the enormous Molossus that sat in the entry and growled as I walked by.

"Whist," the doorkeeper hissed, silencing the dog. Then he inclined his head. "Forgive the beast's manners. Dominus will meet you in the atrium."

I moved through the vestibule and into the spacious atrium, where rays of the setting sun had gilded the painted walls. Slaves had already removed the life-size statue from the crate and placed it on a marble plinth. A trio of slaves were lighting wall torches, sending flickering shadows over the intricate mural of men and women dancing amid an elaborate garden of white-and-crimson flowers.

I studied the scene while I awaited the senator's arrival. I had never met the aedile and had relied on Father's sketches to paint the image. I could only hope the man would appreciate the work Father and I had done. People were often unpredictable—they loved the idea of their likeness in a statue but were repulsed by a realistic result. Father said it was because people tended to imagine themselves as more attractive than they actually were.

The son, Hadrian, crept up on me. "You need not be anxious," he said, his mouth twisting in a wry smile. "It is a true likeness yet flattering. Your father is not only a skilled artist; he is a diplomat in stone."

A matching smile tugged at the corner of my mouth. "You should have introduced yourself when we met on the street. Or do you delight in surprising the merchants who serve your family?"

"I had no idea you were a merchant—or a merchant's daughter. I thought you were on your way to bury a husband."

I tilted my head, conceding his point. "I have never had a husband. But you are generous and kind. And those are traits not commonly associated with public servants."

A snort of laughter escaped him. "While I have always admired forthrightness, perhaps you should emulate your father's diplomacy. I can assure you that all public officials, from the aediles to the emperor himself, consider themselves the epitome of virtue."

"Perhaps they are—and I must beg your pardon, sir. I am a common girl, not a patrician's daughter. I am not acquainted with your father or the emperor, so I cannot judge. But if your father pays the invoice and speaks well of my father's work, I will praise his name among the plebeians."

A flurry of movement caught my attention, so I stilled my tongue as an older man entered, his white tunic edged with an embroidered Greek design. I thought the garment a trifle elaborate for a quiet evening at home, but what did I know of patricians? A quartet of slaves followed their master and stopped when the aedile halted in front of the statue, his eyes narrowing as he folded his hands.

I held my breath and waited.

After a long moment, Cronus Tuscus spoke. "Hadrian?"

"Father?"

"What think you of this?"

The younger man stepped to his sire's side, but not before tossing me an assertive smile. "I am much taken with it. The sculptor has captured your strengths, yet still manages to portray you as a man who would enjoy dining with his neighbors. You appear strong, but not Herculean. Devout before the gods, but not obsequious. This statue depicts a man who is a servant to the emperor, but not to trends or foolish whims."

The aedile dipped his chin in a slow nod. "I do believe you are correct. At first I was not sure the artist had captured my intellect, but now I see the wide forehead . . ."

"Note the gleam in the eye," Hadrian added, smiling at me again. "That tiny speck of painted light reveals that you are a man who understands what is transpiring beneath the surface of any interaction."

"By all the gods, Pericles has outdone himself." The aedile's face lit with a dazzling smile. "I was impressed with the bust he did for Titus Flavius Sabinus, but this work outshines it by far."

Hadrian gestured toward me. "Father, may I present the woman who delivered the piece? She is the sculptor's daughter."

Unprepared for the introduction, my cheeks heated as the aedile turned. "Sir." I pressed my hand to my chest and bowed. "I am Calandra, daughter of Pericles. He bade me deliver this statue into your keeping."

The aedile studied me, then the corner of his mouth twitched. "You are Greek," he said, his tone openly approving. "All the best sculptors are Greek, as are the best doctors."

Startled by his blunt opinion, I nodded. "Thank you, but I have seen many fine sculptures by Roman artists. My father says art is ever-changing because each generation improves upon the work of the former."

"That may be," the aedile said, sniffing. "But I have yet to see a Roman sculptor who could improve on this." He swiveled back to the statue, eager to admire his likeness again, then he threw me a backward glance. "You must wait," he said, offhandedly gesturing to one of his slaves. "I shall send a letter to your father, and I expect a reply within the week."

I was not surprised he wanted to thank the artist, but what sort of reply did he expect?

One of the attendant slaves stepped forward with a writing desk, which the slave placed on his lap as he perched on a stool. Cronus waited until the slave dipped his stylus into the ink, then he began to dictate:

"To Pericles Aemilius Claudus, sculptor of the Aventine, from Senator Lucius Cronus Tuscus:

"I must say that I was surprised beyond measure to behold the likeness you sculpted on my behalf. Truly, you have created a magnificent work, one I shall be pleased to exhibit in my home. I will thank the gods for your skill every time I pass this magnificent piece, and I will recommend your abilities to anyone who asks.

"As a result of viewing this stellar image, the gods have inspired me with an idea, and I am determined that you should agree to my request. I work for the emperor, as do we all, and I wish to give him a gift unlike any other. I want him to be as impressed with his likeness as I am with mine, so I wish to commission you to create a statue of Nero, larger than life, in bronze. I know I owe you a sum of twenty-five hundred sestertii, which I will pay, but I will also pay that sum every month that you are engaged in the work of creating a colossal image of Nero. I have heard of other sculptors requiring eight years to create such statues, so I will give you four years to complete the work. When I present your art to the emperor, I will bask in his gratitude even as you benefit from mine. What say you,

Pericles? Please respond as soon as you are able. May all the blessings of the gods fall upon your house."

He snapped his fingers at the amanuensis. "Seal it and send it with this woman," he said, flicking his hand toward me. He caught his son's gaze. "Will I see you at dinner?"

"Of course."

For a fleeting instant I found myself wishing I could be present at that dinner, but I banished the thought as Cronus gave the statue another appreciative glance and left the atrium, trailed by a bevy of attendants.

The amanuensis remained behind. He tossed a handful of sand onto the wet ink, waited a moment, then shook the sand into his lap desk. While I waited, he folded the letter, then lit a candle and dripped wax onto the overlapping folds. After sealing the letter with his master's ring, the man handed it to Hadrian, who gave it to me.

I accepted the letter and reluctantly turned toward the door, keenly aware that I had failed in my most important duty. Hadrian must have noted my hesitation. "Is there anything else?"

"Payment would be appropriate," I said, lifting a brow.

"Ah." Hadrian pointed to a slave standing near the door, then looked at me. "What was it? Twenty-three hundred sestertii?"

"Twenty-five."

"Of course." He looked to the slave. "Bring that amount from my father's strongbox."

I would have been content to silently stand and reflect upon the perfect proportions of the young man in front of me, but Hadrian released a polite cough as the slave hurried away. "So . . . when your father is working, what do you do?"

I almost laughed. "I do whatever he requires. I work with clay and paint. I am also an artist."

"You make bowls and lamps?"

"And the clay models for my father. One day I will create even more."

He arched a brow. "So you have been blessed by the gods, too."

"I was born under Caesar's Comet, so I suppose I have."

"I know nothing about art," he admitted, "but I greatly admire those who do."

I pressed my lips together, hoping to relieve him of the task of making polite conversation. Fortunately, a moment later the slave returned with a small pouch. When he handed it to Hadrian, I heard the distinctive clink of coins.

Hadrian weighed the pouch on his palm, then gave it to me. "I will send a group of men to see you safely home."

"I have Cassius and Felix."

"An old man and an injured boy? While you would likely be safe in the Palatine District, you are traveling to the Aventine. In darkness." He pointed to a slave waiting near the doorway. "You there. Fetch six armed men to escort this woman to her home."

I marveled at the ease with which a wealthy man could summon almost anything he wanted.

Six

Hadrian could not help but feel that the interesting young woman was eager to be away.

"Thank you," she said. "I will wait outside with my servants."

He frowned. "Are you certain? The night air will be cool, and you have no cloak."

"After the heat of the day, the cool air will bring blessed relief."

"If you insist. But I will escort you to the street."

She strode toward the vestibule, not bothering to wait for him. He was about to warn her about the doorkeeper's beast, but the dog lifted his broad head and gave her a slobbery smile. Hadrian's warning caught in his throat as Calandra scratched the creature's ear and walked out.

Her companions were waiting when she reached the wagon. The boy sat in the back of the vehicle, nursing his injured foot, while the freedman held the mule's reins. Calandra was about to climb onto the wagon when Hadrian caught her arm. She flinched, and he released her at once. "I apologize, but surely you are aware that my father's statue was a test."

She blinked. "What do you mean?"

"For months my father has been searching for a sculptor capable of rendering a unique gift for Nero. My father will enjoy his likeness, of course, but his chief goal is to rise in the emperor's favor. Rome has four aediles; my father wants to be chief among them."

Understanding lit her eyes. "How many statues did your father commission in this test?"

Hadrian laughed. "Our garden holds a half dozen. The other marble likenesses will be broken up for gravel, but your father's work will remain untouched. I tell you this so you can help him understand—my father would do almost anything to achieve his goal, and he has a unique knowledge of the emperor. While other artists would immortalize Nero as a soldier or a god, my father knows that Nero's greatest wish is to be remembered as an artist. *That* is what your father must portray. He must reflect the emperor's dream in bronze."

When her eyes widened, Hadrian knew she understood the challenge in the task. Nero was known to be fickle in his affections.

"And if the emperor does not approve of my father's work?"

Hadrian blew out a breath. "We will not consider that possibility at this point. If my father's offering does not please the emperor . . . well." He forced a smile. "We will pray. If the gods are willing, and your father does his best work, Nero will be pleased. Now, if you will linger but a moment, I will fetch my horse and see you safely home."

"You have already given me an escort. Six slaves are more than sufficient."

"My father's future depends upon your safe arrival. So hold a moment and I will join you." He turned and hurried toward the stable.

Sitting beside Cassius, I pulled my palla more closely around my head and thanked the gods for the darkness around us.

With the aedile's son on horseback, plus extra slaves before and behind, our small party had become a parade through the nearly silent streets. The clopping of hooves on cobblestone, the grinding of the iron-rimmed wagon wheels, and the flapping of canvas awnings disturbed the thick quiet that descended after sunset. When Hadrian's horse shied away from a man who abruptly stepped out of an alley, the stallion's whinny rang like a trumpet.

The aedile's son had mentioned the possibility of a cool night, but the air around us was a damp blanket against my skin. The heat that baked the city during the day remained, stirred only by a fetid breeze that carried the odors of charcoal, sewers, and perspiration. I held my palla over my nose as we passed a butcher shop near the Circus Maximus. The place did a brisk business selling meat pies to those who wanted hot food in the arena, but the stench of blood rose from its gutter.

Under the silver cloak of moonlight, details I overlooked in daylight seemed mysterious and significant: secret niches in stone walls, hidden alleys, mosaic emblems on stately homes. Statues of goddesses seemed to sway to the musical gurgle of fountains and underground sewers. A train of rats scurried into a sewer pipe while a fat cat watched their progress, tail twitching in anticipation.

Finally, we entered the crowded streets of the Aventine, where insulae towered over us. I tipped my head back and stared at a rectangle of black sky, dissected by lines of wet laundry that shimmered beneath a nearly full moon. The sound of horse hooves brought several curious faces to windows, so I lowered my head and hoped no one would recognize the wagon. A woman called out, "From where have you come at this hour, girlie? No place for decent women, I'm certain!"

I wanted to disappear. If Hadrian had not insisted on accompanying us, I would have dismissed his slaves and bade

Cassius to trot the mule so we could get Felix home as soon as possible. The boy did not complain, yet he kept grimacing and rubbing his chest.

Hadrian turned in the saddle. "Which building? I have not visited your father's workshop."

Of course he hadn't. Residents of the Palatine tended to spend their free time at the Forum, the Campus Martius, or the Portico of Octavia, named after the sister of Augustus. Why would he visit my father's work when he could study pieces by famous Greek sculptors, golden representations of gods and goddesses, and an ancient bronze of Alexander the Great so carefully crafted that his hair seemed to blow in the wind?

"At the next building, turn right," I told him, gesturing at the street ahead. "But you need not accompany us. We are only a short distance from the shop."

"A man does not quit until the job is done," he replied. "I will see you safely to your father's home."

I groaned. What would the neighbors think? A young woman did not go out after dark without her husband or father, and a worker's daughter did not associate with patricians.

Hadrian and I were oil and water. We could not mix. Ever.

"Please." I attempted to smile. "You have done more than enough. I have my companions, and we are well . . ."

He turned at the point I had indicated, and we followed, stopping outside my father's shop. The door was closed, of course, as was the wide counter window.

Weary of waiting, I slipped from the wagon before Hadrian could dismount. "Please tell the senator I will deliver his letter and urge my father to respond quickly. Thank you, sir, and good night."

Cassius flicked the reins and drove the mule toward the alley. Hadrian's slaves stood in the street, uncertain, while I pulled the key to the workshop from my tunic and unlocked the door.

"Shall I—?" Hadrian began, but I did not give him time to finish. I stepped into the workshop and barred the door behind me.

"Calandra?" Father stepped out from behind the curtain that led to our bedchambers, his eyes as round as plates. "Did you have a problem with the delivery? Was he pleased? Did he give you the payment?"

I handed Father the letter and the pouch of coins. "We had no problems tonight, but I doubt we will be able to say the same about our future."

He paled. "What do you mean?"

"Congratulations, Father—the aedile wants you to create a statue of Nero. But I am not certain the honor will be worth the cost."

"Why not? Was the man unpleasant? Did he not treat you well?"

I drew a deep breath and smiled, knowing he would never understand. My hesitation sprang not from the aedile, but from his appealing and handsome son. Having to see him regularly would surely be torture, like teasing a puppy with a steak destined for the master's table.

"Never mind. The aedile was perfectly civil and quite impressed with your work. You have done well."

"Why then do you disapprove?"

"I do not." I kissed him on the cheek and turned toward my bedchamber. "Good night, Tata."

Hadrian dropped his toga into the arms of a waiting slave, then went in search of his father. He found Cronus in the *triclinium*, sprawled on a couch and feasting on a platter of dainties.

"You are late," Cronus said, wiping his hands on a linen cloth. "I was starving and could not wait."

"I apologize." Hadrian sank onto a couch while a slave poured wine into a goblet. "But the sculptor's daughter has been safely delivered. She promised to urge her father to reply speedily."

"Remarkable work." His father glanced through the doorway that led to the atrium. "I cannot believe an unknown genius resides in the Aventine. But his obscurity will prove practical—I will not have to pay the current rate for such artistry."

Hadrian leaned back as a slave brought his dinner: a roasted nightingale coated in honey and decorated with rose petals and fresh plums. He picked up the bird and pulled off a section of breast meat. "Are you certain you want a statue?" he asked, plucking the few remaining feathers. "Surely you could find something more unique to impress Nero. The man has a hundred statues."

"That is why I must give him another," Cronus answered. He thumped his chest, belched, and licked his fingers. "The man prides himself on his collection of bronze works, so I will add one he truly loves." He picked up a grape, tossed it in his mouth, and pointed at his son. "You should pay more attention to the art of flattery. One day you will have my chair in the Senate, and you must know how to persuade your opponents. To do that, you must have knowledge."

Hadrian swallowed a bite of plum. "You are not dying, Father. I have time to learn such things."

"No man has as much time as he wants." Cronus picked up his cup, then studied his son over the rim. "I have been pleased with your efforts on my behalf, but when you are a senator, you will have opportunities you cannot now imagine. Rome rules the world, and senators have power. You must learn to use it wisely."

Hadrian swallowed another bite, then propped his elbow on the arm of his couch. "I want to make a difference," he said, aware that he rarely enjoyed such honest moments with his father. "I believe in what Rome stands for—virtue, faithfulness, piety. Like you, I believe our duty to the Empire must be greater than anything else, even love for one's family—"

"Soon *you* will have a family," his father interrupted. "I do not want to rush you, but the law requires that Roman men marry by age twenty-five, so it is time you considered taking a wife. We are descended from the fathers of the Republic, so we must maintain the family heritage."

"Above all, I wish to please you, Father. So you have only to tell me when you have arranged the betrothal. Until then . . ." Unbidden, the image of the sculptor's daughter rose in Hadrian's head. The young woman had surprised him with her honest speech and manner. Most women he met were so intent on not offending him that he never knew what they were thinking . . . or if they were thinking at all.

"We must find a woman of gravitas," his father said, waving a finger. "Someone who reveres the gods and wants children. You must have a son, even two, because life is far too short . . ."

He turned away, ostensibly to sip from his cup, but Hadrian understood. His mother had died five years before, and his father still mourned her loss. And not only *her* loss. In the years before his mother's death, Hadrian had lost a brother and sister to Roman fever.

He and his father were well acquainted with grief.

"As I said," Hadrian said, clearing his throat, "when you have negotiated a suitable match, I will marry. I look forward to experiencing the same happiness you shared with Mother."

His father smiled. "Your mother was an exemplary woman, a true Roman, and I see the results of her efforts every time I look at you."

Hadrian lowered his head, hoping his marriage would be as blessed by the gods as his father's had been.

Seven

THE 19TH DAY OF IULIUS

Father and I did not discuss the aedile's offer after my return from Cronus's house, but he was eager to talk the next morning. He caught me when I emerged from my bedchamber, Cronus's letter in his hand.

"Is he quite serious?" he asked, searching my face. "Or has the man lost his mind?"

I tightened the belt of my tunic. "Have you broken your fast?" I moved toward the cupboard. "Do we still have bread and cheese?"

I found the bread and cheese hanging from a wall hook, then set both on the table. As Father sank onto a stool, I cut two portions of each and set them before us. Fortunately, our pitcher still contained water, so we could eat and drink before I would have to go to the fountain.

"Daughter." Father's voice deepened. "You were at the aedile's house; I was not. So tell me—is this a genuine offer, or does he intend to employ other sculptors as well?"

I sipped from my cup. "He has already seen the work of other sculptors. Apparently this offer is sincere. His son testified to his intention."

"His son?"

"Hadrian, the man who escorted us home last night."

Father glanced into the workshop, a frown creasing his forehead. "Such a commission could end our worries about money. He will allow us four years to complete the work? And he will pay us during that time?"

"Four years is a lengthy commitment. Do you want to work so long on a single project?"

"I do not know." Father shook his head, sending a sheaf of gray hair into his eyes. "But what a project it would be! A colossal statue! How tall should we make it?"

"That is for you to decide. What can you create in four years?"

Father leaned back and closed his eyes, lost in his calculations.

I had just taken a bite of cheese when I heard pounding on the wooden planks that shuttered our shop. I snorted in irritation and rose to open the counter window. We were not so prosperous that we could afford to ignore customers.

"One moment," I called to our unseen visitor, then motioned for Father to help. Together we pulled the horizontal boards out of the grooves along the width of our counter and set them on the floor.

I frowned when I recognized the man peering into our shop. Cronus's son had returned.

"Salve," he said, bowing his head when he saw us. "I have come to see if Pericles has decided to accept the commission."

Father blinked, then flapped his hand at me. "Open the shop, Calandra, and get the man a cup of honey water." Before Hadrian could move, Father dipped his chin in a formal bow. "Have you broken your fast, sir? Would you prefer wine over honey water? Calandra, is there any sweet bread?"

I resisted the urge to groan and opened the door. While

Hadrian stood in the workshop, I poured a cup of honey water for our guest.

"Please," Father said, pointing to the bench at our table, "sit. I have not had much time to think about your father's proposition, and I must discuss matters with Calandra."

A puzzled expression crossed Hadrian's face. "You consult with your daughter?"

"Calandra plays a vital part in my work." Father settled onto his stool and gestured to the counter cluttered with ceramic bowls, platters, and vases. "When I accept a commission, she is the one who must turn out the other wares that keep food on our table. She also paints for me—her hand is far steadier than mine."

From across the table, Hadrian regarded me with new appreciation in his eyes. "You told me the truth."

"Did you doubt me?" I asked.

"My daughter is a talented artist in her own right," Father said. "If I accept this commission, she must agree. I will also need answers to several questions."

Hadrian leaned forward, resting his elbows on the table. "That is why I have come. We thought you might require clarification."

Father turned to me, his eyes softening. "Calandra, what say you? Should we take this job?"

I sat as if glued to my stool, my thoughts darting about like frightened squirrels. The job, if successful, might bring my father the acclaim he deserved, well-earned praise that had thus far eluded him. Furthermore, Cronus had promised regular payments, so those coins would cover our expenses for clay, wood, and other tools of the trade.

But if Father's efforts did *not* please the aedile, his work would never reach the emperor. And if the finished piece pleased Cronus but not Nero, who could say how the emperor would

53

respond? I had heard that Nero had a nasty temper. How could anyone hope to please a man who, by all accounts, lusted for glory and blood?

"I think," I said, carefully choosing my words, "that you should make this statue for Cronus Tuscus. But let the senator give it to the emperor. The idea is his, so let the risk be his as well."

Father's brow crinkled. "As intelligent as she is beautiful," he said, winking at Hadrian. "So yes, I will accept the commission. As to my questions—"

"Speak freely," Hadrian said. "I will do my best to provide answers."

Father folded his hands. "I do not know Nero and have seen him only from a distance. How am I supposed to sculpt the likeness of a man I have never met?"

Hadrian shifted his weight. "Father suggests that you work from an image. Many artists have created commendable portraits of the emperor's visage."

Father frowned. "A painting exists in two dimensions, while a sculpture occupies three. I would not want my work to seem flat."

"You would want an audience with Nero?" Hadrian's expression clouded. "I do not know if that would be possible. My father has been a senator and aedile for years, but he has never had an audience with the man."

"Perhaps I could be one among many? I might be able to sketch his proportions if I could see him from across a room."

Hadrian exhaled slowly. "It might be possible for you to attend some of the games Nero favors. Could you view him from—?"

"My eyes are not strong enough to see from across a crowded stadium."

"Could Father visit the Senate when Nero attends?" I asked.

"He could sit in the back. Or perhaps Nero would willingly agree to—"

"Nero thinks everyone wants to sculpt him," Hadrian interrupted. "And my father wants the statue to be a surprise. If the emperor knows the statue is in progress, he might grow impatient . . . or expect too much." A tentative smile crossed his lips. "I say that not to insult you, but when one expects something amazing, one can be disappointed when it finally arrives. If he is forewarned, Nero might expect the statue to be as tall as a mountain and sing on command."

Father chuckled. "True enough."

"Why do we not ask my father for a solution?" Hadrian finally said. "That is why I have come so early in the day. My father is inviting both of you to dine with us tonight. He says it is the least he can do to thank you for your work on his own statue."

Father looked at me, his eyes narrowing in speculation, but I could think of no reason to refuse. Though Father and I had done work for many wealthy patricians, we had never been invited to a home on Palatine Hill.

I widened my eyes, silently urging him to accept the invitation.

"Tell him," Father said, "that we would be honored to attend."

"Excellent." Hadrian slapped his hands on his thighs. "We dine at the twelfth hour. During dinner, perhaps we can devise a discreet way for you to view the emperor's face. After all, you will have four years to finish the work."

Father stood. "Thank you for this opportunity. Gods be willing, we will see you this evening."

"You shall," Hadrian said. "Father is sending a litter to pick you up."

I had just prepared a ball of wet clay when I realized I had nothing to wear to dinner at a senator's house. The linen tunic I had worn the night before would not do, but it was the best I had. This would be a unique occasion, an honor for my father, and I could not go in a mud-splattered tunic with my hair dangling about my shoulders.

"Father," I called, moving to the washbasin. "I need to go out. I may be gone until midday."

He lifted his head from the accounts ledger and looked at me with a distracted expression. He had heard my voice, but I knew he had no idea what I had said.

"I will be gone awhile," I repeated, speaking slowly. "I need something to wear tonight."

"Oh." His brows lifted. "And what should I wear? Will my red tunic do?"

The red tunic with green embroidery on the sleeves had served Father for years, but since he rarely wore it, it might also serve for this occasion.

"Yes, wear the red. When this is finished, we shall buy you a new tunic, or perhaps two. But I need something that is not spattered with paint."

Father returned to his accounts. "Be careful. Guard your purse."

He did not have to warn me. The crowded streets of Rome teemed with pickpockets and tricksters. I found the purse Cronus had given me and took out twenty-five sestertii, enough to buy a decent tunic and perhaps a necklace. Then I took my blue palla from a hook and left the shop.

The street was choked with people from every part of the Empire. As I pulled my palla tighter around my throat, I spotted Ethiopians with ebony skin, Gauls with blue eyes and red tresses, bearded Jews from Judea, and other foreigners whose origins I could not name. I walked carefully, dodging scampering children, avoiding the wheels of pushcarts, and making a wide arc around legionaries on leave. Their sandals were studded with iron cleats, and I once had my foot pierced when a drunken soldier stepped on it.

I walked past the butcher shop, the tanner, and the man who provided mourners for funeral processions. On the other side of the narrow street, I saw an idol carver, a shoemaker, and an *oculariarius*, who made glass or ivory eyeballs for sculptors. I crossed the street and studied his display. His wares were not as detailed as the eyeballs we had used in Cronus's statue, but perhaps he could improve . . .

"Can I help you, lady?" the owner asked.

I shook my head and moved away.

Finally, I found a shop with an image of a woman on the wall. The owner rushed forward, her face wreathed with a smile. "Salve," she said, her gaze raking me from head to toe. "I am Lupina, and I am an expert *ornatrix*. We are a new business, so I will give you extra value for your coin. How may I serve you?"

A blush burned my cheek. "Tonight my father and I are having dinner with a senator," I said, the words coming out in a rush. "I need something appropriate."

A highly plucked brow rose in an arch. "And your mother?"

"I have no mother." And never had I more keenly felt the need for one.

Lupina took me by the hand and led me into her shop. "I will make certain you have everything you need. A new tunic, of course. Something white, unless you are married . . ."

"I am not."

"Such a shame. Surely you are well past the age."

"My father needs me." I tamped down a rise of irritation. "And I do not need a husband."

"So say you *now*," the ornatrix cooed. She walked to a table, where several lengths of linen had been folded into tidy bundles.

She lifted one and shook it out. "I can imagine you wearing this with gold brooches at the shoulder and perhaps two gold belts—one at the waist, another directly beneath the breasts." The woman's lashes fluttered. "To show off your charms, of course."

I resisted the urge to chuff in exasperation. "I do not want to spend a fortune, but neither do I want to look like a pauper. My father is an esteemed sculptor about to receive an important commission."

"An auspicious occasion," Lupina said. "Stand and I will fit the tunic for you. And then, if you are willing, I shall do your hair in the latest style. If you like, I can add a touch of hair color—"

"I am fine with the color," I said quickly. The woman snapped her fingers, and two slaves stepped forward, removing my tunic with practiced gestures. Soon they had fitted me with two lengths of the white linen, covering my front and back. The slaves fastened the two lengths at the shoulder, then one girl tied a golden cord beneath my breasts while the other fastened a thicker belt at my waist.

"Now," Lupina said, "let me see you walk."

I took a step forward and felt air flowing around my limbs.

"You have attractive legs," the ornatrix said, "but you need new shoes. I have the perfect pair of leather slippers."

I would have resisted the unnecessary purchase, but I could not argue with her selection. My sandals, worn and stained, would not be appropriate for tonight.

Then, before I could protest, the woman had covered me with a rough piece of fabric and pushed me onto a couch. One of her slaves sprinkled ash through my hair while the other placed an iron rod onto the hot coals of a brazier.

While the rod heated, the ornatrix lifted my elbow and peered at my armpit. "A disgrace." She clucked her tongue. "I can tell you have no mother. No self-respecting woman would let her unmarried daughter walk about in this condition." She snapped her fingers at a waiting slave. "Fetch the hair plucker."

I would have risen from the couch, but a slave held me down. I gasped in horror when another slave appeared, armed with a sickle-shaped blade. "This will not hurt," the slave said, her eyes slanting like a cat's. "But if it does, remember that one must suffer to be beautiful."

"Before she begins," Lupina interrupted, "we should decide what to do with your hair." She pulled out a box of coins, each of which had been embossed with an image of a Roman woman. Along a windowsill she had also arranged several small statues, each representing one of our emperor's wives.

"Choose a style," she said, fingering my unruly hair. "Whichever you prefer."

My gaze flitted over the coins and statuettes, then I tapped a statue with tight curls around the head and a bun at the neck. "The Agrippina," Lupina said. "Our emperor's unfortunate mother."

I grimaced, remembering that Nero had allegedly murdered the woman. "Should I choose someone else?"

"You are not becoming the woman; you are only adopting her hair style. But first we must take care of those arms. I cannot apply a hot rod to the head while my client is having her underarms plucked."

I gasped as the first two slaves held me down, using the hair plucker to apply warm tar to my armpits. She scraped the iron blade over the tar, removing the substance and a layer of skin. The blade did not remove the hair cleanly, so she repeated the process, ignoring my yelps as she scraped. Finally, when my armpits were red and sore, she resorted to a pair of tweezers, which she wielded with dogged persistence until my underarms were as bare as my cheeks.

"Much better!" Lupina nodded in approval. "Now you can relax while we arrange your hair."

I closed my eyes, exhausted from having endured the hair plucker. My eyes flew open, however, when I heard the sizzle of hair against the hot iron. When the red-hot rod touched my scalp, I squealed like a pig at the butcher shop.

By the time Lupina and her slaves had finished with me, I felt like a shadow of the woman who had entered the shop. The ornatrix handed me a looking brass.

A stranger stared back at me.

Through the clever use of pomade, water, and woolen thread, Lupina had arranged a row of tubular curls around my face. The length had been gathered into a ball at the back of my neck, though several wavy tendrils trailed behind my ears. My face had been painted, my eyes darkened, my lashes lengthened. Even my angry underarms had been soothed with a mysterious salve.

"I have never appeared so . . . patrician," I said, astounded. "How much do I owe you for this miracle?"

"Twenty sestertii," she said, holding out her palm. "For the tunic, slippers, hair, and ornamentation."

I took every coin from my purse and dropped them into the woman's hand.

❖

As the twelfth hour approached, I calmed my jittery nerves by reminding myself that Cronus had been pleasant at our last meeting. Would he be as pleasant tonight, or would he mention some unexpected requirement for this commission?

And what of the banquet? I had never dined at a wealthy man's home. What if I did something wrong or said something to offend him? What if I spilled food on my tunic, or worse, on my host?

"Father," I said, pulling loose threads from the end of my palla, "perhaps we should not go. Surely Cronus can send a contract for the commission. We do not have to eat at his house to get work."

Concern and confusion mingled in Father's eyes. "What worries you, daughter?"

I shrugged. "I am not accustomed to conversations with educated and wealthy men. I do not want to embarrass you."

"Calandra." Father stood and placed his hands on my shoulders. "You could never cause me embarrassment or shame. Do you not speak with wealthy men at our shop?"

"But they think I am only a shop girl. Perhaps it would be better if Cronus thought of me in the same way."

"You have no reason to doubt yourself. And you have never looked more lovely." He turned when someone knocked at the door. "That must be the litter. Shall we go?"

"Wait." I hurried to my bedchamber and grabbed a comb from my trunk. Then I returned to my father and gestured to a stool. "You look distinguished," I told him, "but sit and let me do this for you."

His brows flickered, but he sat, folding his hands while I ran the comb through his overgrown hair. Most men regularly visited the barber to share jokes and stories, but my father saw no need in ritual vanities. As a result, his hair was overgrown, his face covered with silver stubble. He also carried a soft little belly beneath his tunic, but so did many men of his age.

I combed his hair forward, covering the bald spot, and tucked a few long hairs behind his ears.

"Done," I whispered.

He glanced at me over his shoulder. "Are you certain I will not embarrass you?"

"You could never embarrass me," I said, readjusting my palla. "But I want you to look as handsome as possible."

So, appropriately combed and plucked, Father and I stepped outside and found four slaves in matching tunics waiting at the curb. The double litter was covered with fine linen drapery that stood open, revealing an interior mattress strewn with pillows.

At least the curtains would guarantee our privacy.

After Father locked the workshop, I climbed inside, slid over, and immediately closed the curtains at my right.

"Why close them?" Father asked as he settled beside me. "Do you not want our neighbors to see how we have been honored?"

"This is embarrassing. Here I am, looking like something I am not, while you—"

I closed my mouth, unable to speak over the lump that had risen in my throat. Dressed in his finest garment, his forehead lined with wrinkles and his hands callused from so many years of working clay and stone, my father deserved a night like this. The man had been my mother and father, teacher and nurturer, friend and confidant. He had done so much for me—the least I could do was remain silent and appreciate his joy.

Tonight, at long last, a powerful senator was going to honor the artist who had brought me into the world and taught me to appreciate its beauty. Lucius Cronus Tuscus might see my father as thread-worn and plebeian, but I saw the sensitive artist beneath the shaggy hair and stubble.

Tonight, on the nineteenth of Iulius, in the tenth year of the reign of Nero, my father would be recognized as an exceptional artist.

I would do nothing to spoil this night.

❖

We arrived at the aedile's house a few minutes after sunset. Burning torches bathed the red door in a golden glow as we disembarked from the litter. The doorman admitted us at once, bowing as we passed. The gigantic dog, I noticed, was not in his usual place.

"Welcome, Pericles Aemilius Claudus!" Cronus strode through the vestibule to meet us, his arms outstretched. "I have been eagerly awaiting your arrival. I am honored to offer my hospitality to Rome's most eminent sculptor and his daughter."

Father and I bowed, then my father grasped Cronus's hand. Hadrian appeared and stood behind his father.

"Your home is lovely," I said when Cronus turned to me.

The senator beamed. "Would you like a tour?"

I blinked, but Father did not hesitate. "Of course! I would love to see where the statue now lives."

"Come this way."

Father followed the aedile and Hadrian fell into step beside me. He gave me a nod and asked if our travel had been pleasant.

"Indeed," I said, trying to behave as though I regularly traveled in a litter. "With the curtains closed, I did not even notice the crowd in the street."

We had scarcely taken ten steps when Cronus stopped and pointed to the floor. "The mosaic tiles," he said, "were installed by my grandfather's slaves as a tribute to Jupiter. Have you ever seen anything more artistic? The shiny bits are gold leaf, but I am constantly having to replace them. My grandfather did not realize that it is not practical to walk on one's gold."

"And now . . ." With a flourish, he gestured to a hallway framed by ornate Corinthian columns. Past the columns lay the atrium, its ceiling open to the sky, with a rectangular reflection pool beneath the opening. My father's statue of Cronus stood on a pedestal in the center of the pool while rose petals sailed around it like tiny skiffs.

"I am honored," Father said, "to find my work displayed in such a prominent place."

"As it should be." Cronus gripped the folded edge of his toga. "Come, let me show you something else."

We left the atrium and found ourselves in a peristyle. Framed by palms and flowers, the focal point of the garden was an impressive nettle tree, heavy with the small purple fruits known as honeyberries.

"My pride and joy," Cronus said, beaming. "This tree was bearing fruit when my grandfather built this house more than one hundred years ago. Before that, the land belonged to a consul of Rome, so perhaps he planted it. Every morning I beg Jupiter to watch over this tree, Hadrian, and his future sons so that they may live long in this house."

Father looked at me, and in his eyes I saw an apology. We had no garden, no peristyle, and no tree. But he had given me so much more.

"An impressive specimen." Father turned to our host. "Do you eat the honeyberries?"

"Nearly every day," Cronus said, leading the way back into the house. "As long as the fruit is in season. I believe honeyberries restore health like nothing else. I shall soon celebrate my fiftieth year, and I am as strong as I was at twenty."

Father nodded. "I have not lived as many years, but time has certainly taken a toll."

"Manual labor." Cronus dipped his chin in a sharp nod. "Plebeians will never live as long as patricians because manual labor saps their strength. I have developed a philosophy—if your heart is fated to beat ten thousand times and you overtax it by hard labor, are you not shortening your days? No wonder slaves live only nine or so years after being assigned to the mines. So it is best to live a life of luxury and let slaves perform the physical labor."

He led us through the rest of his house. We were shown his *tablinum* with its desk and strongbox; his ornate *cubicula* with its imposing bed; the *lararium* carved into a wall with niches for the household gods; and the *culina*, where a half-dozen slaves were busy preparing our meal. Throughout the tour Cronus talked nonstop, presenting his views on public service, a man's duty to others, proper reverence for all things Roman, and service to the emperor.

Finally, we reached the triclinium, where four dining couches had been arranged in a semicircle. The walls of the room were crimson with vibrant green tiles skirting the bottom edge.

"I had the walls painted," Cronus said, his eyes gleaming. "With so much light in the atrium, I thought a little darkness might be in order here." He turned to Father for approval. "An artistic touch, is it not?"

"Indeed." Father sighed. "It is an elegant room."

"My intention," Cronus answered, leading us forward. Near the doorway, a trio of musicians played a sprightly tune with flute, lyre, and tambourine.

Cronus took the couch nearest the doorway, while Father and I took the next two. Hadrian sat to my left.

A pair of twin female slaves entered, presenting us with goblets of *mulsum*, a honeyed wine. I sipped slowly, determined to keep my wits about me, and Father pretended to listen to our host. Hadrian's gaze drifted over the room, seeming to light on every surface save my face.

I was glad for his inattention. I had seen more than enough of him in the previous two days, and I did not need to be distracted in the home of an important politician. Men like Cronus could make life difficult for anyone, but this aedile wanted to be Father's patron. And that, at least for the moment, was a gift from the gods.

While Father and Cronus talked, slaves brought platters of artfully arranged food. I leaned forward, my elbows braced on a pillow, and picked up honeyed almonds and Lucian sausages.

"Delicious," I said, nibbling on a sausage. I looked at Hadrian, who seemed to enjoy watching me.

"I am glad," he said, choosing his own finger foods, "you are enjoying the meal."

Had I been overly complimentary? Did he imagine that I had *never* been exposed to almonds or sausages? I wanted to make a positive impression, but I did not want him to think I'd lived my entire life in squalor. We were not slaves. We were hardworking people who sometimes had coin and sometimes did not.

I grimaced when several slaves entered carrying two huge trays, each of which featured a baked flamingo in a nest. Cronus applauded as they stopped before his couch, then he tore a wing from a bird and tossed a few feathers over his shoulder.

I shook my head as the slave offered the platter to me, but I did take a few of the seasoned mussels at the edge of the platter.

When Cronus stopped talking long enough to dip a boiled egg into a bowl of pine-nut sauce, Father leaned toward him. "Can we discuss the details of the statue you wish to commission? Would you prefer that it be set in bronze or sculpted out of marble?"

Cronus paused to swallow, then pressed his hand to his chest. "It must be bronze," he said. "Because it must be huge. The biggest thing Nero has ever seen."

Shock flickered over Father's face. "Bigger is not always better. How is an observer to see the face on a statue if it extends far above his head?"

"It must be visible from a considerable distance," Cronus insisted. "We could mount it on Palatine Hill or perhaps on a base in the river. People should be able to see it as they approach from the sea."

"And you want this in four years?" Father blew out a breath. "This will be quite the project."

"Of course," Cronus answered, "and I insist that you devote

your full attention to it. My son tells me that your workshop offers pottery and other goods."

"Yes." Father reached for the flamingo. "My daughter makes dishes and bowls—"

"You must stop that," Cronus interrupted. "I will not have it said that I hired a common potter for this work. You are about to become the greatest sculptor in Rome, so you must be single-minded in your work."

When Father hesitated, I knew what he was thinking. The pottery provided a steady income for us, and to stop selling it . . .

"Am *I* not allowed to make pottery?" I said, daring to interject. "I am not my father, and the ceramic items bring in much-needed coin."

Cronus squinted at me. "Well . . . I do not want to be unfair." He sighed. "So be it. Your daughter may continue to sell the pottery. But *your* focus should be on the statue alone, as it shall be your prime concern."

Father nodded. "Agreed."

"Now," Cronus said, gripping my father's arm, "tell me about the process. I want to learn every step in the production of a masterpiece."

Father folded his hands. "We begin with a drawing. Because I have not had an occasion to sketch Nero, I will use an image as reference—one of our coins perhaps. Once the drawing is perfected, we will produce the sketch in clay."

Cronus drew in a breath. "How big will it be?"

"The clay model will not be full size, but it will be detailed. Once we have finished the model, we will enlarge it and fabricate the joins—the places where the statue will be fastened together. Are you familiar with a pantograph?"

Cronus frowned. "I cannot say that I am."

"It is a Grecian device," Father said, a note of pride in his voice, "which allows us to scale an image. The movement of one wooden arm produces identical movements in a second, so the result can be rendered larger or smaller. In this way, through a system of wooden braces, we will create a full-size model."

Cronus rubbed his hands together. "I cannot say I understand, but I am delighted you do. Nero will be thrilled with the result, I am certain."

I was not so certain. Even the lowest beggar on the street had heard of Nero's fickle nature, and yet Cronus seemed convinced that my father would create a praiseworthy offering. If his commission allowed us to eat for the next four years, was this not a good arrangement? Few artists enjoyed such security.

"Tomorrow I will send papers to formalize our agreement." Cronus smiled as a slave entered the room with a platter of sweet cheesecakes and pear patina. "I know our relationship will be as sweet as these delicacies."

Unable to resist, I sampled the cheesecake, sighing as the delicious creaminess melted on my tongue.

"And now, Pericles," Cronus said as he rose from his dining couch, "let me show you more of my art collection. You will find I have an extremely discerning eye."

While Cronus led Father away, Hadrian stood. "Would you like to see the garden?"

I was about to remark that we had already seen it, then I realized that he might have intended to separate me from my father. Though I was not certain what this meant—perhaps Cronus thought it inappropriate for a daughter to hear about finances?—I managed a smile and followed Hadrian into the garden, where we stood beneath the stout branches of the honeyberry tree. We were not unchaperoned. Stout male slaves stood at each doorway, and three female slaves were lighting the garden torches.

"When I was small," Hadrian said, stepping around the sprawling roots at the base of the torchlit tree, "my father built me a tree house. Come and see."

A gust of wind billowed, tangling the curls at my neck, but I followed. At the back of the tree, someone had built a circular staircase that wound around the trunk. The lowest steps had been cleverly hidden behind shrubbery.

Hadrian began to climb, though he had to duck beneath several branches to make upward progress. I laughed as I followed. Clearly, this had not been built for the adult Hadrian had become.

"I am surprised your grandfather didn't build this for your father," I said. "Everything else in this house seems to have history."

"Wood rots," Hadrian said, "unless it is healthy and alive."

I rounded the tree and met him on a platform about fifteen feet off the ground. I had not noticed the structure because leafy branches concealed it. The tree house was remarkable—a lovely private room with leafy walls.

The wind gusted again, rattling the nettle tree's leaves while Hadrian extended his arm and lowered a slender branch. The view stole my breath.

The Palatine District occupied one of Rome's seven hills, and this house stood at a high point. From the treetop hideaway, I could look over the adjoining valley, where the Circus Maximus lay in a cleft between two ridges. I could see the stands that could hold 150,000 people, the rooftops of assorted shops, the barns, and the cages for imported animals.

Beyond the Circus I could see the Aventine with its seven-story insulae, each jammed with plebeians who dined by the light of a single lamp, men and women who worked and sweated, their hearts beating twice for every thump of a patrician's . . .

Staring at the moonlit landscape, I saw more in a single glance than I had ever seen from the ground. Was this how the gods saw Rome?

Another hot gust whipped the branches around us. Instinctively, I reached for the trunk, but Hadrian's arm slipped around my waist. "You will not fall," he promised. "I would not let you."

"I was startled." My cheeks burned at his touch. "I did not expect the wind to be so strong."

"Look there." Hadrian released me and pointed. "A lamp burns in one of the shops. Some merchant is working late."

I squinted into the darkness, then spotted the flickering light. "That is so bright—how could it be a single lamp?"

Hadrian's brows lowered when he looked again. "That is fire, and in this wind it could be dangerous. But surely the *tresviri capitales* will put it out."

I pressed my lips together, quite certain that my opinion of the tresviri differed from Hadrian's. Along with the *vigiles*, the tresviri were supposed to patrol their assigned districts during the night and watch for fires, but often they bullied the population and called their actions "peacekeeping." Whenever strife disturbed a district, the Senate commanded the tresviri to tighten their patrols, which only convinced peaceful citizens to bar their doors after sunset.

But I said nothing. Hadrian and I watched, our eyes fixed on the valley, as the orange light lengthened and rippled through the darkness, moving first along the side of the racetrack, then darting away from the Circus.

My pulse quickened. "The fire is coming this way."

"By the crust between Jupiter's toes, I must alert my father."

Hadrian charged toward the staircase, then, as an afterthought, extended a hand to help me descend. I did not need further urging.

I followed close as a shadow as Hadrian burst into his father's office. "A fire has erupted," he said, perspiration beading on his forehead. "At the Circus."

Cronus sighed. "The tresviri will take care of it."

"The wind has already taken hold," Hadrian said. "It is moving quickly toward the palace of Augustus. Toward *us*."

Cronus's countenance shifted from mild concern to anxiety, and I understood why. The aediles were responsible for civil affairs, so if this fire grew, Cronus's reputation would be savaged. "Ajax!"

A slave appeared in the doorway. "Dominus?"

"Tend to our guests and see them safely home. Send Castor to alert the tresviri—we have fire approaching. Send men to all the houses in the Palatine, and see that the slaves have axes, bucket chains, pikes, and ladders. Also send slaves to operate the *sipones*—there is one near every fountain."

Ajax left at once, and Cronus turned to us. "I am sorry, my friends, that this evening must end. You will be safe—the fire is moving north, and the Aventine is south."

Both he and my father stood. "I will wait to hear from you," Father said, bowing. "Until then I will create an artistic design."

"I have complete faith in you." Cronus pulled a leather purse from his desk and dropped it into my father's hand. "For your immediate expenses. Be well."

We found Ajax waiting for us at the front of the house. The litter-bearers wore anxious expressions, and I wondered if they would return after we reached the Aventine. Who would want to return to a fire?

Ajax motioned to the litter. "If you would hurry."

We climbed into the conveyance. I was about to draw the curtain when Hadrian strode out of the house, his face drawn and his mouth tight. "Be careful," he said, peering into the litter. "Take every caution for your safety." He backed away and commanded the litter-bearers. "Be off! At once!"

I pulled the curtains together as the litter-bearers began to jog.

But even behind the closed curtains, the scent of smoke began to tickle my nostrils.

Eight

"Father . . ." I struggled to steady my voice as the litter jolted over the street. "Will the people of the Palatine be safe?"

"Do not worry." He patted my hand. "The Circus Maximus has survived many fires. It burned when I was a boy, and Tiberius compensated the shop owners for the full value of their properties, paying more than a hundred million sestertii. Even Caligula once paid compensation for the losses suffered in a fire."

"But Nero—"

"The fire will not reach the Palatine. If it does, Nero will compensate owners for their losses. Such has always been the tradition."

I was far more worried about being burned alive than being compensated, but Father seemed determined to remain calm.

The scent of smoke grew stronger, and the slaves carrying our litter coughed as they ran. Their steps had slowed, and when I peeked through the curtains, I saw that the western horizon had taken on an orange glow. Golden embers and swirling smoke danced across the sky as people poured into the streets.

I coughed as my lungs rejected the smoke. "Father, the men cannot continue in such foul air."

He opened the curtain on his side. "Slaves! Halt!"

I wondered if they could hear us above the onlookers' rising panic, but the slaves stopped. My father stepped out of the litter. "My daughter and I will walk," he told them. "If you wish to shelter with us, you may. But you do not have to run."

A wide-eyed litter-bearer met Father's gaze. "We will be beaten if we do not obey our master's order."

"I will not tell Cronus about this. And he will not have time to consider you; he will be occupied with the fire." Father turned, his eyes narrowing when he saw that several scattered fires had dotted the hillside. We watched, speechless, as snakes of flame slithered up Palatine Hill.

Father pointed in the opposite direction. "You can shelter at our shop. Leave the litter here."

"But if it is burned—"

"No argument. Better for it to burn than for men to lose their lives. We must get out of this smoke."

We walked, following the road that ran parallel to the Tiber, retracing our path from earlier that evening. I watched the swirling sky and wished I could see beyond the stately houses that frequently blocked my view, but the sight of the fire zagging about on Palatine Hill was enough to spur me toward home.

The night unfolded like a bad dream. We set out with determination and caution, making our way south. We lost sight of Cronus's slaves minutes after beginning our journey, and our progress halted after walking the length of an insula. Multiple buildings had emptied, swelling the streets with a frenzied throng, many of whom clutched children and bundles of cherished possessions. The air thickened with smoke and swirling embers that dropped combustible kisses onto wooden shingles, women's head coverings, and children's clothing.

I clung to my father's hand and realized with sudden clarity that we might die before morning. I could not see flames, but smoke rolled over us, stinging our eyes and burning our throats. The twisting lanes that had guided us to Cronus's house were choked with panicked men, women, and children. Cinders and ashes danced in the chaos while hot clouds swirled above our heads. Amid the pandemonium, the shrill cries of women and children merged with the shouts of desperate men. Looters complicated the situation, gleefully plunging into burning structures and reappearing with stolen treasures.

The congealed mob around us surged toward the Aventine, but Father gripped my hand and dragged me northward, against the tide.

"Father! Why are you leading us into the flames?"

"There is no bridge that way," he reminded me, his voice ragged. "Unless you wish to swim, you must stay with me." He pulled the edge of my palla over my face, then covered his nose with his mantle. "Stay close."

The shrieks of terrified people grew louder as the fire spread. When we reached the western edge of the Palatine, I stared in disbelief as a group of men hurled flaming torches into unscathed homes. I shouted in Father's ear, desperately attempting to draw his attention to the arsonists, but he pressed ahead, shouldering his way through terrified groups.

I turned, my heart in my throat, when a detachment of firefighting vigiles tore us apart. "Father!" I reached for him as the crowd surged and threatened to carry him away.

The fire caught up with us. I watched as golden flames caressed the uppermost windows of a nearby insula. Dense clouds of gray smoke streamed from cracks in closed shutters, and the laughing crackle of flames nearly drowned out the cries of those trying to flee. Flames danced in the darkness, and streams of sparks whirled off into the night, going only the gods knew where.

"Calandra!" Father caught my arm and dragged me forward. I clung to him like a shipwrecked soul, shuddering when a chunk of blazing debris landed on the spot where I had stood a moment before.

I could see no way to escape. Flames had enveloped the buildings on both sides of the street, and the wind was a searing tempest. A woman who had been next to me for several minutes had disappeared when I turned again, her child vanishing with her. Had she been trampled, or had she given up?

The vigiles near us pushed toward the east, their heavy boots trampling those who could not move out of the way. As Father pulled me northward, I clung to his arm and begged the gods for mercy. At one point, I felt something soft beneath my slippers, but could not bend to see what—or who—I had stepped on. A cat? Or a person?

We reached the Via Aurelia and collided with the human tide streaming over the slope of the Palatine—patricians and hundreds of slaves. The memory of Cronus's floating rose petals colored my vision. Without an escape route and unable to see beyond the edge of the mob, we swayed one way and then another, powerless to exercise free will.

At one heart-wrenching juncture, I heard an anguished scream and looked up at an insula. A man, his tunic billowing in the wind, had eased himself onto a ledge on the fourth floor. As flames licked the window frame, he jumped and disappeared into the crowd below.

The wind howled and shifted, sending the flames in another direction. When we set out, the wind had come from the south, but before long it blew from the north. Several insulae loomed ahead of us, their upper stories outlined with flickering flames. I wondered if those who slumbered within had grasped the danger, but surely they could hear the screams . . .

We no longer had a choice—the crowd that engulfed us

surged toward the river and we went with it. Several insulae stood between us and the water's edge, and they too were burning.

The remainder of that night dissolved into a terrifying series of images that would haunt my dreams for years to come.

I spotted a woman sitting beneath the portico of an insula, her toddler cradled in her lap. Though tears streamed down her cheeks, she smiled and stroked her child's hair. For an instant I wondered if she had lost her wits, then I realized she had decided to face the flames rather than risk being trampled in the street.

A mother tossed her children from a fourth-story window in a last, desperate effort—no one caught them. An elderly man staggered through a nearly skeletal structure, calling out for the wife he could not find. A desperate father dipped his baby into the pool of a fountain, then realized, too late, that the water was hot enough to scald tender skin.

I saw houses crumble into ruin and temples succumb to the flames. People burned, their frenzied screams drowned out by the fire's hiss and cackle as they gyrated in agony.

Through an iron fence I saw a mother, her clothing aflame, spread her palla over her children as their stately home crumbled around them. Another child had tried to squeeze through the fence, but the hot iron seared her flesh, holding her in a deadly embrace.

I bore witness to sights that scarred my psyche and visions that left me numb. And as we struggled in the midst of the mob, I heard an ominous snap and crack. I looked up and saw a burning timber break free of a wattle-and-daub wall. My father shoved me forward, then collapsed beneath the falling beam. As debris rained down around me, I searched and finally spotted the sleeve of his tunic. I struggled to pull him free, ripping his tunic in the process, and finally a man stopped to help move the beam. I slipped beneath my father's arm, swatted the glowing sparks that threatened to ignite his hair, and wiped soot from his face. Together we stumbled away, the overheated paving stones scorching our shoes.

I pulled Father into an alley and examined him in the fire-tinted darkness, noting his torn tunic and the blood streaming from his hairline.

"Father, are you—?"

"I am well. We need to go."

"But—"

"No time for that, we must go!"

I wrapped both arms around his waist and pulled him back onto the street. If we were fortunate, we might reach the river . . .

To my dismay, hundreds of others had the same idea. The mob moved toward the yellow waters, and many jumped into the Tiber without thinking. I heard screams and splashes and wondered if those people knew how to swim. I did not.

As we struggled to reach the river, my father spoke again: "Calandra?"

"Yes?"

"Do not let go of my hand."

"I would not."

His lips curled in a lopsided smile. "I am sorry I am not of more use."

A crazed bark of laughter escaped my lips. "No one has been of much use tonight."

"Do not be alarmed, but—"

"What?"

His wide eyes blinked slowly, then he shook his head. "I am sorry to be a burden, but I-I cannot see."

⸻ ❖ ⸻

Through some miracle of Caesar or the gods, I spotted one of the stone bridges that crossed into Transtiberim. I dragged Father toward it and merged with the tide of people streaming westward. I watched in horror as a woman at the edge of the bridge stumbled and dropped her child into the river, then jumped in after him. The woman surfaced, her face contorting as she screamed, then she went under. I did not see her again.

When we reached the other side, I led my father down a narrow street, hoping to find a place where we could rest. The fire had not yet reached this district, but dozens of residents had come out to stare across the river, their grim faces speckled with ash. I pulled Father forward, searching building exteriors and trying to remember if I had visited any of them. But I could barely see through the smoke.

Then a strong arm pulled me into a walled garden. "Come," a man said, helping me with my stumbling father. "Come and rest. You can lean against the wall, and no one will bother you."

"Calandra?" Father's trembling hand sought my shoulder. "Where are we?"

"In a safe place." I guided him to a space beside a young couple and their two children. "We will go home in the morning."

I eased Father to the ground, then sat beside him, our backs to the stone wall. The man who had helped us had disappeared.

Overcome by weariness, I let my head fall to my father's shoulder. I should have been terrified, yet the frantic energy that had fired my blood evaporated, leaving me limp with weariness and haunted by questions.

What was wrong with my father? Was his blindness a trick of the mind? Would he recover soon? If he did not, how was he supposed to earn his living?

I closed my eyes and prayed I would not have to open them again until morning.

Nine

THE 20TH DAY OF IULIUS

I woke to the sound of voices. For a moment I could not tell whether it was day or night, then I realized that the dull glow midway above the horizon was the sun. But the sky was dark, the air gray, the smoke nauseating.

I nudged my father's shoulder, and he woke almost instantly. "What? Is there fire?"

His eyes were round and dazed, but still he could not see clearly. "The fire is not here, Tata. We are safe."

He drew a deep breath, coughed, and wiped perspiration from his forehead. "Surely the fire is out. We should find something to eat and make our way home." He lowered his voice. "I still have the purse from Cronus. If you can find a market, we will eat."

I squeezed his hand. "Can you see anything? Can you see me?"

He squinted, then slowly shook his head. "I shall have to depend on you for a few more days. But do not worry, daughter, the gods will preserve us. All will be well."

I helped him to his feet, and we left the safety of the walled garden. The public areas were packed with people who had fled their homes. The refugees did not move, but sat on fountains or stood in the street, staring toward the east as they whispered prayers to Jupiter, Vesta, and Fortuna.

Father tugged on my arm. "You must ask someone if the fire is contained."

I waved at a man who had just crossed the footbridge. "Sir, does the fire still burn?"

The man, sweat-stained and sooty, gaped at me. "East of the river, it spreads in every direction. Nothing has been spared."

Father gasped. "Nothing?"

"Nothing I could see." The man's lips compressed in a grim line. "Some are saying this is Nero's doing. They say his men are feeding the flames."

Father flinched. "How could that be?"

"I saw them," I whispered. "Last night. I saw men throw torches into unburned houses."

Father pinched my arm, a wordless warning. "Thank you," he told the man who had spoken to us. "Do you know where we can find food?"

"No," the man snapped, irritation flashing in his eyes. "And you would do well to find shelter. The survivors who have lost their homes will soon pour into this district." He trudged off.

I took Father's hand. "Do we know anyone in this area?"

Father shook his head, but then I remembered. "Last month I sold a set of bowls to a tentmaker's wife who wore the most beautiful blue palla. She lives in Transtiberim."

"How can we find one woman among so many?"

"Do not worry. Rome is not overrun with tentmakers."

I looped my arm through his, and together we lumbered through the streets, stepping over families sleeping on walkways, pointing others toward the nearest fountain, and trying to avoid being trampled by those who insisted on riding donkeys and mules in the midst of the crowd.

Finally I spotted a sign. "The tentmaker—I see the sign above the door."

Somehow Father found the energy to quicken his step. "I hope it is our customer, and I hope she is happy with her bowls."

❖

I knocked at the tentmaker's shop, but no one answered. Perhaps the woman and her family had fled the city. Then I heard stirring from within, so I knelt and peered through the keyhole. The tentmakers had made use of their many goatskins. Throughout the spacious room, dozens of people were lying on skins and woolen blankets. I searched for the woman I remembered and spotted her moving along the back wall.

I pounded on the door.

When it opened, a pair of dark eyes studied my face. "I am Calandra," I said, breathless with hope. "From the pottery shop in the Aventine."

"I remember you." The woman opened the door wider, but her smile faded when she saw the blood on Father's head. "You are injured. Come in, please, and let me clean your wound."

I glanced around—every available space in the room was occupied. "Can you take two more? We would go home, but the fire still rages."

"We will make room."

The woman helped me bring Father inside and laid a blanket on the floor in the middle of the shop. We sat, grateful for a chance to rest, while the woman knelt in front of us.

"Sir." She placed her hand on Father's arm. "I am Priscilla, wife of Aquila the tentmaker." She frowned when he did not meet her gaze. "Sir, are you all right?"

He shook his head.

Priscilla turned to me. "Has he always been—?"

"Last night he was hit by a beam. He has not been able to see anything since."

"I will try to find a doctor." She squeezed Father's hand. "You are both welcome for as long as you need to stay. But now I will find something for you to eat."

She stood and walked away, leaving us to sit in amazement and relief.

"The gods have been kind to us," Father said, his voice breaking in exhaustion. "So many will have no place to go."

"We will be here only a little while," I assured him. "We will gather our strength, then we will make our way home."

"Whatever you say, daughter." And with that, Father lowered himself to the floor, closed his eyes, and slept.

As Father took a well-deserved rest, I walked around the tentmaker's shop. Like my father, Aquila and Priscilla had set up their business on the ground floor of an insula. I saw a curtained doorway that most likely led to their sleeping quarters, while a wide masonry counter served as the heart of the culina, or kitchen. On the stone surface, a clay pot sat on a metal tripod above a glowing log.

My stomach clenched at the thought of food.

Instead of a window that opened to the street, customers of Aquila and Priscilla's shop entered through a sturdy set of double doors carved in a Greek design. Though the shop was filled with refugees, it was not difficult to imagine how the place would appear on an ordinary day. Samples of tanned goatskin lay on a table near the door, and papyri on the wall displayed sketches of tent designs. A desk in the far corner held a box of rolled papyri, along with a stylus and several bottles of ink. A locked strongbox stood next to it, bolted to the floor.

Yet one aspect of the shop was markedly unusual. Most

shops, including my father's, dedicated at least part of a wall to the lararium, where stone shelves held sacrificial offerings, and niches displayed replicas of the family's gods. Every morning Father and I dropped bits of bread and fruit on a shelf before a statue of the *Lares*, our domestic gods.

But though a previous owner had built a lararium into the wall, the niches stood empty, the shelves bare. Had the owners been so distracted by the fire that they neglected the daily sacrifices? I did not know and was reluctant to point out that the tentmaker had neglected his religious duties.

I searched for the lovely woman who had shown us such generous hospitality. Priscilla had moved to the culina to stir the contents of the clay pot. I did not know what she was cooking, but a wonderful aroma reached my nose, and my stomach clenched again. I had eaten plenty the night before, but at that moment my belly felt as empty as a pauper's purse.

"Priscilla?"

She turned, a beautiful smile crossing her face. "Calandra! How is your father?"

"He is resting."

"I am sorry I have not yet cleaned his wound. I had water and cloth, but I saw that he was asleep. I will tend to him—"

Without warning, a fountain of tears sprang up and spilled across my face. I did not know why, but her words, her kindness and concern . . .

Last night, in the middle of the nightmare, I did not think I would experience such things again.

"You poor girl." Priscilla drew me into her arms, patted my back, and murmured soothing sounds. I melted in her embrace and might have remained there if she had not stepped back. "You must stop worrying. You are safe now. You are among friends." She bent to peer directly into my eyes. "Did your home burn?"

"We do not know. We were away when the fire began."

"Let me see if I can learn anything." She called to a tall man across the room. "Aquila! Have you heard anything about the Aventine?"

The man glanced at me as he came toward us. "Not yet," he said. "The fires are still burning."

Priscilla poured two cups of water and pressed them into my hands. "Take one of these to your father and make sure he drinks. I will do my best to find a physician."

I stared, astounded that she could concern herself with our needs while Rome was burning down around us. Her world could burn, too. One shift of the wind, a few embers alighting upon these wooden rooftops . . .

"Your home has been overtaken," I said, feeling guilty. "We should not impose upon you."

"Yeshua told us to be prepared for days like this," Priscilla said, stirring her pot. "Take the water to your father, and I will bring you some soup. When did you last eat?"

"Last night." I shook my head, unable to believe we had been away only a few hours.

"You must be famished. Rest now and I will bring soup—in the bowls you made." She gave me a warm smile, and I could not help returning it.

I crossed the room, careful not to step on any of the other guests, and finally sank to the floor next to my father. An inexplicable peace settled over me as I sipped my water. In all the years of my life, I could not remember any woman fussing over me.

The soup Priscilla eventually brought had been stretched to feed a houseful, but the extra spices gave it a pleasing flavor. She brought bread after Father and I finished the soup and broke off generous pieces for us. While I chewed on the hearty crust, she walked through the room, feeding everyone who had found shelter beneath her roof.

I turned to my father, whose sightless eyes seemed fixed on a distant horizon. "Who," I asked, watching Priscilla move through the shop, "is Yeshua?"

He shook his head. "I have never heard of him."

The fires burned all afternoon, but at least the flames remained on the eastern side of the river. Because Priscilla was so busy caring for those who had taken shelter in the shop, I left my father with her and went to look for a physician. Father still could not see, and other than bathing and bandaging the cut on his forehead, I could do nothing for him.

What if he remained blind? His assurances did not allay my fears. What would we do if he could not sculpt? I could help him, but only to a point. I had never sculpted anything but clay.

What would we do if he could not complete Cronus's sculpture?

Smoke and ashes swirled in the air, so I tied my palla over my nose and searched for a doctor in Transtiberim. Refugees filled the streets, many of them sitting on the pavement and staring at nothing, their faces stamped with despair. I did not know if they would ever recover.

After inquiring at several shops, I finally found a Greek slave who had studied medicine under Celsus, an esteemed physician during the time of Augustus. The slave's master agreed to let him examine my father for two sestertii. At first I thought I would not be able to meet his price, then I remembered that the ornatrix had sewn four bronze *dupondi* into the hem of my tunic to weigh it down. I lifted the hem and extracted the coins, then dropped them onto the man's palm. "Four dupondi equals two sestertii," I said.

"He is yours for an hour."

While the slave evaluated my father, I told Priscilla how I had remembered the coins. I thought she would marvel at the wisdom of the ornatrix, but she smiled and said Adonai had provided.

I nodded. "Who is Adonai?"

"The God above all others, the Creator of heaven and earth."

"So this household worships Him?"

"Yes, and His Son, Yeshua."

The hired slave called to me, asking for a candle.

I looked to Priscilla, who shook her head. "We have none."

The slave sighed. "A lamp then."

Priscilla brought me a small oil lamp. With trembling fingers I lit it and handed it to the slave. He held the clay lamp a few inches from my father's eyes and peered into them. He waved his hand before my father's face and received no response, not even a blink. He touched the cut on Father's forehead and pressed the back of my father's head. "Does that hurt?"

Father winced. "Of course."

The slave handed the lamp to me. "How long since the injury?"

"He was struck last night."

The slave folded his arms. "Your father received a blow to the back of the head, which is connected to the eyes. The area is not swollen, but it is tender. Barring a miracle of the gods, your father will remain blind. When the tenderness at the back of his head subsides, your father's vision will remained fixed as it is at that time."

My heart shriveled to a barely beating lump. "But my father *needs* his eyes. He is a sculptor. An artist."

The slave tilted his head. "Art is not dependent on the eyes; it is a function of the mind and heart. Your father remains an artist. As to whether he remains a sculptor"—he shrugged—"that is up to him."

Glancing over the physician's shoulder, I saw a tear trickle over Father's cheek.

I dismissed the slave, not wanting to believe his report. But if he was right . . .

A week ago I was confident my father could carve anything for anyone. Yesterday he had won praise from a senator and his son. He had received the promise of a commission that would make him one of the most famous sculptors in Rome, perhaps the world.

Why had the gods shifted our lives so dramatically?

I looked to the tentmaker's empty lararium. No Roman gods lived there, so I could not pour out my case before them. Apparently, the only God in this place was Priscilla's invisible Adonai.

I lifted my head. "I do not know you, Adonai, but thank you for this shelter. My father has been everything to me, so now I will be everything he needs to continue his work. We will face the future together."

My father, who must have been lost in thought, turned to me. "Is someone there, daughter?"

"No one we know." I gripped his shoulder. "Do not despair, Tata. When we get home, we will find a new way to create art."

Ten

Hadrian dipped his mantle in a puddle, then pressed it to his face. Amid the mayhem of destruction, he stood motionless, letting the wet cloth cool his overheated flesh. A thin ribbon of sweat trickled down his back while his sandals did little to protect his feet from the hot pavement.

How many days had flames ravaged the city? With the sun blocked by smoke, he could scarcely tell day from night. He had not slept in a bed; he had not returned to his home. He had done nothing but fight the fire.

"You there!" He lowered the wet cloth and saw one of the vigile captains pointing at him. "We must topple this wall."

Hadrian gripped his axe and trudged forward. The work of fire-fighting had become a wave of destruction as men labored to create empty spaces that would starve the voracious flames. His group had already destroyed ten homes along the Esquiline and set fire to the rubble. New fires licked at the crumpled wattle-and-daub walls and died down, their appetite sated.

South of Hadrian's crew, the army's military machines had rammed and toppled two stone granaries. Fire-fighters tossed torches onto the exposed grain as residents from the neighborhood surged forward to protest the waste, only to be ordered away.

The people, especially the poor, did not understand that this ravenous inferno could be extinguished only through demolition and counter-fires. If the people wanted to survive, the vigiles needed to offer the monster clear ground and open sky.

Though Hadrian was not an official member of the vigiles, he had valid reasons for fighting alongside them. His father had approved the idea, reasoning that a future senator ought to be seen working for the benefit of Rome. But the most pressing reason for Hadrian's commitment had more to do with the sculptor's daughter than public appearances. He had sent the woman and her father away after the fires broke out. The thought that he might have delivered them to death haunted him.

"Bow before the emperor!"

Hadrian fell to one knee as the sound of tramping feet reached his ear. A moment later, he lifted his head and saw Nero approaching in the midst of his Praetorian Guard. Wearing a red cloak over a soot-stained tunic, Nero surveyed the demolition. "We will work here, there, and there," he said, pointing to several spots. "Lead me to high ground, so that the people may see I am fighting the fire with them."

Nero's entourage moved toward a particularly high mound of rubble, and the emperor mounted it, gingerly stepping over charred stones until he found solid footing. "Let it be recorded," Nero shouted, surveying the vigiles and the people who watched from scorched buildings, "that I, your emperor, worked among the citizens this day, suffering with the people of Rome through this terrible conflagration!"

Hadrian drew a breath through his cracked lips. History would record that Nero had been present, but Hadrian knew the truth. And so did his father . . . if Cronus still lived.

Eleven

THE 23RD DAY OF IULIUS

As the fires continued to devour the city, I helped Priscilla cook, clean, and tend to the needs of others under her roof. Having something to do eased my frustration with our inability to go home, so I carried fussy babies on my hip while their mothers slept, and bandaged limbs injured from falling debris.

When no one needed my help, I listened. Everyone who came into the shop had a unique horror story, and most were desperate to share it. I sat and listened, fear knotting my insides as they spoke of fleeing their homes after doing all they could to save their children and their possessions.

"Everything is gone," a woman in a once-elegant tunic told me. "All our treasure, the death masks of our ancestors, the roses in the garden. We will have to start over."

"At least you are not alone," I said, gentling my voice. "Many are in the same situation."

"Are they?" The woman wiped away fresh tears. "I do not know if we will ever find all our slaves. Such an investment, lost to the flames or escaped to the country."

I blew out a breath. Perhaps she was correct, but not many of the refugees I'd met had to worry about escaped slaves.

When the tentmaker's workshop could hold no more, the refugees spilled onto the portico and the street beyond. People slept on the pavement, in the shifting shade of insulae. I did not know how they knew that Priscilla and Aquila would help them, but they did.

Though the homes in the Transtiberim District had not burned, we still suffered the fire's effects. Smoke hung low in the sky, causing us to cough and stinging our eyes. Soot filtered in through the shutters and doors, and the hot wind of summer did little to dispel the heat that drifted over the city like a shroud.

Priscilla enlisted several women to help her feed refugees while Aquila brought goatskins from his storage room. He wet the skins in a fountain and hung them on the roofs of buildings near the river, shielding the wooden shingles from flying embers. The wind remained erratic, blowing from the south, then from the north, and whooshing through narrow spaces between insulae. The law required an alley of at least two and a half feet between buildings, but that was not enough to keep flames from leaping from one roof to another.

While helping Aquila one afternoon, I climbed through an attic window and surveyed the smoking city east of us. Buildings that had been emblazoned with red, green, and gold paint now stood dark and charred; insulae that once towered above the street had become stubby skeletons against a gray sky.

Was this the end of Rome? Surely not! Rome was the Eternal City, protected by a pantheon of gods and goddesses. But where were our deities and why had they allowed so many of our citizens to be burned alive?

Days passed, and while I carried bowls of soup and distributed bread and cheese, I searched the ever-changing sea of refugees for Cronus or Hadrian. I had heard that most homes on the Palatine were destroyed, including the palace of Augustus. Several temples had also burned, which would not please the gods.

If our gods are so powerful, I yearned to ask, *why did they not preserve their temples and our homes?* But I could not ask anguished people for answers.

As the sounds of coughing and weeping stilled each night, Aquila would stand in the center of the room and pray, his voice booming throughout the shop: "*Baruch atah Adonai,* Creator and Master of all," he would say. "Thank you for preserving our lives and bringing us to a safe place. Thank you for the food you have provided and for the shelter over our heads. We pray your angels would shield us from embers and flames, and that you would awaken the hearts of those who slumber in ignorance. Show us your power, *Adonai El Elyon,* for you alone are worthy of praise and honor. We ask these things in the name of your Son, *Yeshua Mashiach.*"

I wondered what the others thought of Aquila and his foreign God. Many closed their eyes and dozed while he prayed, but several listened, their foreheads creasing as he spoke of provision and protection. Our gods had not protected us, but apparently Adonai had protected the people on this side of the river. Why?

On the fifth day of the fire, I went with Priscilla to deliver bread to other homes in Transtiberim. Since farmers could not come into the burning city, only those with surplus grain could eat.

When she asked if I wanted to join her, I glanced at my tunic, which had become stained with soot and grime. She laughed. "This is not a time to be concerned about one's appearance," she said, wiping her hands on her own garment. "It is a time to be concerned about people. We will wear our soiled tunics and suffer along with the others."

But we weren't suffering—at least not as much as those east

of the river. As we walked, each of us carrying a basket of bread, I gave her a curious look. "If the markets cannot get grain, how did you procure so much?"

A dimple appeared in her cheek. "Adonai provided."

"But how? Did He send grain during the night?"

Her eyes softened. "Several weeks ago, Aquila had a dream. In the vision, a man told him to store up grain, just as Joseph stored grain in Egypt. Aquila did, and now we have enough to share."

"Your God speaks to you through dreams?"

"Sometimes. But however He speaks, we listen."

I watched as Priscilla spoke with several women, many of whom had lost loved ones in the fire. I did not doubt that she was a compassionate woman, but why did her husband believe his dream came from God? I frequently had odd dreams, and I could have interpreted any of them as a warning. I dreamed of a fire once—had Fortuna attempted to warn me of the coming danger? What made Aquila's dream different from mine?

We visited several apartments in an insula, and all were filled with refugees. Priscilla introduced me to the tenants in each dwelling, but after a while the names and faces ran together.

"Are all those people believers in your God?" I asked when we finished our deliveries. "You seemed to know everyone."

"I know Petros and his wife, Hannah, Mariana and Marcus, Titius and Aurora, and Thomas and Lucia," she said. "Many of them are confined to their homes, so they cannot leave to search for food."

I winced at the unexpected answer. "They are prisoners? What have they done?"

"They believe in Yeshua; they have refused to sacrifice to the false gods."

I had heard rumors of a new cult whose adherents called

themselves *Christians*, but I knew little about it. "Who are these people?"

She turned to face me. "We are Jews and Gentiles who believe in Adonai and His Son, Yeshua. We believe Adonai is the only God worthy of worship, so we cannot bow before any other. To do so would be a lie."

She started walking again, so I hurried to keep up. "You and Aquila believe, but you have not been arrested."

"Most of us live quiet lives that draw little attention. But the people you met were subjected to a loyalty test in Corinth, and they could not deny Yeshua. Since they are Roman citizens, they were brought here to await trial."

I digested the information in silence. I knew little of politics, but I could not believe Nero would be upset by the religious beliefs of plebeians. None of the people I had met behaved like criminals; they were as pleasant and kind as Priscilla. Surely Nero would soon release them.

"How long have they been under arrest?"

Priscilla chuckled. "Years. Yet they are content to follow God's will for their lives. If that means they must live in a tiny Roman apartment, they will be satisfied."

As we approached the river we heard shouting, so we stopped to listen to a man who had climbed onto a platform to address the crowd. "Nero walks among us!" he shouted, lifting his arms in the stiff, practiced gestures of a professional orator. "Our divine emperor returned to Rome as soon as he heard about the fire, and now he works to end this calamity. His own house has been destroyed, as well as many temples and monuments. But you have an emperor who loves you and cares for his people."

Was Nero among us now? I scanned the crowd, but saw no one in purple, no Praetorians, and no ensign.

Twelve

THE 28TH DAY OF IULIUS

Rome burned for seven nights and six days. Every morning Aquila climbed into the attic of his building and peered out a window, then brought us reports of the fire-fighters' progress. On the morning of the twenty-sixth, Aquila reported that the fires had been extinguished, so Father and I made plans to go home. Yet those plans were set aside when another scout reported a fresh blaze. That new fire was not contained until the twenty-eighth of Iulius, nine days after the fire's outbreak.

Weary fire-fighters crossed the footbridge and told us that most of the buildings in the Aventine were still standing, a report that gave us hope. But Father and I were not completely reassured. We had placed our hope for the next four years in Cronus, but what if he had perished in the flames? We heard rumors about the Palatine lying in ruins and of patricians who died trying to flee with their treasures. Was our benefactor among the dead?

On the afternoon of the twenty-eighth, as I helped Priscilla feed the refugees one last time, she caught my hand. "I know you are eager to go home," she said, her eyes shining, "but I hope you will visit us again. You and your father have become precious to us, and we would hate to lose your friendship."

"Of course," I said, my heart warming. "After all—" I forced a laugh—"you have some of our bowls."

She gestured to my father, who was talking to Aquila. "I am sorry his condition did not improve. I will keep praying for him."

"I am certain we will find a way to work," I said. "With my help, he will—" I halted, the words catching in my throat, when a familiar figure came through the doorway. For an instant I wondered if I was seeing a ghost, then the man caught my gaze and smiled.

Cronus's son had found us.

As Priscilla slipped away, Hadrian strode forward, grinning with what looked like relief. "You are alive! And your father?"

I pointed toward the table where my father sat with Aquila. "He is well."

"Gods be praised! My father and I worried that you had been lost in the fire."

"Your father lives?"

"As of this morning." Hadrian grinned. "Our house is gone, but Nero has opened his palace at Maecenas for displaced residents of the Palatine, so we are staying there. Once we begin to rebuild, my father intends to formalize his agreement with your father."

I pressed my hand to my chest, my heart singing with relief. "Happy news, indeed. How did you find us?"

Hadrian waved his hand toward the door. "I thought you may have crossed the river, and others said this place was serving as a refuge. I would have come sooner, but I have been helping fight the fire."

I scarcely heard what he said, for I was too busy looking at him. He was cleaner than I was and wore a fresh tunic, but his hands bore cuts and bruises that testified to his work with the vigiles. His eyes had not left mine since he entered the workshop, and I found it difficult to tear my gaze away.

"I thank the gods you are safe," I said, embarrassed that my pulse had begun to pound. "Father and I are eager to go home and see what must be done before we begin the work."

"Would you like me to escort you?"

I almost said yes, then I remembered Father's injury. How could I tell Hadrian that the senator intended to hire a blind sculptor? If Father's injury improved, perhaps I would not need to tell him anything.

But every day I had probed the back of Father's head, hoping his injury was still tender. Until it healed completely, the doctor said, his vision might improve. But one morning he did not flinch when I touched the spot, and yet his blindness remained.

I sidestepped so Hadrian would turn his back to my father. I did not want him to notice how Father stared vacantly as he spoke to Aquila. "I would like you to escort me to our shop," I said. "If the building has been damaged, I want to know so I can prepare my father for bad news."

Hadrian's brow flickered. "When would you like to go?"

"Right away." I pulled my palla over my hair. "If we go now, we should be able to return before dark."

Rubble smoldered as Hadrian and I trudged over what had once been a street. Though the fire had been officially extinguished only a few hours before, the vigiles and civil slaves had worked for days clearing paths through the debris.

Even though I had watched the fire's progression from the other side of the river, my throat tightened when I saw the extent of the damage. Piles of charred stone lay in heaps in spots that had once been marked by beautiful homes. Pieces of people's lives floated in swollen gutters—a blackened necklace, a carved goddess, a child's toy.

After a few moments, I kept my gaze on the ground. Where were all those people? Were they among the displaced or had they died in the blaze? The city's collective grief clung to me like the soot that had permeated our tunics.

As we walked, Hadrian occasionally asked passersby for information: "What remains of the Aventine? What of the insula on the Via Ostiensis?"

No one could give us an answer.

We entered the Aventine from the north and walked toward the insula that had housed my father's workshop. The streets were packed, but none of the faces were familiar. These people had to be refugees, and many had been injured in the destruction. Men and women with oozing, blackened burns lay on mats beneath storefront awnings, moaning in pain and gasping for relief. But I saw no doctors and suspected that most of the city's physicians were tending those who could pay despite the disaster.

Days before, we had traveled the same road and I had been painfully aware of dozens of prying eyes, each pair belonging to someone who knew a patrician's son and a pleb's daughter did not belong together. But those sharp eyes had disappeared, as had the old Rome. All that remained were the starving, the homeless, the injured . . . and the survivors. Hadrian and me.

Finally, we reached my father's shop. I stood motionless in the road and examined the building, stunned by our good fortune. The wooden shutters had been singed in several spots, but our building stood. Hadrian pushed at the door, and it swung open, the lock broken. We walked in.

The workshop was not empty—a half-dozen vigiles sat against the wall, their eyes closed and their faces lined with soot. One of them opened an eye as we approached, then went back to sleep.

I nudged Hadrian. "Should we——?"

"Let them rest," he said. "They may be the reason your building survived."

We walked forward. Every worktable and stool was covered with a layer of gray ash. I would spend weeks cleaning. Hadrian whistled when he saw my father's tools remained on his workbench, along with several clay statues that had served as samples of his art.

He sank onto a stool. "I do not suppose there is any food."

I snorted at the thought but moved to the cooking counter out of habit. I reached beneath it and pulled out my bread box, which held a loaf of moldy focaccia. "There is bread, but I do not think you would want to eat it."

He glanced at the bread and laughed. "Life will return to normal, but probably not for months. Until then, food will be in short supply, so take it when you can find it. But Fortuna has blessed you—you still have a home."

I startled when an unexpected sound came from the living quarters at the back of the shop. I moved forward, about to investigate, when Hadrian stepped in front of me and whispered for me to wait. He pulled a dagger from his belt and crept toward the back, pushing aside the curtain that led to our private space, then he turned into my bedchamber.

His shoulders relaxed, and his dagger returned to its sheath. A moment later he came toward me, a sheepish smile on his face. "I do not know how you feel about sheltering others," he said, "but two families have moved into the bedchambers. Both have small children."

For an instant I was annoyed—how dare anyone invade our private quarters?—then I remembered Priscilla. How could I deny anyone anything when I had been freely welcomed, fed, and made to feel comfortable?

Hadrian moved into the workshop and nudged one of the

sleeping vigiles with his sandal. "Wake," he commanded, his voice husky. "The fire is out, and your efforts have been rewarded. Go. Find your families and feed them as best you can. Now the real work begins."

The authority in Hadrian's voice roused the exhausted men from their stupor. They grumbled, but they rose, and one man even saluted before leaving.

Hadrian closed the door and examined the broken lock. "I ought to repair this before we go. If I do not, you may return to find another dozen people sleeping in your shop."

I sank onto a wooden stool and gazed at Hadrian, my eyes burning from weariness . . . and guilt. "Now that we are alone, I must confess something."

Amusement flickered in his eyes. "What's this? Did your father lose the advance payment in the fire?"

I shook my head. "I wish the problem were that simple."

"Tell me." He pulled another stool over and sat so close our knees touched. "What could you possibly have to confess?"

I swallowed hard. "My father was injured during the fire. A beam hit him on the head, and since that night he has been unable to see. We found a doctor to examine him, but he could not assure us that Father will see again . . ." My voice broke. "I did not want to give you the news. My father is a talented sculptor and deserves this commission from the senator, but your father will not want to hire a blind artist."

Hadrian caught my flailing hands. "Who was this doctor?"

"A Greek slave. I hired him for two sestertii."

"There are better doctors, I am certain." He pressed his lips together, then met my gaze. "Tell me the truth—do you think your father can complete the work in his current condition?"

I blinked. "Can he sculpt . . . without seeing? I think he can. Many times I have found him working in the dark because he was too engrossed to light a lamp. His talent goes beyond what he sees."

"Then for now, we will say nothing of this. My father's plans must be put on hold because everyone in Rome will spend months, if not years, recovering from the fire. My father's first concern will be focusing on the city, not flattering Nero."

"And then?"

He stood, his forehead crinkling in thought. "While my father is involved in the rebuilding, we will have another physician examine your father. We will take him to the temple of Asclepius on Tiber Island. We will do whatever the gods require to restore his eyesight."

"But if none of those things—"

"If those things do not work, you will help him." Hadrian reached out and placed his hand on mine, his touch sending ghost spiders down my spine. "And he will complete the work. Once my father has recovered from the fire, every month I will deliver your payment and report on your progress. As long as there *is* progress, my father will not need to know that your father's eyesight has been . . . impeded."

"Once your father has recovered? Is he ill?"

"He is not ill, but he has lost everything. He will regain it, of course. He will earn plenty as people pay fees and taxes to rebuild their homes, but that will take some time. He may recover some of his treasures from the ruins of our home, but I doubt it. I am sure the area has been thoroughly looted."

I looked at him, and in that moment I felt as though we were united against the world, against the gods, against the fire. Our two souls were inexplicably bound by determination and purpose.

"Thank you." The words rose to my lips on a wave of admiration and gratitude. I could not believe he was willing to go to such lengths for my father, for me. What other patrician would do that? "I will do my best to make certain our work does not disappoint. We will do anything you say, take any step—"

"First we survive," Hadrian interrupted, removing his hand. "Until life returns to normal, we focus on staying alive."

Shivering in a wave of emotion, I wrapped my arms about myself. "I cannot believe—I cannot accept everything that has happened. The destruction of a single insula would be horrible, but so many have burned! How can any of us return to what we were?"

Hadrian gripped my shoulders. "Do not let fear overtake you." He bent until his face hovered inches from mine. "Do not be like those who sat in the midst of the fire and did nothing to escape. You are made of stronger mettle."

"How can you say that? You do not know me."

"I know you better than you think." His grip on my shoulders tightened. "Your character is evident in your countenance, and I see it every time I look at you. I see strength in your eyes, loyalty in the stubborn set of your jaw, and intelligence in your brow. I see *you*, Calandra, and I know who you are. That is why I found you. I knew"—his hands slid from my shoulders and caught mine—"you would survive."

Reason fled my brain as I lost myself in his eyes. No man had ever held my hands like this, and no one, not even my father, had ever spoken as though he had peered into my soul . . . and seen things I had never glimpsed in myself.

No man had ever made me feel like this. I met men every day at the shop, and none of them had ever fascinated me like this. Yes, Hadrian was attractive, perfectly proportioned and a sculptor's dream, but he had also been gifted with a quick tongue, a clear head, and a determination that met and matched my own.

His gaze held me, and in that instant I understood the elemental force that had compelled Paris to kidnap Helen of Troy and wage war for her. I felt as though I had been created for

Hadrian and he for me, and no one else would suit either of us. Though some small voice whispered that we would never have been thrust together if the world had not been turned upside down, I did not want to listen . . .

Only by the strongest of efforts did I tear my eyes from his. I turned my head and noticed a welt along his forearm. I ran my finger over it and heard him catch his breath.

"You were hurt." I met his gaze again. "You are not a vigile, so why did you go out to fight the fires? You could have remained at the palace."

"Truthfully?" He leaned closer. "I went out to fight fires . . . and search for you."

My common sense skittered into the shadows as our lips met, his arms went around me, and I surrendered to the overwhelming yearning that engulfed my heart.

Thirteen

THE 29TH DAY OF IULIUS

Hadrian could not sleep. Though the effects of several days' hard labor bore down on him with an irresistible weight, the significance of what he had just done would not let him rest.

For the first time in his life, he had been honest with a woman about his feelings. Without negotiating through her father or his, he spoke to her while looking into her eyes and heart. She responded with warmth, all the passion in her nature, and something that felt like desperation.

And afterward, as they lay on his mantle amid the ashes on the floor, he realized that the freedom of this interlude would not last. Life would resume in familiar patterns. The patricians' homes would rise again, along with their expectations. In a few weeks or months, his father would build another house and expect Hadrian to resume his role as a future senator.

The Roman way of life had been momentarily upended . . . but it would return.

Once the city recovered from the fire, his father would resume his search for a suitable daughter-in-law. Because Cronus held such important positions, Hadrian would need a wife from a wealthy patrician family, a woman descended from prominent and powerful ancestors.

The odds of Cronus marrying his son to the daughter of a sculptor, however accomplished, were about ten million to one.

Hadrian rolled onto his side, propped his head on his hand, and studied the woman sleeping next to him. When she woke, would she regret this encounter? Or would she wake as he had, with the sad knowledge that no matter what their bodies had promised, they could never be married.

He rolled onto his back and examined the shutters over the nearest window. Unless he was mistaken, the sun was attempting to penetrate the blanket of smoke floating over the city. A new day was about to begin . . . and he had responsibilities to his father.

He sat up and allowed his eyes the pleasure of observing Calandra while she slept—noting the curve of her cheek, the delicate points of her upper lip, the gentle arch of her brow. He ought to escort her back to Pericles, but she had already proven herself capable of surviving a crisis. She would be safe here in her Aventine home.

And if no one saw them leaving together, her reputation would not suffer.

So why did he feel so guilty?

"Forgive me," he whispered, rising from the floor.

Fourteen

THE 31ST DAY OF IULIUS

At the end of the month, Roman officials counted up the losses from the fire, and like many others, I was horrified.

Rome was well-acquainted with fire, but no blaze took as many lives or destroyed as many buildings as the inferno of Nero's tenth year. Of the city's fourteen districts, only four escaped the flames' fury. Three districts were leveled, seven left with the remains of charred buildings and temples.

And who could say how many lives were lost? Over four thousand insulae were destroyed, hundreds dying in each. With their narrow staircases, flimsy structures, and wooden shingles, those buildings became traps. The fire also destroyed historic temples, including the temple of Luna, which had been consecrated by King Servius Tullius in the days before Rome became a Republic. The blaze also consumed the temples of Jupiter Stator and Vesta, both of which stood at the foot of the Palatine.

As we joined our neighbors in the cleanup, Father and I began to hear rumors about the origins of the blaze. According to several witnesses, the fire began at the Circus Maximus. Father believed someone must have disobeyed Nero's order and cooked at the venue. Most of the shops still had cooking areas, and someone might have decided to grill a bit of meat while no one was around to report the illegal activity.

But the explanation of a single disobedient shopkeeper was far too simple to satisfy the outraged survivors. Other rumors began to circulate, stories of uniformed men who had tossed burning torches into unburned buildings, strange men who ignored or threatened anyone who protested their actions. I believed the rumors because I saw those men.

Who could have authorized such an action? Only Nero.

Nero loved spectacle, the gossips said, and what could be more spectacular than the greatest city in the world in flames? Witnesses reported that though Nero *did* fight the fire after returning to the city, when he tired of doing his civic duty, he retreated to the gardens of Maecenas, where, inspired by the beauty of the flames against the night sky, he entertained his closest friends by performing his original song about the glory of the Trojan War. Those who witnessed his performance complimented him. Those who later heard about it despised him.

But not everyone castigated the emperor for his behavior. After the fire, Nero declared he would personally handle the removal of debris. On his orders and at his expense, the civic slaves were commanded to haul rubble and corpses to the Ostian Marshes. To preserve public health, the debris was removed as quickly as possible.

Those who suspected the emperor's motives were quick to point out that his "generosity" allowed him to take his pick of precious items recovered in the debris. "If you had a priceless statue in your home on the Palatine," one wit declared, "you may find it later in Nero's palace."

Father and I returned home at the end of the month of Iulius. We allowed the refugee families to remain with us two weeks, then encouraged them to resume their lives even as we struggled to resume ours.

While I scrubbed floors and walls, Father inventoried his tools and supplies, trying to discover how much we had lost to looters. Several sample pieces were missing, as were a few tools, but Father insisted that we had been blessed. He still had the purse from Cronus, he told me, adding, "Praise Adonai, we did not lose a single sestertius."

I arched my brow—praise *Adonai*? When did my father start praying to a Jewish God?

I, too, had considered Priscilla's God, who had not only spared the Jews and Christians of Transtiberim but provided grain during a time of starvation. After hearing the story of Aquila's dream, my father lifted his hands and declared that henceforth he would worship Adonai. Though I suspected his newfound faith resulted from a portly man's fear of hunger, every morning he knelt at our lararium and asked Priscilla's invisible God for the restoration of his eyesight and success in his new commission.

Since the gods of Rome had utterly failed me, I stopped praying. And though Adonai *might* have fed and sheltered me during the fire, He did not prevent Hadrian from using and abandoning me.

The morning I woke on the floor of our shop, alone, dirty, and ashamed, I knew Hadrian was no Paris. Probably because I was no Helen of Troy, who had been the daughter of Zeus, the wife of a king, and the most beautiful woman in the world.

I was the ordinary daughter of a blind sculptor, and I had no use for a God who cared more for hungry bellies than broken hearts.

Because Rome's gods must have had a reason for allowing the city to suffer such a cataclysm, Nero ordered the priests to consult the ancient Sibylline books. Venerable priests descended into the crypts beneath the temple of Jupiter and brought out the scrolls, then studied the writings so they could absolve the city of its sins.

The priests offered prayers of supplication to Vulcan, Ceres, and Proserpina. The heads of leading families offered sacrifices in the temples. Married women were instructed to perform propitiatory ceremonies on the Capital and the shoreline. Because Rome held mothers in high esteem, patrician mothers were urged to hold ritual feasts and all-night festivals to soothe the angry gods.

Once the gods had been placated, Nero's attention turned to the rebuilding of Rome.

Because Hadrian knew the burden of responsibility would fall on the shoulders of the four aediles, every morning he met with his father and received a list of areas that needed to be evaluated by a team of surveyors.

"I want you to oversee the work on the Palatine," his father told him. "If you find it too difficult to continue your visits to the prisoners, I can find someone else."

"I can continue my visits," Hadrian said. "Why bring in a new man when the prisoners trust me?"

"As long as you can complete the surveying. Nero wants the Palatine cleared as quickly as possible."

"I can do both."

"Fine. Nero plans to pay the landowners for the land he will take to build his new palace, so your appraisal must be exact. And if the workers discover anything of value in the wreckage, set those items aside."

"What sorts of things?"

"Unburned slabs of marble, bronze antiquities, precious stones, jewelry. Anything that can be used for a new purpose."

"I understand. But there remains the matter of the sculptor."

His father blinked. "Sculptor?"

"The statue you wanted to commission for Nero. Pericles the sculptor."

His father swatted the idea away. "That will have to wait, of course. Rome will have to be put back on its feet. Then perhaps I can pursue the idea."

"Of course. But the man and his daughter were waiting on a contract from us. I believe the honorable Pericles may avoid taking on other work that may conflict with your commission."

"So?"

"He will starve if he does not hear from you."

Cronus's brow lowered. "I gave him coin, did I not?"

"You did."

"Then let him live on that for a while."

Hadrian drew a deep breath. "Very well. I will do as you say."

His father smiled. "I know."

<hr>

As the sinking sun signaled an end to another hot day on the Palatine, Hadrian left Lysandros to catalog any valuable items and tally how many hectares had been cleared. While Lysandros toiled, Hadrian took a horse and crossed into Transtiberim.

He was pleased to learn that none of his prisoners perished in the fire. He told Marcus of Corinth that the Christians had been fortunate to avoid the fire's destructive path, but the governor's son only laughed and said that Adonai, not Fortuna, had preserved them.

As always, Hadrian's prisoners were quick to share the little they had, whether it was cakes, dates, or cups of honey water. He was astounded to see that most of their apartments, many of which were small and sparsely furnished, overflowed with refugees weeks after the fire.

At Petros's door he asked the required first question, but when he reached the second—*Have you spread the heresy of*

Christ-worship in Rome?—his throat tightened until he could barely speak. How could he ask that question when he heard the people in Petros's apartment singing praise to the Christ as Hadrian came up the stairs?

He met the elderly Judean's gaze. "Are you now willing to amend your ways and offer incense to the gods of Rome?"

Petros's face split into a crooked grin. "I cannot."

"Right." Hadrian exhaled in a rush. "Then I declare that your imprisonment in this dwelling shall continue until the emperor decides otherwise."

"Are we finished, my young friend?" Petros slapped Hadrian's shoulder. "Then come inside. Hannah has baked fig cakes, and we have honey water to quench your thirst."

Hadrian closed his writing tablet and entered the apartment, nodding at familiar faces. He glanced about as he ate his fig cake, searching for a certain young woman and her blind father . . . but he did not spot them among the believers.

He left the building and hesitated in the street, glancing across the river toward the Aventine. He could easily walk to the sculptor's shop and explain his father's silence, but surely Pericles knew the aedile was busy rebuilding Rome. The commission was a whim, a politician's bid for favor, not a necessity. Surely the artist would understand.

Perhaps he would. But as Hadrian turned toward the north, where he would sleep in one of Nero's palaces, the chiding voice of his conscience spoke the truth. He could not go to the Aventine because he was too ashamed and afraid to face Calandra.

❖

As summer faded into fall, the city of my birth continued to suffer the effects of the fire. While the damaged districts focused on rebuilding, the rest of us tried to feed ourselves.

Without a contract for Cronus's commission, my father

spent hours reconfiguring his workshop to accommodate his blindness. He no longer prayed for the restoration of his sight, but asked Adonai to helped him adapt to a life of darkness. A practical approach, no doubt, but not one that persuaded me to believe in the Christians' invisible God.

One morning I took a basket and went in search of food. The central markets had been destroyed, but farmers from rural areas had been allowed to sell from carts and wagons. I paid two sestertii for a loaf of hard bread and a block of cheese, then tucked them into my basket. I was about to go home when a glimpse of a tall woman reminded me of Priscilla. I had not seen her in three months, and I wanted to know how she and Aquila were faring.

I walked north toward the footbridge and soon found myself surrounded by misery. Starving people lined what remained of the ruined streets—men, women, and children who had little to eat and nothing to exchange for food. Rome had always supplied grain to plebeians, but in the aftermath of the fire, Nero had discontinued the dole.

I hurried past them, feeling guilty because my basket held a loaf and cheese for which I had paid dearly.

Father and I would be hungry if Cronus had not given us an advance payment. We were careful with the coins, not wanting to waste them or attract the attention of thieves. But since Hadrian had not returned with an official contract, I feared Cronus had changed his mind.

I had said as much to my father, who reacted with surprise and indignation. "Hadrian is a good man. He would not allow such a thing to happen."

"But a son does not control his father. And Cronus—"

"Is busy with the reconstruction of the city. Why would he change his mind?"

I had pressed my lips together and said nothing, though I

could think of several reasons. First, Hadrian might have so regretted what happened between us that he had resolved never to see me again. He would not want to visit us for updates on the project, so he might have persuaded his father to find another artist. All he had to do was mention my father's blindness and Cronus could have been convinced to cancel.

Even if Hadrian didn't reveal my father's condition, he could have suggested that his father postpone the project. People were worried about food, not art, and Cronus had to be preoccupied with the needs of the city. The emperor would not expect a statue from Cronus, but he would expect Cronus to rebuild the city.

The last thing Cronus needed was a commission from a blind sculptor. But the sculptor and his daughter desperately needed the commission.

But how could I face Hadrian again? I could not think of him without feeling queasy. Memories of that night in the shop haunted me, no matter how desperately I tried to lock them away. Had I made a complete fool of myself? Had my ignorance embarrassed him? Perhaps I had appeared too eager or even desperate . . .

I wanted to speak to someone about these matters, and I could not talk about such things with my father. What did he know of a young woman's heart? Years before, when my monthly cycles began, I informed my father of the event in a fit of embarrassed stammering. Without replying, he led me to a brothel, where he sent me inside with three words: "Talk to them."

Now I needed a woman's advice again, but I did not want the advice of prostitutes. I wanted answers from someone I could respect. I wanted to talk to Priscilla.

When I reached the highest point of the Aventine, I saw a settlement of tents on the Campus Martius. I had heard of people sheltering in tombs outside the city walls while others, like Cronus, were living in homes belonging to the emperor. Hadrian was probably sleeping in a palace, too.

"You are a fool," I told myself as I struggled to make my way through a crowded street. "To think you might ever find love with a senator's son."

"Do not be so hard on yourself, dearie."

The voice startled me. I glanced down and saw a woman sitting against a wall, her bandaged legs stretched in front of her. "Pardon?"

She grinned, revealing a missing front tooth. "If you want my advice, do not let yourself fall in love. Just find a good man and learn to live with him."

Wasn't that what I had decided to do? Live with my father until . . . until Hadrian.

I gave the woman a quick nod and moved away. I needed to find Priscilla.

———————❖———————

The sun had reached its zenith by the time I reached Aquila's shop. As I approached, the sound of singing reached my ear, and after a moment I realized it was coming from the open door. I had heard choirs before, but never in a tentmaker's shop.

I stood outside as the words of the song flowed over the portico and onto the street: "Come, let us sing to the Lord, let us acclaim the Rock of our salvation. Let us come before his face with thanksgiving, with psalms of joy."

When the singing stopped, Aquila prayed, his voice ringing with depth and authority. I caught the words *Adonai* and *Yeshua*, along with a reference to *Yeshua's death on the cross*.

Their beloved Yeshua died on a cross? I shook my head, losing whatever respect I might have had for the man. Only criminals and fools suffered crucifixion.

I moved aside as several men and women came out of the shop, their faces wreathed with smiles.

When the entrance cleared, I went inside. Aquila's place still seemed more like a center for the homeless than a place of business. Most of the refugees had gone, but a few bedrolls still lay next to the wall. One woman entertained several children in a corner, two busied themselves at the brazier, and another swept the floor. When I asked for Priscilla, the sweeping woman pointed toward the back of the house.

"What has happened here?" I asked, trying to be nonchalant. "A meeting?"

The woman nodded. "The ecclesia meets here."

"What is that?"

The woman stopped sweeping. "A gathering of believers," she said, her eyes narrowing. "We gather for worship."

Sensing that she did not want to say more, I walked to the privacy curtain. "Priscilla?"

The curtain moved aside. "Calandra!" Priscilla drew me into her arms and hugged me, then stepped back. "You look tired, dear girl." Her brow furrowed. "How is your father?"

"The same." I mustered a smile. "But we have managed to clean and organize the workshop. Our area was not heavily damaged."

"God is good," Priscilla said, leading me to a chair. "Sit and let me bring you honey water. Something tells me you could use some refreshment."

I did not protest. An inexplicable tide of exhaustion flowed through me as I sat. My legs felt as though they would not support a dandelion. I could not explain why my energy had dissipated, unless being here reminded me of those horrifying days of the fire . . .

Priscilla set two cups on the table and sat across from me. "Drink," she urged, her voice firm. "And tell me why you are so wan. Have you been able to find food?"

I waved her concern away. "Do not worry about us. We will soon be back to work. My father has a commission, but if that does not proceed, I can make bowls and plates and lamps."

"I may find myself in need of new pots." Priscilla smiled. "Though I have another reason to visit the Aventine. Aquila wants to pray for your father."

I shifted uneasily. "My father would appreciate those prayers. He has also been praying to Adonai."

One of Priscilla's brows rose. "Truly?"

"He was impressed with your generosity. And he could not help noticing that your God protected His people while the Roman gods did little to save the city."

Priscilla's eyes crinkled at the corners as she smiled. "I am sure Adonai protected people on the other side of the river, as well. You, for instance." She leaned across the table and pressed her fingers to the back of my hand. "I see sadness in your eyes, dear girl. Is that due to the fire or . . . something else?"

Before I could answer, a woman who had been working at the brazier came toward us with a plate of roasted meat and vegetables. I had not eaten meat in days, and the pungent aroma struck me like a fist in the stomach.

Horrified, I covered my mouth and ran for the front door, then vomited into the gutter. As I stood there, spitting and clinging to a column, a gentle hand touched my shoulder.

"Come inside," Priscilla said, her voice low and understanding. "Come in, drink, and have some bread to settle your stomach. Then you can tell me about the man who has planted a child in your womb."

Though Priscilla's words had hit me with the force of an avalanche, I knew they were true. The women at the brothel had told me what might happen if I slept with a man—about how my monthly bleeding would cease, and then would come nausea, swollen breasts, and illogical feelings and sensitivity to smells. I had forgotten the details of their lesson, but everything came back to me in an overpowering rush.

I choked back tears as Priscilla put her arm around my shoulders and led me to the private chamber where she and Aquila slept. She sat me on the edge of the bed, then perched on a stool and leaned forward, bracing her elbows on her knees. "Tell me," she said, her eyes soft with understanding. "I will listen."

The story poured out of me. I told her about Hadrian's strength and kindness, his courage, his promises, and his cowardice. "He was gone when I woke the next morning," I said, spilling the bitter words through a stream of tears. "I thought he would at least take me back to my father, but he disappeared."

Priscilla bit her lower lip, then took my hand. "What happened *then* does not matter *now*," she said, silently acknowledging that Hadrian would never be able to marry me. "What matters now is the child you carry within you. Life is a gift from Adonai, even when it is unexpected. You should do your best to care for that little life, and if you need help, call on me. I will do everything I can to support you." A smile curved her lips. "You are not alone. Mariana, another of my friends, is also expecting a child. She and her husband are thrilled."

"But I have no husband." I released another shuddering sob and swiped tears from my face. "How can I tell my father of this?"

Priscilla gave a sigh. "Your father was once a young man, so he will understand. He will not feel kindly toward Hadrian at first, but he might sympathize. You are an attractive young woman, and you had just survived a traumatic experience. You were both alone and vulnerable, and you had witnessed so much death. I can understand why you would want to experience some kind of . . . connection." Her voice softened. "If I had been in your situation, I might have responded in the same way. Then I would feel exactly what you are feeling now."

She squeezed my hand and pointedly studied my abdomen. "According to what you have told me, you will have a child in about six months. Until you do, I would recommend wearing loose tunics. When you go out, cover your belly with a palla. I do not know how observant your neighbors are, but a little disguise may prevent wagging tongues." Her eyes darkened. "But since this is Rome, it is possible no one will care."

Cold reality swept over me in a terrible wave. "I cannot have a child. The baby will have no father to acknowledge him."

"Adonai will acknowledge him. And the Lord will direct your path."

Her words made absolutely no sense. Priscilla insisted the child I carried was a gift from Adonai, but she could not possibly be right.

Fifteen

THE 2ND DAY OF NOVEMBER

Euodia lifted her head when she caught sight of the massive walls at Rome's southern boundary. The gate at the Via Campana appeared sound, but appearances could be deceiving.

Ariston, who must have sensed her foreboding, gave her a smile. "Adonai has brought us safely to our destination," he said, urging the mule forward. "And we will trust Him for whatever lies ahead."

After seeing so many camped outside the city, they left the wagon at a stable and put a few things into straw baskets. As they approached the gates, they spotted a series of blackened mounds that stretched off into the distance. Hundreds of people crawled through the mounds, their bodies and tunics blackened by soot.

"Scavengers," Ariston said. "A nasty business."

Euodia crinkled her nose. A sour stench hung in the air, mingled odors of smoke, death, and decay.

They quickened their steps and entered the city. The narrow cobblestone streets were jammed with foot traffic and tight with farmers' carts, but none of the structures in this area were scorched. "These are insulae," Ariston said. "Hundreds of people live in them."

They were so tall! Euodia tipped her head back and stared at a sliver of sky, all that was visible between two towering buildings. "Like mountains," she murmured. "In the middle of the city."

"Look there." Ariston pointed to a bubbling fountain in a distant clearing. "The genius of Roman architects. The Aqua Appia runs underground, so the fire could not touch it."

They paused at the fountain to drink and wash the grime of travel from their hands and faces. As Euodia dried her arms with her palla, Ariston asked a stranger if he knew of a tentmaker called Aquila.

The man scowled. "You think I know everyone in Rome?"

"He's a Jew," Ariston added.

The man's frown deepened. "Try Transtiberim. Most Jews live across the river."

Euodia sighed. "At least we know where to start looking."

They walked another hour, shouldering their way through crowded streets until they spotted a bridge. After crossing, they could not help noticing that no buildings west of the river had been blackened—a sign that boded well for their friends.

Ariston stopped another man to ask after Aquila and was immediately rewarded. "There." The man pointed to a sign above a shop on the first floor of a tall building. "The tentmaker lives there."

Euodia breathed a sigh of relief and caught Ariston's gaze. "It would appear the Lord has a plan for us in Rome after all."

Euodia and Ariston entered the tentmaker's shop, startling a tall woman who had just set a platter of bread, cheese, and fruit on the table. "Can I help you?" the woman said, wiping her hands on her apron. "Do you need a tent or . . . something else?"

Euodia glanced at Ariston, then took his hand. "We have come from Philippi. We are Ariston and Euodia, believers in Yeshua."

The woman gasped, her hands flying to her face, then turned to the man seated at a desk across the room. "Aquila! They have arrived!"

Euodia's heart sang with delight as Priscilla and Aquila welcomed them.

"Paulos said you would be coming," Aquila said, drawing Ariston into an embrace. "With all that has happened, we did not know when to expect you."

"After hearing about the fire, we were not certain if we should proceed," Ariston said. "But since we had committed ourselves, we pressed forward."

"And now you are here." Priscilla gave Euodia another hug. "Sit, will you, and eat! You may stay with us as long as you please, and you are welcome to share our showroom to sell your fabrics." Her cheeks brightened. "A tentmaker and a seller of purple! A unique combination to be sure!"

"There is a lower-story apartment available across the street," Aquila said. "Very pleasant and close to us, if that matters. But no matter where you settle, know that you can call upon us for anything."

Euodia took Ariston's hand and gave him an assuring smile. "The Lord has a plan," she said, pitching her voice for his ears alone. "Next time I will not doubt it."

❖

Hadrian strode through the atrium of Herod's guesthouse and spotted his father in the triclinium. Several senators had gathered in the ornate dining room, where the center table was crowded with platters of stuffed chicken, stewed hare, and fish. The cooks had prepared the meats with generous amounts of mint, garlic, bay leaf, and cumin, not only to exalt the flavor but to disguise the odor of meat that had lingered too long in the *culina*.

"Father." Hadrian lifted his hand to catch his father's attention. "A word?"

The aedile dismissed his dining companion, then rose and strode toward his son. "How goes the surveying?"

Hadrian pulled a set of papyri from his tunic. "Fine, but I thought I should inquire about another matter—have you forgotten about the commission contract for Pericles the sculptor? We have not discussed the situation in several weeks."

His father rubbed his neck. "I have considered it . . . and Nero will need soothing more than ever once he builds that monstrosity of a house. So yes, the time is right. We will proceed."

"And the terms?"

"Four years, with monthly payments until the work is completed. And write in an exception clause—if Rome burns again—which it might, if Nero decides he needs more land, the project is to be canceled with no need for repayment of any advanced funds." He waved at a senator across the room. "If Rome burns again," he said, returning his attention to Hadrian, "Nero will not survive. The patricians will not endure another fleecing." He wriggled two fingers, signaling Hadrian to come closer.

Hadrian bowed his head, bringing his ear closer to his father's lips.

"Nero has been extracting . . . shall we say, *required contributions*—from provinces, allied states, and cities that were supposed to be immune from tribute. Every day I hear of temples being plundered for their treasures. All that and he demands contributions from senators, patricians, and *especially* the aediles."

Hadrian studied his father. "Does this mean we cannot *afford* to commission a statue?"

"It means"—his father smiled but without humor—"I am glad we do not have to pay the entire amount in a lump sum. Small nibbles from the purse will not impoverish us."

He stepped back. "Finalize the document with my seal and signature and deliver it at your convenience. Keep a copy for my records." He moved toward his dining couch, then hesitated. "Have you eaten? There is plenty of food."

"Thank you." Hadrian bowed his head. "But I should attend to this at once."

❖

The knock startled me. I glanced at Father, then remembered he could not see the question on my face. "Are you expecting someone?"

He shook his head. "Perhaps it is someone seeking shelter."

I bit my lip, afraid we would have to share our meager food and water with a stranger, then cautiously opened the door. Shock stole my voice when I recognized the man outside.

"Calandra," Hadrian said, his eyes gleaming with urgency, "I would have a word."

Stunned by sheer disbelief, for a moment I could not move. He had finally come. For me.

"I will come out," I said, preparing to step onto the street.

"I must speak with Pericles."

I stared, tongue-tied, as he moved past me and entered the shop, his attention focused on my father.

Had he no feeling for me at all? Did he not even remember the night we shared?

"Salve, Pericles Aemilius," Hadrian called. "May the gods bless you."

Father turned toward Hadrian's voice and smiled. "It has been weeks since I heard such cultured tones in the Aventine."

"I apologize for staying away," Hadrian answered, sitting across from my father. "I have been assisting with the reconstruction of the city."

"A big task," Father said. "I have heard much about the new palace."

"That is not my responsibility." Hadrian coughed. "I came because I am certain you would like to know the status of the statue we discussed before the Fates changed our course. Father wishes to proceed with the commission and has asked me to deliver the contract. If you will countersign, I will take a copy, and all will be settled."

I brought my hand to my mouth, stunned.

Father leaned forward. "Cronus is certain of this?"

"He is quite sure, but what about you? If you have found other work and wish to decline the contract, I will understand. My father will be disappointed, but he will not hold it against you, considering your injury."

"My injury is not fatal." Father lifted his hands. "These fingers have not lost their skill."

"Still," Hadrian said, "perhaps you should reconsider. If the finished statue does not delight the emperor, my father's career could be at risk. Even *offering* such a gift is a gamble."

"A gamble the aedile is willing to make." Father nodded. "I will make certain his gift will be favorably received. I can promise that my work will please any reasonable man."

"Do you not understand?" Hadrian thumped the table. "Nero is anything but reasonable, and my father does not know you are blind!"

My breath caught in my lungs as Hadrian's words echoed in the workshop.

My father wanted the job. We needed the coin. But Hadrian was not quite ready to bet his father's life on a blind man's skill.

"My father was not blind when this deal was negotiated," I said, walking to the table. "And the physician said his sight may return."

"What if it does not?"

"I will be his eyes." I lifted my chin. "I have learned many things from my father. If necessary, I will learn how to work in bronze."

Hadrian glanced from me to my father, then chuckled. "I cannot help admiring your determination, but can we trust you to produce a giant bronze in four years?"

"We are not swindlers." I fortified my voice with steel. "By whatever gods you hold sacred, I will swear this to you."

Hadrian studied me, then he nodded. "Let me set forth the terms of our agreement. First, I will visit this shop every month to gauge your progress. If I do not see advancement from month to month, I will tell my father to cancel the contract."

I met his gaze without flinching. "Agreed."

"You will be paid a monthly stipend. When the statue is completed, you will receive a final sum of one million sestertii."

I blinked in astonished silence. We had never made so much on one piece. With that money, we would be able to expand, to create even larger works. I crossed my arms. "Agreed."

Hadrian pulled a pouch from his tunic and dropped it onto the table. "That is additional coin to help you begin the work."

While I watched, surprised by his impersonal tone, he pulled a linen bag from his satchel and pushed it toward me. "If you are going to work, you must eat," he said. "These are desperate times, so let me know if you have trouble. I would rather have you working than running from place to place in search of food."

I opened the bag and found a sizable cheese, a package of nuts, and a bag of wheat—enough to feed me, Father, and Hadrian's unborn child for a week.

My throat tightened until I could not speak.

"There remains the matter of Nero," Father said. "I cannot sculpt what I cannot see. Calandra must be my eyes."

Hadrian's expression grew thoughtful. "Leave the matter to me. For now, sculpt the body and the base. Do everything you can, and we will attend to the face later. Is that feasible?"

I turned to Father, who usually sculpted the face first. "It is," he said. "And since this will be Calandra's first bronze, it is for the best. Small defects will be unnoticeable in the body, but we cannot have an error in the face."

Hadrian unfurled the papyri and turned the pages. "Your father must sign two copies."

I took a sharpened stick and bottle of ink from the desk, then inked the stylus. "Here." I put the stick into Father's hand and placed his hand in the appropriate space. "Sign."

Father inked his name and added a flourish.

"The second copy." Hadrian placed it on the desk, and we repeated the process.

"Done." Father smiled at Hadrian.

"Thank you," Hadrian said, rolling up one of the copies. "I am leaving a copy with you."

He stood so abruptly that he nearly upended his chair. "I must go now, but I will return every month." His gaze shifted to me. "May Fortuna bless you."

Draping the end of my palla over my midsection, I bid him farewell.

❖

Hadrian stopped on a busy corner, then crossed on the raised stones to keep his sandals dry as he walked to the *popina*.

Though several people were dining at tables beneath the shady portico, Hadrian went inside to escape the chaos of the street. He walked past the L-shaped marble counter and took a seat at a table.

A woman walked over to him. "Hungry?" she asked, wiping her hands on her apron.

"Whatever you have," Hadrian said, trying not to appear overly interested. "Olives, bread, anything will do."

"Chicken?"

"Yes. And wine."

The woman walked to the counter, her swaying hips an open invitation to rent one of the upstairs rooms, but Hadrian had not come for pleasure. He clasped his hands and lowered his head, wishing he could restrain his thoughts as easily as he restrained his appetite.

He should have sent Lysandros to handle the contract signing. The business could have been easily accomplished and the slave would not have reported the bewildered hurt in Calandra's eyes.

Hadrian had tried to be detached and businesslike, but like an amateur player on the stage, he had overacted. Calandra must have thought him an arrogant fool.

But how should he have behaved? If he had pulled her aside and apologized for declaring his admiration and taking her into his arms, would he not have been implying a future? She would have assumed his feelings would develop, but there was no hope for any sort of relationship between them. He was a patrician, she a plebeian. He was the son of a senator, and though her father was ascending in prominence, Pericles's lack of noble ancestors would prevent his daughter from ever marrying the son of an aedile.

No, he had done the right thing. He had made a tough choice; he had clarified their relationship with his demeanor.

Business was all they had in common. That one night was an anomaly, the unique effect of a tragedy that temporarily erased the chasm between them. But the boundaries were back, and they both knew it.

He would continue to visit Pericles and his daughter, but he would control his feelings, curtail his words, and refrain from personal remarks.

He had always admired the Stoics—now he would attempt to be one.

The great fire had been extinguished. He could not afford to stir the smoldering embers.

Sixteen

THE 15TH DAY OF NOVEMBER

Priscilla stared at Euodia with horror in her eyes. "You want to buy a *slave*?"

Euodia hurried to explain. "We have been buying slaves for years, as we can afford them."

"But—"

"We free them," Euodia added. "First, we care for them until they are strong, and then we tell them about Yeshua because so many have never heard His story. And when they are ready to be accountable for their own lives, we issue manumission papers, and they are free to go or stay and work with us . . . for proper wages."

Priscilla dropped to a bench, the grim line of her mouth relaxing. "I did not know."

"How do you think I became acquainted with Ariston?" Euodia gave her husband a teasing smile. "Though I was not in the market for a husband, the Lord led me to one. But he was a freedman first. I had to be certain he wanted to remain part of my household."

Ariston grinned at his wife. "In truth, I never wanted to leave it."

Priscilla frowned. "What sort of slave will you buy?"

"We do not know," Ariston said. "But the Lord will show us the right one. He always does."

Euodia relaxed as they stepped into the brightness of a mid-November sun. Rome was far warmer than Philippi, the sky bold and blue with little traces of the smoke that had hovered over the city since their arrival two weeks earlier.

During those weeks, Ariston had focused on setting up a display of their purple goods in the tentmaker's shop, and Euodia had concentrated on making a home out of the apartment across the street. She had hoped to find exotic furnishings in Rome, yet the fire had destroyed so many homes that tables, chairs, and beds were hard to find. The few furnishings that *were* available had become unreasonably expensive, so Euodia resigned herself to living with a bedroll, an old table, and two chairs until life returned to normal. Though she had no idea what *normal* was for Rome, she trusted Priscilla to tell her.

"Aquila says there are two slave markets," Ariston said as they fought their way through the crowd of people, carts, and litters in the streets. "One near the Forum, which may have been burned, and another near the Saepta Julia at the Campus Martius. The latter was not touched by the fire, so we should go there."

"Is this a good time, do you think?"

"Aquila says it is the perfect time. Many families have had to sell their slaves to raise capital. We should be able to find a good worker for a fair price."

They crossed the river, then walked north toward the Field of Mars. Finally, they spotted the Saepta Julia—the place, Ariston said, where Roman citizens gathered to cast their votes.

He pointed to a tent in the distance. "That must be the market."

Euodia felt her stomach sway as they approached the place.

She had bought several slaves in Philippi, but that city was small compared to Rome. What sort of slaves would they find here?

She waited as Ariston paid the entry fee, and together they walked past row after row of metal cages. Men, both young and middle-aged, filled an entire row, followed by a row of women, most of whom appeared to be of childbearing age. The latter rows featured more exotic prisoners—women of breathtaking beauty, children, and some who wore placards advertising their skills in medicine, necromancy, interpreting languages, reading and writing.

After viewing the selection, Ariston turned to Euodia. "Do we need someone with special skills," he asked, "in case they choose to remain with us?"

She paused to consider. "A scribe would be useful," she said. "And medical skills are always appreciated."

"Let us look again," Ariston said, taking her hand. "If you want to stop, let me know."

They moved down the rows again, starting with the young men. Euodia kept her head down, unable to look at the barely clothed slaves. Apparently, Romans wanted to examine every inch of their purchases.

When they came to the women, Euodia searched carefully. So many different faces! Some youthful, some melancholy, some sensual, some jaded. Some women looked as though life had long departed them; others stared at her with hope in their eyes.

She stopped in front of a young woman, tall and thin, whose fair skin magnified the darkness of her eyes. "Do you speak Greek?" she asked, hoping to find someone who spoke her native language.

"Yes, Domina."

"How old are you?"

The girl hesitated. "Twenty years? No more."

Euodia stepped away and turned to Ariston. "Thoughts?"

"She has no skills," he said, noting that the girl wore no placard.

"But she speaks Greek. And something tells me . . . her heart is ready for Yeshua."

He nodded. "If this is the one, we will bid."

An hour later, they collected their slave. Euodia skimmed the records and learned that the girl, Petra, had been enslaved since birth. "She knows her position," her previous owner had written, "and is willing to do whatever is asked of her."

Euodia closed her eyes, knowing all too well what some owners asked of attractive female slaves. But Petra would no longer have to worry because she would soon be free.

❖

While Father slept, I sat at his workbench and lifted a lump of damp clay from an oilskin bag. I had thrown dozens of pots, vases, cups, plates, and bowls on the potter's wheel, but I had never tried to mold a freestanding piece. Better to experiment, I reasoned, while my father slept. Otherwise I might embarrass him.

I sprinkled a few drops of water onto the clay, then rolled it into a tube. Standing it on end, I attempted to broaden the base so it would stick to the table, but the tube kept bending in the middle. I added more clay to that area—this figure's belly would bulge like mine—and attempted to form a head, neck, and shoulders.

After several efforts, I pushed away from the table and wept. What had made me think I could do this? This monstrosity would make Father laugh, then he would despair of ever completing our project. He would want to cancel the contract, but what would we do after that?

I startled when I heard the shuffle of his slippers behind me.

"You are working?"

I attempted to lighten my voice. "I am practicing. I thought I would try something in clay."

"Let me examine it."

I bit my tongue as he slid onto the bench, moved his hands over the table, and encountered my pitiful effort. His brow lowered as his fingertips worked the damp clay. He then took my hand in his.

"Calandra"—a rare tenderness filled his voice—"how do we sculpt a horse?"

"I have no idea."

"We do not sculpt a horse. We sculpt a horse's head, his chest, and his limbs. We do it part by part and bit by bit so the work does not become overwhelming."

His hands returned to my effort and squeezed the clay into a ball.

"Sometimes we start again," he said. He took my hand and placed it on the mass. "So today we will sculpt a head. Only a head, so you will learn that the work is not too difficult."

For the next several weeks, I worked on modeling the clay. I made cat heads, dog heads, bull heads, and bird heads. After making some pitiful heads, I learned what not to do and pulled out a new block of clay.

"Now you are smarter," Father said. "Now you know what you do not know."

"Right." I eyed the clay. Could I shape it to my will?

"What will you make?"

"A bust, I think."

"Of whom?"

"I am not sure."

A parade of faces moved through my mind: the old woman who lived in the attic of our building; the merchant's wife who lived above our shop; the little girl who loved to toss rocks in the nearby fountain. I thought of Priscilla, who had taken us in during the fire, and sweet Mariana, who had tirelessly baked bread for refugees. All their faces had become dear to me, but I yearned to make one face in particular . . . and I had no idea what it looked like.

I tugged on Father's arm, silently urging him to sit next to me. When he was comfortable, I placed my hands on the clay. "Can you describe my mother? I think I would like to sculpt her."

Father folded his hands. "She looked like you, but you have my nose—hers was smaller and rounder. Her eyes shone with kindness whenever she saw someone in trouble, and when she was happy, her eyes tipped upward at the corners. Her lips were full, like yours, and her fingers long and delicate. She was shorter than you and narrow through the hips—" his voice caught in his throat—"but you will not need to sculpt her torso."

"The shape of her face—oval, round, or rectangular?"

"Oval, with a point at the chin. Like a heart."

"Did her hair cover her ears?"

He chuckled. "Only when she let it down. Once we married, she wore it up, as most married women do."

"Was her hair straight or curly?"

"Wavy."

"Brown?"

"Yes, with copper highlights. I used to tease her about being a Gaulish girl." He smiled at memories I could not see. "She was the most beautiful woman I had ever seen. And she was never more beautiful than on the day she told me she was carrying you." He sighed. "I should have sculpted her so you could know what she looked like. I never felt the need, though, because I see her every time I look at you."

I bit my lip as a dozen different emotions collided within me. Though I loved my father dearly, I had always yearned to laugh with a mother, to feel her arms around me, to share my secrets, even the ones I could barely acknowledge. Only through modeling other women had I learned how to dress and walk, behave in a man's presence, and live in a man's world.

So I would sculpt my mother's face. Since Father had lost his sight, no one could tell me if the image was not perfect. I picked up a sheet of papyrus, then went to fetch my looking brass. Propping it on my left, I began to sketch, following the lines of my face, then filling in the features as I imagined them.

How did an artist portray kind eyes or a happy mouth? I did not know, but I would do my best to learn the technique.

Seventeen

LATE NOVEMBER

Nearly five months after the great fire, Hadrian began to see signs of new life throughout the imperial city. Fresh construction rose on Palatine Hill, and crowds returned to the markets, where vendors' stalls brimmed with food from the farmers outside Rome. Nero reinstated the grain dole, which helped feed the hungry plebeians.

After his efforts to appease the gods, the emperor instituted an orderly rebuilding program, carefully supervised by the aediles and other officials. Streets would be properly surveyed and widened. Insulae would be restricted in height as before, but owners of illegal buildings would be severely fined. Open spaces for greenery and future growth would be reserved. In the wealthy areas, no single house would connect to its neighbor, and every new residence would be required to have outer walls of fire-resistant Alban or Sabine stone.

Nero also required the addition of porticoes to tall buildings and agreed to pay for them himself. These columned porches, with their flat and sturdy roofs, were to provide platforms for vigiles to fight future fires. And since many of those who perished in the great fire had been struck and killed by falling debris, they would also provide shelter for those fleeing a tall building. Hadrian did not understand how a ten-foot platform could serve to fight flames on a neighboring seventy-foot roof, but at least the porticoes would provide shade from the hot sun.

The emperor also offered building incentives in the form of grants, based on a person's rank and the value of the destroyed property. As further inducement, the Senate enacted a new law. Any former slave who had acquired his freedom could become a full citizen if he had assets of no less than 200,000 sestertii and spent at least half of his wealth to build a house.

Hadrian thought Nero's attention to detail and careful planning would earn him the love of the people, but it did not. Even as they carried away bags of free grain, the plebs muttered about Nero singing as his city burned.

One afternoon Hadrian and Lysandros were on their way to Transtiberim when Hadrian spotted his father at a familiar site. Hadrian greeted his father, then stepped back to survey the lot where he had been born. "At least the hill remains."

His father barked a laugh, then shaded his eyes from the morning sun. "What are the people saying about the emperor's efforts?"

"Who asks, you or Nero?"

His father cast him a sidelong glance. "Would you answer differently if I were the emperor?"

"Absolutely." Hadrian crossed his arms. "Some people appreciate all he has done—the availability of grain, the removal of debris and the bodies. If left to the citizens, Rome might have taken years to recover from this tragedy."

"You said *some*. Are there a great number of naysayers?"

"Did the sun rise this morning?" Hadrian chuffed. "Rumors about the fire persist. I have heard witnesses speak of men who set fire to unburned buildings. When other citizens protested, they were rebuked."

"They saw vigiles setting firebreaks. Nothing else."

"Others point out that Nero never liked the old city's design. He often called it ugly."

"Certain parts of the city, yes. His opinion was justified."

"The Palatine was not ugly."

"True enough." His father shrugged. "Do they actually blame Nero for the fire?"

"Think about it. I have heard that before the fire, he hired an architect to draw up plans for a huge Golden House near the Palatine, and today the Palatine stands cleared of its former inhabitants. Before the fire, Rome had no land to suit his design, yet today he can take his pick of the lots. He is the emperor, after all."

His father scowled. "Look yonder and tell me what you see—do you not see rows of properly surveyed streets, spacious thoroughfares, and areas set aside for gardens? Are the insulae not being renovated with porches to shelter citizens from the heat?"

"Nero has also decreed that new insulae must be built farther apart, so that the alleys will no longer be shaded. The heat will become *more* oppressive."

Cronus waved the objection away. "The emperor has taken great pains to be sure the owners receive their former lots cleared of rubble. The debris that would have served as fodder for rats has been moved to the Ostian Marshes. The dead have been removed and burned."

"I am not saying the emperor has done nothing," Hadrian said, amused by his father's spirited defense. "But the city has come through a calamity, and the people want someone to blame."

"A scapegoat."

"Exactly. And who better to play that part? We are told Nero is divine, so why did he not stop the flames? He is the first citizen of the Empire, so why was he not here when the fire started?"

"You have just proved my point!" His father whirled, his finger rising to Hadrian's face. "They say Nero started the fire, but he was in Actium when the blaze began."

"An emperor does not have to be present to effect action. He did not draw the sword that struck his mother, but he murdered her nonetheless."

Cronus looked hastily left and right. "You should watch what you say in public."

"No one can hear us," Hadrian said, checking the vicinity. "I do applaud the good Nero is doing, though I suspect the good ideas came from you or one of the other aediles. In a year or two, the citizens of Rome will be grateful for your efforts. But now they are struggling, and they want someone to blame for their trouble."

"Let us hope they do not settle their fury on the aediles. Because I lost my home—as did Nero."

"But you did not have plans to build a palace on nonexistent land," Hadrian pointed out. "And that is a significant difference."

❖

As the days grew cooler, shorter, and wetter, I closed the shutters and tried not to think about the changing world outside the walls of our shop. The city had always been noisy and crowded; now it was even more so. People scrambled not only to eat, but those who had lost their homes were desperate for housing.

The sound of hammers and saws echoed through the valleys from sunrise until well into the night, but hundreds of people still lacked shelter. Nearly every day someone rapped on our door and asked if they could sleep in our workroom, but I turned them away. I always felt a stab of guilt—what would have happened to us if Priscilla had sent *us* away?—but I could not risk anyone taking advantage of a blind man and his pregnant daughter.

Each morning, after making sure we had food and water for the day, I went to the worktable and focused on my project. I had no way of knowing if my sketch was a reasonable likeness. After all, Father could not see it, and none of our current neighbors remembered my mother. So I worked until I was satisfied with the sketch, then I unwrapped a brick of wet clay and began to loosen it.

I decided to sculpt a simple bust, head and shoulders only, then I would ask Father to examine it. Surely his fingertips would find any irregularities.

I had watched Father sculpt hundreds of busts, so I was familiar with the process. After kneading and pounding the clay, I molded it into the shape of a large egg and stuck the base to the table. When the front resembled an oval, I pulled another hunk of clay from the original block and fastened it onto the egg. This would become the face.

I smoothed the clay with my thumbs and added a small rolled tube for the neck. I envisioned my mother's long throat, much like my own, and added two additional egg shapes to build up her shoulders, making certain the mass could support the original mass.

When I had a solid base, neck and head, I took a wooden knife and carved lines to represent the lower part of the skull and jawline. Another two cuts marked the vertical and horizontal centers of the face. With a smaller knife I carved two eye sockets above the horizontal center and deepened the lower half of those sockets, creating indentations that would emphasize the cheekbones. Two more depressions, one on each side of the head, created the woman's delicate temples.

The growing gloom in the workroom reminded me of the

late hour, so I put away my knife and threw a damp cloth over the clay. I needed to set out Father's dinner.

I rose, then sank immediately back to the bench. Overcome by a sudden weariness, I slumped forward, my arm dropping to my swollen belly. I lowered my head to my other hand and felt a vein pulse at my temple.

No. I knew the signs . . . some illness was approaching. If it worsened, I would soon be in bed.

I was not surprised. Since the fire, the sewers had been clogged with debris, dust, and ash, leading to a sharp increase in mosquitoes and rats. Those who lived in elevated areas were spared from such vermin, but since water ran downward, the valleys and riverfront suffered from all sorts of pestilences. Priscilla had recently dropped by and mentioned that some of her friends were sick.

Perhaps I was, too.

I pushed away from the worktable and stumbled to my bedchamber. I needed a few moments to rest and then I would see to Father's dinner.

❖

Before the fire, Hadrian's prisoners had been accustomed to weekly visits, but he knew they would not complain about being interviewed every month while he worked to rebuild the city. In order to discourage them from violating the terms of their house arrest, he told them he would visit unexpectedly.

In mid-November, as a chilly breeze whistled through the narrow streets of old Rome, Hadrian left Lysandros to oversee the surveying so he could visit his prisoners. He saved Petros and Hannah for last.

"Hadrian!" Petros greeted him with a quick embrace. "It is good to see you again. Can we bring you some water?"

Hadrian shook his head, amazed to see several refugees still living with the prisoner and his wife.

"I am here to see if you are upholding the terms of your confinement." He looked around the crowded room, quietly marveling that those who had the least seemed the most willing to share. "Have you ventured outside this apartment in the past month?"

Petros gaped at him. "What an idea! I must ask—would I be allowed to leave if this building was burning?"

"This insula did not burn." Hadrian met the old man's grin with a somber nod. "But I trust you have remained here."

"How can I venture out?" Petros said, tugging on his beard. "We are rather wedged in here, especially at night."

Hadrian nodded at the refugees. "These are friends of yours?"

"Not all. Some were strangers until the fire. But do not worry—when Nero rebuilds their insula, they will return to the other side of the river."

"The emperor is working on it."

"But he is also building a new palace, yes?" The question came from a man sitting on the floor, a man who did not wear a beard like most Jews.

Hadrian met the man's gaze. "Do you resent Nero's desire for a new home? He *did* lose his house on the Palatine."

The man lifted his hands. "I am not critical. I am curious."

"Right." Hadrian turned back to Petros. "Have you spread the heresy of Christ-worship in Rome?"

Petros smiled. "Am I not allowed to mention my Lord and Master in my apartment?"

Hadrian sighed. "Are you willing to amend your ways and offer incense to the gods of Rome?"

"Why would I dishonor Yeshua when He honored me, a simple fisherman, with the gift of eternal life?"

"Then I certify that your imprisonment in this dwelling shall continue until the emperor decides otherwise."

"Will he decide anytime soon?"

"You will be fortunate if Nero even remembers he has prisoners," Hadrian answered, allowing himself to smile. "I will see you next month."

"Of course, my young friend." Petros waved as Hadrian moved into the hallway.

In desperate need of fresh air, Hadrian hurried down the stairs. Once outside, he drank deeply of the cool night air and crossed the Tiber.

The sculptor's workshop was not far, so he turned toward the Aventine. Though the hour was growing late, people still bustled around merchant stalls and haggled with vendors. Hadrian could almost believe that life had returned to normal.

But refugees and the injured still lined the roads, their cupped hands rising at his approach, and the Aventine, which had fared better than most districts, was still crowded with displaced persons.

He found the sculptor's shop, knocked quickly, and opened the door with the familiarity of a frequent visitor. He expected to be greeted by Calandra, but darkness filled the interior of the shop.

A twinge of unease lifted the hair at the back of his neck. "Is anyone here?"

A man's voice called through the gloom. "Who speaks?"

As his eyes adjusted, Hadrian glimpsed movement from the rear of the room. A curtain over the doorway lifted, and Pericles appeared, leaning on a walking stick as he shuffled forward. "May I help you?"

"It is I, Hadrian. I have come for the monthly progress report." He glanced around. "Has your daughter gone out? She should not be outside alone; the streets are filled with bandits and beggars."

"She cannot leave. She is ill."

A crack in the sculptor's voice betrayed his deep concern, and when Hadrian moved closer, he saw that worry had etched Pericles's face with deep lines. The sculptor pointed toward the curtained doorway. Hadrian strode forward, batting the curtain aside as he passed. Peering into the first bedchamber, he saw a figure lying beneath a tousled blanket. An oil lamp burned on a table, and in its dim light he recognized Calandra. Her eyes were closed, her hair loose, her forehead pearled with perspiration.

He sat on the edge of the bed and pressed his hand to her feverish forehead. "Why did you not send for me?"

"You are not responsible for my daughter," Pericles said.

"Have you sent for a doctor?"

"How am I to do that? I can barely find my way across the shop."

Hadrian uttered a curse and strode past the old man. "Get her some water while I find a physician."

❖

"I know this illness," the physician said, returning to the sculptor's workroom. "The Greeks know it as *miasma*, but here it is known as Roman fever."

"Will she recover?" Hadrian asked.

The physician's brow creased. "How long has she been like this?"

"Her father said she was well four days ago. This is the third day of fever."

"*Febris tertiana*." The doctor rummaged in his bag. "I have an herb. Steep it in hot water and make her drink."

"Will she improve?" Hadrian asked. "She is doing important work for the aedile."

"She should recover fully." The doctor pulled out a small bag, sniffed it, and placed it in Hadrian's palm. "Are you the father?"

Hadrian blinked. "I am a friend. The old man—he is the father."

The doctor shrugged. "Very well. Since the old man is blind, make sure he knows where to find this. Will he be tending her?"

Hadrian hesitated. "I could send a slave."

"A good idea."

The physician adjusted his tunic, picked up his bag, and waited until Hadrian gave him four sestertii. "For your trouble."

"May the gods prosper you."

"And you."

When the doctor had gone, Hadrian set the bag of herbs and the monthly payment on the counter. He looked around the workroom, which now glowed with lamplight. Calandra had obviously begun to work on something, but the sketch on her worktable revealed a young woman. Was this a self-portrait?

"She needs to learn technique, so she has begun with something simple."

Hadrian startled. He had expected Pericles to remain with his daughter. "I did not hear you come in."

"A strange thing," Pericles said, a smile playing at the corner of his mouth. "My eyes no longer work, but my ears are keener than ever. I heard you walk the physician to the door, then you hesitated at the worktable."

"Yes. I see a clay form and a sketch, but neither resembles Nero."

"You see Calandra's mother," Pericles said, resting both hands on his walking stick. "I imagine the similarity is remarkable. When I see Calandra—or when I last *saw* her—I could see the mother in the daughter."

Unable to tear his eyes away, Hadrian studied the oval face, straight nose, and arresting eyes. "If your wife looked like this," he said, his voice catching in his throat, "you must have loved her very much."

"I did," the sculptor answered, "but my wife's greatest beauty lay within. Calandra has the same quality . . . for those with eyes to see it."

Reminding himself of the business at hand, Hadrian turned away. "I hope this illness will not stop her progress. You have promised to have the statue finished within four years, but apparently Calandra still has much to learn."

"She is young and strong." Pericles lifted his chin. "We will not fail you."

"Good." Hadrian moved toward the door. "To make sure she recovers quickly, I will send a nurse tomorrow. I have left the herbs and your payment on the counter."

The sculptor dipped his head. "May God go with you."

Hadrian left the shop but hesitated on the portico. What had the sculptor said when they parted? Perhaps he had misheard. No one spoke of only *one* god when Rome offered dozens.

Eighteen

EARLY DECEMBER

Hadrian waited a week before commanding his litter-bearers to take him to the sculptor's shop. He knew he was probably being foolish, but he could not wait a month before checking on Calandra. What if she had not improved? How could Pericles complete the statue without his daughter?

Most important, what would he do if he lost her? The world would seem a more dismal place without her.

He glanced at Lysandros, who walked outside the litter. "What do you think? Can a strong young woman die of Roman fever?"

Lysandros shrugged. "I am no physician."

"But you are Greek, and Greeks seem to have the best grasp of medicine."

"Only certain Greeks, Dominus. Not all."

When the litter-bearers stopped outside the sculptor's shop, Hadrian noticed that the counter window and door remained closed. He shot a look at Lysandros—the closed shutters did not bode well.

Lysandros knocked, twice, while Hadrian waited in the litter. Finally, the Gaulish slave he had sent peered out, her eyes round with wonder.

"Slave." Hadrian stepped out of the litter. "Take me to the sick woman."

The girl blinked, then opened the door and bowed as Hadrian passed.

He stopped inside the workroom, which had not changed since the week before. "How is she?"

The slave bobbed her head. "She eats only when forced and mumbles in her sleep."

"Have you seen *no* improvement?"

The girl shook her head.

"Where is her father?"

"I am here." Pericles appeared, shuffling toward Hadrian from the other bedchamber, his shoulders slumped with weariness. "We were not expecting you today."

"Why is she not better? I have sent a doctor and a nurse."

"And I have not stopped praying." Pericles turned his sightless eyes in Hadrian's direction. "But still she does not improve."

"Have you sacrificed to Asclepius? If you visit his temple, surely the god of health would—"

"I have prayed to Adonai." Pericles drew his mantle around his thin shoulders. "And if He has a purpose in this, I have not yet seen it."

Hadrian suddenly realized how chilly the room was. No fire burned at the brazier, and the November wind whistled through the shutters.

"She needs warmth," he said, gesturing for the slave to light the brazier as he strode toward Calandra's bedchamber. "If she is sick . . ."

"Does the fever not burn hot enough?" Pericles asked.

Hadrian moved into the sickroom and saw Calandra on the bed, swathed in linen sheets. She lay on her side, her knees at her chest, her long hair damp with perspiration. What sort of fever was this?

Helpless, he turned to Lysandros. "Suggestions?"

His slave pressed his lips together. "I have heard . . . but the idea may not please you."

"She has already been visited by a physician. What else can I do?"

Lysandros shook his head in apparent exasperation. "One of your Christian prisoners has been known to heal the sick."

Awareness thickened between them as Hadrian digested the information. His father would not approve, nor would the emperor. But what else could he do?

He could not lose this woman.

His gaze dropped to Calandra's motionless figure. "Which prisoner?"

"Petros of Judea."

Petros, the uneducated fisherman. The man who was forbidden to speak of Christ while in Rome.

But healing Calandra would not be speaking of Christ, would it? Perhaps he could heal silently with a gesture or the waving of incense . . .

"Pericles," Hadrian said as he moved to the bed, "I am taking your daughter to visit one of the Christians. This might be a good time to remind Adonai that you have been begging for His favor."

Pericles stepped from the doorway as Hadrian gathered the bedcoverings, scooped Calandra into his arms, and carried her out of the sickroom.

❖

Hadrian commanded the litter-bearers to hurry. They jogged through the streets as Lysandros ran before them shouting, "Make way!" Hadrian had drawn the curtains to protect Calandra's modesty and to protect himself. He could not allow this story to spread throughout the city.

When they reached the insula where Petros lived, passersby stopped and stared at the ornate litter, as out of place as a bucket under a bull. Hadrian knew they would gossip, but perhaps they could be persuaded to forget what they had seen.

"Lysandros." He opened the curtains. "Give each man you see a sestertius and tell them to say nothing."

He lifted Calandra into his arms. Even swathed in her bed linens, she seemed to weigh nothing, and her face had gone as pale as goat's milk.

After scattering coins among the onlookers, Lysandros went before him, clearing the way as they climbed the brick staircase. Finally, the slave pounded on Petros's door. "Petros of Judea! Hadrian, son of the aedile, needs you!"

The door opened a moment later. Hannah stood in the doorway, her eyes wide. She gasped when she saw what Hadrian carried.

"Where is your husband?" Hadrian demanded, pushing his way into the apartment. The place seemed empty, and he realized why—the refugees had departed.

Hannah pointed to the window, where a narrow shaft of sunlight fell on her kneeling husband's face. Petros turned when Hadrian entered.

"Hadrian." The Judean gave him an assuring smile. "I have been expecting you."

"Indeed?" Hadrian followed Hannah, who hastened to move a stack of rolled papyri from a mattress. When she stood, her arms full of documents, Hadrian lowered Calandra to the bed. "This woman is working for my father, but she has a fever. Lysandros says you have healed people. If that is so, I want you to heal her."

The corner of Petros's mouth lifted. "I have no power to

heal, my young friend. The healing is done by Yeshua, but only if it is His will."

Hadrian ran his hand through his hair. "I do not understand your God. With us, we do something for a god, he does something for us. If we want prosperity, we sacrifice to Proserpina. If we want good fortune, we kill a dove for Fortuna. If we want to curse an enemy, we ask the god of war to do the job."

"Adonai does not live to serve us. We live to serve Him."

"Then how do you know if someone can be healed?"

"We ask Him. I have already asked, and yes, the Lord is willing to heal this young woman. He will do it for your sake."

Surprise siphoned the blood from Hadrian's head. "But I have done nothing for him."

Petros's smile flashed in his beard. "He will do it so you can know His power and His love."

The old man rose and walked to the mattress. Calandra lay on her side, curled into a fetal position. The Judean held his hands over her body, not touching her, and closed his eyes. "Young woman," he said, his voice at once powerful and gentle, "in the name of *Yeshua ha-Mashiach*, be healed."

Hadrian held his breath as an unexpected breeze moved the damp hair at Calandra's cheek. Her eyes shifted beneath her eyelids, and color bloomed in her cheeks. Her chest rose and fell in a convulsive breath, then her eyes opened. She looked at the people around her—Petros, Hadrian, Lysandros, and Hannah—and frowned.

"Where is my father?"

Hadrian laughed out of sheer relief. "Your father is at his shop, where you should be. But you have been ill."

Her frown deepened. "If I were not well, I would not be here. I would be at home and . . ." She pushed herself up and glanced at her thin tunic. Her blush deepened to crimson as she pulled the bed linens over her chest.

"Do not fret," Hannah said, hurrying toward Calandra with a blanket. "Your modesty has been preserved."

Hadrian and Lysandros turned away. Petros went back to his window as Hannah tucked the blanket around Calandra.

Hadrian moved toward the window, where Petros was praying in a low, quiet voice: "Blessed are you, O Lord our God, King of the universe, who shapes light and crafts darkness, who makes peace and creates all things. Everyone will thank you; all will praise you and everyone will declare: there is none holy like the Lord."

Hadrian stepped closer. "You are certain the healing gift lies with your God and not with you?"

Petros chuckled. "Quite."

"And who is this God? I have heard people speak of Christ, who was crucified, but he cannot be a God . . ."

Petros looked Hadrian squarely in the eye. "He is called many things, but most people know Him as Adonai, Creator of heaven and earth. He chose the children of Abraham to be His people and to bless the world. Yeshua the Christ is His Son, and He is not dead."

Hadrian folded his arms. "And how do these Jews bless the world? I have seen many Jews in Transtiberim, and most cannot bless their own families."

"The Jews have blessed the world in many ways," Petros said, his voice softening, "but chiefly through Yeshua, who came to save those who are lost."

Then, while Hannah prepared bread and honey water for Calandra, Petros invited Hadrian and Lysandros to sit at his table and learn how and why Yeshua had come.

"I am here as a representative of Rome," Hadrian said, "so I must be about Rome's business."

"Some other time perhaps," Petros said, smiling. "When you can find an hour to call your own."

❖

Father welcomed me with a warm embrace. "Blessed be Adonai," he whispered, his face lighting with joy. "He is indeed a God who works wonders."

I bade Hadrian, Lysandros, and the nurse farewell, then closed the door and leaned against it. "When I was sick, how many times did Hadrian visit?"

"Twice," Father said. "The first time he brought a doctor. He was most concerned about you."

Was he? Or was he worried about the sculpture? Another thought troubled me. "Was Hadrian in the room when the doctor examined me?"

"No. He remained outside your bedchamber."

I sighed and tried to remain calm. Hadrian had not examined me closely, which meant he had not seen the bulge of my belly. I was wrapped in bed linens when they transported me, so he might not know I was carrying his baby.

In the early days of my sickness, I hoped the fever might rid my body of the child. The prostitutes had told me that illness could often stop an unborn child from developing. "If not disease, certain herbs will do the same thing," a woman said.

"If the herbs do not work," an older woman told me, her eyes dark and somber, "there is always the *Column Lactaria.*"

I could not forget the heavy silence that fell over those women at the mention of the column at the Forum Olitorius. Later, I visited that marketplace and saw babies that had been abandoned at the column's base. Some had been wrapped in blankets with broken coins hanging from a string around their necks. Others had no coins, no blankets, nothing to tie them to the women who had given them life.

The women of the brothel explained that the infants with coins had been left at the column because they needed a wet nurse. Their families would pay a lactating woman to breast-feed the child. When the father wished to reclaim his offspring, he would visit the column and present the matching half of the broken coin to prove his parentage.

If a parent did not claim the child after the age of weaning, the children could be put to whatever use the foster family wished. They could be sent to beg on the street, used for prostitution, or be sold into slavery.

Children deposited at the Column Lactaria without a coin necklace faced a more precarious future. At midmorning, child-sellers would visit the column to collect infants that had not been picked up by wet nurses. These babies would be examined for defects, and the unblemished would be advertised to slave traders and families who wished to adopt an heir. Infants with deformities or undesirable marks were abandoned outside the city.

I shuddered at an all too vibrant memory. Once, after accompanying my father to deliver a statue to a family tomb, we entered the city through the gate at the Via Appia. In front of the imposing stone wall, I spotted an area covered with scattered bones. I asked Father what sort of animal had died there, and by the grim set of his mouth I knew I should have remained silent.

Then I saw a small human skull . . . and realized that the bones belonged to abandoned infants. What had Priscilla told me? She said life was *"a gift from Adonai, even when unexpected."*

Neither the sickness nor the doctor's herbs had removed the child from my womb. Priscilla would point to those failures as evidence that Adonai was protecting this baby, but despite what happened in Petros's home, I could not believe in a God who had been foolish enough to die on a cross.

Yet after experiencing the fire, an illness, and a broken heart, I found it hard to believe in the divine Caesar, either.

After returning Calandra to her father, Hadrian walked toward the river, not toward home. "Did we forget someone?" Lysandros asked. "Can it not wait until the morrow?"

"I think not," Hadrian answered, scanning the horizon. "I have questions that will not let me rest tonight."

Lysandros did not protest when they crossed the bridge and reentered Transtiberim, then returned to the former fisherman's apartment.

Petros answered the door. "We have not, we have not, we cannot." He gave Hadrian an impenitent grin. "Since you did not ask your questions when you were here earlier, I thought I might save you some time."

Hadrian sighed. "We did not come to ask the emperor's questions. This hour is mine, and I have come to ask a few of my own."

Petros's eyes warmed as he invited them to enter.

If Hannah was surprised to see them again, she did not show it. Instead, she offered them a seat at the rough table. "Honey water?"

"No," Hadrian said. "We do not wish to trouble you."

Petros dropped into a chair. "Then why do you keep coming?"

Hadrian was afraid he had offended the man, but then he saw the twinkle in Petros's eye. "I have been watching you," he said, folding his hands. "I have seen how your God spared you during the great fire. I saw how he provided food for you when the rest of the city had none. Today I saw your God heal Calandra when neither the Roman gods nor the doctors could."

"Our God does have great power. He answers prayer according to His will."

Hadrian frowned. "Does he not always save his people? Surely, he must reward your faithfulness and your sacrifices."

"He does," Petros said, "but it is more important that we acknowledge *His* faithfulness and sacrifice. You Romans have a contractual relationship with your gods, but Adonai will not be ordered about by his creations."

Hadrian found the idea of an authoritarian God oddly satisfying. A God who was unlike the changeable, imperfect people he ruled. As the son of an aedile, Hadrian had been educated by one of the finest Greek tutors, a man who taught him about the entire pantheon of gods, their adventures and misadventures. He learned that Jupiter, whom the Greeks called Zeus, ruled all gods and men from his home on Mount Olympus. He had fathered many children, some of whom grew to be greater in reputation and power than Jupiter himself.

When Hadrian's mother had become ill, he offered countless sacrifices to Jupiter, modifying his behavior until he was certain it would be perfect in the eyes of the omnipotent god. But when his mother died, Hadrian had left the bedchamber where his father wept and returned to the temple, where he spat on Jupiter's altar and cursed the god who had done nothing to save his mother. "*If you care so much for your people,*" he had shouted, alarming the priests, "*why do you not honor those who give you the best they have?*"

On that day, at the tender age of fourteen, Hadrian renounced the gods of Rome. He did not broadcast the news, knowing that gossip would hurt his father's reputation, but began to seek other answers to the questions that kept him awake at night. What was the purpose of life? Why had he been born? Why did good people like his mother suffer and die?

Stoicism—the philosophy that moral worth, duty, and justice were to be sought whenever possible—seemed a pragmatic approach to life, far more practical than Epicureanism or Skepticism. Several Roman senators were Stoics, and though Hadrian's father faithfully sacrificed to the gods of Rome, Hadrian suspected that he placed little faith in them. Cronus, like Hadrian, had been disillusioned by his wife's untimely death, but he had an image to maintain and a duty to Rome.

Stoicism served Hadrian well for a few years, but Calandra's illness led him to doubt his philosophy. The concept of changing what he could and accepting everything else left him feeling frustrated and helpless. If a true creator existed, would he not want to help his creations? Surely, he would not be indifferent to their suffering! Surely, he would answer prayers if the petitioner discovered the proper way to reach him.

Hadrian spread his hands on the table and met Petros's gaze. "I have been a stoic," he confessed. "I have tried to accept what I must and change what I could. But I could not heal Calandra, nor could I provide grain when none was available. I could not stop the fire or prevent it from engulfing my father's house. And I cannot be indifferent to the suffering of others."

"Adonai," Petros said, his forehead crinkling, "does what He pleases with His creation. He loves us, protects us, and uses us to bless others in ways we cannot imagine. Yes, Adonai protected us from the flames of the fire, but He could have allowed us to perish."

Hadrian stiffened. "How so? If you have been faithful to Him . . ."

Petros braced his elbows on the table. "His will is bigger than my life because He loves the *world*. If my death can bring someone else to God, I will happily surrender my life. That is what Yeshua did for us. Why should I not do the same for others?"

"If your death means others will live," Lysandros asked, "then why did he not send the fire to Transtiberim and save those east of the river?"

"Perhaps He saved us for your sakes. If we were not here,

how would you hear the good news of salvation?" Petros leaned back in his chair. "Having heard the Gospel of Messiah Yeshua, are you ready to believe in Him?"

Hadrian glanced at Lysandros, then nodded. "What must I do? Do I offer a sacrifice or make a pledge or—"

"Yeshua offered the sacrifice of His mortal body," Petros said, his eyes glittering with passion. "You must offer the sacrifice of your *will*. Surrender it to Him, and you will receive His Spirit, who will guide you in all things."

Hadrian swallowed hard. This was no light decision. His father might not understand, but his father was too busy caring for Rome to give much thought even to his own soul.

Calandra might not understand; she might even mock him. But Pericles would, because he had been patiently praying, certain that Adonai had a purpose for everything.

Hadrian met Petros's gaze. "I am ready."

❖

Two days later, Hadrian greeted Marcus and his wife Mariana, the young couple from Corinth, and their maid, Salama. For prisoners of Rome, they seemed remarkably content to be confined to their second-floor apartment and warmly welcomed Hadrian each time he appeared.

Still ebullient from his recent encounter with Yeshua, Hadrian struggled to resist an urge to hug all of them. He opened his wax tablet and trained his eyes on the prescribed questions. "Have you left this apartment to participate in any forbidden meetings?"

Marcus shook his head. "No."

"Have you spread the heresy of Christ-worship in Rome?"

"We have not."

"Are you now willing to amend your ways and offer incense to the gods of Rome?"

Marcus shared a smile with his wife and picked up his two-year-old son, Ivan. "Why should we offer sacrifices to the gods of Rome when Adonai has so richly blessed us?"

Relaxing, Hadrian nodded toward their living space. "In Corinth, you lived in the governor's palace and could travel anywhere you pleased. Now you are confined to these walls. How can you say you are blessed?"

Marcus reached for his wife's hand. "In a few months we are going to have another child. I cannot imagine a greater blessing."

Mariana blushed, and only then did Hadrian notice the soft mound at her midsection.

"You do not know our history," Marcus continued, "but we lost a baby in Corinth. For years we wondered if we would ever have children, but then we had Ivan." He grinned at the toddler in his arms. "Now Adonai is going to bless us again. So why would we want to forsake Him and worship Roman gods?"

Unable to argue with the man's logic, Hadrian closed his tablet and smiled.

Nineteen

For a week after my recovery, I did not touch my sculpture but spent my days cleaning and arranging our bowls, amphorae, and other pottery. At Father's urging I created several new pieces on the potter's wheel—wider-than-usual chamber pots, delicate perfume vials, and the two-handled containers known as "Greek vases," though they typically held water, wine, or olive oil, not Greeks.

Mindless work seemed the perfect antidote to worry while I pondered the greatest problem of my life.

Because of a single lapse of judgment in a time of calamity, in four months I would bear a child. I could not keep it, and I did not want my father to know about it. I was also determined that Hadrian should not know of it, for why would I bother him when he had a city to rebuild and an emperor to impress? Hadrian lived and worked on a stratum far above my own, so my problem would surely be insignificant in his eyes.

If we lived in another world, or if we had been born to different parents, things might be different. If I were patrician or he plebian, we could marry and raise our child together. But we were not the same.

The day I first felt the baby move, I caught my breath, amazed at the sensation, then closed my eyes and dreamed of a place where Hadrian and I could be together—rich or poor, exalted or debased, I did not care. When the child fluttered within me at night, I caressed the protective dome of stretched skin and imagined myself carrying a perfectly formed son to Hadrian and laying it at his feet. He would smile at me, joy lighting his eyes, and hold the child high, pleased and proud to have an heir.

But those dreams were nothing more than spun gossamer. The Fates had decided our positions, and we were locked in place. If I carried a child to his *paterfamilias* in the spring, Cronus would command that it be sent to the slave market.

No, my dreams of this baby could never come true.

Thinking of Hadrian reminded me of our commission. Father and I had to complete a giant statue in four years, a statue we had not yet begun. But he had signed a contract and accepted payments, so we would soon have to outline a plan and set it in motion.

I was still willing to help him, but my feeble attempts to sculpt a bust had only revealed how much I did not know about the art and method of sculpture. I would have to learn and become more observant. I would have to study people's facial expressions and the way a senator's toga fell in complicated pleats. I would have to learn how to sculpt hair and study men's hands. What jewelry did wealthy men wear? On which fingers did they wear it?

And before the statue could be finished, I would have to study Nero. That might require being in his presence, and the thought was enough to send a chill up the column of my spine. Hadrian did not seem overly concerned about the situation, but I did not see how it could be done.

So many difficult tasks lay ahead, and I had so much to learn. But first I would have to bear this child.

❖

As the month of December drew to a close, I found myself grateful that Father had lost his sight. The bulge at my belly had become undeniable, and though I hid it with my palla and stood behind the counter when dealing with customers, Father would have discerned the truth had he not been blind.

One afternoon I took advantage of the chilly weather and donned a concealing mantle so I could go out. I had not seen Priscilla in weeks, and I knew I would enjoy the brisk walk to Transtiberim.

Priscilla greeted me warmly. "Calandra!" She gathered me into an embrace and remarked that she had heard about my healing from Roman fever. Then she pulled back, her eyes searching my face, and I knew she was hoping to hear that I had also become a believer in Yeshua.

"I am sorry," I whispered. "I cannot explain how I was healed, but it is possible that a priest of Asclepius could have healed me just as easily."

"Then why did no one take you to *his* temple?"

She tossed the question carelessly, then shook her head. "In any case, I am happy to see you looking so well." She lowered her voice. "And how fares your little one?"

My hand dropped to my belly, hidden beneath layers of fabric. "Still with me." I shrugged. "I thought it might go away when I was sick, but—"

"God had other plans." She took my hand. "Come inside and let me feed you. After all, you are now eating for two."

I did not argue because she was correct. Something—either the baby or the fever's departure—had left me ravenous.

Twenty

In the first month of the new year, Hadrian and Lysandros visited the Aventine to check on Pericles and his daughter. Despite the sun's attempt to bathe thousands of construction workers in the usual honeyed sunshine, a chilly wind blew over the city, causing Lysandros to shiver.

A smile tugged at Hadrian's mouth as he thought of the young woman he would soon see. Though he was undeniably drawn to Calandra, after her healing Hadrian limited his visits to one per month. To fixate on the woman, to become a close friend, would be unfair to her and sheer torment to himself. Such a situation, he felt, would not please Yeshua.

Fortunately, his father seemed to have tucked the idea of Hadrian's marriage away. The marriage laws would not be enforced until the next census, and not even the aediles knew when the emperor would call for an accounting. But he would, and soon, because Rome also needed money and the census was the best way to conduct tax collection.

Because Cronus was focused on rebuilding Rome, it might be months before his father realized that his son had not yet taken a wife. Someone could always remind him, of course, as Hadrian had reminded him of the commission for Pericles, but Hadrian was in no hurry to marry. His mind was too full of work . . . and Calandra.

He caught her preparing to go out. She wore an odd mantle over her tunic, one that began at her neck and flowed to the ground, and she carried a tablet with several sheets of papyri. With full cheeks and a rosy complexion, she had never appeared more beautiful.

"Must you go?" Hadrian asked, trying to hide his disappointment. "We have come to see your progress on the commission."

"Do not let me stop you," she said and stepped into the street. "Go inside and speak to Father if you like, but I will be working at the Forums today."

He did not understand what she intended, but he would not let her wander the city alone. He and Lysandros accompanied her to the Imperial Forums, a public square for judicial business. Calandra wandered to a shaded marble bench, where she sat and pulled out a sheet of papyrus. Lysandros sat beside her while Hadrian stood at the end of the bench, admiring the statuary while he greeted fellow patricians. At one point he glanced over Calandra's shoulder and realized she was sketching the men who paraded before her. Many of them were senators, evidenced in her sketches by their luxurious togas with purple borders.

Hadrian locked his hands behind his back and strove to be patient. He was glad he had come. He did not think it wise for a young woman to sit alone in a public place—even one as modestly dressed as she was—because another patrician might discover her talent and try to steal her away from the project. One never knew who might be spying in the Forums.

He turned at the sound of cleated sandals on the tiles. A group of Praetorians approached, guarding someone of obvious importance. Who? He squinted but could not see the man who walked in the center of the procession.

He caught Lysandros's attention and jerked his chin at the Praetorians. "Any idea who walks there?"

Lysandros's brow lifted. "Could it be the emperor?"

Calandra's head rose, but Hadrian caught her shoulder. "Not enough guards. This is someone important, but not the man you want to see."

They waited as the guards drew near, and Hadrian was finally able to glimpse the fellow who walked in their midst. The stranger was short, dark-haired, and bearded, so he was not likely to be Roman.

When the retinue had passed, Lysandros nodded. "I do not know who he is, but I will find out."

For the better part of an hour, Hadrian watched Calandra sketch details of clothing, hands, feet, and hair, furiously scrawling her papyri and ignoring the curious glances of passersby.

When she finally put her work away, Hadrian sat beside her. "Do you still want to see Nero?"

"Not yet," she answered, keeping her attention on something in the distance. "I will sculpt the face last."

"Because it is the most important?"

"Because it is the most revealing."

"Nero does not hide from his people. He reveals himself every day."

She looked at him as though he might be slow-witted. "My father says a man does not truly reveal himself unless he is feeling pressure from an outside source."

"Was the fire not pressure? Is he not feeling pressure about rebuilding the city?"

"He is the emperor," she said, staring at the Forum's marble columns. "The people listen to him, and the Senate votes as he wishes. How can that be pressure?"

Hadrian inhaled slowly, unwilling to engage in a public argument. His father had warned him that artists could be temperamental. They did not think like ordinary people.

"Come," he said, standing. "If we stay longer, people will wonder what we are doing."

He and Lysandros escorted her back to Pericles's shop, halting several times as she stopped to study statues of warriors, gods, and previous emperors. At the Forum of Augustus, which had recently been rebuilt, she squinted at an eight-foot bronze of Tiberius. The statue depicted the late emperor with his toga partially draped over his head, signifying his role as chief priest of Rome. A ring on his left hand was marked with a *lituus*, the curved staff augurs used to discern the will of the gods.

"The previous emperors are all wearing togas," she said, a hint of exasperation in her tone. "Why do they wear the same clothing when they were vastly different men?"

"Because the emperor always wears a purple toga," Hadrian said, suspecting that he had missed her point. "It is traditional."

"But is Nero like the other emperors? Is he of Augustus's temperament? Is he as genial as Tiberius? As clever as Caligula?"

Was she really so naive? "Nero is like none of those men. He is . . . himself."

"And what is he like? Really?"

He turned away, uncomfortable with the question. He did not know the emperor, but his father had frequent dealings with Nero, and what he reported did not elevate Hadrian's opinion of the man.

"He is an artist," Hadrian said, carefully choosing his words. "Like you, he does not think like other people. He takes pleasure in singing and playing the lyre. He writes poetry, designs buildings, and races his own chariots."

"So he is a man who does all things well," she said, her brow arching. "A man the gods have blessed."

Hadrian felt his mouth curve in a sardonic smile. "He is a man who *wants* to do all things well. But when he holds men's lives in his hands, who would dare tell him he is not as accomplished as he imagines?"

The light of understanding filled her eyes. "He is surrounded by a kindly conspiracy."

"The conspiracy is more cowardly than kind," he answered, "for what man wishes to risk his life on the ruler's mood? People encourage him, but not overmuch. They applaud him. But no one eagerly anticipates his company, particularly if he will be performing."

Two senators walked by, their togas marked with the senatorial band. Oblivious to Hadrian, Lysandros, and Calandra, they stepped into a narrow alley framed by cedars. Hadrian could not see their faces, but their voices flowed through the shrubs.

"I tell you, the people grow more convinced each day," the older senator said. "Several citizens have sworn that they saw men deliberately setting fires. Some tried to stop the firebrands, but they were beaten for their trouble."

"They truly believe the fire was Nero's work?"

"Why else would he clear the land of debris and set about building his Golden Palace? Why else would he be so eager to recompense the patricians who lost their homes? Many in the Praetorian Guard are convinced he burned his own city."

"But he was not in Rome."

"Does he not have men who willingly carry out his bidding?" The older senator lowered his voice to the point where Hadrian strained to hear. "The rumors have grown so persistent that the Senate will soon call for action. The people do not trust him, and the higher his Golden Palace rises, the more resentful they become."

"What do they expect of us?"

"They expect justice. They have placated the gods and repented for whatever evil behavior brought the gods' judgment upon us. After confessing and humbling themselves, they expect him to do the same."

"What should he confess?"

"He might begin by confessing the murder of his mother. He has thumbed his nose at the integrity of the family, and our citizens are ready to revolt. But say nothing of this—not yet."

The senators emerged from the alley, their faces flushed, and hurried away.

Hadrian turned to Calandra. "Do you still believe the emperor is not facing pressure?"

She tilted her head. "Perhaps you are right."

"In any case, you must say nothing. Forget what you have heard."

"Can you forget it?"

Hadrian snorted. "I do not know. But one thing is certain. I will hold my tongue until Rome is peaceful again. To speak of such rumors now might spark a revolt . . . or worse."

❖

Something, I told Priscilla the next day, had changed Hadrian. We were sipping honey water at a caupona near Aquila's workshop, and her face brightened at my words. "For better or worse?" she asked.

"I am not sure," I told her. "I cannot put my finger on the difference, but there is something."

I considered the question as I walked home and was not surprised to see a familiar litter and its attendants waiting outside my father's shop.

I adjusted the fabric of my mantle and went inside.

As I suspected, Hadrian had returned. "Forgive me," he said when I entered. "Yesterday I was so distracted that I forgot to leave your monthly advance payment."

I glanced at Lysandros, who was counting out coins as my father sat behind his worktable.

"Salve," I called, closing the door behind me. "I am sorry you had to make the journey twice."

He squared his shoulders. "There is another reason. My father has heard upsetting news and demands reassurance about your progress."

Careful to keep my mantle over my belly, I sat at the worktable. "What has upset your father?"

Hadrian flushed. "Do you remember the man we saw surrounded by Praetorians? That was Zenodorus. The Senate is abuzz with news of his arrival."

"I have heard of him." Father tapped his chin thoughtfully. "In Gaul, he created a giant statue of Mercury—the Arverni community paid him forty million sestertii for the work."

"Over an extended period," Hadrian added. "He needed ten years to finish."

At the sight of Hadrian's unease, a knot formed in my stomach. "How large was this work?"

"Sixty feet tall," Father said. "It depicted Mercury seated on his throne."

I blinked. Such a statue would be nearly as tall as an insula. No wonder the sculptor needed ten years to finish the job! But surely Cronus did not expect us to compete with Zenodorus. We had neither the time nor the budget.

I forced a smile. "So this man created a giant statue in Gaul. Why does the Senate buzz about him?"

Hadrian heaved a sigh. "Because Nero has just commissioned Zenodorus to create a one-hundred-foot statue of himself. Apparently, it is to stand outside his Golden Palace for all time."

I caught my breath as understanding dawned. No wonder Cronus was concerned. Our statue, a mere larger-than-life-size work, would look like a miniature compared to Zenodorus's colossus.

"What should we do?" Hadrian asked, his forehead creasing. "My father is concerned—"

"Let me think." I brought my hands up to my face and closed my eyes. How could we prevent an unfavorable comparison? Art was about more than size. Art was about beauty and design and its ability to provoke thought . . .

"If Zenodorus's commission is to be famous for its size," I said, lifting my head, "then Cronus's statue must be known for something else. Something vastly different."

"Design," Father said. "If Zenodorus plans to portray Nero sitting, we shall have him standing. On a mountain perhaps."

Hadrian sank onto the bench across from me. "But what if Zenodorus creates a standing Nero? How else can we differentiate the works?"

I looked at Father, waiting for input, but he only gave me a confident smile. "Calandra?"

I exhaled the breath I'd been holding. "How do most sculptors depict an emperor?"

Hadrian glanced at Lysandros. "As ruler, of course."

"And gods," Lysandros added, crossing his arms. "They are intended to reinforce an emperor's image of himself."

I nodded. "But even we plebs know that Nero sees himself as more than a ruler."

When Hadrian's gaze met mine, I knew he had intuited my thoughts. "He sees himself as an *artist*," he said.

"Exactly." I opened a wax tablet and picked up my stylus. "Let us portray a common emperor, not wearing a toga, but a simple tunic. Instead of a sword, we will give him a lyre."

Lysandros grinned. "You have heard the story, as well."

"Everyone in Rome has heard the story," Hadrian said. "Nero sang while Rome burned."

I lifted a warning finger. "We should not reinforce that tale if it will provoke him. He also fancies himself an actor, no?"

Hadrian nodded. "He does. I have been forced to attend a few of his performances."

"Then let us have this common man assume an oratory pose. Or build it on a base that resembles a stage."

Hadrian rubbed his chin. "I like the idea. And smaller will be better because my father cannot afford to pay even two million sesterces. But he will have to approve this notion of yours."

"I understand," I said. "Assure the aedile that we will present our work in four years, while Zenodorus will take much longer to finish. Surely a statue on display is more valuable than one in the workshop."

"Which brings me back to my original purpose," Hadrian said. "What progress have you made thus far?"

I hesitated, then stood. "Come with me and I will show you."

I slipped through the crowded street like a cat, trying to stay one step ahead of Hadrian. I did not want his eyes probing the front of my mantle, nor did I want him to think I had time for a leisurely walk.

"Is the city burning again?" he called, panting.

I hurried down the block and turned toward the two massive brick kilns at the pottery. I greeted the guard and strode through the yard, where a dozen slaves and an equal number of freedmen labored at long tables. Atrides, owner of the pottery, was known throughout Rome for his fine ceramics.

I felt like an absolute beginner whenever I visited Atrides, but he was always kind and quick to offer suggestions. That morning, however, I went to pick up a piece that had been fired in his kiln.

Leaving Hadrian to negotiate the pottery yard, I walked past a table of finished products, eager to see if Atrides was offering any goods that might be profitable for our shop. At one table, slaves at potter's wheels were throwing *skyphos*, shallow drinking cups, and bowl-shaped *kraters* for mixing wine and water. At the decoration station, skilled slaves were painting slender-necked *loutrophoros* jars, destined to hold water for wedding rituals.

"Why are the Greeks so fond of painting their vessels?" Hadrian asked, catching me beside an elaborately decorated amphora. "It seems a waste of time."

"Your father has commissioned art for the emperor. Does that seem like a waste of time?"

Hadrian chuckled. "His purpose is clear—and practical. But what is practical about the decoration of bowls and pitchers that will only be used in the home?"

"Beauty casts its own magic." I picked up an exquisitely painted bowl and wondered if I was wasting my breath. "Though it is lost on some, not everyone is blind to it."

He stared at me, then the corner of his mouth quirked. "Beauty is not lost," he said, "on me."

Atrides strode toward me, waving for my attention. "Calandra," he called. "Your piece is ready."

I followed him to a small room, where rows of shelves held hundreds of ceramic objects. "Over here," Atrides said, pointing to a small corner. "I have taken the liberty of shielding the work from curious eyes because I was afraid someone would want to buy it. But your father should be very pleased."

He pulled a square of linen from the shelf, and I stared as if I were seeing the bust for the first time. My mother stared at me, her oval eyes holding mine, her smile warm with recognition.

"It is you," Hadrian whispered from behind me. "But *not* you."

"It is my mother. Or at least how I imagine her."

"Indeed it is." Atrides crossed his arms. "I knew her, and this is exactly how she looked when she married your father. Did he carve the bust for you?"

I drew a breath, about to tell him about Father's blindness, then remembered that few people on the Aventine had heard the news. Perhaps that was best.

"He did not," I said, "but he is trying to teach me. He described her and I carved the clay."

"The gods have shared his talent with you." Atrides smiled as he lifted the heavy ceramic from the shelf. "Take it and prosper. And may the gods go with you."

I reached out to accept the piece, but Hadrian was faster. "I will carry it."

A flicker of apprehension touched my nerves. "Please cover it." I took the linen square from the shelf and draped it over the piece. "I do not want anyone else to see it."

I could not explain why the glances of strangers would feel like an intrusion, but Hadrian did not comment as we left the pottery.

"I brought you here to see how the process begins," I explained. "First, the clay is molded into the appropriate shape, then it is fired in the kiln. We take it back to the shop and enlarge it. We make a larger mold, in pieces, which will be filled with wax and, eventually, molten bronze. It is a simple process, but it takes time."

Hadrian shifted the bust to his hip, pulled away the linen, and again studied my mother's face. "If this is a measure of your skill, I will assure my father that the work is well under way."

We walked back to the shop. And every time I glanced at the shrouded bust, a river of relief ran through me. Father and I just might be able to please Cronus . . . and Nero.

We would not create a statue as massive as the one planned by Zenodorus, but ours would outshine his in beauty.

Twenty-One

EARLY FEBRUARIUS

As the bust of my mother smiled at me, for a full three weeks I focused on creating Cronus's statue. While I was concentrating on the work, Priscilla convinced her friend Euodia to send her maid Petra, a freedwoman, to cook, fetch water, and visit the market for us. She relieved me of my daily duties, but for several days I produced nothing but utilitarian vases, pots, and bowls. I made practical pottery because I could mold such objects without thinking, leaving my mind free to contemplate the statue for Nero.

How did the emperor see himself? As an artist, yes, but also as a charioteer, a musician, a singer, and a ruler. If he could create his own statue, what would he design? I had no idea.

The first week of Februarius was drawing to a close when I heard someone knock on the counter. Neither Father nor I turned toward the sound, assuming Petra would take care of our customer. But some part of my brain noted the soft sound of fine sandals, and I wondered if a patrician had entered the store.

"Exquisite," a man whispered, and I shivered when I recognized Hadrian's voice.

Taking care to hide my belly beneath the table, I turned my

head. He was staring at the bust of my mother with renewed admiration.

"You have already seen that piece," I reminded him.

"And today I see it with new appreciation. It grows more lovely every day."

I searched for some saucy retort, but Father interrupted. "Surely you cannot still doubt us," he said, a smile twisting his lips. "My daughter has the talent and skill to create what your father desires. My lack of sight will not hamper this project."

"I do not doubt you," Hadrian answered, "and every month I assure my father that all is as it should be. But nearly a month has passed, so what progress shall I report?"

"I have been negotiating with freedmen to help us build the armature," Father said. "Calandra has been doing the hard work."

Hadrian turned to me, so I stuttered out a response. "I-I have been thinking."

"About what?"

"About how Nero would like to see himself."

A line creased Hadrian's forehead. "You have already stated your intention to portray Nero as an actor. What more is there to think about?"

"So much!" Aware that I had inadvertently uncovered my midsection, I leaned forward and braced my arms on the table. "I have been considering every detail. What sort of clothing does an actor wear? Should it be a costume or a simple tunic? What sort of shoes, or should he wear shoes at all? And what of the hair—should he wear a wig? Should he look as he normally does? What details would make it clear that we have depicted Nero as an actor? Should I have him hold a mask?"

Hadrian sat across from me. "Have you found answers for your questions?"

"Perhaps." I pulled several sheets of papyri from a satchel.

"These are preliminary sketches. This one shows Nero in a shepherd's tunic while he holds a twig with a bird on it. He is singing—a song about nature presumably."

Hadrian frowned. "Hmm."

"I have just thought of a potential problem," Father said, slipping off his stool. With his walking stick, he tapped his way toward us. "Since actors are always pretending, most patricians believe them to be untrustworthy. Even though Nero takes pleasure in his acting, how will he feel if he overhears people making snide remarks? Because once he is out of the room, they certainly will."

I bit my lip and looked at Hadrian, who appeared as bewildered as me.

"Perhaps—" I said.

"Yes?"

"What if the statue is never displayed in public? Perhaps it could be a gift for Nero's private bath. He would adore it, and the plebs would never have an opportunity to mock him."

"A good idea, but my father cannot stipulate where the statue will be displayed. Nero will put it wherever he wants, and if it is larger than life-size, it will likely have to be installed in a garden or a grand hall. People *will* see it." Hadrian folded his arms. "You are correct, Pericles. Depicting Nero as an actor could be problematic."

"Surely no one would defame the image in the emperor's presence," I said. "No one would be that foolish."

"True, but even Nero has friends who dare to speak the truth." Hadrian sighed, then pushed away from the table. "I will have to talk to my father about this. He may have a better idea."

He offered us a stiff bow, dropped our advance payment onto the table, and departed.

Twenty-Two

SPRING

Knowing that the child was coming—and that, like many women, I might not survive the birth—I worked feverishly through the months of Februarius, Martius, and into early Aprilis. Since we had decided that portraying Nero as an actor was a bad idea, I decided to work on the statue's base until we chose a better concept.

Focusing on the work kept my mind off the growing life at my center. I could not deny it existed because I felt its pressure on my bladder, I saw the child kick at my skin, and sometimes, as I drifted between sleep and waking, I felt it stretching within me.

But I could not keep it. I was not meant to be a wife or mother. Whenever thoughts of the child entered my head, I banished them with a quick prayer to Juno Lucina, begging for a quick and safe end to this trial. I knew Priscilla was praying to her God as well.

One day Petra walked over to my worktable and lowered her head, waiting silently like the slave she used to be.

"You can speak freely," I reminded her, wiping clay from my hands. "You are a freedwoman."

"Forgive my boldness," she said, looking my bloated belly, "but when should your child arrive?"

"I do not know, but I hope you will help when it does."

A slight smile curved her lips. "I would like that."

"Until then we both have work to do."

I was shaping a generous block of clay, forming the plinth, when a sudden thought occurred. Since Nero considered himself many things, why should the statue be an accurate representation of the man? As long as the face was recognizable, I could create a torso to represent all the things he wanted to be—artist, charioteer, singer, and actor.

What was it Hadrian said when he first viewed the statue of Cronus? He said my father was a *diplomat in stone*, and my father always improved his subjects' appearance because people imagined themselves as more attractive than they were.

Why not create a common man, a slender body encased in a simple tunic, ragged at the hem and lacking embroidery at the neck. Instead of polished and rounded fingertips, I could give him plain hands and short nails. Instead of soft arms and pampered flesh, I could mold muscles shaped by labor and carve tendons into a neck that strained beneath daily burdens. Instead of encasing the emperor's feet in supple slippers, I could sculpt open sandals with bunions at the sides of the big toes. The details of the face could wait, but while I waited I would create a beautifully shaped head that could belong to either a patrician or a slave.

Propping my elbow on the table, I settled my chin in my hand, caught up in the idea of a representative figure. When Nero looked at it, he would see himself in all his manifestations. When other men considered it, they might see themselves—if they were free to see themselves as something other than what they were.

I set aside the clay I had been working with and picked up

another block. Since I had never seen Nero's face, I molded an average-sized head with rounded cheeks. I scraped a section of clay with a metal rake, then attached it to the top, sides, and back of the skull. No tightly wound curls for this fellow, but hair left loose and natural, as if tousled by the wind.

I did not think Cronus would allow me to present a statue with nonspecific facial features, so this statue would have to feature Nero's likeness in that regard. Yet I hoped the artist within the emperor would be delighted to know that this image would represent him to all Romans, citizens and noncitizens, patricians and plebeians, slaves and freedmen.

The concept was not without risk, but Cronus already knew his commission would be overshadowed by Zenodorus's work. So why not do something extraordinary?

Twenty-Three

EARLY APRILIS

Hadrian knocked on the sculptor's door and waited until he heard the old man's shuffling steps.

"Salve, Pericles," he said, entering the workshop with Lysandros. "I have come for our usual meeting."

"Of course." The old man bowed as the slave put the monthly payment into his hand.

Hadrian glanced around. "Your daughter is away?"

Pericles gave him a thin smile. "She is exhausted. I told her to rest."

Hadrian frowned. He had not seen Calandra in several weeks, but he had never known her to take to her bed, unless . . .

"Are you sure she is not ill?"

"She is exhausted, but she wanted you to see this."

Pericles gestured toward the table, where a shape had been covered with a linen sheet. He walked over to it, felt for the fabric's edge, and carefully lifted it away.

Hadrian caught his breath. The figure was a clay statue, nearly four feet tall, of a faceless man. The figure wore a loosely belted tunic that could have belonged to a freedman or a patrician. Simple sandals shod the feet. His gaze rose to see a corded

181

neck, a square chin, and untrimmed hair that flowed to the figure's shoulders. But the face was a blank surface.

The figure could have represented anyone in the Empire.

"It is unfinished," Hadrian said, his voice heavy with disappointment.

"The face and other details can wait," Pericles responded. "What matters is the torso—did you note the detail in the arms? I have approved every curve, every mark, and you will find nothing like this in all of Rome. Other sculptors sculpt what they see, but Calandra has sculpted every person who lives in Rome. *This* is what your father should offer the emperor. If Nero would rule *this* man, if he has the courage to be this plebeian, to feel as he feels and suffer what he suffers, then Nero would be a remarkable emperor indeed."

Hadrian studied the statue, trying to comprehend the idea that had gripped Calandra's imagination. He could not deny that the work was detailed. The clay surface had been textured, revealing the warp and woof of the rough tunic, and the hair was impressive, giving the impression of individual strands. But would Nero appreciate it? Would he understand it, or would he search for himself in the image and find nothing?

"Nero will not see himself in it," he said, turning to Pericles. "He will not be pleased."

"It is not finished," Pericles assured him. "Once Calandra has had a chance to sketch him, she will add the face, though she would rather complete the work with anonymous features. But she understands that Nero will want to see himself as this everyman."

Hadrian sat and studied the statue again. Perhaps she was right. With a word spoken in Nero's ear, he could be convinced to see himself as this lanky, rugged creature, this soul who labored by day and prayed by night. With the right words of flattery, Nero could be persuaded to see himself as almost anything.

"She has outdone herself," he finally said. "No wonder she is exhausted."

"Yes." With extreme care, Pericles lifted the fabric and covered the statue again.

"And the next step?" Hadrian asked. "I cannot believe the work is nearly complete."

"It is not." Pericles rested his hands on his walking stick. "This hollow piece is supported inside by bits of wood and metal, so we will carefully divide it into sections. Then we will enlarge those pieces and fit them together again. When we have recreated this statue at twice the size, we will prepare to pour the molten brass. Then we will reassemble the pieces, smooth the seams, and apply a patina. Only after that will the piece be ready for presentation."

"This will take time, of course."

"At least two years, perhaps three. The process is long and tedious."

Hadrian nodded. "I will inform my father that the work is progressing as it should. But I would like to compliment Calandra. Will you wake her for me?"

He frowned when the sculptor stiffened. But the old man gestured to Petra, the servant, who bowed and hurried through the curtained doorway.

A few moments later the servant reappeared, followed by Calandra, who moved slowly, her hand pressed to her back.

If Pericles had not assured Hadrian that his daughter was well, he would have sent for a physician. She kept her head down, her shoulders hunched forward, and she did not meet his gaze. Though the weather had warmed, she wore the voluminous mantle that covered her from her shoulders to the floor.

He stood and forced a smile. "Calandra, you have done well. The statue is impressive."

She looked up. Her face, which had always been heart-shaped, had become round and soft. "Thank you. Now, if you will excuse me, I am overtired."

"Of course, you deserve your rest. But know that my father will be pleased with your work."

"Good, but there is much yet to do."

She turned, and as she walked away with one hand pressed to the small of her back, Hadrian recognized the gait and posture. The puffy face, the voluminous clothing, the waddling walk . . . Calandra was with child!

He lurched forward, about to pursue her, when Lysandros raised a hand of warning. When Hadrian shot him a sharp look, the slave pointed to the old man.

Comprehension seeped through Hadrian's shock. Calandra was pregnant, and her father might not know. Had she hidden her condition to avoid shaming Pericles? Or Hadrian?

He stood like a man rooted to the floor, drowning in guilt, until Lysandros released a discreet cough. "We will take our leave," the slave called, loud enough for half the building's residents to hear. "We will not return until next month."

As the events of the last hour collided in his head, Hadrian followed Lysandros into the street.

"She did not tell me." Sitting in a tavern with his slave, Hadrian repeated the words again, shaking his head as he stared across the table. "Why did she not say something?"

Lysandros lowered his cup. "What would you have her say?"

"I thought we were well-acquainted. I thought we were friends."

"Friends are equals. She is not your friend."

"Is she not? I have worked with her for months."

"So?"

"What about us? We are not equals, yet we are friends."

Lysandros snorted. "At the risk of offending you, Dominus, we are not friends. I am your slave; you are my master."

"Do we not speak freely to each other? Do I not confide in you?"

"You confide in me, yes. You speak freely to me. But you do not ask about my feelings, and I do not share them."

Hadrian gaped at his slave. "Why not? Are we not now brothers through Yeshua?"

"We are. But why would I share my feelings with a man who could beat me for my honesty? I said it once, but apparently my words have not penetrated your skull: friends are equals. Calandra is your employee, not your friend."

Knowing he could not win the argument, Hadrian lifted his cup. "The child may not be mine. It could be anyone's."

"True, but highly unlikely."

"The woman travels through the streets without an escort. She could have been attacked. She could have been mistaken for a—"

"You have made your point. The child may not be yours."

"Still . . ." Hadrian closed his eyes as memories of their visit to the Aventine resurfaced. The city had been a ruined wreck, the future uncertain. The boundaries that kept them apart fell away, and they reached for each other in a moment of desperation, attraction, and fear. He sighed. "The child is mine. The fire . . . was nine months ago."

"You need not worry. She is not likely to seek you out."

"I wish she could."

Hadrian imagined the scene. When a child was born, every Roman wife or female slave brought her newborn to the paterfamilias and laid it at his feet. If the head of the family lifted the child, he acknowledged it and assumed responsibility for its care. If he ignored the baby, someone would quietly take it to the slave market or expose it outside the city walls.

Hadrian was not the paterfamilias of his family. Even if Calandra were brazen enough to take the child to Cronus—which she was not—the aedile would be astonished, disbelieving, and offended.

Lysandros was correct—Hadrian could not imagine any circumstance in which Calandra would approach him with her child. And he had no idea how to help her when she was obviously trying to hide the child's existence from him.

What, then, would she do with their baby?

Twenty-Four

The first pain struck as I was painting a set of ceramic bowls. I gasped, held my breath until the birth pang passed, and called for Petra.

"I need you," I said, "to go to Transtiberim and find Priscilla. Tell her my time has come." I could tell from her round eyes that she had grasped the significance of my situation.

"Yes, Domina."

"I am not your domina," I gasped as another pain ripped at my back. "But you should not delay. Go."

The girl threw a palla over her head and hurried away. Not knowing when I would be able to return to my work, I took a few moments to clean my brushes.

On the other side of the room, my father was smoothing areas of our clay model with a damp sponge. "Father," I called, keeping my voice light as I waddled toward him, "Priscilla is coming to visit. I trust you remember her."

"Of course!" His countenance brightened. "Will Aquila be with her?"

"I think not. Priscilla may stay awhile."

His smile faded, replaced by a somber expression. "Are you well, daughter?"

"I am." I took his hand and squeezed it. "You must not worry about me."

"I do not worry, Calandra, because I have been praying that Adonai will protect you . . . during your time of labor."

Surprise stole my voice. I thought I had managed to hide my condition, but apparently Father had realized the truth. He had always been able to see through my attempts at disguise.

"Oh, Tata!" For the first time in months, I fell into his arms, my façade crumbling like brittle clay. "I am so sorry! I wanted to tell you, but I did not want to bring shame upon your good name."

"I could never be ashamed of you." He patted my back, his chest rising as he gulped a deep breath. "I have been praying for you, daughter. I have begged the Lord to protect you and the life within you. I have asked Him to give you wisdom."

I bit my lip, resisting the urge to tell him that his prayers had not been answered. I had neither wisdom nor answers. I could see nothing ahead but misery.

I clung to him a moment more, then straightened my spine. "I must be strong now. Priscilla will soon be here."

"Calandra . . ." His voice held a note of entreaty.

"Yes?"

"You could lay the child before me. I would claim it and be responsible. I would trust Adonai to provide."

In my father's tear-streaked face I saw his willingness to be mocked, questioned, scorned and ridiculed. People would think the worst of us, my father's rising star would plummet, and I would remain forever unmarried. People might buy my bowls and platters, but Pericles the sculptor would never receive another commission. And Hadrian would wonder if the child was his or someone else's.

No. This child was my doing and my responsibility. I loved my father, but I would not allow him to bear this burden.

"Thank you, Tata, but I cannot do that. When Priscilla arrives, please send her to my bedchamber."

Then, moving in the uneven, slow shuffle that had probably revealed my secret, I held my breath through another ripping pain and staggered to my room.

❖

"It is time—push!"

Straining, leaning against Petra's chest as she knelt behind me, I gritted my teeth and bore down as my child slid into the world on a tide of blood and foamy water. Priscilla caught the infant and lifted it.

"A boy," she cried, her voice vibrant with joy. "You have given birth to a healthy son."

I acknowledged her words with a nod and turned my head. I could not look at the baby. I would not want it, nor miss it, if I had never seen it.

"Let me clean you up," Priscilla crooned, speaking to the infant. "I will find you a warm blanket and then your mother will nurse you."

I swallowed the lump that had risen in my throat and struggled to rise from the floor. My loins ached and my legs felt as though the bones had dissolved, but somehow I managed to crawl onto my bed. I buried my face in a pillow and yearned for sleep, but some part of my brain would not disconnect from the sounds in the room—Priscilla's soft murmuring, water splashing in the basin, the baby's mewling cry.

A cry that scoured my heart.

Poor baby. Son of a patrician father, a *good* man, this infant should have been celebrated, welcomed, and joyfully laid at Hadrian's feet. I could well imagine the light of joy that would enter his eyes as he picked up the baby, brought it to his chest, and marveled over the miracle of bright eyes, ten fingers and ten toes.

But I was not worthy of bearing a patrician's child, and my unworthiness would be this baby's downfall. The gods might yet guide him to a safe harbor, even a good place, but I could do nothing for him.

I thought about praying to the goddess Lucina, protector of newborns, but she might take offense if I petitioned her without first making an offering. I had made no offering to any god, but perhaps there was one who would listen to the cry of an anguished woman in need . . .

I covered my face with my hands. "I beseech you, listening God, heed my prayer! I place my baby into your hands and beg you to protect him. Keep him safe, show him love, and let him become as noble as his father. I beg you to hear me and answer."

I heard no response from the heavens, yet the room seemed to fill with the soft sound of suckling. I turned and opened my eyes enough to see that Priscilla had swaddled the child and placed her finger in its mouth. "Your baby is hungry," she said, her voice warm and inviting as she came over and sat on the edge of the bed. "Will you not nurse him?"

She nudged my shoulder with the warm bundle, but I turned away. "Thank you for coming," I said, my voice as ragged as my emotions, "but I have kept you from your husband long enough. Leave the child with Petra."

"Are you sure? I could stay if—"

"You should go now," I rasped, closing my eyes more tightly. "I need rest."

I heard Priscilla instruct Petra before leaving—she was to keep the child warm and let it suck on a wet cloth until a wet nurse could be found. She continued with further instructions, but I put my hands over my ears and refused to listen.

Finally I heard retreating footsteps . . . and the soft, gasping sounds of a newborn.

I forced myself to sit up. "Please . . . take him away."

"Domina, surely you do not mean—"

I covered my ears. "Take him to a Column Lactaria. His fate rests in the hands of the God who listens."

Petra pulled the child into her arms and stared at me, her eyes damp with sorrow. "Adonai could provide a way," she said. "Can you not trust Him?"

"I have already made my prayer." I closed my eyes and waited until she left the room. When I heard the squeak of the front door, I released a shuddering breath and heard my heart break—a piercing sound, like the snap of living bone.

❖

For the next several days I felt as if there were hands on my heart, slowly twisting every ounce of energy from it. My body felt empty without its warm, moving weight, and I did not want to leave my bed. Petra brought me bread, fruit, and cheese, but I ate little.

My body rebelled against what I had done. My aching breasts grew tight with milk. My abdomen continued to cramp, and my mood remained dark and somber. Petra brought in a midwife, who said my discomfort was normal.

"Your body is adjusting," she said. "In time it will realize your child is gone, and it will return to the way it was. The cramps will ease, and your discomfort will fade. Soon it will be as if you never had a baby."

I did not see how that could be possible.

Two days after the birth, Petra brought me a letter from Priscilla. "She wanted to come see you," Petra said. Her faint smile held a touch of sadness. "But she thought you might not feel up to having a guest."

I took the letter and tossed it in my trunk, certain of its contents. Priscilla would have written that she was praying for me, she cared about me, and she hoped I was well, but how could anyone expect me to be unaffected by what had happened? My feelings for the baby surprised me. I had not wanted to attach to it or even to want it. I understood that married women yearned to provide heirs for their husbands, but why should I desire a child? I who had never known a mother was surprised to feel an inexplicable yearning to hold my baby.

Yet there had been nights, as I lay in bed and waited for sleep, when I caressed the mound of my belly and felt answering movements. By some miracle of the gods, Hadrian and I had created a life. If I had been Hadrian's wife, the child would have grown to be a senator, an aedile, or even the emperor. I had been born under Caesar's comet, so why had I not been born a patrician?

But I would never be Hadrian's wife, so I had done the best I could for my baby. He stood a decent chance of survival at the Column Lactaria. Other illegitimate children, including at least two of our past emperors', had been exposed outside the city, where they were certain to perish.

My father, who had always been proud of his Greek heritage, once told me of the three Fates, daughters of Zeus. Clotho, the first sister, spun the thread of life for each child born. Lachesis, the second, measured the thread, determining how long each child would live. Atropos, the last, cut the thread, determining the death day of every living person.

What joys and sorrows had Clotho spun into my child's thread? How many days had Lachesis allotted for his life? Had Atropos already cut the thread, or was she allowing my child a few more months of life?

Perhaps my ignorance of his fate was a blessing.

For two weeks I mourned in my bedchamber, allowing my body to adjust as my mind cleared. I grieved for the child, but as the days passed, the practical side of my nature chided my softer self. How could I ever have imagined that Hadrian would accept our child as his son and heir? He could never acknowledge a child from an unmarried woman, especially a woman of the working class. His father would not allow it, and no proper Roman son would rebel against his father. A son who dared to do so risked dishonor and death.

And how could I imagine raising a child myself? Only prostitutes and widows raised fatherless children, and most prostitutes ridded themselves of babies either before or after birth. Those who abandoned their offspring found hope in the fact that noble families often adopted healthy male infants and wealthy families always needed slaves.

Fourteen days after giving birth, I rose, bathed with water from the basin, and put on a fresh tunic. Seeing that I had decided to rejoin the world, Petra offered to arrange my hair. Resigned to the necessity, I allowed her to do so.

When she had finished my hair, she pressed her hands to my shoulders. "Before you go to work—"

"Yes?"

"I wanted to give you this." She reached into her tunic and pulled something from her *subligaculum*, the undergarment worn around the chest. She gestured for me to put out my hand, and when I did, she dropped a coin onto my palm. Not a perfect coin, but one that had been broken.

"Forgive me if I have overstepped," she said, misery coloring her face, "but I could not bear to see you give your baby away without recourse. So I wanted you to have this."

She did not have to explain the significance of the object in my hand. I had seen babies at the base of the Column Lactaria with half coins tied around their necks, their only link to the mothers who might want to reclaim them.

"I do not want it."

"Keep it." She thrust her hands behind her back. "The child is yours. As long as you have this, you will remember him."

Why did she think I could forget?

❖

Father looked up when he heard me enter the workroom. "Calandra! You are recovered?"

I pulled out a chair and sat across from him, noting that anxiety had deepened the lines in his face. "I am sorry for having stayed so long in bed. And for not wanting to see you . . . after."

Love and tenderness twisted his face as he turned toward me. "You have been very brave."

Though sorrow throbbed like a knot inside my chest, I nodded through tears. "Can a woman be brave when she has no choice?"

"She can. Your mother was brave until the end, as were you." His chin quivered, and I saw a geyser of emotions threatening to break through his fragile composure.

I placed my hand on his. "I had a healthy baby, Tata. A boy."

"Petra told me."

"So you know she took the child to the Column Lactaria."

"I do." His voice broke. "And I am to blame for your sad decision. As a blind old man, you did not feel I could adopt your child."

"No, Tata." I patted his hand. "It would not have been fair for me to place the burden of a child on you. You are not to blame for anything."

"I should have known what you were going through. But I did not see."

"How could you?"

"I should have known. I knew you and Hadrian—I know he loves you."

"He cannot love me. We can never be together."

194

"You should not lose hope, daughter. You should never stop praying."

"I *did* pray. To any god who would listen."

"That is good. Adonai listens, and I have seen Him do amazing things. I have heard stories of miracles—"

"You are still blind, Tata, and my baby is still gone. So let us say no more about this."

He drew a breath as if he would speak again, then he nodded. "As you wish."

"What's done is done. Now I am ready to help you complete the statue."

"My dear girl." His hand turned and caught mine. "How I wish I could have been of more help to you. If only your mother had been here."

"I had Priscilla and Petra to help. Now I am ready to work."

"Are you certain? I could send someone to inquire about—"

"Please, Tata." I firmed my voice. "I cannot have you picking at this wound. I need to think about something else."

He squeezed my hand, swallowed hard, and gestured in the direction of the clay model. "Now we shall enlarge the clay figure. Our calculations must be exact, or the new model will not have the proper proportions."

I leaned forward and focused on our statue . . . still as faceless as the child I had abandoned.

❖

Hadrian stood in the middle of the Aventine street, ignoring those who shouted for him to move out of the way. Finally, Petra came out of the sculptor's workshop and gestured for him to meet her by the fountain.

Hadrian followed, his heart pounding. "Is she well?" he asked when he caught up to the servant. "Has she asked for me?"

The servant gave him a sad smile. "She is well, but she has not said much to anyone. For days she would not even speak to her father, who stopped by her room every morning."

"I have never known Calandra to be at a loss for words. Are you sure she is not ill?"

"Her sorrow, sir—it has stolen her words. Now she speaks only of getting back to work."

He drew a deep breath and turned toward the workshop. Everything in him wanted to stride into the place, take Calandra into his arms, and offer the solace and comfort she surely needed, but would that be fair? How could his comfort help when he could not offer the things she needed most—namely, marriage and a home for their child? Surely that is what Yeshua would want him to offer.

"What of the child?" he asked.

Petra folded her hands. "She was safely delivered of her baby. She told me to take it to the Column Lactaria, so you need not worry about it showing up at your home."

He sank to the stone wall around the base of the fountain. The girl spoke the words so easily, but she had been a slave, accustomed to people, even children, arriving and disappearing at the whim of the master. Calandra would not be so casual about the child, he was sure of it. But being thoroughly Roman, neither would she want to discuss it.

"Rome is far from perfect," he said, thinking aloud. "We boast of our freedom, but how can we be free when a man cannot marry the woman he loves?"

"I have heard there is a law against a citizen marrying a former slave," Petra said, her eyes narrowing. "Yet there is no law against a citizen marrying another citizen."

Her words caught him off guard. "You know Roman law?"

"I am a freedwoman," she said, her tone sharper than before. "So yes, I have learned about what I can and cannot do.

I cannot marry *you*, but there is no law against you marrying my mistress."

Hadrian sighed. The girl was right, of course. But while Rome had the rule of law, the patricians had the rule of *practice*. And to maintain the purity of the first families and the nobility of the Senate, patricians always married other patricians.

"Thank you," he said, standing. "Tell Calandra and Pericles I will make my regular visit soon."

"If I may, sir—" The girl bit her lip.

"Yes?"

"My mistress is in a fragile state. Perhaps . . . I know it is bold of me to suggest such a thing—"

"Speak, Petra."

"Perhaps you could send your servant in your place. For a month or two. Give my mistress time to recover."

Hadrian exhaled slowly. Petra knew Calandra's condition better than he did, so the girl was probably right. Perhaps Yeshua was speaking through her, revealing a way He could demonstrate mercy to Calandra and ease his own troubled heart.

"Yes, that is wise. I will send Lysandros."

Petra exhaled in relief. "Very good, sir. But do not say I told you to stay away."

"I will not."

"Thank you, sir." The servant stood and hurried back to the shop. Hadrian watched her go, struggling to swallow the lump that crowded his throat.

Twenty-Five

Spring surrendered to summer and summer to the cooler days of autumn. With each succeeding month I found it easier to hide my heartbreak and focus on the building of Cronus's statue. Because the work would literally be larger than we were, Father hired several skilled freedmen to help us in the enlargement.

The process of creating the new model took over the workshop. The freedmen constructed a pantograph, a mechanical device that would expand our original clay model. The tool consisted of four jointed arms, two short and two long. The short arms were connected to each other with a pointer, and their opposite ends were connected to the two longer arms. One of the longer arms was stationary, while the other moved freely.

At first I did not understand how the pantograph worked, but Father explained that when we positioned the pointer on our existing model, its movement caused a corresponding motion in the longer arm, which moved over a greater distance and thus enlarged our model.

I watched, amazed, as Father put the pointer at the head of our original model. The pointer on the long arm moved to a point on the armature, a three-dimensional frame the freedmen had built. One of them marked the spot with a nail, then Father moved the pointer to the base of our model's chin. Again, a freedman marked the corresponding spot on the wooden frame, and so the enlargement began. Working from side to side and back to back, the workers painstakingly marked out new dimensions for our original model.

Father had decided that our statue should be ten feet tall—large enough to be impressive, but not so large that it would not fit in our workshop.

"It will appear as a gnat compared to the behemoth Zenodorus is building," Father said, "so it is good we will be finished long before he is."

When Hadrian and Lysandros dropped by the workshop in late October, we had nearly completed the framework of the enlargement. Hadrian whistled when he saw it. "Impressive."

"The work is coming along," Father said, stroking his stubbled chin. "Once we have mapped the entire model with nails, we will apply clay to the structure. The nails will support the clay as we sculpt the enlarged model."

"It will be impressive," Hadrian said. "Father is convinced that his gift will be offered so far in advance of Zenodorus's work that it will be well appreciated." He glanced at me. "I would not have believed that a woman and a blind man could work so well together. But I see what you have accomplished, and I am quite pleased."

I lowered my eyes, afraid Hadrian might read my emotions. "I am glad you and your father have retained your confidence in us."

"I am happy to see you looking so well." He smiled, yet a note of uncertainty echoed in his voice. He had to be referring to the months when I hid behind tables and counters, my face puffy from the pregnancy.

I gave him what I hoped was an indifferent shrug. "I am fine."

"Well enough to come with us?"

"Where are you going?"

"We have to visit Transtiberim. I know you have friends there."

My heart leapt. Father and I had been so busy that I had neglected my friends across the river. They had not neglected me—Priscilla had visited several times since the baby's birth, and during her last visit she asked if I would consider allowing Petra to return to Euodia, the woman who had arranged the girl's manumission. I felt guilty for having commandeered someone else's servant and immediately sent her back to work for the woman from Philippi.

I wanted to see all of them again. "Of course I will come."

"Make yourself ready, and we will go."

❖

I did not realize that going with Hadrian and Lysandros meant I would accompany them on their rounds, but that is what we did. We visited so many imperial prisoners that their names ran together in my mind: Titius Justus and Aurora from Corinth, Petros and Hannah from Judea, and several couples from Ephesus. Marcus and Mariana, also from Corinth, had two young sons, a toddler and an infant. I looked away, blinking, and tried desperately to think of something else.

In each household, no matter how humble, Hadrian treated his prisoners with consideration and respect, quietly listening to their answers as Lysandros recorded them on his wax tablet. I marveled at Hadrian's attitude. Though he and his father were employed by Nero, Hadrian seemed to admire them even though they had taken a stand against the Empire. Both he and Lysandros treated them with a gentleness I did not expect from representatives of Rome.

I received the shock of my life when we entered a shabby apartment on a high floor of an insula. A tall older man opened the door when Hadrian knocked, then Hadrian stepped forward and greeted the man with a hug. I stared in utter amazement as the prisoner, whom Hadrian addressed as *Petros*, patted Hadrian's back.

Since when had the aedile's representative and these prisoners of Rome become as close as family?

In Petros's apartment, we received news that clearly caught Hadrian by surprise. I did not catch the words at first, but when Hadrian startled, I focused my attention on the elderly Judean fisherman. "*Who* is coming to Rome?" I asked.

"Paulos." An eager light flashed in the old man's eyes. "Apparently Adonai is leading him back to us."

Hadrian did not reply, but his brow furrowed when we left the apartment.

"Who is this Paulos?" I asked, struggling to match his pace. "And why does his return upset you?"

"I am not upset," Hadrian said, pinching the bridge of his nose. "I am only surprised."

"Why?"

He halted in mid-step. "The man is a respected rabbi and follower of Yeshua. He has been imprisoned before, and he left the city when he was released. But if he is coming back . . ." He shook his head.

"Is he not allowed to come back to Rome?"

"It is not wise for him to return. Wherever he goes, trouble follows."

Hadrian resumed walking, and I struggled to keep up. I did not know anything about Paulos, but apparently Hadrian did not want him to get in trouble again. Why? Was he dreading the thought of having to visit another prisoner?

I tugged on his sleeve as he headed toward the bridge. "You mentioned that I have friends here," I said, gesturing to another insula. "I need to visit them before we return to the Aventine."

"Need to?"

"I *want* to." I gave him what I hoped was a convincing smile. "You may recall Aquila the tentmaker and his wife. You visited us when we sheltered with them after the fire."

Hadrian squinted at the building. "I remember."

"I should stop to see how they are doing."

He glanced at the sky to check the hour, then gestured toward the tentmaker's shop. "Lead the way."

I strode forward, pleased by the thought of seeing Aquila and Priscilla. Though they were Christians, the tentmakers were not prisoners, so they were free to earn a living. They were not only prosperous; they provided a valuable service to the community.

A doorkeeper stood outside Aquila's shop and dipped his head in a respectful bow as we approached. "May I tell my master who is calling?"

"I am Calandra, daughter of Pericles, and this is—"

Hadrian lifted his head. "Hadrian Cronus Tuscus."

"Son of the aedile?"

"The same."

The man smiled and stepped aside. "You may enter."

I gasped when we walked into the workshop. Aquila's shop had been clean and attractive when I last visited, but the place had been transformed. Now only a few tables held goatskin samples; the others were swathed with displays of glorious purple linen and silk.

I pressed my hand to my chest. "What happened here?"

A lovely woman came out from the back room. "May I assist you?"

"I-I . . ." I stuttered, overcome by the unexpected sight of such elegance among the goatskins. "I wanted to give my regards to Aquila and Priscilla."

"Calandra?" Priscilla stepped out from behind the curtain, a piece of bread in one hand and a cup in the other. "Praise Adonai, it *is* you! I thought I recognized your voice." She set her lunch on a nearby table and hugged me, then gave Hadrian an appraising look. "And who is this?"

"Hadrian," I said. "He was kind enough to allow me to leave the workshop for a breath of fresh air."

Priscilla laughed. "I do not blame you for wanting to venture out." She reached for Hadrian's hand and held it between her own, an astounding gesture of familiarity. "I have heard about you. Petros told us of your decision to follow Yeshua."

I gave Priscilla a glance of disbelief. "Surely you are confused. This is Hadrian Cronus Tuscus, son of the aedile."

Priscilla nodded. "And I am delighted to call him my brother in Messiah Yeshua."

Paralyzed by astonishment, I stared at Hadrian. "How?" I asked. "When?"

He locked his arms behind his back. "When Petros healed you," he said. "I knew no man could perform such a miracle. So I went back to talk to Petros about Yeshua."

"And you have——?"

"I have chosen Him above all other gods."

I transferred my gaze to Priscilla as the change in Hadrian suddenly made sense. "You trust this man?"

"Don't you?"

I snapped my mouth shut. I *did* trust Hadrian, but I was not a member of an unpopular sect. "Priscilla, he is warden to your imprisoned friends."

"And we thank Adonai for him." She released Hadrian's hand and nodded to her elegant guest. "This is Euodia, my friend from Philippi. She is the woman who sent Petra to help Calandra."

Hadrian bowed to the woman. "I am honored. Welcome to Rome."

Ignoring my incredulous expression, Priscilla touched my arm. "And how is your father?"

"He is in good spirits . . . as long as the work progresses on schedule."

"Will you join us for a meal? Euodia and I were enjoying a bit of bread and cheese."

"I do not want to disturb you." I took a step toward the door. "We have just come from Petros's apartment, so I suppose you have heard his news."

"Indeed we have." Priscilla lowered her voice. "We know who is coming, and we will be delighted to see him."

"I met Paulos years ago," Euodia said, her eyes glowing. "I count him as one of my dearest friends."

I caught my breath. I had never met the man, yet I was growing more curious by the moment. But this was not the time to hear all the details.

"We must go," I said, remembering my manners. "Euodia, thank you for sending Petra to help me. Priscilla, I am so grateful for your kindness. I can never repay you."

"You will always be welcome here," she said. "Hadrian, on the first day of the week, the ecclesia meets in our shop. You are welcome to join us."

Hadrian pointed at Lysandros, who waited outside. "My slave is also a believer."

"He is welcome as well. We are all equals in the ecclesia, for the ground is level at the foot of the cross."

I gaped at them, unable to make sense of what I was hearing, but how could I fault Priscilla for her beliefs? Her tender compassion, her reassurances during my pregnancy, and her practical help in those horrible days after the fire combined to form a knot in my chest. Unable to speak, I flapped my hand in a weak wave, then darted through the doorway, desperate for fresh air.

I did not say much as we walked back to the Aventine, and Hadrian spoke only when we reached my father's shop. "I did not decide to follow Adonai *only* because of your healing," he said, gripping the edge of his toga. "The people themselves convinced me. Despite what others have said, I can find no fault in them. How can they be enemies of Rome when they care so deeply for Romans?"

I pressed my lips together, unable to argue.

"Until next month." Hadrian bowed, an unexpected sign of respect, and turned. I stood on the portico and watched him go, my heart contracting as he and Lysandros walked away. Why did Hadrian affect me so deeply when there could never be more than friendship between us? And why did his decision to worship Adonai feel like a betrayal?

"She looks better," Lysandros remarked as he and Hadrian walked back to the Forum.

Hadrian grunted, not in the mood for conversation. Calandra had been a puzzle—happy one moment and irritated the next. He had no idea why she should be irritated with him, but he would have sworn she was. Yet her eyes had shone with tears when they left the tentmaker's shop, and he could not understand why her friends would make her sad. Priscilla and Euodia had been gracious, and he had done his best to be discreet with the news about Paulos. He wanted to assure them that though he knew about the rabbi, he would do nothing to threaten the man or even reveal his whereabouts unless directly asked.

In that case, he would probably tell the truth. Duty demanded it . . . but did Adonai?

"She was glad you asked her to accompany us," Lysandros said. "Did you not see the warmth in her countenance?"

Hadrian blinked. "You saw warmth?"

"In the beginning, yes."

Hadrian shrugged. "I do not understand the woman. She is more changeable than the wind. I never have any idea what she is thinking."

"She admires you or she would not speak so freely in your presence. She also trusts you."

They walked in silence, dodging merchant carts, children, and beggars, then Hadrian clenched his fist. "*Does* she trust me? If so, why did she not tell me about the baby?"

Lysandros shook his head. "Who am I to know such a thing?"

"I did not know about the child until she was ready to give birth," Hadrian said, spitting out words he had locked inside himself for months. "She should have told me."

"Children are a woman's business, and she is not your wife. Legally, the child is nothing to you."

"But it was mine!" Hadrian whirled, halting their progress. "Should I not know what became of the child that sprang from my loins?"

Lysandros held up his hand. "Careful, Dominus. Perhaps you should not be saying such things in the street. Even to inquire about such a child—if it still lives—might incur responsibilities you do not want."

Hadrian hesitated, then gripped his slave's shoulder. "You shall make inquiries. Discreetly. Do not let Calandra know what you are doing."

The slave's expression shifted to one of pained tolerance. "And if I find an answer to your question?"

"Keep the knowledge to yourself." Hadrian lifted his chin. "For me it will be enough to know that you know."

Twenty-Six

DECEMBER

With mixed feelings, my father and I—indeed, all of Rome—watched a glittering phoenix rise from the ashes of the great fire.

Our former emperors had built palaces among existing homes on Palatine Hill, but Nero built his *Domus Aurea* on Palatine Hill, Oppian Hill, *and* Caelian Hill. His architects oversaw the removal of massive amounts of rubble and debris, then surveyed the land and divided it according to its intended use.

On Oppian Hill, Nero established the complex dedicated to his dining rooms and art galleries. To the south, Caelian Hill featured an expansive terrace with several fountains and gardens. The largest complex, with more than two hundred rooms, rose from Palatine Hill.

In his early years as emperor, Nero had focused his architectural attention on structures that would benefit the people—first, a substantial market, then a theater and baths. After the fire, he concentrated his energies on building a house to prove he ruled the world.

Every day we watched goods and building materials from

throughout the Empire move through our streets—exquisitely carved columns of yellow marble from Africa and slabs of green marble from Sparta. Though I had loved color since childhood, I never imagined seeing hues like those destined for Nero's house. His lavish spending—while the citizens of Rome still struggled to feed themselves—rankled.

On festival days, when only slaves and day laborers worked, we were able to walk the two roads that led through the area devoted to the Golden House. Hadrian often escorted me, and we marveled at the sheer number of bricks required to construct the massive structure.

"Nero wants this building to stand forever," Hadrian once said, watching as a team of slaves mixed lime with sand from volcanic rock. "See there? The concrete will be poured between those two brick walls. Only God could knock down a wall five feet thick."

I noticed his mention of a singular God but did not remark on it.

"I have never seen walls of such height," I said, tipping my head back. "The artists who paint these ceilings will be dizzy."

"They are designed to make us feel small. We are to marvel at the emperor's wealth and realize we are only ants."

"At least we are grateful ants," I countered. "Father says Nero's palace has employed thousands who would otherwise go hungry."

"A man who is busy working cannot be part of a mob. Nor can a man who spends his day at the games. Nero knows how to keep the plebs happy, but he is less skilled at satisfying the patricians."

"The Senate does not support him? I would have thought that what is beneficial for Rome is beneficial for the Senate—"

"The senators are too wise to openly declare their frustration." Hadrian stopped and leaned against a column. "But

consider all the men who lost their homes on Palatine Hill—
yes, they were compensated for the loss of their property, but
that paltry compensation could not compare to what they lost.
Now they are being taxed almost beyond their means. The
provincial governors are also reporting that their people are
unhappy with the new taxes. Why should the provinces pay
for the fire in Rome?"

I shook my head. "People always complain about taxes.
Surely this will pass, and Nero has put people to work."

Hadrian pulled himself off the column and resumed walking.
"What if I told you that in the last few months alone, nineteen
high-ranking individuals have been put to death or commanded
to commit suicide? One of them was Seneca, Nero's former
tutor."

I startled, having heard wonderful things about the esteemed
philosopher. "What did he do?"

"As I said, the senators and equestrians are unhappy about
the financial burdens they have been forced to bear. One man,
Calpurnius Piso, actually led a conspiracy to kill the emperor.
But his plan fell apart when one conspirator was tortured. He
named the others, and now all of them are dead. In days to
come I would not be surprised to hear those men named as the
arsonists who started the great fire."

"Did they?"

Hadrian barked a laugh. "Of course not. But Nero is looking
for someone to blame." He shrugged. "So why not them? The
dead cannot deny the charge."

Seeing that Hadrian had become agitated, I cast about for
a more pleasant subject. "Surely time will repair the losses suffered by the patricians—"

"Annius Vinicianus led another plot. He planned to murder
Nero when the emperor passed through southern Italy on his
way to Greece, but someone in his retinue revealed the plan.

Nero ordered Vinicianus to kill himself, along with Scibonius Proculus and Scibonius Rufus. My father says Nero seems determined to kill all men of rank and virtue."

The frown shadowing Hadrian's face had not lifted, prompting me to ask the unthinkable: "Is your father still loyal to the emperor?"

He gave me a humorless smile. "My father is a high-ranking official, but his virtue tends to be flexible. He suffers like the others who lost their fortunes in the fire. Still, he is not foolhardy."

When Hadrian fell silent, I knew better than to ask anything else.

Twenty-Seven

IANUARIUS
THE 12TH YEAR OF NERO'S REIGN

Father and I finished the framework of the enlarged statue, so the new year found us smoothing the resulting figure. Father worked on a scaffold with railings, and though I worried he might fall, the railings helped him keep his balance as he examined sections that needed smoothing, cutting, or alteration.

I often thought he had developed eyes in the palms of his hands. Simply by running his fingers over the damp clay, he knew exactly what had to be done to make each area fit into the statue.

As I watched the image take shape, I wondered which would be finished first, our statue or Nero's Golden House?

Since meeting Hadrian, I had begun to understand the politics of government, and what I learned elicited equal parts admiration and dismay. Rome prided itself on being a republic, with people who were represented by senators, but in reality the senators only represented patricians and wealthy families. No poor men wore senatorial purple, and no noncitizens sat in that vaunted chamber.

For years I had heard Father praise Julius Caesar, who had

been murdered because certain senators feared his power as dictator, but was Nero not a dictator? He ordered, and people obeyed. He taxed, and people paid. He did what he wanted and eliminated all those who opposed him.

At least Caesar had wanted to give foreigners an opportunity to become citizens and senators.

From living on the Aventine, I saw how the common people loved Nero. He sponsored gladiatorial games on festival days, and people thought the necessary coin came directly from Nero's purse. Yet Nero did nothing to earn money. Instead, he took it from the patricians, the provinces, and those who sold slaves from conquered lands.

After Hadrian told me about the tension between Nero and the ruling class, I became a better observer and eavesdropper. When I went to the Forum with my wax tablet and stylus, no one noticed the woman sketching faces, hands, and the intricate swirls in patrician hair styles.

No one noticed the woman who overheard conversations that echoed Hadrian's concerns. That is when I learned that people throughout the Empire, including my father and me, were being robbed without our knowledge.

The realization came to me one afternoon when Hadrian and I were walking in a terraced garden. Suddenly he put out his hand and turned, halting our progress. Two men approached, each of them wearing a senatorial toga. When they had passed, Hadrian lowered his voice: "They are involved with the Treasury. Let us remain close."

"Why?"

In answer he pressed his fingertip to his lips and led me behind a tall hedge that stood between us and the senators.

"So how does the emperor plan to meet this enormous demand?" the older man asked, his voice cracking with age. "He seems to think silver grows on trees."

"He has a plan," the second man said. "He has ordered the Treasury to change the denarius."

"How so?"

"The weight of the coin will be slightly reduced. Instead of being pure silver, each coin will be mixed with copper. Beginning this year, our denarii will be only eighty percent silver."

When the second man did not answer, I turned to Hadrian, who wore a look of astonished consternation. After a moment he took my arm and led me away.

"I do not understand," I said when we had left the garden. "They are changing the size of the coins?"

His face darkened. "They are changing the *worth* of the coin."

"How so? If I paid one denarius for a palla last year, will I not pay one denarius this year?"

He drew a patient breath. "Nero is shortchanging coins at the mint. Since the time of Augustus, a denarius has been required to be pure silver. But this year if you sell a bowl for one denarius, you will only receive eighty percent of what you are owed. Your bowl has been devalued, and you did not even know it."

"But what is the harm? If I do not know it—"

"People *will* know it in time. When we pay taxes at the next census, the tax collector will ask for old coins, not the new ones. Smelters will realize the change when they melt down the coins. Soon everyone will know the new coins are worth less. If Nero persists in this venture, one day the denarius may be worth nothing."

"So I should—"

"Accept only old coins in your business," he said, taking my elbow. "And if you want to make a profit, you must increase the price of your pottery."

The thought troubled me as we walked back to the Aventine.

The patricians had felt the effect of Nero's taxes, but now we plebeians would feel it, too. Prices would rise and . . .

I halted in mid-step. The smelters will be among the first to realize the truth. Their prices would rise, though we still had to buy bronze ingots for the statue. Father had calculated the expense months ago.

"Calandra? What is wrong?"

I shook my head. "Nothing." We resumed our walk, but my thoughts kept whirling.

When we were engaged to create the statue, my father signed a contract and agreed upon the monthly payment. He could not now demand more coin, but the cost of bronze ingots would soon rise. The cost of *everything* would rise, and we were helpless to stop it.

In months to come, Father would have to hire helpers and foundry workers. He would have to rent a wagon and donkey. We would have to purchase eyes from the oculariarius. So many expenses awaited us, yet our payments would not stretch nearly as far as they had in the past. We might find it difficult to pay the rent or even to buy food.

But we had signed a contract, so we could not complain.

❖

Hadrian stood outside the sculptor's shop and wondered if he should send Lysandros with Pericles's monthly payment. He knew the sculptor was making progress on the statue; he had seen it during his last visit. The enlarged model, still faceless, was nearly complete, and would have made a fine statue in fired clay.

But, Calandra assured him, a clay statue could never withstand years of exposure to the elements, and they were still months away from pouring the bronze.

He braced himself for the coming encounter. Visiting Calandra was not easy, especially because he had no words to define their relationship. Lysandros had been correct—they were not friends and could never be, not with the difference in their social status. Calandra might make a fine match with a wealthy merchant, but she would never be wed to a patrician. Just as he could never marry anyone but a patrician's daughter.

And therein lay a potential problem. He was now twenty-five, and Rome expected him to take a wife and produce a family. If the emperor called a census and he was discovered to be unmarried, his father would pay a great price, both in additional taxes and personal embarrassment.

But the same law required all female citizens to marry by age twenty, so Pericles would face the same penalty if Calandra did not marry. Perhaps she should. Perhaps it would be best if they resolved never to see each other again. But life without her would feel . . . empty.

He squared his shoulders and walked into the shop, then peered at the wall farthest from the bowls and assorted pottery. Pericles stood facing the statue, one hand pressed to his hip, the other lifted as he directed a freeman helping with the work. Odd that a sightless man could see more than the others.

"Pericles?"

The sculptor turned, his broad face lifting in a smile. "Hadrian! How good of you to come."

Hadrian strode forward. "I have brought your payment." He dropped the purse onto a nearby table. "And I have no need to inquire of your progress, for I see that the work is progressing nicely."

"All due to Calandra," Pericles said. "Do you see her? She said she might go out, but I do not know if she has."

Hadrian scanned the room. "Your daughter is not here."

"Ah. You have missed her." His bushy brow lifted. "I wonder if you would do a service for me?"

"Anything."

215

"I could use a breath of fresh air, and Calandra usually guides me through the street. Since she is out, would you?"

Hadrian blinked, then turned and offered his arm. "Did you wish to visit someplace special?"

"No, no need." Pericles took his arm. "It is enough that I exercise these legs of mine."

They set out, Hadrian shortening his stride to accommodate the older man. Pericles had been blind for two years, but Hadrian had never seen a man better accommodated to living as a blind man. But surely he must have prayed to receive his sight . . .

He halted as a child darted into the street. "May I ask you a question?"

Pericles chuckled. "You are my employer. Ask anything you like."

"Calandra tells me that you follow Yeshua, as do I. Which makes me wonder . . . did you never pray to receive your sight?"

The man's brows rose like twin birds in flight. "What man would not?"

"But you are still blind."

Pericles chuckled. "I prayed for Adonai to change my poor eyes, and He changed me instead."

"I do not understand."

"At first I prayed to receive my sight. Then I prayed for Adonai's will. And that is when I realized a truth." A smile lifted the corners of his mouth. "When I had sight, I was blind to the Creator of the world, but as a blind man I began to glimpse His hand. Now I see Him working every day."

Hadrian struggled to understand. "You could have gone to Petros. He healed Calandra, so surely he could have—"

"Would I return to the way I was?" Pericles interrupted. "I would not. I am content." He hesitated, then leaned closer. "May I ask you a question as well?"

"Of course."

Uncertainty crept into Pericles's expression. "Your father . . . certainly he has given thought to your marriage. As pater-familias, it is his duty to see that your family line continues."

"I know he has considered it."

"Surely you are near the age when marriage is required. Do you not wish to marry?"

For the first time, Hadrian was glad Pericles could not see. A dozen different emotions had to be playing across his face. He drew a deep breath. "Like you, I am trying to understand what it means to follow Yeshua. And since marriage is such an important matter, I am in no hurry. I would rather pay the tax for disobedience than rush into a union with the wrong woman."

"Ah." Pericles probably had more to say but did not feel free to say it.

Hadrian guided the older man into a quiet alley, where they were alone but for a rat scurrying along the gutter. "I know Calandra had a child," Hadrian said, his voice rough with barely checked sorrow. "And I know she could not keep it."

The corner of Pericles's mouth twisted. "Does this upset you?"

"Of course! Every time I see a maimed baby, I wonder if the crone sitting next to him injured my child so she could be a more effective beggar. Every time I hear that a senator has adopted a child, I wonder if the new heir is my offspring. Because it upsets me, I beg Adonai to keep my child safe, wherever it is. And then I beg Adonai to allow me to know its fate."

Pericles's expression remained smooth with secrets, but then the old man spoke. "A boy," he said, a tear dropping from his lower lashes. "Calandra bore a son. I have a grandson. Somewhere."

Hadrian stared into the street beyond, where men, women, and children churned the afternoon air. He focused on a baby strapped to a woman's back. Could that be his son? Or was he father to the one-legged baby in the beggar's arms?

Or, more terrible still, perhaps what remained of his child rested outside the city, among the abandoned bones.

Only Adonai knew.

Twenty-Eight

EARLY APRILIS

Nero called for a census.

We heard the news from the *praeco*, who stood on a podium in the center of the Forum and broadcast the details. "Beginning at the Ides of Aprilis," he called, gesturing dramatically with his free hand, "the paterfamilias from all citizen families of Rome will report to the censors at the Villa publica. Citizens are to bring records of their possessions and family members. Citizens are also to come prepared to pay all appropriate taxes for property, possessions, and sales. Those who have inherited property shall pay the inheritance tax. Slaves who have been granted freedom since the last census are to pay the liberty tax. And any citizen of childbearing age who remains unmarried shall pay the *Aes Uxorium*. Rome's future lies in its families."

As the praeco moved on to another announcement, Father's hand tightened on my arm. "We have been blessed to escape this inevitability thus far, but—"

"We will set some coins aside. I would rather pay the tax than leave you now."

"But—"

"I mean no disrespect, Tata, but did you not do the same

thing?" I turned, wishing he could see the accusing look on my face. "After Mother died, you did not remarry, so you must have paid the tax at every census. Would you do less for me than you did for yourself?"

He sighed, and I knew I had won the argument. He had been unable to marry again while his heart remained full of love for my mother, so he could not blame me. How could I take a husband when my heart and mind considered no one but Hadrian?

❖

On the fifteenth of April, a long line of Roman men stretched from the double doors of the Villa publica through the grounds of the Campus Martius. The census always proceeded by tribe, beginning with Rome's founding families and continuing until every free citizen had reported to the two censors. In addition to paying the annual poll tax, the heads of Roman families put one percent of their wealth into the Roman treasury, along with additional taxes and penalties.

The censors, who were held in high regard, were attired in the stately, purple-bordered togas worn only by consuls and emperors. Their word had the authority of law, and no one dared dispute their decisions. Any head of family who did not show up for his accounting was deemed *incensus*. If his absence was not excused by military duty or some other crucial endeavor, he could be sold by the state as a slave.

Every afternoon I went to the Forum to see how far the censors had progressed. When I heard that they had reached the plebian families, I told my father we would have to report on the next day.

Since the families were called alphabetically, we found our place in line and waited outside the double doors until Father's name was called: "Pericles Aemilius Claudus!"

Father leaned on my arm, and I led him forward. The two

censors sat in their official curule chairs, their purple togas draped over their shoulders. Behind them a trio of scribes furiously made notes of the proceedings.

The eldest censor, whose age revealed itself in deep crevices at the corners of his mouth and nose, jerked his chin at my father. "Pericles Aemilius Claudus, you are required to give an account of yourself, your family, and your property upon an oath declared from the heart."

My father straightened. "With respect I will do so. I am a sculptor and live with my daughter, Calandra Aemilia Claudus. We own little property other than our tools and the pottery wares we create to sell. We have forty sestertii in our strongbox, a few tunics, and I have one plain linen toga. White, of course. My daughter has four tunics and three pairs of shoes; I have two."

The second censor peered up from a papyrus document. "You are a citizen of Rome, correct?"

"Yes, my father was born in the city."

"You have never been a slave."

"I have not."

"Do you own land inside or outside the city?"

"I do not."

The man shifted his gaze. "The woman with you—she is your wife?"

"My daughter."

"Is she married?"

"I am not," I answered quickly, risking their irritation to spare my father discomfort.

The second censor studied the page. "Your daughter is twenty years old. You must pay the tax on unmarried women of childbearing—"

"Wait." The first censor picked up another papyrus and showed it to the second man. The second read it, then nodded.

"Your penalty has been paid. You owe only the poll tax; one sestertius for each of you."

My fingers trembled as I opened our purse and pulled out two sestertii. What an unexpected blessing, but who had been our benefactor?

I had my suspicions, of course, and Father confirmed them as we left the Villa publica. "Hadrian," he said, lifting his face to the sun as we began the walk home. "Cronus and Hadrian have already reported, so they must have paid your unmarried tax."

I wanted to deny it, but who else would have? Who else could have afforded to pay his tax and my own?

"I am sure he paid the tax for business reasons," I said, keeping my voice light. "He does not want me to be distracted from working on his father's commission."

Father laughed. "I think he had another reason."

"Such as?"

Father's smile broadened. "Because he loves you; the man is praying for a miracle."

I snorted in response, but as we walked, I hoped Father's words were true.

Twenty-Nine

MID-IUNIUS

By the Ides of Iunius, Father and I had moved into another stage of construction. We smoothed and perfected the enlarged statue, then we covered the surface with several light coats of plaster. Before the material hardened, we divided the statue into manageable sections by sliding thin brass strips into the soft covering until they stood perpendicular to the surface. We supported these strips with additional coats of plaster, leaving a ribbon of brass exposed.

After the mixture had set, we reinforced it with iron bars. Once the covering dried completely, we would separate the pieces at the brass strips and pull the individual sections away from the clay statue.

We were debating how to remove the separate pieces when Hadrian and Lysandros arrived for their monthly visit. Lysandros dropped our payment onto the worktable as Hadrian leaned against a pillar. "The emperor," he announced, his voice grave, "plans to address the Senate next month."

Father turned, his brows lifting, and I put aside all thoughts of our plaster puzzle. Hadrian would not have made such an announcement if he did not feel we needed to know about it.

"Well?" Father steadied himself against the table. "What is on the emperor's mind?"

"Even my father does not know. But the senators are worried."

"Surely whatever it is will not affect us," I said.

"Everything Nero does affects Rome's citizens," Hadrian said, straightening. "Yet we can do nothing but wait." He gave me a polite smile. "I have to make my rounds through Transtiberim. Would you like to accompany me?"

My heart leapt at the invitation. I had not spent any real time with Hadrian in months, and I missed our conversations. But I could never confess that I had yearned to see him.

"Father? I would love to visit Priscilla."

"Go." He waved his hand toward the door. "I will have our problem settled by the time you return."

"Before you go," I told Hadrian as I picked up my palla, "you should examine the progress we have made."

He stepped forward, his forehead creasing as he gazed up at the ten-foot rectangle of plaster, iron, and brass. "Am I supposed to be impressed?"

"This is the outer shell. The beauty lies on the inside."

"I will trust you," he said, turning away. "I look forward to seeing the beauty, and my father will be pleased to hear that you have made progress." He waved toward the door, where Lysandros waited. "Shall we go?"

❖

I could not help admiring the rebuilt streets as we walked to Transtiberim. Though the roads were wider than before the fire, the extra space only seemed to invite more traffic.

Thinking of Rome reminded me of the unsolved mystery. "You are aware," I said, tossing the words over my shoulder as Hadrian walked behind me, "that the census comes every five years or so. Are you planning to pay my unmarried tax forever or just until the statue is finished?"

"What do you mean?"

I turned and caught his hand. "I am grateful, truly. So is my father. But I was willing to pay the tax myself."

One brow rose. "Why do you think I paid your tax?"

"Because you had to pay it as well. It was only logical to assume that you want me to focus on the statue and not on marriage."

He smiled, but I thought I saw a flicker of hurt in his eyes. "What can I say? You have found me out."

"I wanted to thank you. And to say that you will not have to pay at the next census."

I released his hand and resumed walking but could not help feeling that I had blundered. If my father was right, Hadrian had paid the tax because he wanted to marry me, but such an idea was nonsensical. Even though he would be my first choice for a husband, my only choice, surely it was better to release him from his foolish prayers.

I sighed when we crossed the river's blond waters and entered the less-crowded Transtiberim District.

We visited several prisoners on Hadrian's list: an older couple from Corinth; a young man from Ephesus; and a young Corinthian couple. Marcus and Mariana lived with a servant and two boys, and my heart twisted when I saw their youngest child, a toddler. My baby would be about the same age.

"Ivan and Chaim," Mariana said, noticing my gaze. "Our sons."

I forced a smile.

"I remember," Hadrian said, clapping Marcus on the shoulder, "when you told me you were expecting. God has blessed you."

"Indeed." Marcus smiled at his wife. "He blesses us every day."

"You have friends in common," Hadrian said, gesturing to me. "Marcus and Mariana are acquainted with Aquila and Priscilla."

"We have known them for years," Mariana said, shifting her toddler to the opposite hip. Her eyes narrowed slightly, as if she were trying to determine if I was friend or foe.

"I met them during the fire," I said. "They are wonderful people. Very generous."

Mariana turned to Hadrian, who proceeded to ask the prescribed questions. When he reached the last one—"Are you willing to amend your ways and offer incense to the gods of Rome?"—Marcus pointed at the family's table, where Mariana had set out fruit and cheese. "No, but I would happily offer food to *you*, my friend."

Hadrian waved away the offer, smiled at their sons, and bade them farewell.

I was the first through the doorway, my mood drastically darkened by the sight of the boy in Mariana's arms. I needed to think about something else.

"Are there many more visits?" I asked. "I ought to get back to work."

Hadrian cocked a brow. "Did you not want to visit the tentmaker?"

"Not today." I tapped my fingertips to my temple as if a headache pounded there. "I would like to go home."

"One more visit, then Lysandros will escort you."

We walked to another insula, moved past the kosher butcher on the first floor, and climbed to the second. The landing outside the second-floor apartment was decorated with an ornate design of black-and-white tiles. Fresh flowers filled the niches beside the door. Mariana's apartment had been nice, but this was far more lavish.

"A slave trader," Hadrian said, nodding. I breathed in the

heavy scent of lilies—probably an attempt to mask the smell of blood from the butcher shop—and followed Hadrian until we reached a humble sixth-floor apartment.

I blinked when Petros of Judea opened the door.

Petros and Hannah greeted Hadrian with a friendly smile and beamed when they saw me. "Calandra," Hannah said, pulling me into the apartment. "We have not seen you since the day you were healed! How are you, and how fares your father?"

"We are both well," I replied, a little bewildered by her warmth.

"Calandra and Pericles are impressive," Hadrian said. "Their work is progressing well."

"Adonai be praised." Hannah released me and walked toward a table. "I have been weaving, so you must take a sample before you go." She picked up a palla woven in soft browns and light blues. "I wove this one in the colors of Judea. I hope you will think of my homeland whenever you wear it."

I accepted her gift reluctantly, embarrassed that I had nothing to give in return.

"Have you heard the news?" Petros said, a smile flashing in his silver beard.

I glanced at Hadrian, but he shook his head.

"Sha'ul is returning to Rome," Petros said, clearly delighted. "We received a letter from him last week. He is coming to encourage the believers."

Hadrian frowned. "Who?"

"Ah—Sha'ul, but you probably know him as Paulos. He is coming back to 'finish the course.'"

Hadrian's brow furrowed. "What does he mean?"

Petros clapped Hadrian's shoulder. "Relax, my friend. It is not code for a revolution. Sha'ul is saying that he intends to serve Yeshua until the end of his life, and no one would describe him as a young man."

Petros pointed to a pitcher on the table. "You must be thirsty. Have a cup of honey water before you ask your questions."

I accepted the cup of water, but did so with a guilty heart, knowing Hannah had to carry a heavy jar up and down six flights of stairs to provide water for her household. I sipped the lukewarm liquid and smiled.

Hadrian asked the required questions: "Did either of you leave the apartment this month to participate in forbidden meetings?"

Petros clasped his hands. "We did not leave the apartment at all."

"Have you spread the heresy of Christ-worship in Rome?"

When Petros hesitated, Hadrian arched a brow. "You received a message from Paulos, did you not?"

"He is not an enemy of Rome; he is a brother in Christ. He is also a Roman citizen." Petros folded his arms. "Next question?"

"Are you willing to amend your ways and offer incense to the gods of Rome?"

"I am not, and neither is my wife."

Hadrian sighed. "Then I declare that your imprisonment in this dwelling shall continue until the emperor decides otherwise."

"We are happy to remain here until Adonai moves us elsewhere." The old man grinned. "Is that all, my young friend?"

Hadrian nodded. "Until I come again next month."

"You are always welcome." Petros opened the door, and the corners of his eyes crinkled when his gaze met mine. "As are you, Calandra. Bring your father to see us. We have been praying for him."

I thanked them for their hospitality and followed Hadrian to the staircase. On the landing, Lysandros took out his wax tablet and made a note.

"Why did the name of Paulos upset you?" I asked, trying to keep my voice light.

When Hadrian hesitated, Lysandros answered for him. "The aedile will want to know about Paulos. That man never fails to stir up trouble."

I looked from one man to the other, confused. Every Jew I had met, including Petros and Hannah, spoke of Paulos with nothing but love and regard.

How could such a one cause trouble?

Thirty

SUMMER

Over the next three months, Father and I continued our work. With help from hired freedmen, we carefully chiseled away the pieces of the bulky plaster and set them on worktables, the floor, any available surface in the shop. Then we checked the interior of the pieces to be certain every crevice and corner, bump and dimple of the clay had transferred to the plaster. Surrounded by these front and back molds for the base, legs, lower torso, upper torso, neck and head, we cleaned and oiled the pieces of what would become our molds for the bronze.

Father and I stood back and watched as our hired workers broke the enlarged clay statue into a thousand pieces. And with mixed emotions I stood outside and watched the hired men sweep the broken bits into a cart, which would then be dumped as rubble outside the city.

Father placed his hand on my shoulder. "You are pensive."

I patted his fingertips. "I am fine. Just sad to see a beautiful piece reduced to dust."

"Like our bodies, it was only a shadow of the finished work." He squeezed my shoulder. "Wait and see. The transformation has only begun."

I turned, ready to go back to work, but glimpsed a familiar face in the street. "Aquila?" I waved to catch his attention. "Over here!"

His face brightened as he shouldered his way through the crowded street. "I am surprised to see you," he said, wiping sweat from his brow. "I thought you would be on your way to hear Paulos."

"He is in Rome? The man who has caused so much trouble?"

"The man who has done so much *good*," he said, gently reproving me. "He is planning to address the people of our ecclesia at midday."

"Father—" I turned, but my Father was already at the door. "You may go," he said. "As long as Aquila escorts you."

Aquila and I joined the throng heading to Transtiberim. I marveled that so many had heard of Paulos the rabbi, but apparently he was well known throughout the Empire. The Christians had become a source of fascination for me, and the Roman Christians seemed to have two things in common— their devotion to Yeshua, the Jewish Messiah, and their love for Paulos, the rabbi who had carried the Gospel to those outside the family of Abraham. Priscilla had told me that Paulos had stood before governors and judges, courageously testifying that he saw Yeshua *after* His crucifixion in Jerusalem.

I wanted to hear the story for myself. I wanted to meet the man who had met the resurrected Son of an invisible God.

Thirty-One

On a warm afternoon in the twelfth year of Nero's reign, Paulos of Tarsus returned to Rome. Despite his wish to enter the city quietly, word spread among the believers and leaked to the authorities. Alarmed by the possibility of turmoil, the aediles posted lookouts near every synagogue and instructed them to send word of any unusual public gatherings.

When Aquila and I entered Transtiberim on the first day of the week, I was not surprised to see a crowd outside the tentmaker's shop. Everyone knew Paulos had once worked with Aquila and Priscilla, but the shop remained shuttered that morning. Euodia and Ariston, the purple merchants who shared space with the tentmakers, stood next to a small cart parked by the road, but they had not pulled out any samples to sell. I blinked in surprise when I saw another familiar face—Lysandros. I did not see Hadrian.

While Aquila went into his shop to check on his wife, I sat on the low wall around a fountain and waited, occasionally shading my eyes from the hot sun. The crowd stirred in the heat, but no one complained.

Then the tentmaker's door opened, the crowd turned, and

Aquila and Priscilla came out with an old man. The stranger crossed the portico in two quick steps, strode into the street, and squinted in the bright sunlight. Someone offered an overturned bucket as a podium.

That's when I realized I was watching Paulos, emissary to the Gentiles, known to the Jews as Sha'ul.

The bald man ignored the bucket and surveyed the crowd. The space around him emptied as others shrank back, intimidated either by his reputation or the power in his gaze.

"Friends," he called, smiling despite the weary slump of his shoulders, "grace, mercy, and shalom from God the Father and Messiah Yeshua our Lord!"

A ripple of pleasure moved through the crowd. Faces that had been tight with concern softened with smiles.

"I thank God," Paulos continued, slowly circling to address his audience, "whom I serve with a clear conscience as my forefathers did, when I continually remember you in my prayers night and day. I remember your tears, and I have longed to see you so I might be filled with joy."

I stood to better see the rabbi. He was no taller than me and probably weighed less. Thin and frail, he seemed lost in his tunic. The jut of his bearded chin suggested a stubborn streak, but laugh lines radiated from the corners of his dark eyes.

"I would urge you," he said, lifting his hands, "to not be ashamed of the testimony of our Lord, or of me, His prisoner, but share in suffering for the Good News according to the power of God. He has saved us and called us with a holy calling—not because of our deeds, but because of His own purpose and grace. This grace was given to us in Messiah Yeshua before time began, but now has been revealed through the appearing of our Savior."

He turned and faced me. I took in his untrimmed beard, threaded with silver, and felt his gaze lock on mine. His eyes softened with seriousness.

"For this Good News," he said, his voice both vibrant and gentle, "I was appointed a herald, an emissary, and a teacher. For this reason I have suffered many things, but I am not ashamed because I know in whom I have trusted and am convinced He is able to safeguard what I have entrusted to Him . . . until that Day."

A murmur rose from the listeners, and I remembered Priscilla's stories about Paulos's sufferings. Apparently the man had been scourged several times, imprisoned, stoned, even shipwrecked. But he had never stopped sharing his story.

What would cause a man to willingly endure so much? I might suffer willingly for my father. For someone I loved.

Paulos's eyes roved over dozens of rapt faces. "Therefore, my children, be strengthened in the grace that is in Messiah Yeshua. What you have heard from me among many witnesses, entrust to faithful people who will be capable to teach others. Suffer hardship with me, as a good soldier, for no one serving as a soldier entangles himself in the activities of everyday life. And if anyone competes as an athlete, he is not crowned with victory unless he competes according to the rules. Consider what I am saying, for soon the Lord will give you understanding in everything."

I examined the faces around me. Was anyone else as confused as I was? Paulos was free and standing among people who loved and admired him. What hardship was he referring to?

"Remember Yeshua," he continued, "who suffered and was raised from the dead. For this testimony I will suffer hardship, even to the point of chains—though the word of God cannot be chained. Therefore, I endure everything for the sake of the chosen, so they might obtain salvation in Messiah Yeshua.

"Trustworthy is the saying: if we die with Him, we will also live with Him; if we endure, we will also reign with Him; if we deny Him, He will also deny us; if we are faithless, He remains faithful, for He cannot deny himself."

His words made absolutely no sense, but at that point Paulos bowed his head. His lips moved soundlessly as a heavy silence fell over the gathering, broken only by the trickle and splash of the fountain.

I caught a flurry of movement at the back of the crowd, followed by the faintly metallic crunch of approaching Praetorians. The crowd fell away as the guards cut through the listeners and surrounded the elderly rabbi.

"Paulos of Tarsus," the chief Praetorian barked. "For disturbing the peace of Rome, you are under arrest."

How had he disturbed the peace? I glanced around, wondering if I had missed something, but no one moved, not even Paulos. As the chief guard stepped forward, the rabbi turned, a faint smile glinting through his beard.

"The time has come," he said, his gaze lighting on Aquila, "for my departure."

He lifted his hands in a gesture of surrender, and the guards dragged him away.

The crowd roiled in confusion, some retreating, some following the guards, others standing like witnesses to a fatal accident. I ran across the open space and clutched Lysandros's arm. "What did he do? Why have they arrested him?"

"I cannot say," Lysandros answered. "But it seems he was anticipating their action."

"I saw no disturbance," I said. "We must speak to Hadrian, who can speak to his father. If this arrest is allowed to stand, justice does not exist in Rome."

<hr />

After Paulos's shocking arrest, I remained with Aquila and Priscilla, hoping to provide some comfort and discover answers. They were concerned about their friend, but I saw no anxiety in their eyes. Compassion, certainly, but not fear, even though Paulos had probably been taken to Mamertine Prison.

Priscilla said Paulos had been kept under house arrest during his previous imprisonment, not in the Mamertine. I had never been inside the notorious place, but I had seen the rough stone structure on the slope of the Capitoline. The ancient prison had been built during the time of Rome's kings and reportedly consisted of two roughhewn chambers, one above the other. Prisoners were lowered through a circular opening into the lower space, which had little light and even less ventilation. Their only source of water was a trickling sewer.

I thought about the Praetorian conspirators who had undoubtedly been held in the same dungeon. Were they terrified when their treachery was discovered? What did they feel as they awaited execution? Did they trust the gods of Rome to save them? How could they when they had conspired against the divine Nero?

What would Paulos feel in such a place? And how had he known what would happen to him? He had spoken of suffering in chains . . .

I asked Priscilla how Paulos knew he would be arrested, and she only shook her head. Aquila said the Spirit had told him, but I could not believe in a Spirit who spoke without words.

Finding no answers in Transtiberim, I returned to the Aventine, where Father and I went back to work, though both of us found it difficult to concentrate.

The city was rife with tension. We saw it in strained faces and heard it in curt voices. Even people who knew little to nothing about politics had noticed the dramatic increase in prices. The bag of wheat that used to cost half a sestertius had decreased in size, as had a bowl of soup at the caupona. And the tunic that used to cost fifteen sestertii now cost seventeen or more.

"The people are restless," Father said as we oiled the interior of our plaster molds. "First the fire, then Nero's excessive building, and now an increase in the cost of everything. Rome reeks of discontent, and discontent breeds revolt."

I was about to say no one would revolt as long as Nero was surrounded by Praetorians, but were his guards loyal? Some of them had already been executed for conspiracy.

"You should tell Cronus we need more coins in our monthly allotment," I said, melting the wax that would soon cover the interior of the plaster pieces. "This beeswax costs more than it did before the fire."

Father grunted, but I knew he would say nothing. In a time of ubiquitous uncertainty, he was grateful to be employed.

❖

Hadrian hurried to the Curia Julia, where the Senate had convened. The guard at the door recognized him and allowed him to enter. Hadrian stood at the back of the room, scanning the rows of hoary heads as he searched for his father.

On the second row, Cronus was speaking to another aedile. As Hadrian debated whether to interrupt the conversation, Nero strode into the chamber, surrounded by armed Praetorians.

Silence, as thick as wool, descended upon the assembly.

"Citizens of Rome," Nero said, his high voice echoing in the vaulted chamber. Ever the actor, he stood in the center of the room and assumed a pose—one hand uplifted, the other extended to the men on the front row. "Honorable senators, I have longed to speak to you, but duty required that I be vigilant before presenting my case. I have come today to answer a question that has occupied our thoughts since the pernicious flames of betrayal destroyed so much of our imperial city. I have come, honorable senators, to unmask the nefarious criminals who set the flames."

Cronus turned to the other aedile, and Hadrian saw consternation on the man's face. Hadrian knew what he was thinking—what they were *all* thinking. Rumors about Nero's involvement in the fire had circulated for years, and the emperor's extravagant Golden House had only increased the whispering. Was the emperor finally going to admit his role in the disaster that had destroyed so much, impoverished so many, and killed so mercilessly? Or would he accuse the patricians who had attempted to overthrow him?

"A growing pestilence has taken root among us," Nero said, tucking his free hand into the folds of his purple toga, "stemming from a people who are not like us. For years I have heard about them, but they seemed small in number and of no great consequence. But their numbers have increased, and the pestilence has become more pronounced."

The senators murmured among themselves, then looked to the emperor, their faces fraught with tension.

"Governors in other provinces have judged them, often harshly," Nero continued, "but still they spread like weeds, remaining devoted to a strange and vicious superstition. They are accursed and hated for their shameful offenses, and chief among them is their refusal to worship or acknowledge the gods that bless and defend our empire. They are known troublemakers and enemies of public order. They continually clash with those who worship the Jewish God and cause headaches for the provincial governors. They call themselves Christians, and they are dangerous because they are haters of humanity. They must be rooted out, tried for their offenses, and condemned to death."

The chamber rang with the roar of absolute silence. Hadrian noted stunned expressions on several venerable faces, including his father's.

"I therefore adjure," Nero continued, "the city prefect, Titus Flavius Sabinus, and the Praetorian prefects, Ofonius Tigellinus and Faenius Rufus, to commence judgment so our city can enjoy the peace of Rome. I give these men my authority to arrest and interrogate those who call themselves Christians. They are guilty, and they deserve exemplary punishment so others will learn not to follow their example."

With a final flourish of his hand, Nero pivoted and swept out of the room. A moment of stunned silence ensued, then the Senate erupted.

Hadrian hurried toward his father, shouldering his way through astonished senators.

"Order!" the consul shouted. "The emperor has spoken!"

A senator on the first row rose. "But what did Nero intend? Has he decreed the Christians guilty of arson? What proof did he offer?"

"We have all heard eyewitness reports of men who set fire to untouched buildings," another senator said. "And everyone knows Christians cause trouble. What is arson, if not trouble?"

A younger senator leapt up. "Even if they are not guilty of arson, they are thoroughly disagreeable. By not worshiping our gods, they reveal their cold and callous hatred of the human race."

"They caused such trouble with the Jews that Claudius expelled both groups," another senator proclaimed. "I recall the incident as clearly as if it were yesterday."

"Haters," another man echoed. "Anyone who refuses to placate the gods of Rome exposes us to danger, destruction, and starvation. If that is not a hater of mankind, what is?"

"Order!" The breathless consul stood until the others had retaken their seats. He gripped his toga, clearly trying to maintain a semblance of dignity. "The Senate must agree to this action before we can proceed. What say you?"

"The emperor has instructed us to prosecute the guilty," a senator called. "So let us proceed!"

Hadrian felt his stomach tighten as a ripple of agreement moved across the room.

The consul nodded. "So be it!"

Hadrian waited to catch his father in the flood of exiting senators. "What is this?" he whispered, pulling Cronus aside. "Are we now prosecuting people because they worship a foreign god?"

The aedile held up a wagging finger. "We are prosecuting arsonists."

"But what proof did Nero offer? I have met several Christians, and they are the least likely people to commit a crime—"

His father cut him off with a sharp gesture. "Have you wondered why so few of the homes in Transtiberim suffered damage? Perhaps it is because the area is infested with Jews and Christians."

Hadrian sputtered in frustration. "Their homes did not burn because the fire did not jump the river."

"But Christians have no trouble crossing the river, so perhaps they set fire to homes in the Palatine, including *our* home."

"For months they fed and sheltered those who were left homeless! Would haters of mankind do that?" Hadrian lowered his voice. "You cannot seriously believe that Christians set the fires that destroyed Rome. It is far more likely—and logical—that Nero intends to deflect criticism by offering them as a scapegoat."

"In truth, I do not know what happened." Cronus shrugged. "But Nero is the emperor, so what can we do? The common people will accept his explanation and stop grumbling about his Golden House. If we lose a few foreigners who have never adapted to our ways, what of it?"

"Not all of them are foreigners," Hadrian said, thinking of Pericles. "Mark my words, Father, this will not end well."

"But it will end." Cronus gave him a grim smile. "And the

responsibility, whether good or ill, will rest upon Nero, as it should."

I was closing the counter window when I saw Hadrian and Lysandros on the street. Lysandros waited as Hadrian strode toward me, lines of concentration creasing his forehead.

"Something happened today," he said, his voice pitched for my ears alone. "I am deeply troubled."

"Do you speak of Paulos's arrest?" I asked. "The man barely had time to greet his friends before Praetorians took him away."

"My news is not of Paulos, but Nero. The emperor addressed the Senate and blamed the Christians for burning Rome. They are to be arrested and tried."

Though I was no Christian, a wave of shock slapped me. "They are to be tried? For what?"

"Arson perhaps? Or hating mankind. The facts will not matter. Our emperor has decreed that the Christians are guilty of destroying the city. And since he wants the public to have someone to blame . . ." His voice broke as he looked away.

"Someone who is not *him*," I said, daring to speak freely. "He knows the people blame him for the fire, so he will kill Christians instead."

Hadrian did not deny my statement, and my heart twisted when I thought of all the Christians I had grown to love. Aquila, Priscilla, Ariston, Euodia, and Petra—all of them had shown kindness and grace in my hour of need. Even though I did not accept their faith, they continued to love me. In my darkest hour, Priscilla had come to deliver my child and comfort me through that searing heartbreak. Euodia had sent her maid to serve me, without asking for anything in return.

My father, Hadrian, and Lysandros called themselves Christians. What would this mean for them?

I pointed to the leather satchel hanging from Hadrian's shoulder. "You are delivering messages for your father?"

He swallowed hard. "I . . . have been ordered to carry out the will of the Senate."

"What does that mean?"

He exhaled heavily. "Go inside, Calandra. Night is coming, and you will not want your father to be on the street."

"What about you?" I looked at him, blood pounding in my ears. "You should renounce this foreign faith. It is important to me that you are safe."

"I cannot renounce Yeshua," he said, the look in his eyes piercing my soul, "any more than I can renounce you."

I learned the specifics of Hadrian's dark errand later—not from him, but from a visitor to our shop. Two nights before, the Christians under house arrest in Transtiberim had been forced from their apartments.

The elegant woman in search of a set of matching vases did not notice when I gripped the counter as she shared the news. "It is about time," she said, adjusting her palla so it shaded her pale skin. "Some of them have been confined for years. They have enjoyed the fruits of our city long enough."

"The Christians who were taken," I whispered, my voice catching in my throat. "What were their names?"

The woman made a face. "How am I to know? I do not make a habit of crossing the river. I would not have gone there at all if not for the woman who sells exquisite purple."

When the woman had gone, I threw a palla over my hair and left the shop, ignoring Father's warning to remain inside. I hurried to the footbridge and crossed it, then made my way to the tentmaker's shop.

The door was closed and locked, but still I knocked. A moment later, Priscilla opened the door—thanks be to her God!—and drew me inside.

"You are here!" I threw my arms around her. "They did not take you."

She held me for a moment, then released me. "My movements are not restricted," she said, meeting my teary gaze. "Aquila and I are safe, as are Ariston, Euodia, and Petra, but many of our friends are not."

She wiped moisture from her eyes and led me toward her desk. A lamp pushed at the stubborn gloom, and I could see that her eyes were red-rimmed.

She sat. "They took all the house prisoners. Your friend—the aedile's son—came with warrants for their arrest, and Praetorians gathered them. We have not seen any of them since."

"Petros and Hannah?"

She nodded. "Marcus and Mariana, Titius and Aurora, and so many others . . . everyone who had been sent from the provinces to await judgment. Fortunately, Mariana's maid, Salama, had gone to the fountain, so she is safe with us. So are Mariana's two little boys."

I bit my lip, trying to imagine how Petros would react to his arrest. He had always seemed content with his situation, so perhaps he would remain unflappable. "At least they are with Paulos," I said. "He will encourage them."

Priscilla pressed her fingertips to her lips. "I doubt they are with Paulos. He is in the Mamertine, and that place cannot hold so many."

I closed my eyes, realizing that Priscilla had not been able to say Hadrian's name. How could he have arrested people who believed as he did? How could he have betrayed them? What would I do if he came for my father?

I shoved my thoughts in a different direction. "If our friends are not with Paulos, where are they?"

"At the Circus Maximus."

A shiver climbed the ladder of my spine. The Circus Maximus, the first structure to burn in the great fire, had been rebuilt in the valley between the Palatine and Aventine hills. Beneath the sandy racetrack of the new Circus, iron cages had been installed to hold wild animals as they awaited their turn in the arena.

A sob escaped my chest. "Have they already been condemned?"

"We must pray." Priscilla clasped my hands. "Paulos said we would suffer as he had, so we must be as faithful and constant as he is. Above all, we must pray that everything will happen as Adonai wills."

She said *we*, though I had never professed to believe in her Yeshua. But she saw me as one of them, and in that moment I was both gratified and horrified by her words.

❖

Aquila escorted me home. Father startled when I came through the door, so I soothed him and said everyone in Aquila's household was well. But that night I paced for hours, amazed that the justice of Rome had been twisted to trap people who had done nothing but love and care for their fellow Romans.

The next morning, the looking brass revealed smudges of fatigue under my eyes. Not caring, I opened the counter window and set out a selection of bowls, pitchers, and vases. Then I sat and waited for the hours to pass while my thoughts swirled in confusion.

How could I make a statue of Nero while so many good and honorable people languished in cages? I could not sit at my workbench and polish the molds. I could not even *look* at my sketches without wanting to spit on them.

My father, however, seemed especially industrious. He did

not go near the plaster molds but sat at the potter's wheel, frowning, while his fingers deftly molded amphorae—two-handled pots with narrow necks and big bellies. He had always been a skillful potter, and I knew he had turned to the wheel out of a simple desire to be productive. He was fond of the Christians he knew, and his newfound devotion to Adonai seemed to give him affection for anyone, Jew or Gentile, who prayed to Yeshua the Christ.

For the next few days we went about our daily routine. I rose and prepared food; Father went to the baths and came back to his potter's wheel. Though disturbed by the Christians' arrests, he said little, but his voice overflowed with anguish when he said his morning prayers.

Neither of us approached our massive work in progress. The plaster pieces lay on the tables and floor, covered with linen, silently reminding us that we depended on the coins from Cronus's commission. Hadrian had been faithful to bring our monthly payments, but how could we continue? What would Cronus do if we refused to finish? He could demand repayment, and since we could not pay, he could sell us both into slavery.

Yet even that realization did not compel either of us to approach the unfinished molds. Instead, we spent the next few days attending to housekeeping, recording payments and debts, and selling pottery.

When we were not working, we sat at the counter window and listened to snatches of conversation from the street. We heard gossip about senators, gladiators, and the emperor. We heard about the colossus Zenodorus was creating for the Golden House. The project had evolved into a work depicting Nero as the sun god, a statue one hundred and twenty feet in height.

That particular news gladdened my heart. Our statue, if we finished it, would depict Nero as an ordinary man, which he certainly was. He was less than ordinary, less than noble, if he continued to insist that Christians had started the fire.

We also heard reports about the imprisoned Christians. News of the arrests had energized the citizens of Rome. Some were jubilant that the arsonists would finally be punished; others wept as old emotional wounds were torn open. But few lamented the Christians' fate, and no one openly criticized Nero. He was the emperor, his word would be obeyed, and he had found those responsible for the Great Fire of Rome.

A short distance away, the ever-enlarging profile of Nero's Golden House mocked us.

Thirty-Two

FEBRUARIUS
THE 13TH YEAR OF NERO'S REIGN

Five months after the Christians had been removed from their apartments, a group of slaves delivered the bronze for Nero's statue. I directed the slaves to stack the expensive ingots in a corner of the shop, then draped a piece of linen over them.

Father sat at the potter's wheel and listened intently as the slaves came and went. When we were alone again, he stopped his wheel. "What troubles you, daughter?"

"My heart is no longer in the work," I said, sinking onto a stool. "In the beginning I was thrilled to learn something new and amazed we would earn this commission. Knowing I could help you gave me tremendous joy."

"And now?"

"Now I can think of nothing but Petros, Hannah, and the others who were arrested. I cannot imagine what they must be enduring at the arena." I turned to look at him. "How can we complete this work?"

Father's eyes closed, and when he spoke again, his voice was ragged. "Being an artist is a wonderful thing," he said, as if he were pulling words from some deep and secret place, "but it is also a hard thing. Because an artist must work even when the heart is broken and the well is dry. If you would eat, you must work. If you want to live, you must fulfill your obligations. There is no shame in earning your living from art. But in the private space of your work, often there is no glory either."

He kicked the wheel beneath his feet, spinning the wheel head, then dropped a mound of clay onto the center. He dipped his hands into water and cupped the clay, letting his fingers mold the mass.

My heart sank. Nero's actions had indirectly forced my father, a sculptor fully as talented as Zenodorus, to make common bowls for poor families. I knew I ought to get to work as well, but in that hour I could do nothing but sit and watch the hands that had molded me.

Thirty-Three

THE 16TH OF IUNIUS

Standing beside the Basilica Julia's white pillars, Hadrian watched officials move up and down the broad staircase. Lawyers loitered on the steps, eager to find clients who lacked representation. Citizens lurked there, too, looking for harried men in need of a someone willing to testify for appropriate compensation.

He stiffened when he saw the line of prisoners coming from the south. Nine months after being taken to the Circus Maximus, the Christian prisoners were being escorted to their trial. They were chained together, a long line of men, women, and children in dirty tunics and bare feet. The women's hair was matted and unkempt, the men were bearded and shaggy. Roman matrons gasped and covered their noses as the prisoners passed.

Hadrian moved into the courtroom, reflexively lifting his gaze to the large upper windows that lit the space below. Ordinarily curtains would have divided this vaulted chamber into units for small trials, but for this the curtains had been raised. Nearly every man in Rome wanted to see this *cognitio extra ordinem*, an extraordinary legal procedure.

At the end of the room, Titus Flavius Sabinus, the city prefect,

249

waited to investigate, prosecute, and judge the prisoners. Hadrian stood with other observers, most of whom had been drawn by curiosity and spectacle. He wiped perspiration from his forehead and noticed that the men on the raised platform were sweating like dogs. The only ventilation came from the open doors, which had been blocked by the crowd.

Sabinus presented his case. The Christians refused to sacrifice to the gods that protected and served the city and therefore the Christians hated Rome and its citizens. And since only people who hated Rome could have been involved in setting the fire that destroyed so much property and took so many lives, the Christians must be guilty of arson.

As Sabinus droned on about the importance of supporting the old gods, Hadrian studied the faces of the accused men and women. They had come from all over the Empire—Corinth, Ephesus, Thessalonica, Philippi, and Athens. He recognized the faces of men and women, slaves and freedmen, elders and couples in the prime of life. Mariana of Corinth stood next to her husband with a new baby in her arms. Her two young sons, he was glad to see, had avoided arrest. Would her innocent baby be condemned?

Hadrian could not consider the question without feeling the sting of guilt. He had also come to believe in the power of Adonai and His Son, so should he take his place among the prisoners? He had pondered the question through many long nights, knowing that any of the condemned men could give the officials his name.

But they did not name him, even under torture, so he had kept quiet.

Finally finished with his summary, Sabinus pronounced the Christians guilty and decreed that their executions would begin at the Festival for Venus and continue during the month of Augustus until "the Christians are no more."

Hadrian swallowed to choke back the bile that rose in his throat. Death would come to all of them. Not only would they die, but they would be executed in public while Romans celebrated.

Hadrian left the Senate chamber with a heavy heart, knowing his father would not approve of the guilty verdict. But Cronus could not protest because he, like Sabinus, had to follow Nero's orders.

❖

Hadrian waited, his heart thudding in his chest, until a guard brought Petros into the office at the Circus Maximus. The old fisherman seemed more hunched than usual, yet his swarthy face brightened when he recognized his visitor.

"Hadrian!" Petros lifted his arms, but the chains prevented a proper embrace. "Have you come to ask your questions?"

"Not this time." Hadrian pointed to a bench. "Please, sit. I want you to be comfortable."

"What is comfort to a prisoner?" Petros laughed. "His rod and his staff comfort me, and that is enough."

"Pardon?"

"You should read the psalms of David. They will help you in the days ahead." Petros dropped to the bench, his chains rattling. "You have waited a long time to visit. What brings you now?"

Hadrian swallowed hard. "I was at the trial this morning. When they pronounced you guilty, I realized I was as guilty as you."

A corner of Petros's mouth curled upward. "*You* set Rome ablaze?"

"No, but I am a Christian. So I thought I would ask—should I confess and join you? I am willing to do so."

Petros's smile softened, as did his eyes. "Ah, my young friend . . . you are serious."

"I am."

"I am glad to see it. But no—if Adonai has spared you thus far, do not hand the enemy a victory he does not deserve."

"So I should say nothing."

Petros lifted a warning finger. "But neither should you betray the Lord. I did that once, much to my regret. Continue as you are until the Lord leads you down a different path." He shrugged. "Who knows? You may find yourself with us tomorrow, as I have heard rumors of spies and torture. But if you are safe, do your best to remain so."

Hadrian exhaled slowly. "Then I will pray for you."

"Good. I will pray for you and your father. And for your friend, the lovely Calandra. The Spirit is preparing her heart."

"And that means?"

"You will see." The old man regarded Hadrian for a moment, then his brow wrinkled. "Will you promise me something?"

"Anything within my power."

"I have written a letter to all who believe in Yeshua. When my time comes, you will find it among my things. Will you see that it is distributed to the believers?"

"I do not know how to do that."

"The Spirit will show you the way."

Hadrian nodded. "I will do it."

"Thank you." Petros clapped his hands on his bony knees. "Is that all, my friend?"

Hadrian's heart contracted in anguish when he realized he might never hear Petros speak those words again. "Yes."

"Then carry on." Petros attempted to stand, staggered, and Hadrian caught him. A moment later, the guard led the prisoner away.

❖

When Calandra answered the door without a smile, Hadrian realized she had heard about the trial. She stepped aside without speaking, so he walked to her workbench and slid onto the bench.

She sat across from him and arched a brow. "You were there?"

He nodded.

"Tell me."

Without preamble he gave her the news: "The imprisoned Christians have been condemned to die during the festivals of Augustus."

She snatched a breath. "So soon?"

"The emperor wants them gone. Most will die during the games of Venus."

"*Most?*"

"Those who are Roman citizens will most likely be beheaded or hung."

Her eyes welled with tears. "Is this how your Adonai demonstrates his power? Is this how he rewards his followers for their devotion? Our Roman gods are more reasonable. We do things for them; they do things for us. These Christians do everything for their God, but what does he do in return?"

Hadrian hung his head. "I do not know, but I have seen Adonai's power. You were nearly dead when Petros healed you in Yeshua's name."

"You cannot be sure of that. The physician's herbs may have healed me. I could have been healed by Vesta or Jupiter."

"The physician did nothing for you. I sacrificed to Jupiter on your behalf, but you did not improve."

"If Adonai healed me, then why has he not healed my father? Why does he not free his followers from prison?"

Hadrian released an exasperated breath. "I do not always

understand His will. I have just come from meeting with Petros. As my father's representative, I thought I should check on his welfare."

"Let me guess." Her eyes sharpened. "You asked if he wanted to recant his testimony."

"I asked if I should confess to belief in Yeshua and join him in prison. Why should they lose their lives while I remain free?"

A tremor passed over her face. "Surely you jest."

He shrugged. "There are things I cannot yet understand, but I want to learn more. Petros said Adonai's Spirit would teach me what I need to know."

She rose in one fluid motion. "I cannot believe what I am hearing. Priscilla is bright and has the good sense to remain quiet. When she hears that the others will die for their belief, she will recant—"

"I do not think she will," Hadrian interrupted, "though she is wise to remain silent. If you care for Priscilla and her husband, you should pray that the imprisoned remain strong. If Flavius Sabinus needs more bodies to satisfy the vengeful crowds, the guards have been instructed to torture prisoners for additional names."

Calandra swallowed hard. "Perhaps I should caution *you* to keep quiet. I should not like to hear that you have been arrested."

"I came to caution you with the same words." Hadrian stood. "Because today I heard that the Praetorians have noticed your frequent visits to Transtiberim."

Hadrian's parting comment haunted me. In a city of thousands, why had the Praetorians noticed *my* trips to Transtiberim? They must have investigated people associated with Cronus, which led them to my father. Yet he did not cross the river as often as I did.

Had my visits to the tentmaker's shop endangered Priscilla and Aquila? Would they be betrayed by a member of the ecclesia that met in their home?

Though I had assured Hadrian that Priscilla was too bright to admit to being a Christian, I knew she would never recant. Her entire world revolved around service to Yeshua. Though Aquila usually remained in the shop to run the business, Priscilla was constantly visiting those who were confined, taking them food and water, praying with them, encouraging them.

Why had the spies *not* noticed her? While I found it hard to believe the imperial guards had noticed *me*, I had been keeping company with a senator's son, and the Praetorians often guarded senators. Hadrian's visits to our shop might have drawn attention, and on many occasions he had escorted me throughout the city.

A few days later, I heard that Lupina the ornatrix had been arrested and charged with being a Christian. Her hair plucker, a slave, had been arrested with her. Who would the Praetorians arrest next?

Thirty-Four

As the month of Iunius drew to a close, Flavius Sabinus's men went through the city, arresting additional men, women, and children. Those who were willing to offer incense to Jupiter were released almost immediately; those who would not were sentenced and sent to the Circus.

One day a slave delivered a message to my father. Recognizing Hadrian's seal, I unfurled the papyrus and read the words aloud: "Lysandros has been arrested. Pray for him."

Father groaned while I took a deep, quivering breath to still the leaping pulse beneath my breastbone. If they arrested Lysandros, surely they suspected his master as well. So why hadn't they questioned Hadrian?

For three days I worried about Hadrian, Priscilla, and Aquila. Finally, just before sunset on the third day, I set out for Transtiberim, hoping I would not be noticed in the dim light of dusk.

I had just crossed the footbridge when two Praetorians accosted me. "Calandra, daughter of Pericles," one of them said, his broad hand closing around my upper arm. "We have questions for you."

"W-what questions?" I asked, my words tripping over one another. "I am not a thief. I am a citizen of Rome."

"You are not under suspicion," the guard said, "but you have been associating with questionable company."

❖

The Praetorians escorted me into the vestibule of a decaying insula. The doorman darted away as we approached, so the guards pushed me into the abandoned first-floor apartment.

"Your father, the sculptor," one of them said, resting his hands on his sword belt. "We have heard that he is a Christian."

I stared, blinking, until a question bubbled up from some place deep inside. Where had they heard this report? Hadrian knew about my father, and so did Priscilla and Aquila, but none of them would betray my father to Sabinus. Priscilla would not betray anyone, and Hadrian needed my father to complete the commission for Nero.

If not them, then who? I closed my eyes, seeing my father in his workshop, carefully running his fingers over the surface of the plaster molds. When he was working, Father could be amiable, even talkative, if someone entered the shop. If he spoke to a customer while I was out, he might have mentioned that Adonai healed me from Roman fever or tell of how he had benefited from the faith of the Christians who had fed and clothed us after the fire.

In those days no one cared if the Christians worshiped another God. Rome's citizens needed the Christians, relied on them, and were grateful for them. Any passerby could have heard my father profess his belief in the God of the Jews. But I could more easily cut off my arm than betray my father.

I looked the most senior guard in the eyes. "My father is a proud Roman citizen."

The guard gripped the hilt of his sword. "Very well," he said. "Perhaps it is *you* who follows this Christ."

I snorted in a most unladylike manner. "Your information could not be more inaccurate."

The guard chuckled. "Perhaps. But we were given two names, and a prisoner under torture was certain that at least one of the names belonged to a Christian. The first name was Pericles the sculptor, and the second was Priscilla, wife of the tentmaker."

The name struck me like a blow. I stared at the dirty tiles of the mosaic floor as the words rang in my ears. Pericles and Priscilla, Priscilla and Pericles. I loved both of them.

My heart congealed into a lump. "I do not believe either—"

"One of them or both," the guard said, his voice like steel. "If you do not confirm one name, we will arrest both." He leaned forward until his sour breath tickled my nose. "Consider yourself fortunate that we will only take one. Two names were given to us, but we know the aedile's son considers you a favorite. We would not want to offend him."

My stomach twisted at the sordid implication. I did not want to owe Hadrian anything, but if he could help, I would beg for even a shred of mercy.

My father had lived a full life, but he was responsible for my *existence*. He had been mother and father to me since the day of my birth.

But Priscilla had taken me in when I had no safe haven. She was the mother I needed when I had no one else to talk to. Without judgment she listened to me confess my greatest shame and comforted me. She helped deliver my child and consoled me when I had to send him away.

What to do? I closed my eyes, wishing I had the certainty of Petros or Paulos, that my God would simply *tell* me what to do. But my Roman gods had never told me anything. Even when I once sacrificed a lamb and stared at the bloody entrails, I saw no message there, only the loss of an innocent life.

I lifted my head as a pearl of perspiration traced a path from my armpit to my rib. "I cannot do this."

"You must."

"These people are kind and loyal—they do good in the world."

"Christians hate the gods who keep the Empire safe."

I wanted to ask what the gods were doing the night Rome burned, but such a comment would not be well received.

"My patience grows thin." The guard gripped his sword again. "Speak or we will take them both."

Do you protect your own, Adonai?

I closed my eyes and gave the guard a name.

I slipped into our workshop, staggering under an overpowering weight of guilt. I heard Father call out, so I answered in as calm a voice as I could manage, then went into my chamber and fell onto the bed.

I deserved to die. I should have died the night I gave birth to my son. I could have slipped easily into the afterlife, where I would—what? I had no idea, but anything would be easier than bearing the grief that undoubtedly lay ahead.

I lay awake for hours, anticipating the sound of men at our door. What if the guard ignored our bargain and came for me and my father? What if they took Priscilla and Aquila?

When exhaustion finally overwhelmed me, I slept fitfully. In the grip of dark visions I tossed and turned, resisting specters that rose to accuse me: the neighborhood girl I purposely tripped because she mocked my dead mother; the woman I overcharged because she insulted Father's work; the baby I abandoned at the Column Lactaria. All of those trespasses, ugly as they were, faded in the light of what I had done hours before.

I had betrayed someone who loved me. Someone who had done nothing but show me mercy and kindness. Someone who had been exactly what I needed when I needed love. Worst of all, I knew she would forgive me.

But would Aquila?

Thirty-Five

THE 8TH DAY OF IULIUS

For two endless weeks I wrestled with guilt and despair, then I gathered what remained of my courage and walked to the tentmaker's shop. Looking through the open door, I saw Aquila's household and many of his friends in prayer. They did not pray before the lararium, but in the middle of the room, joined in a circle as they prayed to their invisible God.

I knew, better than anyone, what had sent them to their knees.

One of the servants noticed me and tugged on Aquila's sleeve. The tentmaker stood and came toward the doorway, his face impassive. A small voice reminded me that he might not know I had been the one to name Priscilla as a Christian, but if he did not know, I was prepared to confess.

I steeled my resolve, willing to endure whatever punishment he wanted to deliver.

Aquila crossed the portico. Even in his grief, he managed to give me a weary smile.

"Calandra," he said, his eyes reddened by sorrow. "I suppose you have heard about Priscilla's arrest."

"I came to warn you," I said, unable to wait a moment longer. "Flavius Sabinus has not finished his investigation. You should not be praying where people can see you. If you must pray, stand before the lararium, so people will assume you are praying to Vesta."

"Why would I adopt such a pretense? I cannot pray to any God but Adonai."

I clenched my hands. I had already betrayed his wife; did he want *all* his friends to be executed? "Do you not understand? You should leave the city. At the very least, come stay with my father. Sabinus would never look for you on the Aventine."

Aquila reached for my hand and held it between his own. "I appreciate your concern, but we are not afraid. When we die, we will be with Yeshua. What could be better than that?"

I snatched a frustrated breath. How could I reason with a man—with anyone—who considered death a reward for living?

"You and Priscilla have been like family to me. Please, let me help you. Come stay with us. You and your household can stay as long as you need to hide yourselves."

"All of us? You do not have room for Ariston, Euodia, and our servants. We also have children to care for—"

"Father and I will sleep on the floor, or I can find you a place in our insula. But if you remain here, Sabinus will surely find you."

Aquila patted my hand. "Whether the Lord wills for us to live or die, we are content, and so is Priscilla."

"There is something else." I squared my shoulders, bracing for the scorn I deserved. "I was the one who named Priscilla. The Praetorians stopped me, and I confirmed that she worships Yeshua."

Aquila's brow flickered, then the corner of his mouth rose slightly. "Thank you for telling me. I wondered."

I flinched, his words stinging like the bite of a whip. "Do you not understand? I *betrayed* her. If you want to beat me, I will submit. I would deserve every blow of the lash—"

"Why should I beat you for saying what Priscilla herself would have said?"

"Because . . ." A tear trickled over my cheek, and I swiped it away. "Because they gave two names, Pericles and Priscilla, and I spared my father."

Aquila's eyes softened. "You made the right choice. Priscilla's faith is more mature than your father's."

Part of my brain—the bit not consumed by astonishment and disbelief—wondered if Aquila had lost his reason. I had heard that people under tremendous duress could lose touch with reality.

"While you are here," Aquila said, "I would ask something of you."

I would have agreed to anything in an effort to right my wrong, but I was still uncertain of his sanity. "What would you have me do?"

A young boy toddled out of the shop and clutched Aquila's leg, then looked up at me with soft, brown eyes. One of Mariana's boys, no doubt. My heart contracted. A child who would soon be an orphan.

Aquila rested his broad hand on the boy's head. "It would not be wise for one of us to ask to visit the prisoners, but could your friend Hadrian arrange for you to see them? We want to assure our brothers and sisters of our prayers."

I gulped, hot tears slipping down my cheeks. "Surely Priscilla will know you are praying."

"My friends are strong, but even our Lord asked friends to keep Him company during His travail."

Though the thought of encountering more Praetorians shook me to my core, I nodded. "Do you want me to deliver a letter, or should I simply assure them of your prayers?"

"We will write." Aquila squeezed my hand. "I will have letters ready for you tomorrow."

I brushed away my tears. "I will pick them up at midday. I will also pray to Caesar, promising to sacrifice an entire ox if the guards agree to release Priscilla."

"Thank you." Aquila pressed a kiss to my forehead, a gesture that twisted my heart. "Though our God does not delight in such sacrifices, I know He is pleased that you are willing to do this for us."

Thirty-Six

THE 9TH DAY OF IULIUS

Mariana joined her husband at the iron bars of their prison cell, waiting for an answer that had not yet come. The baby in her arms yawned and flailed, then settled back to sleep.

"Will you not sit?" she asked, slipping her free arm through her husband's. "Watching the stairs will not make help arrive sooner."

"I have no need to sit," he said. "If the Romans carry out our sentence, we shall soon enjoy an eternal rest."

"But we have not yet entered eternity, and your father could still send a letter." She smiled, silently reminding him that his father, the governor of Acacia, might still be able to influence Nero.

If the emperor was in an affable mood.

Ten months had passed since Mariana, Marcus, and their newborn daughter were pulled from their apartment. After so many weeks in an iron cage with no furnishings, no cosmetics, and only a bucket in which to wash, Mariana felt a bit like an animal herself.

She did not worry about her older boys. Their apartment had been filled with guests when the soldiers came, and it had been a simple matter to let the older children remain with those who remained in her apartment. But the baby needed to nurse.

"I cannot believe this is happening in Rome," Marcus said, staring into space. "Rome is the city of my birth. I used to consider its laws my heritage. But now I do not recognize this place. I no longer belong here."

"Since our arrival you have seen little of the Rome you knew," Mariana pointed out. "You have been confined in a crowded insula, and now this."

"I cannot believe Rome has fallen so low," he said. "My father always said the Republic was the birthplace of honor, loyalty, and freedom. I still hold those virtues, but Rome does not believe those qualities compatible with Christianity."

"They do not know Yeshua. They know only what they have heard or what they imagine. If they *knew* Adonai's Son, they would welcome us with open arms."

"Like my mother and my brother?"

Mariana sighed. Marcus had family in Rome, but neither his mother nor his brother had come to visit since his return to the city.

"I love you," she whispered, leaning her head on his shoulder. "Never doubt it."

He pulled her closer, an affectionate public gesture he would not have allowed himself if they were not waiting to die.

"How are the other women?" he asked. "I saw you speaking with Aurora and Priscilla."

Mariana's mouth twisted. "They are tolerating the circumstances. Hannah comforts the younger ones and Priscilla rations the food, so everyone has something in their belly."

She lifted her head at the sharp sound of cleated sandals on the stairs. Torchlight flickered over the stone wall, followed by a guard's shoes. The burly man stopped at the foot of the stairs and glanced over his shoulder. A man and woman descended the narrow steps, the woman's face concealed by a palla. She stood motionless at the bottom of the staircase, then pressed the palla to her nostrils and turned away.

"I know that fabric." Priscilla stood and moved toward the iron bars. "Calandra? Is that you?"

When the woman's companion moved from shadows into the light, Mariana recognized the aedile's son. Hadrian's face was somber, his eyes dark as he gestured to the young woman who had accompanied Hadrian on one of his visits to the apartment.

"Greetings," Calandra said, her voice thin. "We have brought letters for you."

Calandra pulled several sealed papyri from the belt at her tunic and passed them to Priscilla through the bars. The guard watched, his eyes wary, but he did not stop her from distributing the letters.

"What I would give for a lamp," an older man said, lifting his letter to a stray beam of sunlight from the high window.

Marcus opened his letter, read it, and looked at Mariana. "Aquila writes that he has contacted the aedile about the children arrested with us. Since they are Roman citizens, they may soon be released. Cronus is working on it."

Mariana shivered in a thrill of hope. "May Adonai's will be done." She kissed the top of her daughter's head. "I do not want to let her go, but I would not have her share our fate."

She glanced around as her fellow prisoners began to read their letters aloud. One woman wept silently as she heard the words of encouragement and consolation.

Mariana looked at Priscilla, who was reading her letter, her lips forming the words in a soft whisper. When she had finished, she pressed the papyrus to her breast as a tear slipped over her cheek.

Mariana touched her friend's arm. "From your husband?"

"Yes."

"Is he well?"

"He is, and they are praying for us. He also asks us to pray for Calandra."

At hearing Priscilla's words, the young woman looked as though she might run up the stairs, but Priscilla slipped her arm through the bars. "Calandra," she called, her voice firm.

The young woman shuffled forward, her head bowed.

"Do not be afraid," Priscilla told her. "Aquila has told me what happened, and I do not hold you responsible for my arrest. You are a daughter to me and always will be."

A sob burst from Calandra's throat, shaking her thin shoulders.

"I love you." Priscilla thrust both arms through the bars and caught Calandra's hands. "You may not believe it, but Adonai is working in your life."

From the shadows against the wall, Petros stepped forward and beckoned to the man who had come with Calandra. "Hadrian, my young friend, have you news for us?"

Hadrian turned. "What would you like to know?"

Petros gave the man a lopsided grin. "Ha! Now it is *my* turn to ask the questions."

A grudging smile curved Hadrian's lip. "Ask."

Petros rested his arms on the iron bars. "First, do you know when we will be released from this place?"

Hadrian mumbled in a voice so low Mariana strained to hear. "Three weeks from now, your exodus from this place will begin."

"Ah." Petros's eyes glinted in the dim light. "And so it begins—our following in Messiah's footsteps."

Mariana caught her breath, recognizing the words. Petros had written something similar in one of his letters.

"I am prepared," Petros said, his voice smooth and steady. "After Yeshua's resurrection, He told me the day would come when I would stretch out my hands and someone would dress me and carry me where I did not want to go. That day will come . . . soon."

"Is there anything—" Calandra's voice broke—"you would have us share with the others?"

An inner light glowed in the old man's eyes. "Say this: beloved brothers and sisters, do not be surprised at the fiery ordeal taking place to test you, as though something strange were happening. Instead, rejoice insofar as you share in the sufferings of Messiah." Petros's gaze seemed to rest on something in the distance, then he smiled. "And after you have suffered a little while, the God of all grace will himself restore, support, strengthen, and establish you. All power to Him forever!"

Mariana swallowed the lump that had risen in her throat and squeezed Marcus's arm. When she glanced up, he was wiping a tear from his eye.

"Are you ready?" she asked.

He nodded. "I am."

"So am I."

❖

While Calandra spoke with Mariana and Priscilla, Hadrian moved toward the shadows and found Lysandros sitting on the floor with a group of men.

"I almost did not recognize you," Hadrian said. "I have never seen you with a beard."

Slowly, Lysandros stood. "It is good to see you, Dominus."

Hadrian swallowed the lump that had risen in his throat. "It is good to see you as well. How did this happen?"

A wry smile crossed Lysandros's face. "I was at the wrong place at the wrong time. I found an ecclesia not far from your father's house. Sabinus's men interrupted our meeting and arrested everyone."

"I am sorry."

"I am not." Lysandros spoke with his usual deference, but a spark lit his eyes, a flame Hadrian had not seen before. "These people have been imprisoned for nearly a year. I have been here only a month, but I am honored to suffer with them." Lysandros moved closer to the iron bars. "I am happy you have come. I need to tell you something."

Hadrian nodded. "What is it?"

"Months ago, you asked me to inquire after your child, but not to tell you what I learned."

"You *found* him?"

Lysandros's chin dipped. "I did."

"Where is he?"

"I know where he *was*, but I cannot say where he is now."

"You cannot or you will not?"

"You are my dominus, so there is nothing I would not tell you if I could."

Hadrian's thoughts spun. If Lysandros found the child months ago, the boy must have been sold at a market. Families often bought babies to keep as pets and sold them when they were no longer helpless and adorable.

"I thought you should know your son lives," Lysandros added.

Tears sprang to Hadrian's eyes. "Should I search for him? Could he ever think of me as a father?"

Lysandros gripped the iron bars. "That is a question only Adonai can answer."

Hadrian shifted his gaze to Calandra, who was calmly speaking with the women. What would *she* do if he searched for and found their son? Would she be grateful . . . or horrified?

"Is there anything else, Dominus?"

The question brought Hadrian out of his confusion. "Yes. I have something for you. Two things." From his belt he pulled a sheet of papyrus and a *pilleus*, the cap of liberty worn by every freedman. "I have been to the magistrate and recorded your manumission. As of today you are no longer a slave."

He extended his hand through the bars. Lysandros took the document and the cap, then gave Hadrian a bewildered look. "So now you are no longer my dominus, but—"

"I am your *patronus*," Hadrian finished. "Now I can call you *friend*."

Lysandros examined the document, then met Hadrian's gaze. "You've made quite an effort for a man who will soon die. An unnecessary effort because through Yeshua we have been brothers for months."

"I know. Manumission may not seem like much, but as your patronus, I am responsible for you. If—*when*—you die, I am required to pay for your funeral and bury you with my family members. I will care for you, Lysandros, as you have always cared for me."

Lysandros's face darkened, then he reached through the bars and clasped Hadrian's neck, pulling him forward. "May Adonai watch between us," he whispered, his voice brimming with affection, "until we meet again."

Thirty-Seven

AUGUSTUS

Mariana woke to the sound of a rooster's crow. She smiled, remembering the oft-told story of how Petros denied Yeshua so many years ago, then pushed herself up from the floor.

Three weeks, Hadrian had said when he visited. Three weeks before.

She turned to her baby girl, who lay at Marcus's side, swaddled in his mantle. "Please, Abba," she whispered, "save my little Zera and bless our boys. May Ivan and Chaim find good homes, safety, and shelter with your people. Do not let them die before they have begun to live."

Several of the others began to stir. Not everyone had been fortunate enough to hide their older children. A young couple from Ephesus had been arrested with toddling twins. They sat on their parents' laps, silent and sleepy. Another couple had a young son, and a couple from Ephesus had a little girl who had just lost her first tooth. Mariana wasn't the only one who had realized the significance of the day.

A few moments later, she stiffened at the sound of creaking iron, followed by the metallic sound of cleated sandals. Two guards entered the room, their faces grim. The first man consulted a bit of papyrus in his hand.

"Petros of Judea, noncitizen," he barked.

Petros stepped forward. "Yes?"

"You and your wife are to come with us."

Mariana's heart contracted as Petros opened his arms and the others embraced him with tears. She did the same, hugging him and Hannah, then she moved to Marcus's side, weeping silently as the couple from Galilee walked out of the prison cell.

"We will see you soon," Petros called, tossing a triumphant smile in their direction. "Until then, be faithful!"

⬥

Euodia, who was staying with us, along with Ariston, Aquila, Mariana's sons, Petra, and Salama, refused to eat on the eighth day of Augustus, when Rome would celebrate the festival for Venus. When I shot her a curious look, Euodia answered my unspoken question.

"For the Jews, today is the saddest day of the year," she said, a grim expression on her face. "It is Tish'a B'Av, the ninth day of their month of Av. For the Jews it is a day of mourning and fasting. I am observing the date for their sake."

I sat at the table. "Why is it the saddest day of the year?"

"It is the day when the Babylonians destroyed Jerusalem and the Holy Temple. It is also the day when the Hebrew spies returned from looking over the Promised Land and gave Moses a bad report."

"Bad things happen on this day," Aquila added, ignoring the food I had set on the table. "So we have set this day aside for suffering."

Father had convinced Aquila to stay with us. Though Priscilla caught the Praetorians' attention with her many visits to the Christians under house arrest, we knew the authorities could easily shift their interest to her husband. Father went with me to visit the tentmaker and begged Aquila, with tears, to stay with us. Aquila finally agreed, as long as we could shelter his entire household.

I had never realized how small our living quarters were until Aquila and his friends arrived. Salama and the two boys shared my bed, while Father gave his room to Euodia and Ariston. He and Aquila slept on pallets in the workshop, and Petra slept in a hammock suspended from the ceiling.

Though I did not regret our hospitality, we *did* pay a price. Our budget, already strained under rising costs, stretched to feed so many additional mouths. And though I never mentioned it, I suffered an exquisite agony every time I heard the high-pitched squeals of Ivan and Chaim, Mariana's lively little boys.

Where was *my* son? Was he laughing as well? Was he suffering under the rod of a cruel taskmaster? Was he even alive?

So I did not complain when on the ninth of Av we went about our work in somber silence, ignorant of other events in the city. Aquila worked on his bookkeeping. Euodia and Ariston wrote to friends in Philippi, and Salama helped me with household duties as she watched young Ivan and Chaim.

But after sunset, Hadrian arrived. One look at his face told me that he had witnessed something horrific. As he sank into a chair, the others gathered around for news.

"I went to the Circus," he said, glancing at Aquila. "My father had to attend, so I went with him. We arrived early to make certain the days' events were properly arranged."

Then, as Salama brought him a cup of wine, Hadrian told us what had happened.

Early that morning, as I was setting out bread and fruit, Petros, Hannah, and three other Christians had been taken from the underground cells at the Circus. Because the Venus games featured chariot racing, the sands of the oblong arena had been cleared and raked. On the elongated *spina*, the elevated structure at the center of the track, obelisks stood at the northern and southern ends, while golden statues of Roman gods filled the remaining area.

In the middle of the spina, a space had been emptied and five holes dug into the earth. Petros must have realized his fate as soon as he glimpsed the stack of wooden beams because he calmly asked the guards if they would position him head down—he was not worthy to die in the same manner as his Lord.

The soldiers obliged. They did not oblige Hannah, who fainted when she realized how she would die. "In that way," Hadrian said, "Adonai provided her with mercy, as she did not feel the nails piercing her wrists and ankles."

Three other Christians bravely bore their fates on the rough beams, their lives fading as the midday sun blazed overhead, the merchants sold refreshments, and the crowd filled the arena. The executioner had timed the event perfectly. By the time the races began, stirring the dust and thrilling the crowd, the half-starved Christians were struggling for breath.

As chariots flew, hooves pounded the sand, and the crowd roared, the believers blinked dust from their eyes and wept for the world their Messiah had come to save. While Nero awarded laurel crowns to the winners of the races, Peter and Hannah must have recalled the thorny crown used to pierce Yeshua's head. And after sunset, as slaves swept dust from the spina and shoveled manure from the sand, the five martyred Christians breathed their last.

Some speculated that Petros's unusual position had hastened his end, but he and Hannah died in the same hour, just after sunset. The others surrendered their spirits in darkness.

After hearing this dire news, our guests tore their tunics and wept. Hadrian sat next to my father and stoically endured his grief as Aquila, Ariston, Euodia, and Salama rocked with sorrow.

Hadrian looked at me, his countenance dull with despair. He had held genuine affection for Petros and Hannah, I realized, because they loved him.

I loved him, too. My heart swelled with the truth I had long tried to deny, but there it was, as real as my love for my father and the child I could not forget. I struggled mightily to resist the urge to walk over, cup his face, and kiss away his tears. I knew how to comfort him, but I did not know how to make him stop following a God who would certainly lead him to destruction.

Though new prisoners arrived daily, some of them weak and wounded from torture, Mariana thought the iron cells seemed far emptier after Petros and Hannah had been taken away. She had not realized how much they counted on the aged apostle to encourage them, and the days following his death were dark. Hannah's influence had been a steady support to the women, and Mariana could not bring herself to even glance at the corner where the fisherman's wife used to sit.

With Petros and Hannah gone, Mariana realized with startling urgency that her own days were numbered. When a slave brought food, she begged the man for papyrus and a pen, even a piece of charcoal. "I must write to my mother and sister," she told him, her voice breaking. "Please."

She was not sure he would help, but later he returned with several sheets of papyrus. He handed them to her, along with a sharpened stick and a bottle of berry ink. "I will return later," he said, his eyes softening. "Write quickly."

Mariana took one sheet of papyrus and passed the rest to the others.

To Hester and Prima, beloved mother and sister:

I pray this letter reaches you before winter. This may be my last chance to share the feelings that have been crowding my heart.

Mother, how can I thank you for all the ways you have loved me? You led me to faith in Yeshua, and you guided me with wisdom and encouragement. I fear you may be troubled by guilt that you are not with me, but do not allow yourself to grieve. You did what you felt was Adonai's will in that moment of testing, and now you are with Prima and your husband, both of whom need you to shine the light of Yeshua. Keep the faith, Mother, and know that I love you with all my heart.

Prima, I apologize for not being a better sister to you. I should have been more faithful to share the Gospel, and I should not have let you feel isolated. When you tried to hurt me, I withdrew when I should have listened to your grievances. Forgive me, sister, and know that I rejoiced to hear that you survived the anguish that led you to leap from the Acrocorinth. I cannot understand that depth of despair—I do not despair, not even in the face of death, because I am assured that Yeshua has prepared a place for me, and I will see my children again. I would give anything, even my life, to know I will see you in Adonai's heaven.

Please tell Narkis that I will always be grateful to him for providing for me. Marcus sends his abiding affection to all of you, and our three children do as well. The boys are with trusted friends, and the baby is with me, as Zera has not yet been weaned. I entrust her life to Adonai and am certain He will restore her to me.

In the name of Him whose love is far greater than my fear,

Mariana

She stoppered the ink bottle, then handed ink and stylus to Priscilla, who waited to write her own letter. Mariana blew on the paper until it dried, then folded it. She would give it to the servant the next time he brought food.

She lifted her head as the baby began to fuss in Marcus's arms. She unfastened the tunic clasp at her shoulder so the baby could nurse. As she took the child, sandals slapped the stairs. The guards were coming again.

Dread settled in her belly as Mariana turned away. But when she saw relief on the others' faces, she knew it was not a guard who descended.

She turned and saw a woman dressed in the short tunic of a slave. She walked to the door of the cell, then her gaze caught and held Mariana's.

"I have come for the children," she said. "The prefect has ordered that all children under the age of twelve are to come with me."

Tightening her grip on Zera, Mariana glanced behind her. Mordecai and Jerusha had risen at the woman's approach; now Jerusha's hands were firmly fastened to their ten-year-old son's shoulders. Beside them stood Dovev and Chana, who clung to their four-year-old daughter. And the young couple from Ephesus with the twins—Mariana had not yet learned their names.

"W-what will happen to my daughter?" Chana asked. "Will she be sold at the market?"

The slave's face crumpled with unhappiness. "I was told to gather them. Nothing else."

Tears blinded Mariana's eyes as she studied her tiny daughter. She blinked them away, desperate to imprint Zera's beautiful little face on her heart. Would she be sold into slavery? Would she be adopted? Either situation was possible, but boys were adopted far more often than girls.

A guard came down the stairs and saw the prisoners clinging to their children. "Come now," he said, his keys jangling as he unlocked the door. "Is it not better that they live than die with you?"

Was it?

Mariana turned to her husband. "Should we keep her?"

Marcus looked at Zera, his chest heaving. "We will choose life . . . and entrust her to Adonai." He opened his hands, and Mariana lowered her baby into his arms.

The guard grunted. "You do not have to die. A little toss of incense to Jupiter and you are free. Both of you, if you are willing."

Ignoring the guard, Marcus took a moment to study his daughter's face, then he pressed a kiss to her forehead and surrendered her to the slave.

Bracing herself on Marcus's shoulder, Mariana gave way to the sharp sobs that tore at her heart.

❖

In the days that followed, Hadrian frequently visited, reluctantly supplying details about the deaths of our friends. We needed to know what had happened and how they had fared. Hadrian did not relate specifics, but I was familiar enough with the festivals that my mind had no trouble supplying details.

On the ninth of Augustus, games at the Circus Flaminus had honored Sol, god of the sun. Ten Christians were herded into the arena.

Hadrian's jaw tightened as he recalled the circumstances. "They had been stitched into fresh animal skins," he said, perspiration beading on his forehead. "Even a boy who could not have been more than thirteen. Only their feet remained unbound, and guards used their spears to push them to the north end of the track. Once they were in place, *my father*"— the words were tinged with bitterness—"announced that they would die for starting the fires that killed thousands of Roman citizens." Hadrian swallowed hard. "A moment later, the guards released packs of starving wild dogs."

He squeezed my hand. "I am glad you did not see it, Calandra. With your gift for memory, I would not want you to carry that image in your head."

At the end of the worktable, Father clenched his fist. "I am ashamed to think how many times I sat in the stands and watched such things. I believed I was watching the punishment of criminals who deserved to die, but I *know* the people who died today." He sighed. "If I had been there, I would have thanked Adonai for my sightless eyes."

While the entire city stopped working to celebrate the festivals, Father and I sat with our friends in the workshop. The Christians, including my Father, prayed for those who faced death, and I paced like a nervous cat, wondering at the audacity of our emperor. How could Nero link the gods of Rome with the deaths of innocent people?

Hadrian did not visit during the next few days, but I heard about the games from chatter on the street. On the twelfth day of Augustus, Christians were executed at three different festivals—one to honor the birthday of Isis, one to honor Venus, and another to honor Hercules. Citizens who went to honor Isis saw a dozen Christians face six hungry lions. Those who honored Venus, goddess of love, saw five Christian women face five *gladiatrices*, female gladiators. The Christians had been given wooden swords, but they dropped their weapons to the sand after one of the women cried out, "Fear not, sisters! Messiah Yeshua waits for us!"

After that, a breathless customer told me, the Christian women formed a circle, their arms around each other, and refused to even look at the gladiatrices. Even as they were struck from behind, they did not waver in their resolve.

"The crowd cheered when the last woman was run through," my customer told me, her eyes as round as the moon, "but their cries swiftly died. They had come to witness a fierce fight, yet the Christians did not even raise their weapons."

After surreptitiously loitering outside the Hercules Invictus event, Aquila told us that ten Christians, all of them Roman citizens, had been beheaded. Because they had been under Hadrian's supervision, I knew their deaths had devastated him.

Eight different festivals fell on the thirteenth of Augustus—ceremonies to honor Jupiter, Vertumnus, Hercules, Fortuna, Caster and Pollux, Camenae, Flora, and Diana. Executioners spilled the blood of Christians at each event, their deaths artfully arranged to reflect the theme of each celebration.

On the first night of the full moon, Romans celebrated the Nemoralia, or nighttime festival of torches. Traditionally, participants wore garlands and wreaths while offering sacrifices to the lunar goddess.

Nero decided to commemorate the festival by having several Christians sewn into tunics that had been saturated with pitch. These unfortunates were crucified in Nero's garden while the emperor feasted. When the full moon rose, Nero had the Christians set afire and then commented on the outstanding quality of the light.

As Aquila told the story, I quivered with horror and guilt. I used to believe that only criminals and fools suffered crucifixion. How wrong I was.

The next day Aquila returned from roaming the city and dropped onto the bench at Father's worktable. "A day without festivals," he said, dropping his head into his hands. "I pray it is a day without death."

"Have you heard anything," I asked, carefully choosing my words, "about Priscilla?"

He regarded me with a bleary gaze. "No one has seen her, so I trust she still lives."

Father lifted his chin. "Has Nero's lust for blood been sated? If he continues this search for believers, there will soon be no Christians left."

"Not so," Aquila said, his voice heavy. "Adonai always preserves a remnant. Always." He drew a slow breath. "Our Scriptures record the story of Elisha the prophet. A man from another city brought him twenty loaves of barley bread, and Elisha told him to give it to the people. 'How can I set this before a hundred men?' the servant asked. But Elisha said, 'The Lord says they will eat and have some left over.' So the servant obeyed, they ate, and there was bread left over, according to the word of the Lord."

"I have heard," Salama said, her voice almost a whisper, "that Yeshua did the same thing."

"He did," Aquila said, his eyes gleaming. "Adonai will preserve a remnant and not lose a single one of His own."

❖

The city did not observe any festivals on the twenty-ninth of Augustus. I prayed—to whom, I was not certain—that Nero would find another obsession to pursue in September.

But after coming in from the Forums, Aquila said he'd heard the praeco declare that Nero would observe the traditional thanksgiving festival the next day. "The Charisteria," he added, the corner of his mouth drooping. "We are supposed to be grateful for all we have *enjoyed* this month."

We were both thinking of Priscilla. "What of those who are still imprisoned?" I asked.

Aquila shook his head. "No word about her or Paulos, who remains in the Mamertine."

I woke the next morning with a feeling of foreboding. Most

shops remained closed on festival days. Even so, I removed the planks from our windows to listen to the talk on the street. I had no intention of going near the Circus Maximus, but if something happened to one of my friends, I wanted to know about it.

Thirty-Eight

THE 29TH OF AUGUSTUS

"I do not understand why you did not want to come," Cronus said, leading the way to two choice seats down front. "This event will undoubtedly be one of the month's best."

"I came only because you insisted," Hadrian answered, following. "But I have been to dozens of festivals. Why should I sit through another?"

With that said, Hadrian clamped his lips together. His father had to know he had friends among the Christians, but he had never asked Hadrian about the sect. He had professed shock when Lysandros was arrested, then promptly asked the Senate for reparation, as the man had been a valuable slave.

Hadrian dropped into the seat next to his father and propped his elbow on the armrest. To give thanks for having rooted out and executed the Christians, Nero had dedicated this thanksgiving festival to Vesta, Roman goddess of hearth, home, and family. Hadrian knew several Christians still waited in the underground prison, but he hoped he would not be acquainted with any who appeared today.

The director of the games, another aedile, stood and lifted his arms. "Welcome, citizens!" he called, his words echoing in the oval. "To honor our beloved emperor and the goddess all of Rome holds dear, at tremendous expense I have assembled a vast variety of wild beasts, some of which you have never seen! Enjoy the day and give thanks to Vesta for granting us many blessings!"

Hadrian sank lower in his chair as the crowd roared in approval. With a flurry of trumpets, the opening ceremonies began. Seven priestesses from the temple of Vesta approached an altar on the spina, where a male slave stood with a flower-bedecked ram. As the trumpets blew a three-note signal, he held the ram by its horns while the priestess cut the animal's throat with a swift stroke. Blood spilled, the crowd cheered, and Hadrian averted his gaze.

Music played, lyres and trumpets and drums, as the priestesses danced and two teams of horse-drawn chariots trotted around the oval. Scantily dressed female slaves threw flower petals from the chariots while acrobats followed the horses, leaping and cartwheeling over the sand.

When the horses returned to their gates, the trumpets blew again. Hadrian sat up, surprised that the emperor had not appeared. "Is Nero coming?"

Cronus shrugged. "If he does not, this will be the first event he has missed this month."

Hadrian turned toward the end of the oval, where the gates were opening. Two lines of men and women entered the arena, all of them filthy and wearing the rough garments of slaves. The women's hair flowed wild and loose, and most of the men wore beards. At first glance they appeared to be criminals and barbarians. No wonder the people had found it easy to hate those who called themselves *Christian*.

Though he did not want to look, he squinted to search for familiar faces. He exhaled in relief when he did not recognize the first few, but then a suffocating sensation tightened his throat. The Corinthians—all of them—were present. Titius

Justus walked forward, firmly clutching his wife's hand. Behind him came Marcus and Mariana, and behind Mariana, Priscilla.

He turned away, the heaviness in his chest like a millstone. How was he going to tell Calandra about *this*? He ought to be on the sand with them. He ought to stand and confess that he followed the Christian God and Nero had lied to every Roman citizen. Christians did not hate mankind but believed in a living God with power to change men's lives.

"By all the gods, I never thought to see this."

His father's whispered oath caught Hadrian's attention. He followed his father's gaze to the sand and felt his stomach twist. Lysandros, his former slave, stood near Priscilla, his hands clasped and his head bowed.

Jeers and insults rose from the crowd. Some spectators threw rotten fruit, readily available from vendors who carried baskets through the aisles.

Another trumpet blew, and from the opposite end of the oval more gates opened. The director had mentioned wild beasts, and the first to appear were a half-dozen scrawny lions. The animals crept into the arena, their tawny hides marked with bloody cuts from guards, who had tormented them in their cages. The beasts prowled over the sand, their eyes locked on the Christians huddled at the other end of the arena.

The lions lifted their heads, parsed the atmosphere, and sensed no threat. Then they lowered their heads, their golden eyes staring at the vulnerable humans. They were hunters, they were hungry, and they had spotted prey. They circled the Christians, who were praying audibly, calling upon Adonai for mercy.

Hadrian braced his head on his hand, shielding his eyes. No stranger to lions, he knew they worked as a team. They would circle, the flanking females worrying the group while larger females separated one vulnerable victim from the others.

Then the male would charge.

"Tell me," I said, gripping Hadrian's hand. "I must know what happened."

An aura of grief radiated from his face, so he did not have to tell me others had died.

"It was carnage," he finally said, clenching and unclenching his free hand. "I did not know all of the prisoners, but I did see—"

"Priscilla?" My voice broke.

Hadrian looked, not at me, but at Aquila, who sat across the table, his face pale. "Not only Priscilla," he continued, "but Mariana, Marcus, and the others from Corinth. Many of them were citizens. Nero will be soundly criticized for feeding Romans to wild beasts."

"So they are dead." I felt foolish for stating the obvious, but I had to be certain their God had not worked another miracle.

"Who dares criticize Nero?" Euodia said. "He is the emperor."

"He is," Hadrian said, his voice strained. "But he made a mistake. He could not have foreseen the result of these deaths— one in particular."

He pressed his fist to his mouth, apparently unable to speak. What fresh horror were we about to endure?

Aquila leaned forward. "What? Speak, man."

Hadrian lowered his hand. "When the first lion charged, our friends ran, screamed, or fell to their knees. But Priscilla, Marcus, and Mariana stood together, their arms around each other, their faces lifted toward heaven." He exhaled in a rush. "I have never seen such bravery, not even from gladiators. Then someone in the audience realized that the front of Mariana's tunic was wet. A woman shouted, 'Look—her body weeps for her infant!'"

Grief welled within me, black and cold. I had forgotten that Mariana was still nursing her baby girl.

"After that," Hadrian continued, "the crowd went silent. Every eye focused on Mariana, and in that instant Rome realized that those in the arena did not hate mankind. Mariana was a woman who loved her husband and children, just like the virtuous mothers of Rome."

Aquila's face rippled with anguish. "And then?"

Hadrian shook his head. "A lioness took Marcus, and the male got . . ." He shook his head. "Yet Priscilla did not fall, but remained upright, looking to heaven and smiling."

We sat in a silence so thick the only sound was my father's uneven breathing.

"I am sorry." Hadrian looked at Aquila, whose cheeks were slick with tears. "Your wife died well. When a lion finally took her, the crowd remained silent. That's when even my father knew that Nero had lost his war against the Christians. Some might even say that in that moment he lost his hold over the people of Rome."

Thirty-Nine

Nero's bloodthirsty campaign ended with the month of Augustus. The Christians who had not been arrested slipped back to their homes, but no longer would they gather openly in synagogues or public buildings. The ecclesia that had met in Aquila's shop continued to convene there, though they sang their hymns in hushed whispers. I know because on the first day of every week, I escorted my father to that meeting. Hadrian also attended, but now he attended without Lysandros.

From talking to those in the ecclesia, I learned that many Romans who witnessed the Christians' deaths had quietly inquired about Yeshua. They slipped into believers' meetings, and many decided to abandon the old gods.

From the Mamertine, Paulos sent a message to the believers through Luke, his physician and companion: "I know you have sorrow, but rejoice in the Lord! Let your gentleness be known to all people. Do not be worried about anything, but by prayer and petition let your requests be made known to God. And the shalom of Adonai will guard your hearts and minds in Messiah Yeshua."

When the scattered ecclesiae outgrew their meeting places, many of them moved to tombs outside the city walls. Because the Jews preferred burial over the Roman practice of cremation, many Jewish Christians opened their family crypts to the eccle-siae. I found it odd that people who spoke so often of joy would want to meet among the dead, but then their faith had never made sense to me. Hadrian began to believe when Yeshua healed me, but my Father believed in the Son of Adonai even though he was *not* healed. Either their God healed or he did not, and I could not make sense of their reasoning.

In those days, *nothing* made sense to me. Aquila stopped by the workshop every morning to pray with my father, but I was so enshrouded in guilt over Priscilla's death that I could not find the energy to utter a single prayer. Neither could I work on the statue commissioned to honor the emperor who had killed so many innocents.

Whenever I could not focus on any useful endeavor, I crossed the bridge and visited Aquila, Ariston, Petra, and Euodia. Their consolation and gentle conversation did much to soothe my troubled soul.

Though the surviving Christians wore somber faces when they spoke of the recent persecution, they did not lose hope. Even Aquila carried on with strength and purpose. He contin-ued to speak of Yeshua to anyone who would listen, explain-ing how Adonai, creator of heaven and earth, chose a man, Abraham, and a nation—Abraham's descendants—to bless the earth and save people from their own evil.

"Even Nero," Aquila said one night as Father and I joined his household for dinner. "If the emperor would humble himself, repent of his evil ways, and turn to Adonai, he could be saved."

I gaped at him. "Nero?"

Aquila nodded. "We have all sinned, but the believer is set right as a gift of God's grace. Paulos has preached this mes-sage for years."

I blinked. "What of Paulos? Has he been executed?"

Ariston shook his head. "Paulos was not in Rome during the

fire. He was accused of arson, but multiple witnesses swore he was not in the city at the time."

I sighed. "At least *he* lives."

"And he writes," Aquila added. "Even though he wastes away in the Mamertine, he remains determined to redeem every misspent moment of his life. He has also led several Praetorians to Christ."

"Luke visits him daily," Euodia said. "Prisoners in that pit have little to eat but gruel and moldy bread, so we send food with Luke."

A small head appeared in the opening that led to the living quarters. "Euodia?"

"Chaim." She rose, a smile dimpling her cheek. "We must have awakened him."

My heart twisted as Euodia went to check on the child. "Mariana would be happy to know her boys are here. But what of her baby girl?"

Aquila shot Ariston a sharp look. "Any word?"

"We do not yet know what happened to Zera," Ariston said. "We are still searching for her."

I enjoyed being with my Christian friends and had to admit that our workshop seemed unnaturally quiet now that Aquila and his household had gone back to Transtiberim. I missed the sound of the boys' laughter and the warmth of their little bodies on my mattress. While they were with us, I awakened many nights to find that either Ivan or Chaim had looped his arms around my neck, and it had seemed better to leave him as he was than to peel him off.

Ariston stood. "I must see Paulos on the morrow. He has written another letter to Timothy, his young disciple. I have to post it after I deliver a bolt of purple fabric."

His words came to me as if through a fog, for I could not stop thinking about Mariana's baby girl. "Wait." I lifted my hand. "Hadrian has a letter from Petros. He promised to distribute it."

"He has done it," Ariston said, "and already that letter has been an encouragement to many."

I sat back and marveled at the two men. Even with a pantheon of gods at my disposal, I had never been as strong as the people around that table.

Forty

Like the stillness after a violent storm, a dense quiet filled our workshop. Father and I were both overtaken by ennui, so we did not work on the statue for months. We rose every morning and made pottery or went to the Forum to feel the breeze on our faces. One month slid into the next until we found ourselves in a new year.

Hadrian continued to bring our monthly payment, but he did not press us to do the work. Like us, his enthusiasm for the project had faded, and our statue remained unfinished. I had never had an opportunity to sketch Nero, and I had no desire to seek one.

I had no idea how Hadrian filled his days. The prisoners he used to visit were dead. The only Christian prisoner remaining was Paulos.

One cold night, Hadrian came to the shop. Surprised to see him, and knowing that my father was sleeping, I quietly let him in and led him to my worktable, where a single lamp burned.

"I am glad you have come," I said, watching as he pulled off his mantle. "I do not think I will ever be able to sketch Nero.

293

My father and I will understand if you want to stop making the monthly payment."

As embarrassment overcame my weariness, I sat and rested my head on my hand. "I know we will have to repay your father the money he has advanced us, but what if we cannot find the will—or a way—to finish?"

My question rose from simple courtesy because I already knew the answer. If Father and I had to repay Cronus, Father's reputation would be ruined, and we would be impoverished.

Hadrian's gaze slid over the untouched plaster molds, then swung back to my face. "The executions are still haunting you."

"How did you know?"

"Because they haunt me as well."

He sat beside me and leaned forward, propping his elbows on the table. "When I close my eyes to sleep, I see their faces on the backs of my eyelids. I have seen traitors beheaded and criminals torn to pieces. I have watched as runaway slaves were flogged to death. But until a few months ago, I had never watched Rome kill people because of what they *believed*."

I shifted to face him. "But everyone thinks the Christians were guilty of arson."

He scoffed. "That is what they were told, but that is not what they believe. They learned the truth when they saw Mariana and Priscilla and Lysandros. They recognized that our friends were men and women of *honor*. Now the people rumble with discontent."

"What good will it do? Nero is not listening."

"How could he? For the last several months he has been relaxing in Greece. But he is returning soon to celebrate the dedication of his Golden House."

I caught my breath. "He has no idea that the people murmur against him?"

"I am sure he has his spies, but who knows if they are honest with him? I think he left when he realized that the executions did not accomplish his desired effect." Hadrian shook his head. "I still mourn the loss of those good people. I met regularly with many of them, and they were never anything but kind. And Petros . . ." His voice broke. "The Judean was unique among men. At first I thought he was dull-witted because he could not speak Latin. But then I saw the soul beneath that bearded face and felt ashamed for judging him. He was wiser than most of Rome's senators. He was brave . . . and yet never afraid to say what was on his mind."

"I still cannot believe he is gone," I whispered. "And Hannah. Why did they execute her? She did not hate anyone."

A muscle flicked at Hadrian's jaw. "I have noticed the people with evil intent accuse others of the dark deeds lurking in their own hearts. Nero is the hater. He hates because he is afraid— and now he has reason to fear." Hadrian glanced at the shadows, as if expecting a spy to emerge at any moment. "I have heard rumblings. Nero has cut the grain supply again, so the working people of Rome are starving. The army grumbles because he has drained the treasury, and the senators openly complain about his taxes. My father says rebellion is in the air, and soon we will see its effects."

"But what happens if he is removed? The man has no heir."

Hadrian tented his hands. "Many in the Senate yearn for a true republic, but as long as men hunger for power, the temptation to rule will prove irresistible. But one thing is certain—the people may have loved Nero's games and gifts, but they will never forgive what he did to the Christians. When Mariana stood before those lions without flinching, people noticed. Romans do not kill virtuous mothers. When the crowd saw her standing tall, her tunic wet with milk . . ." He paused and shook his head. "Mark my words: no one will ever forget it."

I should not have been surprised when Hadrian dropped by our workshop two weeks later. "I know your feelings about the statue," he said, leaning on the window counter as he watched me dust the pottery. "I also know only one thing is stopping you from finishing and receiving full payment, which you need. So I have arranged everything."

I arched my brow. "You have arranged for me to be more talented?"

"I have arranged for you to study Nero. The emperor returned to Rome last week, and today he will attend the chariot races, probably in an attempt to win the people's favor. My father has been invited to sit in the imperial box, so you and I will be his guests."

All coherent thought left my head. "*What?*"

Hadrian lifted a reassuring hand. "You need not worry. We will be seated in the back, but I am certain you will be able to study Nero's face and features, as he tends to be animated during the races. Bring papyri and charcoal, and you shall have exactly what you need to finish the work."

Shaken, I sank onto a stool. "I cannot sit in that box. I have nothing to wear."

"I doubt Nero will have eyes for anyone but the horses."

"But others will see me and know I am a plebeian. I would like to go unnoticed, but that will be impossible if I am dressed"— I spread my hands so he could better see my paint-spattered tunic—"like *this*."

His brows lowered. "How should you dress?"

"You tell me; I have no experience in these matters. Can you not find me a place *outside* Nero's box? Some spot where I can see him without being noticed?"

"From any other seat you would only see the back of his head."

His frown deepened. "For months you have insisted on seeing Nero, but when I arrange the time and circumstance, you protest. I understand your feelings about the man, but if you do this, you will be able to finish and keep everything you have earned."

I sighed, realizing he was right. He disliked Nero as much as I did, yet he had no power to change our contract with his father. If I sketched Nero's face, I would have to shape clay into the features of a man who had murdered people I loved. If I did *not* sketch his face, Father and I would be ruined. Our commission would end, we would have to repay a tremendous debt, and I might never see Hadrian again.

The last thought saddened me most.

I lifted my gaze, intent on memorizing the lines of his face, and saw him pull a purse from his toga. "For your problem." He dropped eight denarii into my palm, enough for a silk tunic and a matching palla. "Go find something to wear."

"Where am I to go? It takes time to have a proper tunic made."

Hadrian waved my words away. "Eight denarii is enough to encourage idle hands to work quickly. I shall return at midday, and we will go to the Circus. After that I will not tolerate any excuse regarding your lack of access to the emperor."

I sighed as I wrapped my fingers around the coins. Very well. If Hadrian was so determined to be rid of his obligation to me, I would not stand in his way.

I was out of breath and perspiring by the time I reached the tentmaker's shop.

Euodia took one look at my face and poured me a cup of honey water.

"What is wrong?" Ariston asked, coming over. "What rumor have you heard?"

I gulped a mouthful of water. "Hadrian insists that I go to the games today. I am to sit in the imperial box so I can sketch the emperor."

A look of horror crossed Euodia's face. "I do not suppose you have any choice."

I shook my head. "I do need to see the man, but I have nothing suitable to wear."

Euodia turned to Aquila, who was cutting fruit for Mariana's sons. "We must help her."

Aquila nodded. "Priscilla would agree. Go through her trunk and take whatever is appropriate."

My heart contracted at the mention of Priscilla's name. Though she was no longer with us, she would help me once again.

"Come." Euodia led the way to a bedchamber behind the shop. She lifted the lid of a large trunk and pulled out several silk garments.

"This is lovely," she said, shaking out a white tunic with gold stitching along the edges. "There is a matching outer tunic, also trimmed in gold."

She held it up to measure the fit, then nodded. I took the garment as Euodia lifted a light blue palla from the trunk. I recognized it as the one Priscilla was wearing when I first met her. I had never seen a fabric that matched the color of the sky.

"Not that one," I protested. "It should remain with Aquila."

Euodia chuckled. "Aquila would never wear a palla, and Priscilla would want you to have it. My ladies dyed it."

With the mention of her *ladies*, I knew Euodia was referring to the Philippian women who harvested rock snails to produce the rare purple coveted by highborn Romans.

"That shade of blue," Euodia said, "is *tekhelet*, the color used in Jewish prayer shawls. It is the color of nobility, and the Jews wear it to remind themselves that they are a kingdom of priests intended to bless the world."

My eyes welled with tears as I draped the fine silk over my fingers.

"Fear not, dear girl," Euodia said, pulling me into a warm embrace. "Do whatever God has given you to do. We will be praying for you."

"How can I honor a vile man like Nero?"

"He is not my favorite person," Euodia said, releasing me, "but before I met Yeshua, *I* was vile in the sight of our holy God. But Adonai knew His love would change me." She clasped her hands. "If you are meeting Hadrian for the games, we must get you dressed."

"Wait." I pulled the coins from my tunic. "Hadrian would want me to pay you."

She folded my fingers over the coins. "You can find a better use for that silver. Now step out of your workday tunic. We must get you ready, and then"—her dimple winked at me—"I will curl your hair."

<hr />

I must have been almost unrecognizable when I met Hadrian at midday. Euodia had adjusted Priscilla's tunic so it would fit me, and the beautiful fabric shimmered in the sun. The blue palla sat atop my dark curls, framing my face and neck.

Hadrian stared at me, then swallowed. "You look different."

I glanced away as my cheeks burned. "I do not want to draw attention, but Euodia assures me this would be appropriate."

"She would know better than I. Have you drawing materials?"

I picked up the soft leather pouch I had filled with papyri and bits of charcoal. "Yes."

"Let us be off then."

We entered the street, Hadrian leading the way while I followed in the wake of his broad shoulders. As we walked, I could not help remembering the night we stood in the garden and spied the first flickering flames of the fire. Since that night, the Circus Maximus had been destroyed, rebuilt, and baptized in the blood of Christians.

I had not visited the Circus in years. I remembered it as an aging racetrack with wooden seats, small shops, and rudimentary gates, but now the Circus was the largest and most ornate arena in Rome.

As we descended into the valley, I glimpsed shimmering statues of gods and goddesses atop columns in the center of the oval. My gaze scanned the track, and for an instant I saw Priscilla, Marcus, and Mariana standing on the sand, their faces averted from an approaching lion.

I blinked the image away.

The wooden seats had been replaced by fire-resistant stone. The imperial box, a covered hall set apart by four tall pillars, had been built across from the finish line, facing the Aventine. Immediately across from it stood the temple of Sol, a covered hall that faced Palatine Hill.

We passed through several checkpoints, but the Praetorians allowed Hadrian to pass as soon as he mentioned his father's name.

Finally, we climbed to the imperial box.

"I thought it best to arrive early," Hadrian said as we walked across the grand space. "Neither of us will have to make an entrance."

I appreciated his thoughtfulness and immediately strode to an empty chair against the back of the structure. A solid wall stood at my right, blocking my view of the crowd—and their view of me. From where I sat, I would be able to see the man sitting in the elevated seat in the front row. As Nero turned to watch the race, I would catch sight of his profile and features, although I would not see his full face unless he swiveled toward us.

Hadrian must have read my thoughts. "You will have to study him," he said, keeping his voice low, "as the emperor enters. If that is not sufficient for your purpose, we can stay until he leaves. He will turn then, and you can examine him again."

"I will sketch quickly," I said, not wanting to remain a moment longer than necessary. "And if I finish before the race ends, I would be happy to leave."

Hadrian snorted in disapproval.

"We cannot leave early?"

He pointed to the entrance, located near the emperor's chair. "We could not slip out unnoticed. Last year a woman gave birth in the theater rather than leave and risk offending the emperor."

I sighed and settled back in my seat, resigned to waiting out the ordeal. A cold sweat dampened my hairline, my heart thumping unevenly.

As the sun tipped toward the west, the arena swelled with sound and activity. From the northern gates I heard the neighing of agitated horses and shouts from stablemen and charioteers. Occasionally a driver—recognizable by his colorful tunic—would stride across the sand and wave as the crowd cheered his name. "I have ten denarii riding on you," one man called to a charioteer. "May the gods speed your horses and preserve your life!"

Though I had heard about the chariot races, I had never attended one, and never could I have imagined this view. From our seats I could see the entire oval. I nudged Hadrian. "Who are the men on the sand? The ones with the bowls?"

"They are the *sparsores*. When the horses begin to run, the sparsores sprinkle the sand with water to keep down the dust."

"Is that not dangerous?"

"Occasionally. But most of them are slaves, so they must do as they are told."

Without warning, the tenor of the noise changed. I heard shouts followed by shushing and a blare of trumpets. I slipped lower in my seat as people entered the box. I recognized Cronus, then two women entered, followed by . . .

Nero. The boy who followed him, I assumed, was the boy Nero had married a few months before—a situation, Hadrian assured me, that had set the tongues of the senators to wagging.

I expected the crowd to cheer at the emperor's appearance, but all I heard was the resentful silence of an unhappy and intimidated people.

❖

Clearly displeased with his reception at the racetrack, Nero lifted his hand, undoubtedly expecting to hear cheering. Yet the silence only seemed to thicken. Worse yet, several people turned their backs to him . . . and I trembled for them.

The emperor turned as if to see what had cast a spell over his people. His gaze met mine, and a flicker of curiosity flitted over his odd face. Even as I recoiled from his probing eyes, the artist in me noted his average height, prominent belly, thick neck, and thin legs. Irregular brown spots covered his bare arms, and even from where I sat, I sensed a peculiar odor emanating from him—a vague mixture of incense and pig fat. His reddish-blond hair lacked luster, and though his blue eyes were bright, they were small and resided in deep caves of bone.

He was no Adonis.

When Hadrian nudged me with his elbow, I quickly lowered my gaze, not lifting my head until Nero had turned to face the track.

I sat, pulled out a sheet of papyrus, and sketched with haste. I drew the face and body, noting with gratitude that my molds featured a torso in a shapeless tunic—the garment of a wanderer or a singer. I would not have to rework the plaster molds, but the existing neck would have to be thickened.

I thrust the first sketch into my satchel and drew the right profile in which his hawklike nose featured prominently. Then the left profile, which featured his protruding brow.

I frowned. The fringe of hair at Nero's forehead gave the impression of a man who lacked intelligence, and the fuzz beneath his chin irritated me. If he wanted to wear a beard, why did he not grow one on his face?

Hadrian must have noticed my expression. "Your attitude shows in your art," he whispered, so softly I barely heard him. "Temper it, sweet friend, or the subject may not appreciate what he sees."

"Hadrian?" Cronus, seated behind Nero, turned to see his son. "Have you greeted the emperor?"

"Not yet, Father."

"You should before he gets too involved in the race." Cronus gestured toward Nero's chair, and Hadrian rose and descended to the royal seat.

I slipped the papyri and charcoal back into my satchel.

Cronus went to join Hadrian at the emperor's side. "Honored Nero, do you remember meeting my son?"

A flash of irritation crossed Nero's face as he squinted at Hadrian. "Did we meet?"

"Once, sir." Hadrian bowed. "I was honored to hear you perform one of your songs at the Theater of Marcellus."

Nero's face brightened. "Then you were indeed blessed." He leaned sideways and peered at me. "And who have you brought with you?"

Cronus stepped forward before Hadrian could answer. "Her name is Calandra, sir, daughter of a talented Greek sculptor. His workshop is located in the Aventine."

Nero squinted at the aedile. "Do I own any of his works?"

"Not yet, sir."

"We shall have to remedy that." Nero pressed his lips into a thin line. "You should now return to your seats lest you disturb my enjoyment."

Hadrian backed away and gave me a smile of pure relief.

Forty-One

Working with fresh determination, I used the upper front and back pieces of the plaster molds to create a clay copy of the faceless head. Days later, after it had thoroughly dried, I affixed generous lumps of clay to the head and molded Nero's nose and protruding brow. I added striated clay for his hair and created a softer ridge of scruffy beard beneath his thickened neck.

I gritted my teeth as I worked. Father often sat beside me, occasionally running his fingertips over the clay, making small adjustments or suggesting ways to texture the surface.

When the piece was finished, I stood, grateful to put some distance between myself and Nero. "I think it is ready," I said, stretching the stiffness from my limbs. "Do you agree?"

Father let his fingertips dance over the clay and frowned as he touched the fringe beneath the neck. "Not an attractive man, is he?"

"He is not. And though it pains me to do this, we will finish this job."

Father smiled. "During these months, you have learned much about art and about life. When you marry—"

"Father—"

"You cannot avoid marriage forever," he continued, cutting me off. "When you marry, let it be because you admire your husband's character. Make sure he is genuine and honest and that he fears Adonai. Because even if you do not, a man who worships the one true God with his heart and soul will be a good man."

I crossed my arms, my heart welling with affection for the man who had been everything to me. "I am perfectly content to remain as I am, as long as I can work with you."

"You have been a blessing," he said, "but lately I have been feeling my age, and I do not want you to be alone. So find a good man and be married. Raise a family. And though I know you are strong, none of us is immortal. And when you come to the end of your strength, my daughter, seek Adonai."

He rose from the workbench and leaned on his walking stick. "Give me a kiss and wish me a good night." He turned his cheek in my direction. "I will see you in the morning."

Forty-Two

FEBRUARIUS

Hadrian arrived late to his father's dinner, but the older man seemed not to mind. "Son," he said, extending an arm in welcome, "I was about to send a slave to search for you. How fares your work?"

Hadrian dropped onto his dining couch and propped his arm on the curved armrest. "Overseeing tax collectors is not my idea of work. I sit at the Forum, examine records, and gather coins. My belly is growing soft from inactivity."

"It is important work and necessary to the Empire." His father dropped an oyster into his mouth, swallowed, and tossed the shell onto the floor. "You cannot tell me you would rather run up and down stairs in Transtiberim. Nero did you a favor when he executed your prisoners."

"They were innocent people."

His father's jaw tensed. "You should not say that."

"Can I not be honest even with you?"

Cronus lowered his voice. "Must I remind you that slaves have ears?" He snapped his fingers to command the two slaves standing near the doorway and waved them away. When they had gone, he leaned closer to his son. "The nobility are unhappy."

"The plebs are content. They are enjoying Nero's games and the increased distribution of grain."

"But the patricians are paying for the emperor's largesse. He has taxed them to their limit, and they cannot—*Rome* cannot—continue in this way."

Hadrian met his father's gaze. "So what would you have me do? Return the tax revenue when no one is looking?"

Cronus glanced over his shoulder, then shook his head. "I am warning you to be careful. You have always been a free thinker, and I know you have latterly entertained certain unconventional ideas. I know you are friendly with others who hold the same beliefs. Your regular attendance at an *ecclesia* has been noted."

"Am I in trouble? Are my friends?"

"No—but I do not know how long I can dissuade further interest in your actions. The air in the Senate chamber grows hot, and I would not be surprised to see a firestorm erupt."

"You have spoken of such things before. What makes this time different?"

His father picked up another oyster. "I have a feeling—call it a premonition. The tension in the Senate chamber will soon be resolved . . . one way or another."

Hadrian had just crawled into bed when a servant pounded on his door. "Dominus! Your father needs you!"

He threw off the covers and ran to his father's chamber. The aedile lay on the bed, his chest supported by pillows, his eyes bulging. But half of his face had gone slack, and saliva dripped from a corner of his mouth.

Hadrian turned to his father's personal attendant. "Have you sent for the physician?"

"I did, Dominus. I sent two slaves in case one of the physicians could not come."

Hadrian sat on the edge of the bed and met his father's frightened gaze. "Father, can you hear me?"

One of the eyes blinked, and a trembling hand rose from the bedcover.

"Good." He caught his father's fingers. "I am glad to know you are still with us. Try to rest and we will see what the doctor has to say."

❖

The doctor shared many words and opinions, but none of them seemed adequate in the face of Cronus's sudden illness. Hadrian sat and listened as the physician reported that the brain was the seat of emotions and higher functions. "There are four humors in the body," the man explained, "phlegm, blood, yellow bile, and black bile. A man is healthy when the four humors are in balance, but as you can see, your father has experienced an imbalance. If balance is restored, health will be restored as well."

"What, exactly, is out of balance?" Hadrian asked.

"In this case"—the physician waved his hand over the affected half of the aedile's body—"we see an imbalance of blood. The body is weakened by thickened blood on one side."

"How did the blood become thick?"

The physician emitted a nervous laugh. "It is a complicated process involving the four cells of the brain. I do not expect you to understand."

Hadrian stared at his father, who seemed to stare at nothing. Or perhaps he stared at something no one else could see. "Will he recover?"

The physician pressed his hands together. "His fate rests in the hands of the gods."

But I knew better. My father's fate rested in the hands of only one God.

Forty-Three

MARTIUS

Once Nero's clay head had thoroughly dried, Father and I coated it in plaster, seamed it with brass strips, and let the plaster set until firm. When it had reached the desired hardness, we broke it open and chiseled the clay away. While Father oiled and smoothed the interior of the new plaster molds, I swept every last bit of Nero's head from our floor.

"We are nearing the end," Father announced. "We are ready for the wax."

The next day we fitted all the pieces of the cast together in sections and sealed them. Then we poured wax into each section. After giving the wax time to harden, we broke the plaster molds apart and fitted the resulting wax pieces together.

I gazed in wonder at our ten-foot wax statue. "Examine it carefully," Father told me, resting his hands atop his walking stick. "The wax is soft enough to carve, so if there are any fine details you want to add, now is the time."

I went over the piece carefully, wanting it to be perfect—not for Nero's sake, but for my father's. This would be the most famous of his works and would be seen by more people than all his other works combined. I wanted it to be far more detailed than anything produced by Zenodorus, and I wanted it to bring honor to its creator.

I ran the soft tip of a feather down the creases of the tunic, cleaning tiny pieces of wax from a pleat in the fabric. I pressed a ridged seashell into the sandal straps, creating a pattern similar to one I had once seen in expensive leather. I smoothed the skin on the legs, wanting them to appear polished. And on the eyes I used the hollow shaft of a feather to create an indentation for the pupil, so it would appear darker without the obvious use of paint.

Father usually purchased eyeballs from the ocularist, but perhaps, with paint and technique, we could make these eyes appear lifelike without the added expense.

When I was certain the statue was as perfect as I could make it, I asked Father to examine it again. He climbed a ladder and ran his fingers over the wax, sometimes nodding in approval, sometimes grunting, always guiding me to make subtle changes.

When we were both satisfied with the work, we covered the wax pieces with more clay and brass strips, repeating our earlier process. But this time, while the clay was still flexible, we inserted small brass tubes at certain junctures so that the wax, when heated, would have a way to escape.

Once again we carefully pulled the sections apart along the brass seams.

"Almost there," I whispered as I stared at the pieces of our greatest work.

"It has been a joy to work with you," Father said, extending his arms. I hugged him, happily breathing in the scents of sweat, dust, and beeswax.

"Tomorrow we will deliver the pieces to the foundry," Father said. "Then we can rest until the process is finished."

"How long will it be at the foundry?"

He blew out his breath. "They will dig a hole deep enough

to bury the molds, then cover them with wood. The fire will burn for days, the wax will run out through the tubes, then molten bronze will be poured into the new molds. They will leave everything in the ground until the bronze has cooled. It will take days, so do not be in a hurry. Then you must go to work again."

"Only me?" I gently poked him in the ribs. "Will you not be working as well?"

"My work is done," he said.

The next morning, I cut up some dried figs and set bread on a platter, then mixed a fresh pitcher of honey water. I heard a noise and turned, expecting to see Father, but it was only a cat that had crawled in through the open window.

Father had to be exhausted. He rarely slept past dawn, but the last few weeks had drained both of us. Fortunately, once we delivered the statue molds to the foundry we could sleep all day.

I ate some figs and bread, then dusted the pottery display. With the statue away from the workshop for a while, I could focus on our vases, dishes, bowls, and pitchers. I had ideas for new designs, and Father could teach me how to shape them on the wheel.

When the sun reached its peak and Father had not come out, I went to check on him. He was still abed, his thin frame covered with a sheet, but his skin was damp with perspiration. I touched his forehead and found it hot. Why had I not checked on him sooner? He needed water.

I grabbed a pitcher and hurried to the fountain, dodging merchants, beggars, litter-bearers, and a couple of vigiles intent on interrogating a slave. I filled the vessel as quickly as I could, then lugged it home.

I took a cup to Father's room and forced him to drink. After he took a few sips, I went into the shop and closed the counter window, but left the door unlocked in case someone came by.

Then I sat and surrendered to the nauseating sinking of despair. Oh, how I needed a friend! Someone to help, someone to fetch water, someone to tell me Father would soon be all right.

But Priscilla was gone, Hadrian had no reason to visit, and Euodia was busy with the children in her care. I wiped my tears away and went back to Father's room.

About an hour later, I heard movement in the shop. I left Father and found Aquila in the shop with Ivan and Chaim.

Aquila greeted me with a smile. "We were wondering if you had a small dish for children, something with ridges to keep foods from mixing. Chaim does not like his foods to touch one another."

I ignored his request and asked him to pray for my father. "He has fever," I said, struggling to keep the fear from my voice. "I am sure he will be better soon, but if you want to pray for him . . ."

Aquila's eyes darkened with concern. "I will ask Adonai to work His will in Pericles's life."

I turned to watch the boys. *Don't ask for Adonai's will*, I wanted to shout, *and promise you'll do something for him if he does something for you.* But Adonai did not operate like the Roman gods. Adonai demanded that his followers surrender everything to his control. My father had been willing to submit to the Jewish God's authority. So had Hadrian, Priscilla, Aquila, and all those who suffered and died in Nero's games. Yet I could not surrender so easily. If Adonai wanted me to follow him without holding back, surely he could heal my father first. Healing was a small thing for such a powerful God. After all, he healed me when Petros prayed. Petros was no longer with us, but Paulos was.

I whirled to face Aquila. "Can we take my father to the prison? I know the Mamertine is horrible, but—"

"It is no place for a sick man. But I will have Luke ask Paulos to pray for Pericles."

Fresh tears sprang to my eyes. "Tell him it is important that my father recovers. He is all I have in this world."

Aquila shook his head. "That is not true, Calandra. You have Euodia, Ariston, Petra, and so many friends."

"Please pray," I pleaded. "Now, if you will excuse me, I must tend to my father."

<hr />

For the next several days I vacillated between hope and despair. Father's fever would break and his shivering stop, but after a day or two his fever and chills would return, accompanied by a severe headache and coughing. He would breathe in quick, shallow gasps, his heart pounding. I could see his pulse in the veins of his throat, and even though I pressed my hand against his chest, his heart did not slow.

I sent for a physician, and Aquila and his friends prayed, yet Father did not improve. I left sacrifices of wine, honey, and a pigeon at the temple of Caesar, but the divine Caesar did not answer my prayers.

After nearly two weeks, I tiptoed into my father's chamber and saw that the light in his eyes had brightened. Was he better?

He must have heard me come into the room because he smiled. "Calandra."

I moved to his side, not wanting him to waste precious energy. "I am here, Father. What do you need?"

His face glowed in the flickering lamplight. "I need nothing . . . except to tell you farewell."

I sat on the edge of his mattress and took his hand. "What foolishness comes from your lips! This sickness will pass—did it not leave me after a few days? You are breathing better, and soon you will—"

"I am not afraid, daughter, and you should not fear either. Death is not our enemy; it is a journey to Adonai. I will soon stand before His Son, and I cannot think of anything more wonderful."

I covered my mouth and blinked back tears. Aquila and Ariston, who had recently visited, must have filled his head with these thoughts.

"You are *Roman*," I reminded him. "Let the Jews keep their God while you remain loyal to yours. After your last breath, you will meet Mercury, who will escort you across the River Styx. You will be judged according to your good deeds, which benefited many people. You will then be escorted to the Fields of Elysium—"

"No." He turned his head and coughed. Once he caught his breath, he settled back on his pillow. "The things I did to please men are worthless in the eyes of Adonai." His grip on my fingers tightened. "But my wrongs have been covered by the sacrifice of Adonai's Son, so I will stand guiltless before Him. I will wait until . . ." Another fit of coughing seized him. When he had finished, he inhaled a wheezing breath. "I entrust you . . . to our friends . . . and to our Lord," he said, his voice fading.

Then, while I waited for him to continue, his face brightened, and his eyes widened.

"I see them!" His voice echoed with wonder. "Like lights descending from above."

"You can see?" Tears stung my eyes as I clasped his hand. "Can you see *me*, Father? Can you see how much I want you to stay?"

He was not looking at me; his eyes were fixed on something beyond my field of vision. At the sight of someone—who, I could not imagine—he smiled. "I will," he murmured, the words rising from cracked lips, "I will follow."

His chest rose and fell, then the light in his eyes winked out.

I waited, his hand in mine, to see if his soul would return, but it did not.

❖

I do not know how long I sat by Father's side, but his body was cold when I finally left his bedchamber. With stiff strides I went into the front room, took my palla from its hook, and walked to the tentmaker's shop. There I found Euodia, Ariston, Aquila, and Petra. They must have been praying because their faces lit with expectation when I walked through the doorway.

"My father has died," I said, my words flat and final. "Your prayers accomplished nothing."

Euodia rose and pulled me into her arms.

"Not nothing," Ariston said, coming to stand beside his wife. "Adonai has always had a plan for your father."

"Was it Adonai's plan to leave me fatherless?" I wanted to glare at Ariston but could not summon the energy for anger. "Your God has left me alone. Why would he do that?"

"I am so sorry," Euodia said, stroking my hair. "But you do not need to fear. I will send Petra to help you manage your shop."

I shook my head. "You need Petra to sell your purple."

"I can hire someone else," Euodia said, "but you need someone you can trust. Petra will remain in my employment, of course, but let her spend a few months with you. I would feel better knowing you are not alone, and Petra enjoys your company."

I looked at Petra, who was openly eavesdropping behind her mistress. I had relied on her during my pregnancy, so bringing her into the shop would awaken all kinds of painful memories. But what choice did I have?

"Do you want to work with me?" I asked. "Working at my shop is not as easy as selling purple."

A smile crossed Petra's face. "I like the Aventine, and I would enjoy serving you again." She lowered her voice. "As long as you do not plan to have another baby. *That* day was not easy."

I closed my eyes, remembering how Petra had knelt on the floor behind me, letting me claw her arms as I strained to deliver the child. I caught a breath, about to ask the question that had floated at the top of my thoughts for three years, then changed my mind. I would not ask about the baby; I would not think of him. Like a woman who carries a feather pillow to the top of a mountain and opens the seam, my child was irretrievable.

"Thank you," I said. "When you are ready, I would appreciate your company."

Euodia and Ariston pulled on their cloaks and walked me home. We viewed the body, then Ariston nodded. "I will take care of the funeral. Do you have a family tomb?"

I had not visited the place in years, but I knew the location. "Yes—my mother's ashes are there."

"Good. Euodia will help you prepare him, and I will return in a few hours."

I had never prepared anyone for a funeral, but from the sorrow in Euodia's eyes, I knew she had. She pulled the sheet from my father's frame, then turned to the pitcher and basin on his table.

"We will wash him and straighten his limbs," she said, dipping a towel into the water. "We will close his eyes and anoint him with oils. We will dress him in his finest tunic, and when Ariston brings the funeral couch, we will place your father on it. Then we will carry him to his rest."

Following Euodia's lead, I washed the legs that had guided me through city streets, the arms that had balanced me as I learned to walk, the hands that had taught me how to work the clay. I closed his sightless eyes and lifted the back of his head so his mouth would remain shut.

"Who—" my throat tightened—"did you lose?"

Euodia sighed. "My husband and daughter. Years ago, before I moved to Philippi. With them gone I felt like a petal drifting on the surface of a pool."

I nodded, grateful that she had put my feelings into words. "I have no one—" I began, but she cut me off.

"You have *us*," she said, her voice firm. "During the fire, do you think you walked into the tentmaker's shop by accident? Adonai guided you to Aquila and Priscilla. Your father became a believer as a result, and you acquired friends. You are not alone."

Her words were a balm to my wounded heart, but my grief was a long way from healing.

"Now." She dropped the wet towel onto the floor. "What should he wear?"

I opened his trunk and immediately saw the red tunic with green embroidery on the sleeves. He had worn it to our dinner at Cronus's house and through the long days of the fire. It was no longer fine, and I could not believe he had kept it. He always said he would replace it as soon as we finished the statue for Cronus.

I picked up the tunic, pressed it to my face, and breathed in the scent of the father I loved. "He should wear this."

The message from Aquila arrived as Hadrian finished his work for the day. He read the letter, dismissed the scribe who had been recording the day's tax deposits, and went immediately home.

He could not believe he and Calendra were losing their fathers. Aquila's letter said that Pericles died quickly, in his sleep, which seemed far better than the death by degrees affecting his own father. Yet both were old men, and both had borne a great deal of stress in preceding months.

He stopped in the vestibule to inquire about his father's health. "Your father is the same, Dominus," the doorkeeper told him. "And yes, the physician has been to see him. Nothing has changed."

"Is he eating?"

"I do not believe so."

Hadrian went immediately to his father's chamber. Cronus lay in bed, propped up on pillows, a female slave at his side. The slave held a bowl of gruel, which she attempted to hold to the aedile's lips.

Hadrian jerked his chin toward his father. "Any success?"

"No, Dominus."

"Has he spoken today? Attempted to speak?"

"I am sorry, Dominus."

Hadrian peered into his father's brown eyes, hoping to spot a glimmer of recognition. "Father? The physician wants you to eat. You must eat to stay alive."

One eye blinked. Drool dangled from the corner of his mouth.

Hadrian sat on the bed and took his father's hand. "Father," he said, searching for signs of recognition, "I have become a Christian. I suspect you have known this for some time, but I tell you now because Christians have no fear of death. You watched them in the arena, so you know I speak the truth. Yes, they suffer as all people do, but they are confident of living beyond the grave."

Hadrian smiled when one eye blinked. "I tell you this because I suspect you may be near death, and I do not want you to be anxious. Yeshua, the one they call Christ, was crucified but came out of the tomb alive. He wields power over the grave and shares His victory with all who follow Him."

He glanced at the slave, who had bowed her head and backed away from the bed. But she was listening.

319

He bent closer to his father's ear. "I want you to live, Father. But if you cannot summon the strength, I want you to live after death in the victory Yeshua offers. Believe in Him, trust Him to save you. That is all He asks."

He waited, listening for any change in the sound of his father's breathing, but heard nothing. But when he lifted his head, he saw that his father was blinking, his eyelids rising again and again and again . . .

It was an answer. Perhaps the best Hadrian could hope for. He stood and said to the slave, "Keep trying to feed him. Preserve his dignity. I shall return this afternoon."

He went to his bedchamber, pulled off his white toga, and handed it to a slave. Then he opened his trunk and pulled out his *toga pulla*, the dark garment worn for somber occasions.

When death came for his father, Hadrian's life would not be greatly changed. He would step into his father's position, take possession of his father's house, and become the master of his father's slaves.

But what of Calendra? Her father was gone, and she had no protector, no paterfamilias, no property other than that which her father left in the workshop. That property was rented from a landlord, who might not be inclined to rent to an unmarried woman with uncertain prospects.

Troubled by these concerns, he left the house and followed the winding streets to the southernmost gate of the city. He had things to do, but he did not want to be late for Pericles's funeral.

❖

As Ariston, Aquila, and others from the ecclesia carried my father's funeral couch, I followed, my sense of loss beyond tears. A crier led our procession, calling, "Pericles Aemilius Claudus has surrendered to death. For those who find it convenient, it is time to attend the funeral."

Hired musicians would ordinarily accompany the crier, but I had no money to hire them. So my father's funeral couch followed instead, where he lay dressed in his soot-stained tunic and surrounded by a surprising number of flowers. I gasped when I saw the great quantity of blossoms, but Euodia squeezed my arm and said an anonymous friend had provided them.

We had just passed the tanner's shop when I spotted Hadrian. He stood in the crowd of onlookers and acknowledged me with a nod, then he joined the procession, walking with his hands behind his back and his head bowed. He had, I realized, honestly respected my father. And though they were very different men, they had both found reasons to abandon the Roman gods in favor of Adonai.

We walked through the Aventine's winding streets until we passed the city walls, then we followed the Via Ostiensis past dozens of tombs with stately porticoes and decorative columns. When the crier reached the point I had indicated, he turned and led the procession to our modest family tomb. The rectangular structure had no portico or columns and would be just spacious enough to hold my father's funeral couch.

The men lowered the body to the ground outside the door as Aquila turned to face the mourners. "We have gathered to honor our brother, who has gone to be with his Savior," he said, his eyes solemn and serene. "Pericles was a loving father to Calandra, a friend to those of us in the ecclesia, and an artist to the patricians who hired him to grace their homes with beauty. But our Lord loved Pericles and chose him before the foundation of the world to be holy and blameless before Him.

"As our brother Paulos wrote to the believers in Corinth, 'We are always confident and know that while we are at home in the body, we are absent from the Lord. Yet we prefer rather to be absent from the body and at home with the Lord.' Which is where our friend Pericles is now."

Then Aquila prayed, commending my father's spirit to Adonai. When he finished, I waited for the people around me to weep and wail, as was customary. Instead, with joyous smiles they began to sing:

> "Blessed is one whose strength is in You,
>   in whose heart are the pilgrim roads.
> Passing through the valley of weeping,
>   they make it a spring.
> The early rain covers it with blessings.
> They go from strength to strength—
>   every one of them appears before God in Zion."

As they sang of going from strength to strength, a glimmer of understanding pierced my shroud of sorrow. We had experienced so much loss in the last few months. Nero's persecution had devoured far too many people we loved.

But the people with me had not despaired at the thought of death and neither had their loved ones. If anything, those deaths had strengthened the faith and fervor of those who remained behind.

Could my father's death do the same for me?

Forty-Four

I was not surprised to see Hadrian the next day. "I know we need to talk about the commission," I said, skipping the usual greeting as he entered the shop. "Your father may not want to continue now that my father is gone, but I cannot afford to repay the advances he has given us."

Hadrian frowned. "I would not discuss payment while you are in mourning."

"Why, then, have you come?"

"My father is also ill," he said, his mouth twisting. "The physician does not think he will recover."

I winced. "I am sorry. I had not heard."

"You have had other things on your mind." He gestured to the stools at my workbench, so we sat. "The statue is nearly complete, correct? You are ready to cast the bronze?"

"The pieces are ready to be delivered to the foundry."

"I want you to continue." He rapped the table. "If anyone asks, we will say—truthfully—that your father completed most of the work before he died. The statue will be credited to Pericles Aemillus Claudus."

"Thank you. It should be finished within a few months. At the end of summer, perhaps."

"Excellent." Hadrian clasped his hands. "Even if my father

is no longer with us, I will honor the terms of our contract. But . . ." He hesitated.

"What is it?"

"I am confident of your ability . . . I am not confident of Nero."

"What do you mean?"

"Julius Vindex, one of the provincial governors, has refused to pay the new taxes. Nero sent legionaries to convince him to do so, but Vindex has persuaded other governors to join his revolt. The Senate fears the rebellion may be too widespread to overcome."

"Do you think Nero will fall?"

"In the past, rebels have been quickly discovered and executed. But the governors are out of Nero's reach, and time is on their side. They can prepare to defend themselves before Nero even hears of trouble." He lowered his voice. "I recently learned that Flavius Sabinus has turned against Nero . . . because of Poppaea."

I had heard about the death of Nero's wife, yet no one seemed to know the details. "Why would the city prefect be upset about the emperor's wife? Was Sabinus in love with her?"

"Apparently he saw Nero kick the woman to death."

I closed my eyes as memories of my pregnancy flooded over me. I spent those days in an almost constant state of anxiety, but at least I was not married to a man like Nero. His cruelty to his wife, coupled with the executions of so many Christians . . .

"He is a monster," I whispered. "I do not understand how the people can cheer him."

"They do not know him," Hadrian said. "They cheer him because he lavishes the Roman treasury on games and public parks around his Golden House. The people say the palace reflects Nero's glory, but senators and patricians know that house reflects nothing so much as Nero's madness. Some predict he will not be emperor at the end of the year."

I absorbed the startling news in silence, then looked at the tools scattered around the workshop. "If that is so, what will you do with a statue of a despicable brute?"

"I want you to keep working," Hadrian said, and when I glimpsed the warmth in his eyes, I experienced an epiphany. He wanted me to keep working because he wanted to support me. The compassion he had always exhibited toward my father was now offered to me.

Or had his concern been for me all along?

❖

Before sunrise the next morning, I rented a cart and loaded it with a few bronze ingots and plaster molds. Petra closed the workshop, then we pushed the cart to the foundry near the city gate.

Fausto, the soft-bellied owner, looked up when I lowered the cart handles and wiped sweat from my eyelids. "I am bringing bronze ingots and molds to be poured."

His eyes tightened in a squint. "You are Pericles's daughter, no?"

"I am."

The man chuckled. "Have not seen him in a while. He has you doing the heavy work?"

"My father has died. Now I must finish his work."

Fausto's face creased in unspoken apology as he approached the cart. "Quite a load. A statue, is it?"

"Yes, and this is only the first load. We will be back with more."

"How tall?"

"Ten feet."

He whistled. "That should earn you a bagful of sestertii."

"Perhaps. If the client approves."

Fausto called for slaves and told them to unload the wagon.

"I will pour in two days," he said. "I will send a slave to let you know when the pieces are ready."

"Could you deliver them?"

"Will you pay extra?"

I weighed the work against the number of coins in my purse. "Yes."

Fausto shrugged. "Then I will deliver them. Should I crack the molds?"

I hesitated. Allowing Fausto's men to remove the plaster meant risking damage to the bronze beneath it, but I was less skilled than they were.

"Yes," I told him. "Remove the molds and deliver only the bronze."

I thanked him as Petra picked up the handles of the cart. I turned when a sudden thought entered my head. "Fausto?"

"You forget something?"

"How do you feel about the emperor?"

His brows rose. "Why do my feelings matter? Nero is going to do what he's going to do, is he not?"

I gave him a rueful smile and joined Petra at the cart.

Forty-Five

MAIUS

On a warm afternoon, two months after I had taken the molds to the foundry, Fausto delivered the sections of our bronze statue. My satisfaction at seeing the pieces in our workshop was dimmed only by the overwhelming regret that my father was not able to see this stage of the process.

I ran my fingers over the details of the sandals and felt the creases in the tunic that covered the torso. The legs were thinner than I remembered, but Nero had always been more inclined to the arts than athletics. The bust was well-made, the neck slender and smooth, the shoulders of medium width, the arms well-formed. I had designed the figure to hold a scroll, hoping it would appeal to Nero's love of the theater, and the scroll had come out amazingly well, the center page as thin as I had hoped it would be.

The upper section was so realistic I did not want to look at it. Every time my gaze crossed the oversized head, my stomach twisted. So I found a long square of linen and covered the piece, resolving to look at it only when necessary.

I examined the remaining sections for dents or scratches from the foundry workers' tools and found none. So all that remained was for me to remove the brass tubes we had attached to drain the wax. I would smooth the bronze that had supported the tubes, then polish and apply a patina. For the final step, I would hire freedmen to assemble the sections and fasten them together with bolts.

Filled with a sense of accomplishment, I told Petra to close the shop and pull on her palla. We were going to visit friends.

As we set out, for the first time I felt as though I might actually cross the finish line. In a few weeks I would deliver the statue to Hadrian, who would give it to Nero in his dying father's name. The emperor, Hadrian had recently assured me, had solidified his position. The imperial forces, led by Virginius Rufus, had defeated the rebellious governor Vindex. Even though Virginius's men had attempted to proclaim *him* emperor, Nero still held the reins of power.

The thought of Hadrian being in close contact with Nero was enough to pebble my skin, but I needed the tyrant to survive until I finished the statue. With the final payment of one million sestertii, I could keep the shop open and buy supplies. I was not sure what I would create next, but the possibilities seemed endless.

I pushed thoughts of Nero out of my mind as we walked toward the river. I had packed two baskets with decorative bowls for Euodia, knowing how she loved to entertain. But when we arrived at Aquila's shop, the door was locked, as was the front window. This was not a festival day or Shabbat, so I could not think of any reason for the shop to be closed.

A cold hand passed down my spine. "Could someone be sick?" I asked. But Aquila would not close the shop for illness.

Petra knocked, and we waited. A moment later, young Ivan opened the door. I looked past him and saw Ariston, Euodia, Salama, and Aquila sitting at a table with several other believers.

"Should we come back?" I called.

Euodia came to greet us, yet her smile seemed forced. "Come in," she said, planting a kiss on our cheeks as we entered. "Forgive us for not being more welcoming, but we have just received sad news."

My uneasiness swelled into alarm. "Has someone been arrested?"

"It's Paulos," Aquila said. "The Romans executed him. Luke"—he pointed to the man sitting next to him—"brought us the news."

I studied the bearded stranger sitting next to Aquila. I had heard about the Greek physician but had never met him. "When?" I asked.

Luke's dark eyes met mine. "This morning," he said, his deep voice cracking with weariness. "I met him at the Mamertine and was almost too late to say goodbye."

Aquila exhaled a heavy sigh. "Did he say anything?"

"He gave me a copy of a letter he had written to Timothy and said I should read it as he was led to the executioner. I think he wanted the guards to hear it."

"Would you?" Euodia asked. "I would like to hear what he wrote."

Luke pulled the letter from his tunic, unfolded the papyrus, and began to read: "'For I am already being poured out like a drink offering, and the time of my departure has come. I have fought the good fight, I have finished the course, I have kept the faith. In the future there is reserved for me a crown of righteousness, which the Lord, the righteous Judge, will award to me on that day—and not to me only, but to everyone who has longed for His appearing. The Lord be with your spirit. Grace be with you.'"

I sat with the weeping believers, brokenhearted and amazed at the faithfulness of the aged rabbi. I had seen him only once, but his earnestness, zeal, and bravery deeply impressed me.

329

❖

Hadrian found his father's scribe waiting in the vestibule. "Dominus." The slave lowered himself to the floor. "I have unfortunate news."

Hadrian did not need further details. Cronus had dangled between the worlds of the living and the dead for days. "My father is gone?"

The slave raised his head, his face a mask of perfect seriousness. "You are now the master."

Though Hadrian had been preparing for the inevitable, the confirmation sent his heart into his throat. He swallowed hard, then walked to his father's bedchamber, where several torches burned.

Lucius Cronus Tuscus lay covered in a purple quilt, a plain linen tunic visible above the fold. His face, half of which had been slack for several months, was uniformly relaxed. Someone, probably a slave, had closed his eyes and combed his few remaining hairs over the top of his bare head.

He was gone, and in the silence Hadrian keenly felt his absence . . . and the looming responsibility he had left behind. Hadrian was now a senator and would serve as an aedile until the time of election. If he paid even scant attention to his duties and scattered a few sestertii among the common people, the position would undoubtably remain his. But did he want it? Did he want to live his father's life?

He waved at the two slaves keeping vigil. "Leave me." When they closed the door behind them, he gripped the rail at the foot of his father's bed.

"Thank you," he said, bowing his head. "For supporting me in all things. For demonstrating the best of Roman virtues— loyalty, honor, and strength. But though you have left behind a good name and enviable wealth, I cannot live the life you intended for me. I am not the man I used to be, and my life is no longer my own."

Hadrian moved to the side of the bed and studied his father's patrician profile. "Rome is no longer the Empire of Augustus and Caesar, and I cannot change it from a senator's seat. My road lies not in the Senate, but in the world. I want to be like Petros, like Paulos. I want to travel and spread the story of Adonai and His Son."

He stopped, half afraid his father's head would rise from its pillows in protest.

"After the period of mourning," he continued, his voice cracking, "I will write a letter to the emperor and tell him I plan to vacate your Senate seat. Then I will leave Rome with Yeshua Messiah as my one and only God and King. I hope you will understand, and I hope I will see you when I enter the life beyond this one."

He leaned forward, pressed a kiss to his father's cool brow, and straightened. Then he squared his shoulders and went outside to summon the proper officiants.

Forty-Six

THE 9TH DAY OF IUNIUS

For more than a month I sat at a worktable with three freedmen, a portion of the statue before us. Each of us held bits of dried fish skin, which we used to smooth the spots from the brass tubes. The work was tedious and slow, but necessary.

When we were finished with the smoothing and polishing, we would construct the statue by joining the pieces with rivets. Hired freemen would also do this work because I lacked the required skills. But I would ask them to teach me so I would be prepared for my next commission.

"Petra," I called, "is there more fish skin?"

Petra, who had been dusting the pottery, gasped when someone opened the door. I looked up and saw Hadrian standing in the doorway, his face drawn and pale.

For an instant I thought of his father, but then I remembered that Cronus had already been cremated.

I walked toward him. "Hadrian?"

He grabbed my hands and pulled me into a corner, as far from the others as he could manage.

Premonition lifted the hairs at the back of my neck. "What has happened?"

He pulled me close and whispered, his breath tickling my ear. "The emperor is dead."

The news hit me like a slap. If the emperor was dead, why had Father and I spent years working on his statue?

"Are you certain?"

"A few days ago, Nero tried to flee the city, hoping to find shelter in a loyal province. But when the army officers refused his command to accompany him, he returned to his house, but woke in the middle of the night and found that all his guards had deserted him. He called for a gladiator to kill him, but no one came."

I sorted through my racing thoughts. "He knew he was in trouble."

"Of course." Hadrian rose and sat beside me. "At that point he disguised himself and left the palace with Sporus—"

"Who?"

"The boy Nero married. Nero and Sporus left the palace with three freedmen. The next morning Nero learned that the Senate had declared him a public enemy and ordered his arrest. Ever the coward, Nero commanded his secretary to kill him."

"Did he?"

Hadrian shook his head. "It is unclear how the monster died, but when riders from the Senate found him, he was past saving. His final words were, 'Too late! This is fidelity.'"

I covered my mouth, paralyzed by shock. Nero had possessed everything a man could desire—wealth, power, and status, yet he had nothing when he died. How swiftly the man had fallen!

"Soon everyone in the city will know," Hadrian said. "Because he did not leave an heir, men will struggle for power. The days ahead will be tumultuous."

I absorbed the news in silence, then lifted my head. "What should I do? I have a nearly completed statue no one will want."

Hadrian took my hand, compassion stirring in his eyes. "I

will pay you what you are owed. As to the statue, sell it, melt it, or destroy it. The decision is yours alone."

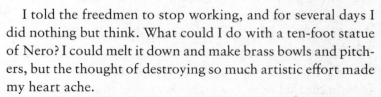

I told the freedmen to stop working, and for several days I did nothing but think. What could I do with a ten-foot statue of Nero? I could melt it down and make brass bowls and pitchers, but the thought of destroying so much artistic effort made my heart ache.

Hadrian was correct—once word of Nero's death reached the city, the streets filled with people. The patricians rejoiced, openly celebrating the tyrant's passing. But the plebeians, who had enjoyed his theatrical events and games, genuinely mourned his loss.

I was not surprised to hear of brawls in the streets. Some hurried to deface Nero's monuments while others bravely defended them. One night Hadrian told us that a portrait on a wall in the Forum had been reworked. Someone had painted over Nero's face, replacing it with a likeness of Servius Sulpicius Galba, the first man to claim Nero's position.

That rebellious painter's act inspired me. Why should I destroy the statue when I could simply rework the statue's head?

Two days later, I sat and stared at Nero's bronze head in despair. This was the last work my father had touched, and I wanted to honor him by creating something memorable and beautiful.

But how could I do that? If I reworked the head, who should the statue depict? Not Galba, who had already stained his reputation by killing everyone who had been friendly with Nero. I considered honoring Hadrian's father by replacing Nero's face with Cronus's, but my father had already sculpted a statue of the aedile, so why create another? Furthermore, the body of the statue had been designed to represent a free spirit, not a staid politician. The torso was clothed in a simple tunic, and no senator would dare be seen in public without his purple-striped toga.

I considered the problem for days, my indecision compounded by increasing frustration and grief. Petra had relieved me of my daily chores, but I missed my father desperately. If he were here, he would have cured this painful inertia by giving me a direct answer.

One night, overcome by melancholy, I went to my room, lit a lamp, and sat on the floor. I had not been able to part with Father's belongings. His tools were still in the workshop, his papyri still littered the desk, and when Petra moved into his room, I put his clothes in my trunk.

I wiped away a solitary tear, then opened the lid and took out one of his tunics. When I heard the sound of something striking the wooden interior, I lifted Father's mantle and saw the half coin Petra had given me after the birth of my baby.

I dropped the mantle and turned away. I ought to get rid of the coin, my father's clothes, and everything attached to a painful memory, but I could not. Not yet.

I rubbed Father's tunic against my cheek. How many times had this garment caressed me? Each time I hugged him, each time he leaned in to observe my work, each time I hovered at his shoulder, bending to see the deft progress of his fingers in the clay.

I shook the garment, intending to properly put it away, but my attention was distracted when a sealed letter fell from a fold. I picked it up and saw that it had been addressed to me . . . in Priscilla's handwriting.

A memory, long repressed, bubbled to the surface. Priscilla had sent this letter a few days after my baby's birth. I had not wanted to read it then, but on that dark night I would have given anything to hear her voice. I broke the seal.

Priscilla, wife of Aquila and servant of Yeshua the Messiah:

My dearest Calandra, you have been ever-present in my thoughts these last few days. I would have come to see you, but circumstances prohibited me from leaving the shop. Yet I have been praying for you.

What brought us together when we met? I believe the Spirit of Yeshua knew we would need each other, so Adonai decided we should be friends. I have watched you grow during these past few months, and I am convinced that the Spirit of Adonai is working in your heart and mind. He loves you, dear one, and so do I. Yet Adonai loved you before the creation of the world, before men created gods to take Adonai's rightful place. You are indescribably dear to Him. You may feel alone, but Adonai knows you completely and has counted every one of your tears.

When you are tempted to dwell on your sorrows, consider the boundless love of Adonai instead. He has given you life, a loving father, many friends, and a man who loves you. And yes, I speak of Hadrian, who has demonstrated that he loves you more than he loves himself.

Trust Adonai, dear one. Surrender your life, with all its attendant sorrows to Him, and watch as He transforms it.

Her words, written years before, pricked my heart. I dropped the papyrus and covered my face as hot tears of regret burned my fingers.

Forty-Seven

The golden gleam of torchlight crept through the cracks around my door and roused me from sleep. I heard the soft sound of Petra's footsteps and the lively little tune she always hummed in the morning.

I was lying on the floor, my cheek pillowed by Father's tunic, my head crowded with a hundred different thoughts after reading Priscilla's letter. After years of resisting the gentle pull of Adonai's Spirit, I had come to the end of my strength and surrendered. Father realized the truth after experiencing the love of those who cared for us during the great fire. Hadrian realized it after seeing Adonai's healing power. I realized it only after a long and protracted struggle in which I flung every possible objection at the irresistible and unchanging reality of Yeshua's love.

Had I not prayed to Him when I had to let Petra take my baby away? Had I not entrusted my father into His hands? I had unknowingly depended on Him without acknowledging His care, behaving like a stubborn child who refused to admit she needed help.

After realizing that every good and perfect thing in my life had come from the hands and hearts of those who followed the only true God, I had lifted my face to heaven and acknowledged the One who had been steadfastly pursuing me. "Yes, Adonai. I *believe*, and I surrender. You are the only true God, and from this day forward I will follow your Son."

I sat up, blinked until my eyes focused, and looked around. Priscilla's letter lay on the floor atop my father's tunic. I picked up the letter and smoothed the crinkled papyrus, then placed it in my trunk.

I *would* finish the statue, and soon. Because I had awakened with an inspired idea of who it should represent.

❖

I worked all day, sculpting the new head from memory. It was a beloved face, one I knew well, but several times I had to stop, close my eyes, and revisit a memory. How far apart were the eyes? How pronounced was the curve of the jawline? And the beard—how should I sculpt the beard?

Petra noted my deep concentration and silently took care of the daily chores—fetching water, handling customers at the window, dusting the pottery wares. At midday she brought me a glass of honey water and a plate of cheese and fruit. I thanked her and continued working, eating only after I stopped to wash the clay from my hands.

By the time the sun dropped in the west, I had finished the clay model. I smoothed the last line and covered the head with a damp cloth, then blew out the lamp.

Someone knocked on the door, and Petra went to open it. I turned to see Euodia, Ariston, Aquila, and Hadrian.

"We are concerned about you," Euodia said, walking toward me with a no-nonsense light in her eyes. "Petra said you have not been eating properly."

I pointed to the empty plate on the worktable. "I am eating."

Euodia regarded me, then turned to Hadrian. "She *does* appear better."

He folded his arms and grunted.

Aquila nodded. "She does not seem as melancholy as before. Something has happened."

Hadrian leaned forward. "What would that something be?"

I gave him a measured smile. "I found an answer to my problem," I said, wiping my damp hands on a towel. "And I have made a new head for the statue."

"I thought you had already—"

"Nero is no more," I said. "This statue will represent someone others *want* to remember."

Hadrian stepped toward the worktable. "May I?"

I moved out of his way. "It is your commission."

He lifted the cloth from the head. All four of my visitors stared at it, then Euodia sighed. "You could not have chosen better!"

Tears glinted in Aquila's eyes. "He would be humbled by this. As for the rest of us"—he pressed a hand to his chest— "we are delighted."

"A wise choice," Hadrian said, his eyes glowing. "His face will remind everyone of what Yeshua said and did throughout his life."

My heart warmed at his words. "Your father paid for this work, so you own it. What will you do with it?"

Hadrian smiled. "When the piece is assembled, I will make sure the statue is seen by as many people as possible. Better to have him remembered this way than hanging upside down on a cross."

My heart swelled with quiet joy. "I only hope Yeshua is as pleased by my effort as you are."

Euodia caught her breath. "Did you say *Yeshua*?"

I ducked my chin and smiled. "Last night I went in search of comfort and found a letter from Priscilla. In it she urged me to believe in Yeshua. I finally decided to follow her advice."

I turned, not to Euodia, Aquila, or Ariston, but to the statue. The loving, confident expression on Petros's clay face—an expression I had seen before—assured me I had made the right choice.

❖

Euodia, Ariston, and Aquila left at sunset, while Hadrian remained. Petra set out a platter of cheese, boiled eggs, and bread, then discreetly retired to her bedchamber.

"So," Hadrian said, his eyes dark and contemplative in the lamplight, "what will you do now that you have almost finished the statue? Are you set on creating other sculptures?"

I sighed, too weary to consider the future. "I still have to pour the wax mold for the head. Eventually the bronze will have to be poured, smoothed, and fitted to the body."

"That should not take so long." Hadrian popped a bit of cheese into his mouth. "I am thinking of the years ahead. Now that your father is gone, what will you do with your life?"

My smile faded. "What *can* I do, other than what I am doing?"

"Do you intend to pay the marriage tax every year?"

I scowled. "Do *you*?"

"I have a suggestion." His eyes probed mine. "Since I am now paterfamilias of my family, I believe you should marry me at the earliest opportunity."

Amazed, I sat and listened to the heavy thump of my heartbeat. For so many nights I had dreamed of this moment, all the while knowing it was impossible.

"We are not equals," I finally said. "You would be criticized for marrying beneath your station."

"Who would criticize me for marrying a brilliant sculptor?"

"Now you are mocking me."

"I have never been more serious." He reached across the

340

table and caught my mud-stained hands. "In case you have not noticed, you have become precious to me—so precious that I cannot imagine life apart from you. So precious that if you refuse to marry me, I will haunt your door day and night, irritating your neighbors and frightening the rats away."

I studied his face. A flush of excitement had colored his cheeks, and his eyes glowed with sincerity. He believed the things he was saying . . . but no one else would.

"Ridding the building of rats would be a good thing. Our marriage? Definitely not."

"Why would you say that?"

"You are a senator of Rome. You are a patrician. You are acting as an aedile, and you will soon be working with the emperor. I am no one."

"To me you are the most important person in the world."

"That is . . . unfortunate."

"Calandra." He cupped my hands, as if doing so could bind us together. "I am no longer a senator. I am no longer an ae-dile. I have already written to the emperor and resigned both positions. I am a servant to Yeshua my Lord, and I want to be a husband to you."

I stared at him, stunned into silence.

"Marry me," he said, his grip tightening. "Tomorrow or next week, whenever you prefer. Aquila has already said he would say the necessary words and pronounce a blessing."

My thoughts darkened at the mention of Aquila's name. Priscilla had kept nothing from her husband, so Aquila had to know about the child I had abandoned. He also knew I betrayed his wife, so how could he agree to marry me to Hadrian, a man he admired?

Shame burned my cheeks. "I cannot marry you."

"You have *other* reasons?"

"I cannot marry you because I bore your child and sent it

away, knowing you could never claim it. I do not know what happened to the boy or even if he still lives, so I will understand if you cannot forgive me—I have not been able to forgive myself. I thought Aquila knew about it, but perhaps he has forgotten. Because he would never agree to marry us, knowing what I have done. Not only did I abandon our child, but I named Priscilla to the Praetorians."

Hadrian's grip on my hands relaxed. "Answer me this," he said. "Do you truly believe Adonai is the only God worth serving?"

Tears blurred my vision. "I do. No other God could have given my father peace with his blindness. No other God could have given Priscilla and Mariana the strength to stand boldly in the arena."

"I have seen barbarians die with courage," Hadrian said. "But what I have seen only in Christians is the strength to forgive heinous wrongs. Aquila holds nothing against you for naming Priscilla. And about our child . . . I forgave you long ago."

Surprise stole my voice. He knew?

He leaned forward, his finger rising to tenderly trace the line of my cheekbone and jawline. "As regarding *us*," he continued, "what did Paulos say? 'In Yeshua, we are neither Jews nor Greeks nor slaves.' I think he would also say we are neither patricians nor merchants, but we are all one in Yeshua. Marry me. Tomorrow." He grasped my hands again. "At the tenth hour, meet me at Aquila's shop, and I will marry you without reservation. But be warned—in the future I will obey the Spirit of Adonai, even if that leads me away from Rome. If you are resolved to stay here and make statues for Roman patricians . . ."

He was willing to leave Rome? I studied his face. I saw no evidence of guile, no deceit, nothing that would cause me to doubt him.

"I have never aspired to be the wife of a senator," I said. "I rarely thought of marriage at all. But whenever dreams of a man filled my head, the man was always you."

"Does this mean—?"

"Yes. Yes, I will marry you."

Before he could say anything else, I tipped my face toward the ceiling. "Adonai," I whispered, hoping my voice would reach heaven, "will you give my father this news? I am to marry this excellent man on the morrow."

Laughter floated up from Hadrian's throat as he leaned across the worktable, cupped my chin, and soundly kissed me.

Forty-Eight

Petra woke me at sunrise, a broad smile on her face. "Let me help you dress," she said, opening my trunk. "Do you have an orange veil?"

I sat up and rubbed the sleep from my eyes. "Why would I have an orange veil? I never expected to marry."

"It matters not. Euodia will have something for your head. Here is a clean tunic with pretty embroidery. What do you think? Will it do for your wedding?"

I blinked, amazed that she had already heard the news. Then again, last night she could have stood behind the curtain and eavesdropped. "That tunic will suit," I said, throwing off the bed linens. "But first we need water."

"Of course." Petra smiled. "We must scrub the clay from beneath your fingernails. Your neck could use a thorough washing, too."

I sighed, pretending resignation, but my heart had already begun to pound in anticipation. Long ago I dreamed of marrying Hadrian, but I held no real hope for marriage. My feelings for him had not abated, but I had forced myself to recast him as a friend, not a potential husband.

My friend Hadrian never disappointed me. Would he be as dependable as a husband?

At the tenth hour, Petra and I threaded our way through the crowds and finally crossed the footbridge. The streets of Transtiberim were busier than those in the Aventine, but Shabbat was approaching. The Jews were rushing to complete their chores before sunset.

We were breathless and perspiring by the time we reached Aquila's shop. The window had been closed, but someone—probably Euodia—had decorated the doorway with flowers. As we approached, Aquila stepped out. "Welcome!" he called. "The groom was beginning to wonder if you had forgotten."

I walked inside and took a quick breath. The displays and goatskin samples had been moved aside to create an open space in the shop. Benches lined the area while Aquila stood in the center. Dozens of people had joined him, some familiar and some not. I saw Euodia and Ariston, Fausto, Salama, and several people I met while visiting Priscilla. Some of the guests were patricians, some freedmen, and some slaves. Mariana's two boys, the youngest guests, stood between Ariston and Euodia.

Euodia came forward with a circlet of flowers and gently placed it on my head. "Blossoms for the bride," she said, her eyes shining. "May every day be as joyful as this one."

I drew a slow breath to calm my heart and turned toward Hadrian, whose gaze I had been too shy to seek. An unexpected, eager look flashed in his eyes, then he extended his hand.

I stepped forward to marry the only man I had ever wanted. Aquila stood in front of us and joined my hand with Hadrian's.

"My brother and sister in Christ," Aquila said, his gaze shifting from Hadrian to me, "why have you come here today?"

"To be married," Hadrian said.

Aquila nodded. "Then you know what to say."

I turned to Hadrian and whispered the words of consent: "Where you are Gaius, I am Gaia."

Hadrian smiled. "Where you are Gaia, I am Gaius."

Aquila cleared his throat. "Yeshua said, 'He who created them from the beginning made them male and female. For this reason a man shall leave his father and mother and be joined to his wife, and the two shall become one flesh. They are no longer two, but one. Therefore what God has joined together, let no man separate.'" He smiled at Hadrian. "I believe you are free to kiss your bride."

When our lips met, happiness bubbled up from a well I had long presumed dry. Hadrian caught my hand, held it against his cheek, then pressed his lips against my palm. Then, though I had no desire to leave Hadrian's embrace, Aquila spoke again.

"Three years ago," he said, speaking as though he was carefully searching for words, "our servant Petra brought a baby to our house."

My field of vision darkened. *What was this?*

"My wife, Priscilla, took the child and cared for it," Aquila continued, his eyes roving over the guests. "A few days later, our friend Mariana gave birth to a little boy, but the child died. Because the infant in Priscilla's care needed a wet nurse, she gave the child to Mariana. The boy remained in Mariana's care until she and Marcus were arrested."

My heart pounded so violently I feared Hadrian would hear it. My knees turned to water, but Hadrian's grip on my hand tightened, holding me upright.

"Since that time," Aquila went on, "the little boy and his brother have been cared for by Euodia and Ariston. Adonai has protected those children, but Euodia and Ariston feel it is appropriate that the boys be placed with a younger couple." Aquila turned, his eyes now piercing my soul. "Would you, Hadrian and Calandra, agree to love and care for those children?"

The onlookers must have thought this a preplanned addition to the wedding, but my thrashing heart was about to break out of my chest. I looked at Hadrian, who appeared as surprised as I, and saw that he understood. Aquila was offering us *our son*. Priscilla had guarded him, Mariana had nursed him, Ariston and Euodia had saved him from Nero.

Adonai had returned the child I lost . . . and was asking us to care for another as well.

I looked at Chaim as if for the first time. In his round face I recognized the arc of Hadrian's eyes, and in the center of his face I saw my father's nose. And lest there be any doubt, on his chest I saw the half coin Petra had tied around his neck the day he was born. The matching half lay at the bottom of my trunk.

A tear slipped over my cheek. "Hadrian?" I asked, unable to look away from our son.

"Yes," he said, his voice tinged with wonder. "Yes, we will adopt both boys."

I gripped his hand. Anyone could abandon a child in Rome, but once a child was adopted, his rights were secured by legal agreement. Aquila was discreetly giving us an opportunity to undo what I had done three years before.

This was complete and unexpected forgiveness.

I sank to one knee and held out my arms. "Boys?"

Euodia prodded them forward. They walked toward me with slow and uncertain steps, but they came.

Hadrian knelt beside me and drew all of us into his arms. "Today Adonai has created a family," he said, smiling. "And if the Lord is willing, we will not be parted."

Forty-Nine

With Aquila's blessing, Ivan, Chaim, and I moved into Hadrian's home on Palatine Hill. Because the emperor had not accepted Hadrian's resignation, he continued in his father's position while I focused on learning how to run a large household and be a mother. Petra went back to work for Euodia, and I waited for Hadrian to determine the best course for our future.

I knew he wanted to leave Rome, but developments in the city disturbed him. Galba had only a tenuous grip on power, and Hadrian was certain he would be ousted before the year ended. Other would-be emperors waited in the wings, and none of them were sympathetic toward Christians. The belief that Christians hated mankind persisted, and when Hadrian erected the statue of Petros in the Forum, few people remembered the man's heroic example.

As for me, I was in love—with Adonai, with my sons, and with my husband. Hadrian was the friend I had always depended on, but as a husband, he became far more. I had never understood all the ways in which a man and woman could come to know each other—not only physically but emotionally and spiritually. I came to know Hadrian's moods, his dreams, his fears, and his weaknesses, and he knew the same things about me. After only six weeks of marriage, I finally understood why my father mourned my mother for so many years. My father had been wise, for all along he had known that Hadrian was a good man.

Ivan and Chaim were shy around us at first, but we took them to visit Aquila, Ariston, and Euodia often. Within a few weeks the boys relaxed. At night, after the boys had dined, I would tuck them into bed, kneel at their bedside, and lead them in prayers to Adonai. They asked God to bless everyone they knew, even the slaves and the dog, and I delighted in their sweet and sensitive hearts.

About two months after our wedding, Euodia and Ariston came to visit. I eagerly invited them in, but Euodia's face had a pinched look. "What is it?" I asked, looking from her to Ariston. "What is wrong?"

Ariston answered, "For several months we have been searching for Zera, Mariana's little daughter. We know she was taken from the prison and sold at the slave market."

My stomach dropped, leaving me with a terrifying feeling of emptiness. I had been a mother only two months, but the thought of having to surrender either of my boys . . . "And?"

"She was bought by a senator's family. She has been much coddled and petted, yet she is available if you want to buy her. But the price will be high. The senator has learned of our interest, and he knows we are connected to you."

"I am so sorry." Euodia's eyes welled with tears. "He might have been reasonable, but when he learned we are friends with the aedile—"

"How much does he want?"

Ariston flexed his jaw. "Two million sestertii. He knows the price is ridiculous, especially for a toddling child, but he will not accept less."

"We will pay it." I spoke without thinking and without

consulting Hadrian. But I knew what he would say. "She is sister to our boys, and she needs to be with them."

"I thought that is how you would feel," Ariston said. "I will speak to the senator and tell you what he says."

Three days later, after Hadrian had sold several of his father's treasures and emptied our strongbox, Ariston and Euodia brought Zera to our home. She wailed for the first hour, undoubtedly overcome by the sight of so many strangers, but Chaim and Ivan fascinated her. Soon she was content to watch them play.

We signed manumission papers for her and adoption papers for all three children, so they would never be taken from us again.

A few weeks later, Hadrian's instincts proved right. After only six months as emperor, Galba was murdered by Otho, who had been disappointed that the childless and elderly Galba did not adopt him as heir. A few months later, Vitellius defeated Otho in battle, and Otho committed suicide. When Vitellius was killed by an angry mob, the Syrian legate Vespasian became emperor.

Hadrian was not happy with the tumultuous changes. "Rome is no place to raise children," he told me. "Nor is this a city where we can worship freely."

So we consulted with Aquila, Euodia, and Ariston. "I am wondering if we should go to an area with a strong ecclesia," I told them. "A city where those who carry the Gospel are free to shine."

"Why not go where the light does not exist?" Ariston countered. "Why not go into the darkness?"

"The apostles of our Lord are dying," Aquila said, doubtless thinking of Petros and Paulos. "The Lord needs new emissaries to spread the good news of Yeshua. Why should we not be those people?"

His words sent chills down my spine. I wanted to serve Adonai, I truly did, but I did not have the strength of Priscilla or the knowledge of Paulos.

"We could go together," Hadrian said. "Jews, Romans, and Greeks—all of us grafted into the Lord's olive tree. Let us show the world that we can work as one."

Fifty

Two months later, Euodia and Ariston, Aquila and Petra, and Hadrian and I sold most of our belongings, loaded wagons, and left the imperial city, determined to design tents, create art, and sell purple wherever the Spirit of Adonai led us. Our first stop, we had prayerfully decided, would be Pompeii, a wealthy town in the shadow of Mount Vesuvius. Once there, we would set up our shops and begin to share the Gospel with the people of that city. Like Paulos, we would stay until the Spirit prompted us to move on.

Aquila left behind a thriving ecclesia, a group that had already come through one storm and was prepared to face another. Aquila promised to pray for them, and they promised to support his ministry. Petra rode with Aquila, and though I wondered about their relationship, in time I realized that Aquila thought of Petra as a daughter in the Lord. She was blessed to have him as an influence in her life.

Purple fabrics and bundles of wool filled Ariston and Euodia's wagon, and every time we stopped at a body of water, Euodia waded into its depths and searched for snails. "You can take a woman out of the purple shop," Ariston joked, "but you can't take the purple dyer out of the woman."

As for me, I was delighted to leave Rome behind. In all my twenty-two years, I had rarely ventured beyond the city, so the rolling hills, verdant with olive groves and vineyards, captivated my artist's imagination. Charming villages dotted the landscape, along with expansive estates owned by Rome's patricians. In the distance, Mount Vesuvius dominated the horizon. I felt like a prisoner who had unexpectedly been freed to explore a strange and beautiful new world.

One day we decided to stop at Herculaneum, a beautiful seaside village, for lunch. We parked the wagons outside the city and walked inside. The sight of so many marble-clad homes stole my breath. Clearly this was a retreat for the wealthy, not for the working class.

As Aquila went to buy food, Hadrian and I visited a shop whose window featured small statues and beautiful jewelry. With Zera on my hip, I walked behind Hadrian, who held the boys' hands. "Be careful," I warned him. "I would hate for them to break something in this place."

I was wiping drool from Zera's lower lip when Hadrian spoke. "Calandra, you will not believe this."

I turned and saw him standing before my father's statue of Cronus. Most of the paint had been burned away and one marble hand was missing, but the work remained in remarkably good condition.

The shopkeeper noticed our interest. "Amazing, is it not?" He hurried over and smiled. "A true work of art, at least a hundred years old. It was plucked from the bottom of the Great Sea."

I blinked. "Truly?"

The shopkeeper turned his dazzling smile on Hadrian. "You, sir, are clearly a man of great elegance and taste. This masterpiece can be yours for three hundred sestertii. Imagine how it would enhance the beauty of your garden."

"This work has already been in my garden," Hadrian said, mischief twinkling in his eyes. "What say you, Calandra? Would you enjoy having this treasure in our future home?"

I widened my eyes, drinking in the sight of Father's work. Oh, how I missed him! But his influence remained with me, and I did not need a reminder.

"It is a lovely piece," I said, nodding at the shopkeeper. "Thank you, but we have living treasures to care for."

After lunch I rode beside my husband in the wagon, my hand on his thigh and my eyes on the horizon. Behind us, the children played together, the boys stacking their wooden blocks while Zera babbled.

Hadrian's hand warmed my skin as his fingers interlocked with mine. He leaned toward me, his shoulder lightly brushing my hair, as a small smile played on his lips. Completely happy, I sighed and lifted my eyes to the brilliant blue bowl of sky above us.

Adonai—He alone—had done so much for me. He had brought me out of darkness, given me true friends, and sent me an understanding husband who cherished and understood me. God had restored what I lost and turned my grief into joy.

What for so many years I deemed impossible, Adonai had turned into reality.

For the first time I understood the true nature of deity. A god who could be commanded or bribed was no god at all. Adonai asked for the surrender of our lives, but in exchange for our suffering, He gave us comfort. For our trials, He blessed us with patient endurance. And for our losses, He poured out unmerited, unfathomable joy.

Author's Note

Because readers occasionally have questions about practices or events I reference in my novels, I've supplied answers to a few anticipated questions. If I haven't answered yours, feel free to email me.

Q. In the beginning, Calandra paints her father's sculptures. Why would she do that? Weren't all the sculptures either bronze or white marble?

A. Actually, no. We think of Greek and Roman statues as being natural marble, but that's only because we are seeing them long after the paint has been worn off by time and neglect. But experts have found minuscule flakes of paint on these ancient statues, and we know the Romans loved color. They painted their marble temples and their homes, so why wouldn't they paint their statues?

Q. Sha'ul, Paul, Paulos, Paulus, Saul—what *was* the apostle's name?

A. All of the above. To the Jews, he would have been called Sha'ul. The Greeks would have called him Paulos; the Romans,

Paulus. We know him, in English, as Paul or Saul. In Acts 13:9, we learn that throughout his ministry he was known by both names.

Q. Did Peter (Petros) really spend time in Rome?

A. Scholars disagree on this point, but I believe he did. In 1 Peter 5:13, he obliquely refers to his location as *Babylon*. Some believe he was writing from Babylon in modern Iraq, and others say he was writing from the Babylon that was a small Roman outpost in Egypt. Still others believe he was referring to Rome as Babylon.

I believe he wrote his epistle from Rome for several reasons. First, he *does* use a great deal of "fire" imagery in his writing, so he might have witnessed the Great Fire of AD 64 from the safety of Transtiberim, where most of the Jews resided. Second, the early church firmly believed Peter ministered in Rome. Another reason is the written testimony of Clement, who wrote a letter to believers near the end of the first century.

In 1 Clement 5:4–6, we read, "There was Peter, who by reason of unrighteous jealousy endured not one nor two but many labours, and thus having borne his testimony went to his appointed place of glory. By reason of jealousy and strife Paulos by his example pointed out the prize of patient endurance. After that he had been seven times in bonds, had been driven into exile, had been stoned, had preached in the East and in the West, he won the noble renown which was the reward of his faith, having taught righteousness unto the whole world and having reached the farthest bounds of the West; and when he had borne his testimony before the rulers, so he departed from the world and went unto the holy place, having been found a notable pattern of patient endurance.

"Unto these men of holy lives was gathered **a vast multitude**

of the elect, who through many indignities and tortures, being the victims of jealousy, **set a brave example among ourselves"** [emphasis added].[1]

Clement writes that Peter and Paulos were joined by a "vast multitude," a phrase that probably referred to the believers martyred under Nero. He says all those who died "set a brave example among ourselves," referring to Clement's own church, which was in Rome.

Q. Apparently, the patricians were the wealthy leaders of Rome. Am I missing something?

A. Your feeling is correct. The word comes from *pater*, Latin for *father*. The patricians were descended from the first citizen families of Rome, and over the years they accumulated considerable wealth and power. There were many ranks within Roman society, but the opposite of patrician was *plebeian*, or commoner. Beneath the commoners were freedmen, who had once been enslaved, and at the lowest point were slaves.

Q. Did Nero really fiddle while Rome burned?

A. Not literally because fiddles/violins were not invented until the early sixteenth century. Nero might have played a lyre while Rome burned because he was fond of singing his own compositions, but he did spend at least *some* time fighting the fire. Yet the fire burned for several days and nights, so he might well have picked up an instrument and performed while he watched his city burn.

Nero was at his summer home in Antium when the fire

---

1. Joseph Barber Lightfoot and J. R. Harmer, *The Apostolic Fathers* (London: Macmillan, 1891).

began, but he returned to Rome when he learned his home on the Palatine was being threatened by the flames. A Praetorian tribune, Subrius Flavus, would later describe how Nero, without the protection of his guard, rushed from location to location during the night as the city burned.[2]

Ancient historians have told us that several citizens reported seeing men setting fire to buildings and saying they were acting under orders, but those men could have been establishing firebreaks. Historians are certain the fire originated at the Circus Maximus. Because the Circus had burned previously, Nero had outlawed the selling of cooked foods at that venue, hoping to keep flames away from the shops and upper seats, which at that time were wooden.

Conspiracy theories were as popular in the first century as they are now. When Nero built a huge palace after the Great Fire of AD 64, people theorized that he ordered men to burn the city to clear the land for his "Golden House," or *Domus Aurea*. As with most conspiracy theories, the truth cannot be proven without more information.

Q. Did God really send Aquila a dream about storing grain?

A. Aquila's dream is fictional, but since God warned Joseph about a grain shortage, I thought He could do the same for Aquila.

Q. Could a person actually succeed as a blind sculptor?

A. Yes. I did some research and discovered sculptor Michael Naranjo, who lost his sight in the Vietnam War. Aided by his

---

2. Anthony A. Barrett, *Rome Is Burning: Nero and the Fire that Ended a Dynasty* (Princeton, NJ: Princeton University Press, 2020), 73.

memory, he sculpts amazing work with his fingertips. I'm sure other sculptors have learned to do the same thing.

Q. Did Nero build the Golden House you described?

A. Yes! The mammoth complex occupied two hundred acres in the heart of Rome and would be extraordinary even today. It had revolving dining rooms and was designed to reflect the sun's beams.

But Nero's dream house was buried by his successors, who built on top of it. Ironically, part of the palace was accidentally discovered during the Renaissance. Artists lowered themselves into a portion of the buried palace and discovered beautiful paintings on the high walls. Those paintings may have inspired some famous painters of the Renaissance period.

Suetonius, who may have seen this house with his own eyes, wrote that Nero's Golden House had a pool "as big as a sea, and was surrounded with buildings made to appear like cities; and there were also tracts of land of different sorts—tilled fields, vineyards, and woods—with large numbers of domestic and wild animals of all kinds.

"In the other areas of the structure everything was overlaid with gold and studded with precious stones and mother-of-pearl. The dining rooms had ceilings made of ivory panels that could rotate so that flowers could be scattered from above and fitted with pipes for dispensing perfume. The principal dining room had a dome which, day and night, was continuously revolving, like the heavens; and there were baths running with seawater and with sulfurous water."[3]

Nero's house must have been amazing, but it didn't last long.

---

3. Anthony A. Barrett, *Rome Is Burning: Nero and the Fire that Ended a Dynasty* (Princeton, NJ: Princeton University Press, 2020), 265.

Q. Did Rome really require people to marry by a certain age?

A. Yes. In an effort to raise the level of morality and increase the number of native Romans, Augustus passed a series of laws known as *lex Julia de maritandis ordinibus*. These laws required men between the ages of 25 and 60 and women between the ages of 20 and 50 to marry. Widows had to remarry within two or three years of their husbands' deaths, divorcées within eighteen months. Those of the pertinent ages who remained unmarried had to pay a special tax, the Aes Uxorium. Married couples who had children were rewarded, and adultery was made a criminal offense.[4]

Q. Did Nero devalue the coins after the fire?

A. Just as our government simply prints more money when needed, thus devaluing the worth of the dollar, after the tragic fire Nero ordered that the silver denarius should contain less silver than before the event. But when he collected taxes, his tax collectors made sure to collect only older, pure silver coins.

Q. Why did Nero blame Christians for the Great Fire of Rome?

A. I don't think anyone believed Christians started the fire, but they made convenient scapegoats. Why? Because, according to Roman thinking, they offended the gods of Rome by not offering sacrifices to them.

The Christians were convicted and found guilty by this skewed reasoning:

---

4. "The Julian Marriage Laws," https://www.unrv.com/government/julian marriage.php, accessed February 19, 2024.

1. The Roman gods protected the city from harm.
2. Christians refused to sacrifice to the gods (who protected the city) because they hated the Roman people.
3. By not sacrificing to the gods, Christians caused the gods to stop protecting the city.
4. Because the gods had stopped protecting the city, the fire raged and took thousands of lives. So the Christians were guilty of arson and murder and deserved capital punishment.

The ruling class must have known that Christians didn't really hate the Roman people, but because the plebs believed Nero ordered the fire, the emperor needed someone to blame. The Christians were an easy target. With their conviction, Nero had enough victims to provide a season of violent sport. The Roman people enjoyed the entertainment until they began to realize that the Christians were not haters after all.

Tacitus, who lived through the martyrdoms of Nero's reign, wrote that the emperor persecuted the Christians "more [because] of their hatred of mankind than because they were arsonists. As they died, they were further subjected to insult. Covered with skins of wild beasts, they perished by being torn to pieces by dogs; or they would be fastened to crosses and, when daylight had gone, set on fire to provide lighting at night.

"Nero had offered his gardens as a venue for the show, and he would also put on circus entertainments, mixing with the plebs in his charioteer's outfit or standing up in his chariot. As a result, guilty though these people were and deserving exemplary punishment, pity for them began to well up because it was felt that they were being exterminated not for the public good, but to gratify one man's cruelty."[5]

5. Anthony A. Barrett, *Rome Is Burning: Nero and the Fire that Ended a Dynasty* (Princeton, NJ: Princeton University Press, 2020), 264–265.

Nero did not institute laws against Christianity, nor did he expel the Christians from Rome as Claudius had expelled the Jews. But future emperors would enact laws against Christianity, and though Christians were sometimes allowed to live in peace, persecution occasionally flared until the ascension of Constantine in AD 324.

Q. Is Tish'a B'Av a real occasion?

A. Yes. Tish'a B'Av is the ninth day of the Hebrew month Av, which does not correspond to an exact date on our calendar because the Hebrew calendar is based on lunar cycles. Not only was Tish'a B'Av the date when the Hebrew spies returned from Canaan with a bad report (read the story in Numbers 13), but it was the date when the Babylonians destroyed Solomon's Temple in 423 BC. The Romans destroyed Herod's Temple on Tish'a B'Av in AD 70.

In AD 133, well beyond the time of this novel, the Bar Kochaba revolt against the Romans ended in defeat on Tish'a B'Av. On Tish'a B'Av in 1290, the Jews were expelled from England, and on that date in 1492 they were banished from Spain.

We do *not* know if Peter and his wife were crucified on Tish'a B'Av. Since it is impossible for us to know exactly when Peter died, I thought it would be fitting to have him crucified (traditionally believed to be the method of his execution) on Tish'a B'Av.

Q. What was the fever that afflicted both Calandra and Pericles?

A. Malaria. Much of Rome was built on swampy land, so malaria, or "Roman fever," was a real threat. The wealthy people living on the higher elevations did not suffer from it as much as the poor who lived in the lower, wetter areas where mosquitoes abounded. Some scholars believe an epidemic of malaria during the fifth century may have contributed to the fall of the Roman Empire.

Q. Did a nursing mother called Mariana actually stand before lions in the arena?

A. Yes and no. I took the story of an actual martyred nursing mother and gave it to Mariana. Perpetua was martyred in AD 203 after giving birth to her baby. Her brave death and refusal to renounce Christ influenced thousands.

Q. The process of building a statue in ancient times seems complicated. Are your descriptions accurate?

A. Mostly. I watched several videos on the process of *lost wax casting* and tried to write out all the steps so a real sculptor wouldn't think I was a complete fraud. But the process is somewhat repetitive, so I eliminated a few steps to avoid repeating myself. I hope what I have written gives a good idea of how the ancient sculptors worked. The information about Zenodorus is historical, and his sculptures were *gargantuan*.

Reading Group Discussion Guide

1. Had you ever heard of the Great Fire of Rome? We have tragic fires in contemporary times, but not usually in places where hundreds of people live in one tightly compacted space. Can you name any modern tragedies that are similar?

2. What surprising things did you discover about life in ancient Rome? Some aspects of ancient Roman life are similar to modern life in Western countries. What aspects of Roman life did you find interesting or odd?

3. Have you ever tried sculpting? Sculpting a small statue is a challenge, but the ancients were capable of building bronze statues over one hundred feet tall and without modern equipment! What did you think of Calandra's process?

4. What had you heard about Nero before reading this book? Were you familiar with his famous "Golden House"?

5. Why do you think it was so hard for Calandra to trust Yeshua? Why was it easier for Pericles and Hadrian?

6. The Roman practice of leaving a baby at a Column Lactaria was well-established. Did this practice shock you? As you read the story, what did you think became of Calandra's child?

7. Were you surprised by the statue's final resting place? Do you think its honoree would have been pleased?

8. How did Pericles see more clearly than Calandra? What themes resonated with you as you read the novel?

9. Nero hires Zenodorus to create a statue that will "stand for all time." The work by Zenodorus, which stood ninety-eight feet tall, was modified by Vespasian to look like Sol, the Sun god. In AD 128, Emperor Hadrian moved it to another location, and later Commodus had the head replaced to portray himself as Hercules. If statues symbolize permanence in the novel, what is the author saying about man's attempts to build something "that will stand for all time"?

10. At the beginning of the story, Calandra's dream is to create "images that would last forever. Works of beauty. Works that would shine through the ages." She is thinking about statues and artistic objects. At the end of the story, has God fulfilled her dream? What is she creating with Hadrian?

11. If you've read the first two books in the series, how did this book compare? What did you think about the inclusion of characters from the first two novels: Euodia and Ariston, Marcus and Mariana? Were you happy with the outcome of their situations?

Read on for a *sneak peek*
at the next book from
Angela Hunt

RESCUED HEART:
THE STORY OF SARAH

*Book 1 of the compelling
Old Testament series*

THE MATRIARCHS

❖

Available in the fall of 2025

Sarah

Since I had agreed to marry my grandfather's choice, I stood in his chamber and waited, my faith minuscule and my confidence nonexistent. My empty stomach twisted as Milcah's hands tightened on mine. "The time has come," she whispered, her eyes bright. "Soon we will *both* be married women."

I exhaled a trembling breath. "I cannot believe the wedding is finally happening. I was beginning to think I would have to live with my father and brother forever."

"No longer! Now that Abram has come, you will discover the joys of married life."

"I hope it is as joyful as you say."

"Of course it is. What could possibly stand in the way of your happiness?"

A thousand things, I wanted to answer, but my sister would not understand the reason for my anxiety. She had grown up with Nahor, her husband, who was also our uncle. My future husband was a kinsman to us, though long ago he had been sent away for reasons I never fully understood, and no one wanted to explain. I was better acquainted with the neighborhood butcher than with my betrothed.

I sighed as Milcah reached for my embroidered veil. Amthelo, my grandfather's wife, had spent years adorning the linen square with delicate stitches depicting butterflies, flowers, and birds. The veil, now nearly covered with embroidery, had become something of a joke between me and my sister.

"Finally Amthelo's work is finished, and there is still space enough for you to see through it," Milcah said, draping the fabric over my braided hair. She stepped back and clasped her hands. "Unbelievable," she whispered. "Despite all the adornment, your beauty shines through the veil. Abram will be speechless when he sees you."

"You are being silly," I chided, "and I need you to be serious. I may be coming to you for advice in the days ahead."

"What advice could you possibly need? In your thirty-nine years, surely you have heard women talking about marriage."

"I have, but . . ." I bit my lip.

"What is it?"

"I do not know the man, so I do not know what he expects of me."

Milcah chuckled. "You will find out within a few hours."

I released an exasperated sigh. "Do not mock me. I know what is expected on the wedding night, but I do not know Abram. I saw him for the first time yesterday, long enough to realize he is different. What if he does not like me? What if he decides that waiting for me was a waste of his time?"

My sister raised a finger. "I cannot deny that he seems odd compared to the men of Ur. But the men in our family have always been good husbands. You will not be sorry you married him."

"I hope you are right." I stepped back and braced for the future. "So? Have you any advice for an older bride?"

She crossed her arms, ran a critical eye over me, and nodded. "You will not disappoint him. But if I were you, I would have a baby as soon as possible. Even with the blessing of the gods, older women find it more difficult to conceive."

You are an older woman. The unspoken words dangled in the space between us.

I went to the door and peeked out, allowing a flood of voices to swirl into the room. As the king's vizier, my grandfather knew nearly every man in the city. Dozens of guests had come to witness the marriage of his kinsman, the mysterious Abram who had come from the north to marry Terah's granddaughter.

"No sign of Father yet," Milcah said, closing the door. "We will have to wait."

Frustrated, I dropped onto a stool, careless of my new silk tunic. "Perhaps Abram has changed his mind. Perhaps he has gone back to his home in the north. He might have a woman there; someone he did not want to leave behind."

"Grandfather signed a betrothal contract, did he not? Abram would be breaking the king's law if he does not fulfill his responsibility."

"A betrothal arranged before I was weaned. He might not have known he had a wife waiting for him in Ur."

"Grandfather would have made certain Abram knew. He would have sent one of the king's messengers with the news."

Her mention of the king only heightened my anxiety. Nimrod, ruler of the Chaldeans, was well acquainted with our grandfather. But my father had always taken pains to keep me hidden from the king's gaze, reasoning that the king did not need a woman from our family in his harem. Grandfather had received many gifts from the ruler, including a fine house, but I had never been allowed to visit the palace or even walk the streets of Ur without wearing a veil.

I understood why. Our king had the right to take any unmarried woman he found appealing, and both my father and grandfather were afraid I might appeal to the king. I found it hard to believe a king would covet an older woman, but even my sister advised me to wear a veil whenever I left the house.

If only my life had been like Milcah's. At forty-two, she had eight sons and two daughters, who kept her busy and gave her a sense of purpose. What was my purpose? To keep my father's house tidy while I waited for an absent groom?

Waiting had never been easy for me. Yet, like a good daughter, I had waited patiently for Abram and for my life to begin. I shivered as an unbidden thought sent a ghost spider scurrying up my spine. "You do not think the king would come to the wedding, do you?"

Milcah laughed. "The king, in his vizier's house?"

"He respects our grandfather. And he sent a gift to your wedding."

"He will probably send a gift to yours as well, but he will not come. A king does not concern himself with the private lives of his servants."

We stilled at the sound of voices outside the door, and I rose as my father stepped into the room and looked at me. "Are you ready? Your bridegroom has arrived."

Milcah nodded. "Iscah has been waiting for years," she told him. "Your daughter is more than ready to become a wife."

Father stepped forward, placed his hands on my shoulders, and drew me close. "I know you were often frustrated because I forbade you from marrying at a younger age, and I know other women mocked your status as a virgin."

Other men mocked you, I wanted to say, *for holding me in reserve as if I were some priceless treasure.* But I held my tongue out of respect.

"Soon you will understand why I kept you for Abram." Father's smile flashed in his beard. "My brother will prove himself worth the wait."

"I hope so," I whispered.

He released me, and I walked toward my future on legs that felt as unsteady as a baby's.

The scent of incense—cinnamon, ginger, and jasmine—filled my head as my father led me into the great hall. I blinked back tears and struggled to smile as the many guests murmured in approval, though they could not see my face. Their soft whispers must have assured my bridegroom, who wore an intense expression of curiosity as he watched me walk toward him.

Father's elbow poked my rib. "So? Do you think him worth the wait?"

From beneath the safety of my veil, I studied my betrothed. The man who waited for me was taller than my father, more tanned than Grandfather, and not as young as I had imagined because gray laced his hair and beard. His eyes were dark, intense, and more than a little intimidating.

I looked away and shook my head, then realized Abram might interpret my movement as disapproval. "I do not know him, Father. But I am ready to commence the next stage of my life."

Father chuckled. "No one will ever again refer to you as overripe fruit. You will be a wife and then a mother, and everyone will forget that you married at an advanced age."

I bit my lower lip, resisting the urge to shush him.

When we reached Abram and Terah, my grandfather, Father took my hands and placed them in Abram's. My groom's hands were rough, his nails untrimmed. From what sort of uncivilized place had he come? Even the slaves of Ur were better groomed.

The intensity of Abram's gaze seemed to burn through my veil as Grandfather recited a prayer to Sin, lord of the moon. Though the groom was not supposed to speak—*never* had I heard of a bridegroom praying at his wedding—Abram raised his voice and asked an unfamiliar god to bless our union. When he finished speaking, he lifted my veil and took a half step back, wearing the look of a man who had been knocked over by a runaway cart. I did not know whether to be flattered or offended. Was he so stunned by my appearance—?

"Bless ADONAI the LORD God," he whispered, his gaze intent upon my face. "I, his humble servant, do not deserve such beauty."

A wave of mirth rippled through the assembled guests. Then my grandfather cleared his throat and said, "Abram, will you take Iscah, daughter of Haran, as your wife?"

"I will."

Grandfather turned to me. "Iscah, will you take Abram to be your husband and lord for as long as you live?"

"Yes." I blushed when my voice came out in a terrified squeak.

Grandfather nodded. "What gift, Abram, do you bring to honor the covenant of marriage?"

Abram spread his hands, which were as large as Grandfather's. "I have neither gold nor silver," he said, his eyes focused on mine. "What would be the use of such a gift, since any gift I bring into the marriage would remain mine? I will give you something to be yours alone: a new name. From this moment forward, you will no longer be known as Iscah, but as *Sarai*. For a *princess* is what you will be to me."

I blinked, simultaneously startled and touched by his offering. I had not expected an expensive present, but I thought it would at least be something tangible. Instead, he had given me a new name, a majestic name that settled over me like an uncomfortable cloak.

"A wonderful gift," Grandfather said. "Sarai, attend to your husband. Abram, you may claim your wife."

Abram stepped forward and kissed me on the cheek, a gesture that elicited shouts of congratulations from the wedding guests. Then he took my arm and led me toward the door.

The crowd surged toward us and shouted their congratulations as we moved to the feast waiting in the courtyard. Some of the guests had traveled for days to celebrate the union of Terah's kinsman, and they needed to be honored with good wine and hearty food.

As the musicians began to play and the guests surrounded Terah and Abram, the men of the hour, Milcah tugged on my sleeve. "Sister," she shouted, "how are you enjoying life as a married woman?"

I leaned closer to be heard above the clamor. "It is not much different from life as an unmarried woman. The men still get all the attention."

"My advice? During the meal, ask Abram what he thinks of the food. If he is complimentary, he'll be an agreeable husband. If he complains, he will tend to be critical."

I regarded her through narrowed eyes. It was probably a trick, a ploy to help me relax.

"Go," she said, giving me a gentle push toward the head table. "You must not keep your husband waiting. Take your place beside him." She smiled. "And do not forget to ask about the food."

Abram and I barely spoke during the feast. He ate, accepting congratulations in between bites, while I nibbled on the roasted meat and vegetables. A few women came to wish me well, casting curious glances at Abram. The butcher's wife leaned forward and whispered, "Unlike the vizier, he has the look of a wild man."

I forced a smile, though her remark had done nothing to assure me. "He does not look like my father or Nahor, but Abram had a different mother."

"So I have heard. Are you certain he did not come from another family?"

I shrugged, but her question lingered in my mind. I knew so little about the man I had married, and the little I knew came from family members who did not seem eager to talk about him. What if the butcher's wife was right? What if I had married a man with whom I had *nothing* in common?

When the congratulations finally faded and the platters were all empty, my pulse quickened. If I did not speak soon, Abram would begin to wonder if I could converse in anything but a whimper.

"My lord," I said, "what do you think of the feast?"

Abram turned to look at me. "What do I think? I think we should go now."

I gasped. "Leave our wedding banquet?"

"Look there." He gestured to a table of giggling women who could barely hold themselves upright. "As long as we remain, they will continue to drink. Better that we leave so they can collect their wits."

Though his suggestion surprised me, I do not think anyone noticed when Abram took my hand and led me out of the courtyard and onto the street. I drew my veil over my face and followed him until we reached the small house where we would live. The orange-tinted structure, which looked like a score of other mud-brick homes in the area, appeared unremarkable.

I shivered when Abram unlatched the door and stepped back, allowing me to enter. A rough coat of plaster covered the walls, and narrow clerestory windows allowed light and air into the space. The house held only a chair, a small table, and a bed, but someone—almost certainly Milcah—had draped garlands across the headboard and around the bedposts. Roses perfumed the air, and a single oil lamp glowed on the table, gilding the room with soft light.

Milcah had brought beauty to the humble house. I smiled at her thoughtfulness and luxuriated in the scent of the flowers, but Abram had other things on his mind.

He bade me sit on the edge of the bed, then tugged on the

corner of my veil. When it fell onto the floor, he stared at me so intently I wondered if he was having second thoughts about the marriage. "Is something wrong?"

"No," he whispered, falling to his knees. "I am simply amazed that ADONAI has chosen to bless me with such a treasure."

A flush warmed my cheeks. "I am far past the age—"

"You waited for me," he said, his voice husky. "I am sorry you had to wait so many years, but I could not leave until ADONAI told me to go home."

I studied his face, wanting to know more about him and this mysterious ADONAI, but perhaps this was not the time for questions. We were married, and we had both waited far longer than was customary or even desirable.

Abram took my hand and pressed a kiss into my palm, then slowly slid his lips up my arm. My skin pebbled beneath his touch, and my heart fluttered. But as he shifted to continue his upward journey, he must have seen the small statue of Inanna, goddess of love and fertility, sitting among the flowers by the bed. Milcah must have placed it there, hoping the queen of heaven would help us conceive on our first night together. The corner of my mouth quirked as I imagined my sister's reasoning: *As a woman of thirty-nine, you have no time to waste.*

I was about to remark on Milcah's thoughtfulness when Abram dropped my arm and grasped the statue. He strode to the door and hurled the statue into the street. I stared, blinking, as the clay shattered.

Abram closed the door, dusted his hands, and returned to me as if nothing had happened. He bent, pressing his lips to my neck, but I could not ignore the astonishing act I had just witnessed. "You do not care for Inanna?" I asked, pulling away. "You are not afraid she will repay your violence by cursing me with a barren womb?"

Abram straightened, taking my hand in his. "You should

know, *Sarai*," he said, stressing my new name, "that I worship ADONAI, the Creator of heaven and earth. I will never allow a graven image to enter my house. As my wife, you should understand and honor my wish."

Stunned, I pulled my hand from his. "You learned to worship this ADONAI while you were away?"

"I did."

"But now you live in Ur, and in Ur we worship the king's gods. We do not know this ADONAI."

"Then I will introduce you to Him." He slipped his arm around my shoulder. "I do not expect you to know this, but the LORD God becomes jealous when we take what is rightfully His and give it to someone else. Our worship and our prayers belong to Him alone. We should not incite Him to jealousy by giving those things to another."

Confused, I averted my eyes. "I did not know."

His fingers caught my chin and lifted it. "I will teach you, but all in good time. For tonight I must focus on getting to know *you*, my princess."

Angela Hunt has published more than 165 books, with sales nearing six million copies worldwide. She's the *New York Times* bestselling author of *The Tale of Three Trees*, *The Note*, and *The Nativity Story*. Angela's novels have won or been nominated for several prestigious industry awards, such as the RITA Award, the Christy Award, the ECPA Christian Book Award, and the HOLT Medallion Award. American Christian Fiction Writers and Romantic Times Book Club have presented her with Lifetime Achievement Awards. She holds ThDs in Biblical Studies and in Theology. Angela and her husband live in Florida, along with their mastiffs and chickens. For a complete list of the author's books, visit AngelaHuntBooks.com.

References

"The Burning of Rome, AD 64," EyeWitness to History, www.eyewitness tohistory.com (1999), accessed June 28, 2023.

"Roman Taxes," https://www.unrv.com/economy/roman-taxes.php, accessed February 20, 2024.

Angela, Alberto. *A Day in the Life of Ancient Rome*. New York: Europa Editions, 2009.

Barrett, Anthony A. *Rome Is Burning: Nero and the Fire that Ended a Dynasty*. Princeton, NJ: Princeton University Press, 2020.

Betz, Hans Dieter. "Paulos (Person)." Ed. David Noel Freedman. *The Anchor Yale Bible Dictionary*. New Haven, CT: Yale University Press, 1992.

Bonvalot, Elizabeth. *The Sculpting Book: A Complete Introduction to Modeling the Human Figure*. Atglen, PA: Schiffer Publishing, 2019.

Bruce, F. F. *The Spreading Flame*. Milton Keynes, UK: Paternoster Press, 1958.

Byfield, Ted., ed. *The Christians: Their First Two Thousand Years: The Veil Is Torn, A.D. 30 to A.D. 70*. 1st edition. Vol. 1. Altona, Manitoba, CA: Christian History Project, Friesens Corporation, 2003.

Cottrell, Jack. *Romans*. Vol. 2. Joplin, MO: College Press Publishing, 1996.

Field, Taylor. "Aquila and Priscilla." Ed. Chad Brand et al. *Holman Illustrated Bible Dictionary*. Rev. ed. Nashville, TN: Holman Bible Publishers, 2003.

Fiensy, David A. *New Testament Introduction*. Joplin, MO: College Press Publishing, 1997.

Goodman, Martin. *The Roman World: 44 BC–AD 180*. New York: Routledge, 2012.

Johnston, Harold Whetstone. *The Private Life of the Romans*, revised by Mary Johnston. Northbrook, IL: Scott Foresman and Company, 1903; 1932.

Kurian, George Thomas. *Nelson's New Christian Dictionary: The Authoritative Resource on the Christian World*. Nashville, TN: Thomas Nelson Publishers, 2001.

Lampe, Peter. "Prisca (Person)." Ed. David Noel Freedman. *The Anchor Yale Bible Dictionary*. New Haven, CT: Yale University Press, 1992.

Leon, Vicki. *Working IX to V*. Somerville, MA: Walker Books, 2007.

Mallon, Elliot. *Sculpting a Head in Clay, Part 1*. YouTube, https://www.youtube.com/watch?v=_wg-ejixB8k, accessed July 14, 2023.

Melvadius. "Status of Illegitimate Children in Rome." December 3, 2007. https://www.unrv.com/forum/topic/7729-status-of-illegitimate-children-in-rome/, accessed February 15, 2024.

Mills, M. S. *Colossians: A Study Guide to Paulos's Epistle to the Saints at Colossae*. Dallas, TX: 3E Ministries, 1993.

Opper, Thorsten. *Nero: The Man Behind the Myth*. London: The British Museum, 2021.

Richards, Larry. *Every Man in the Bible*. Nashville, TN: Thomas Nelson Publishers, 1999.

Ryken, Leland. "Reading the New Testament Letters: What You Need to Know." *Lexham Context Commentary: New Testament*. Ed. Douglas Mangum. Bellingham, WA: Lexham Press, 2020.

Stern, David H. *Jewish New Testament: A Translation of the New Testament that Expresses Its Jewishness*. 1st edition. Jerusalem, Israel; Clarksville, MD: Jewish New Testament Publications, 1989.

Vincent, Marvin Richardson. *Word Studies in the New Testament*. Vol. 1. New York: Charles Scribner's Sons, 1887.

Vos, Howard Frederic. *Nelson's New Illustrated Bible Manners & Customs: How the People of the Bible Really Lived*. Nashville, TN: Thomas Nelson Publishers, 1999.

Weisweller, John. "The Heredity of Senatorial Status in the Principate," Cambridge University Press, September 7, 2020, https://www.cambridge.org/core/journals/journal-of-roman-studies/article/heredity-of-senatorial-status-in-the-principate/, accessed October 5, 2023.

Zondervan Academic Blog, https://zondervanacademic.com/blog/death-afterlife-greco-roman-antiquity, accessed August 4, 2023.

Sign Up for Angela's Newsletter

Keep up to date with Angela's latest news on book releases and events by signing up for her email list at the website below.

AngelaHuntBooks.com

FOLLOW ANGELA ON FACEBOOK

 Angela Hunt, Novelist

More from Angela Hunt

Three Philippians whose lives were changed by Paul—a jailer, a formerly demon-possessed enslaved girl, and the woman referred to as Lydia—find their fates intertwined. In the face of great sacrifice, will they find the strength to do all that justice demands of them?

The Woman from Lydia
THE EMISSARIES #1

Chief magistrate Narkis Ligus sees a golden opportunity to propel himself to greater power and fortune by marrying one of his beautiful daughters to the new governor's firstborn son. Yet Mariana's faith in Yeshua makes her as reluctant to wed a man who worships Roman gods as her jealous and status-obsessed stepsister, Prima, is determined to wed him.

The Sisters of Corinth
THE EMISSARIES #2

BETHANYHOUSE

 Bethany House Fiction

 @BethanyHouseFiction

 @Bethany_House

 @BethanyHouseFiction

 Free exclusive resources for your book group at BethanyHouseOpenBook.com

 Sign up for our fiction newsletter today at BethanyHouse.com